Small Talk

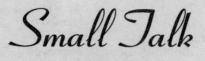

"I know so little about you," Diana said.

"Ask me anything." Travis pulled out a chair and motioned for her to sit down.

"Who's your favorite singer?" She had no idea why she cared or why she'd asked that question.

"It's not the singer so much as the song."

"Television program."

"You got me there. The set I had gave out on me a couple of years ago."

He was the first person she'd ever met who didn't own a television set.

"Okay, if you were stranded on an island, what one thing would you take with you?"

He gave her a wicked grin. "That's too easy...."

She'd read about people's toes tingling, but not until then had she experienced the sensation herself. "I'm serious."

"So am I."

He leaned down and gave her a kiss that left no doubt just how serious.

Books by Georgia Bockoven

A Marriage of Convenience

The Way It Should Have Been

Moments

Alone in a Crowd

Far From Home

An Unspoken Promise

Published by HarperPaperbacks

An Unspoken Promise

GEORGIA BOCKOVEN

HarperPaperbacks
A Division of HarperCollins Publishers

HarperPaperbacks

A Division of HarperCollins*Publishers*
10 East 53rd Street, New York, N.Y. 10022-5299

This is a work of fiction. The characters, incidents, and
dialogues are products of the author's imagination and are not to
be construed as real. Any resemblance to actual events or
persons, living or dead, is entirely coincidental.

ISBN 0-06-108439-5

HarperCollins®, ®, and HarperPaperbacks™
are trademarks of HarperCollins*Publishers* Inc.

Cover photograph by Chad Ehlers/Tony Stone Images

First printing: January 1997

Printed in the United States of America

Visit HarperPaperbacks on the World Wide Web at
http://www.harpercollins.com/paperbacks

❖ 10 9 8 7 6 5 4 3 2 1

This book is dedicated to the loving women and men everywhere who have adopted children and gotten it right. Most especially to those who make up my own extended family.

Acknowledgments

A special thanks to Dixie Reid for her insights into the life of a newspaper reporter.

An Unspoken Promise

One

Diana fought to keep her mind off her burning thighs as she waited for the timer to tell her she was to leave the stair machine and move onto the treadmill. When the bell finally sounded, she stepped down and grabbed the towel she'd tossed onto the chair earlier, burying her face in the terry cloth. At the same instant a crashing sound came from the kitchen, followed by Stuart's voice. "The *bitch*—"

She didn't wonder at the outburst. After two years of living with Stuart, she was as familiar with his eruptions as the list of irritants that invariably ignited them.

This early in the morning the source was undoubtedly the newspaper and the subject financial, something she could let him rant and rave about without getting involved in the conflict. Considering the less than wonderful state of their relationship the past couple of months, she decided to indulge him by listening.

She found Stuart in the breakfast nook, bent over, picking up his prized podocarpus from the floor. Thin green leaves rained on the linoleum as he righted the plant. The back of the chair caught on the corner of his maroon silk robe, pulling it open to reveal legs that were bronzed from a tanning machine. He freed the robe with an angry gesture before going back to the podocarpus. When he discovered a broken branch he yanked it free and tossed it toward the sink.

Diana scanned the room, taking in the crumpled newspaper in the corner, the spilled coffee, the overturned chair beside the table. This was not one of Stuart's run-of-the-mill temper tantrums, an explosion that simply needed an agreeable listener to be defused. Whatever had set him off this morning would most likely last all day. Her time would have been better spent on the treadmill.

Stuart glanced up and caught Diana trying to back out of the doorway. The force of his fury stopped her cold.

"She's gone too far this time."

There was too much emphasis on the "she" for it to have been some obscure politician or entertainment figure who had offended him. This was personal. "Who's gone too far?"

He snapped off a second branch and tossed it in the direction of the first. "All I need is for one person to make the connection and the entire office is going to know." He paused. "Jesus, just thinking about it makes me sick."

"I have better things to do than stand here and play guessing games with you, Stuart. Either tell me who you're talking about or I'm going to take my shower."

Her seeming calm goaded him to a new outburst. "Don't play dumb, Diana. Who else but that goddamned sister of yours could get me this upset?"

Sudden, overwhelming fatigue hit Diana. "What's Amy done now?"

"The bitch got herself arrested last night."

"Stop calling her that." It took a second for the rest to sink in. "What do you mean, 'She got herself arrested'?"

He made her wait, seeking maximum impact. "For prostitution."

Her ambivalence turned to anger. Stuart loved to bait her. "I don't believe you."

For some perverse reason, her reaction seemed to please him. He failed to suppress a smile as he said, "You don't have to believe me. See for yourself—it's in this morning's paper. Along with her family background. Amy wasn't content just to take herself down, she had to take the rest of you with her."

"There has to be some mistake. Amy would never—"

"There's no mistake." He picked up the overturned chair and shoved it back under the table. "She propositioned a cop."

Diana dismissed the charge. "She was just fooling around."

"She gave him a price."

"That doesn't mean—"

"Give it up, Diana," he interrupted, bending to grab the newspaper. He tossed it to her. "Since you obviously don't want to believe me, read it for yourself."

As long as she didn't look, she could convince herself it was someone else who'd been arrested, possibly someone with the same name, a coincidence. Amy had done some questionable things in the past, but never anything like this.

"Well?" Stuart prompted.

He knew exactly which buttons to push. She straightened the wrinkled newspaper and scanned the headlines.

"It's near the bottom, on the left side."

Diana shot him an angry look. "You don't have to sound so damned smug."

"Hey, don't even think about trying to take this out on me. I'm not the enemy here."

"And Amy is?" Oh, God, there it was, right where he'd said it would be. DAUGHTER OF PROMINENT TWIN CITIES' PHYSICIAN ARRESTED FOR PROSTITUTION. What was it about actually seeing something in print that made it seem so much worse?

"I see you found it," Stuart said.

She read the first two paragraphs and skimmed the rest. It was enough. Diana didn't doubt for a minute that Amy had been playing one of her stupid games again, only this time she'd let it go too far. The thought of her sister actually selling herself was as farfetched as her checking into a nunnery.

"You know, it could just as easily have been your name in there," Stuart said. "Or mine. At least your father's position at the hospital is secure. I can kiss my career at Cunningham's good-bye if Ellsworth sees this and realizes her association with me."

Diana almost laughed out loud. The investment company where Stuart worked had been involved in half a dozen lawsuits over the past five years. "If Gerry Cutter could 'borrow' funds from a client's account and still keep his job, I hardly think Stanton Ellsworth is going to give you grief over my sister."

"It's precisely because of what Gerry did that the rest of us have to keep ourselves above reproach."

"No one is going to connect you to any of this. How could they?"

"God—you can be so unbelievably dense at times. Half of my clients are people I met through your father."

Diana glanced at the clock. "It's almost seven,

Stuart. If I don't get to the jail now, I'm going to have to call work and take the morning off."

"You can't be serious. I would've thought you'd learned your lesson by now."

"She's my sister. I can't abandon her any more than you could abandon John if he were in trouble."

"The difference is my brother would never ask for my help. Amy expects yours. She knows no matter what kind of mess she makes of her life, you'll always come running to clean up after her."

"That's not true." She scrambled mentally for an example to prove him wrong. "I had nothing to do with getting her into that drug rehab program. Amy did that all by herself."

"She was the one who decided to stick that crap up her nose all by herself, too."

It was an old argument, one Diana refused to get into again. She was about to leave when he asked, "What about your parents? Don't you think it's time you took their feelings into consideration? Have you thought what it must be doing to them to see their names constantly dragged through the sewer by Amy?"

She didn't have to think, she knew. Her father would storm around the house in a rage, her mother would take to her bed with a migraine. "It isn't Amy's fault Mom's and Dad's names were in the paper."

"Would you take off those goddamned blinders? If Amy didn't fill the reporters in on the details, who did?"

"She wouldn't do something like that."

"What better way to get even?" Diana wavered only for an instant, but it was enough for Stuart to pick up on her doubt. "At least now you can understand why I'm not going to let you go down there to see her. She'll make sure you—"

"I don't remember asking your permission," Diana said coolly.

"Don't push me on this one, Diana. There's too much at stake."

"Amy's in *jail*, Stuart. You can't expect me to just leave her there."

"Maybe a few nights behind bars will do her some good." His eyes grew animated as he warmed to the idea. "Nothing else has worked. You know as well as I do that if she keeps this up, she's going to wind up in the morgue one of these days."

There were nights she'd lain awake haunted by the same fear. Still, no matter the provocation, she couldn't turn her back on Amy. "I'm going to take a shower."

"Do you want me to drop you off at work? I have to go that way to meet a client this morning."

The invitation had the subtlety of cigar smoke. "I hate it when you do that. If you want to know my plans, just ask."

"Maybe I didn't make myself clear on this, Diana. There's no way I'm going to let your sister drag me down with her."

Again she glanced at the clock. "We're going to have to finish this later."

"Just tell me what you intend to do."

"I don't know yet." She was lying.

"Don't say I didn't warn you," he said with an eerie calm.

After all the time they'd lived together, she'd become accustomed to the idle threats Stuart made in the heat of an argument. They'd bothered her in the beginning, but not anymore. "All right, I'm warned."

"It's me or Amy."

Even at Stuart's annoying worst, she invariably felt the need to placate him. "Why don't you meet me at Charlie's after work? I'll buy you dinner and we can talk about this then."

"I've made other plans for my dinner."

She waited for him to tell her what they were. After several seconds she realized he wasn't going to say anything more. "I guess I'll see you when you get home, then."

An hour later Diana was on her car phone, telling her assistant she would be arriving late and to clear her schedule. She had no idea how long it took to bail someone out of jail. It wasn't a subject that ever came up in her circle of friends.

One minute she was furious with Amy for getting herself into yet another mess, the next she could hardly breathe past the heartache over the demons that drove her sister. It was important to be good at something when your entire life you'd been told you were second best. Through circumstance and personality Diana had left Amy only one role in which she could excel, and she was doing a hell of a job of it.

Diana knew where the jail was—she'd lived in the Minneapolis/St. Paul area all her life—but she'd never had occasion to go inside. Simply getting out of her car and walking through the visitors door put her on the defensive. From the moment she entered she found herself battling an irrational urge to stop everyone she passed and tell them she really didn't belong there, that her sister had been arrested by mistake, that no one in her family, that no one she even knew, had ever been in the kind of trouble that would land them in jail.

It took several minutes to connect with the person who collected the bail and to discover that someone had already paid for Amy's release. She'd been gone for more than an hour. Dumbfounded at the news, Diana asked the policeman a series of questions that he either couldn't or wouldn't answer. Finally she gave up and left.

Amy's mysterious benefactor had saved Diana the embarrassment of having her name and address listed on an official police record. She should have been relieved, even grateful; instead she was suspicious. No one had been there for Amy when her drinking changed from social to excessive or when she moved from an occasional joint to hard drugs. Why now?

Despite an overcast sky, she stopped to dig her dark glasses out of her purse and put them on. When she looked up again she saw Frank Pechacek, an old friend of her father's, headed her way. If he spotted her, he was sure to ask what she was doing there. After all, the local jail was hardly the place one would be expected to find Carl and Eileen Winchester's daughter.

Then it hit her. Frank wasn't just her father's friend, he was his attorney. A partner in one of the best firms in the city. He was there to help Amy.

The thought no sooner formed than Diana realized how crazy it was. Her parents had severed their relationship with their wayward adopted daughter years ago. They might show up if she were in the hospital dying, but there was no way in hell they would come anywhere near her under these circumstances.

Diana put her hand up to her face, pretended to adjust her glasses, and headed in the opposite direction. Too late.

"Diana, is that you?" Frank called.

She turned and forced a smile. "Frank—I didn't see you."

"The hell you didn't," he said, coming up to her. "But then if you're here for the reason I think you are, I don't blame you for trying to avoid me."

"You know about Amy, then?"

"Her arrest was on the front page, Diana. Lawyers tend to notice those things."

"Have you talked to Dad?"

"No, and I don't think I want to. Not about this, anyway."

"I thought maybe you were here to . . . Actually I guess it was more that I hoped my parents had sent you to help Amy." She gave him a quick smile. "When I'm wrong, I'm wrong big time."

"I'd be happy to do what I can, but this kind of thing is usually pretty straightforward. Assuming this is the first time she's been caught, she should get off with probation."

The first time she's been caught? A surge of anger shot through Diana. All Amy's life people had presumed her guilty no matter the charge. If the last of the milk was gone, Amy drank it. If the dog ran away, Amy left the gate open. In the fifth grade when Jimmy Randall said someone stole his lunch money, Amy was the first person questioned. It was always someone else who took or forgot or stole, yet not once did anyone apologize to Amy.

"It's not just the first time, Frank," Diana told him. "The whole thing is a colossal mistake. I wouldn't blame Amy if she decided to sue the police department for false arrest." Her protest was vehement when it should have been indignant.

"I don't understand how this happened," she went on in a more reasonable tone. "The only thing I can figure is that she was joking around with the cop and he took her seriously. I'm sure she's not drinking again, so it couldn't have been that she was drunk. Maybe she was just feeling a little crazy. She gets like that—" She stopped when she saw the look on his face.

"I'm sorry, Diana. I thought you knew."

She went cold. "Knew what?"

"Amy's been at this for a while."

Admitting she didn't know what he was talking about didn't come easily. "She's been at what for a while? I don't understand."

Visibly upset, he started to say something and then stopped. "I shouldn't have brought it up. It would be better if you talked to Amy. She should be the one to tell you this, not me."

"If there was something she wanted me to know, she would have told me already." She could see she hadn't convinced him. "I can't help her if I don't know what's going on."

"A couple of months ago Darren Harris—you remember him, he was president of the Fordham Club the year your dad was secretary-treasurer—anyway, Darren had a couple of clients in town for a convention and they asked him if he could get them some girls for a little party at their hotel. Darren called a friend of his who does that kind of thing. The friend made a couple of phone calls, and . . ." He left the rest for her to fill in for herself.

"And?" she prompted.

"Amy was one of the girls who showed up."

He might as well have told her no flowers would bloom that summer. "What made him think it was Amy?"

"I asked Darren the same thing. I knew how hard something like this would be on your family, so I wanted to be sure he knew what he was talking about. He reminded me that Amy and his daughter had been on the swim team together in high school." Frank looked away, as if to shield himself from her reaction.

If she had arrived a few minutes sooner or left home just a little later, she and Frank Pechacek would never have crossed paths and she would have had the rest of the morning to believe in Amy's innocence. Now she was left with a hundred questions, and no desire to hear the answers.

Two

After Diana left Frank Pechacek she didn't know where else to go, so she headed for her office. She should have gone to see Amy. The longer she stayed away, the more awkward it would be when they finally saw each other again. But she couldn't face her sister. Not yet. She needed time to deal with the news, time to try to find a way to keep the confusion and, more important, the revulsion from showing on her face and in her voice.

Why would Amy do such a thing?

The question rolled through Diana's mind like a ricocheting boulder, crashing into every thought, shattering every control. Amy couldn't need money. The trust fund from their grandmother was as large as Diana's own. But if not money, then what? In a way the drinking and drug problems had been understandable. Experimentation was integral to an evening's entertainment with the friends Amy had kept from high school. Prostitution wasn't something you dabbled in because you wanted to be part of the crowd. To sell yourself to strangers took premeditation and a knowing willingness to participate in intimate, degrading behavior.

When Diana had driven by streetwalkers in the past she'd given fleeting thoughts to how someone might wind up selling their body. She'd read about actors who hired call girls, or paid women for drive-by sex, but to be told her own sister was a part of that scene was incomprehensible.

Diana pulled into the turn lane in front of the Sander's Food Building. She looked at the gleaming structure and realized the last thing she wanted to do was go inside. Eventually she would be able to handle the sidelong glances and questioning looks from the people she worked with, but not yet. Most of all she didn't want to see sympathy or pity in anyone's eyes. If someone should actually go so far as to try to commiserate, she'd be hard-pressed to be civil.

After checking for a break in traffic, she pulled back onto the main road and drove away without thought to direction or destination. An hour later she was in Stillwater. From there she headed north, stopping in Taylors Falls to pick up a sandwich at a deli.

Surprisingly there weren't many tourists at the park where she went to eat her lunch, but then it was early May, and the middle of the week, and a storm had been forecast for later that day. After dumping her half-eaten sandwich in the trash, she wandered along the river, stopping to watch a couple in a rented canoe. The man struggled with the paddle, but the woman looked on as if he were an Olympic champion. The two were obviously lovers, in a world of their own, one filled with touching, and intimate glances, and laughter. Had she and Stuart ever occupied such a world? She glanced down at the obscenely large engagement ring he had given her for her birthday. She would gladly trade it for just one day like the one being shared by the two people in the canoe. Diana felt a wave of envy so fierce, she had to turn away.

From the day she'd escaped her playpen by stacking her toys in the corner and climbing over the bars, she'd thrived on finding solutions to seemingly impossible problems. As kids Amy had never been in trouble that Diana hadn't been able to intercede on her behalf. When they'd been in school together and Amy was failing a class, there wasn't a teacher Diana couldn't talk into giving Amy extra credit. Even now at work Diana was considered a genius at finding paths around brick walls. Stuart said she manipulated. She preferred to think she was creative.

Whatever her skills, they were useless to her now. This time Amy had gotten herself into a situation that couldn't be talked or manipulated or wished away.

The thought stopped Diana cold. No wonder she'd left town rather than face Amy. She was running from her own sense of impotence.

On the ride back to town Diana rehearsed what she would say to Amy. But as she drew closer to her sister's apartment, the words became trite and meaningless and the doubts returned. She found a parking place on the street right away but couldn't make herself get out of the car. She was afraid if she went in still battling the resentment and frustration, she was going to say something she'd regret later. The pain and disappointment were too new to hide and the last thing Amy needed to see after everything that had already happened.

A lovely sentiment, but leaning more toward self-serving than altruistic.

When had she become such a coward?

Diana got out of the car. The breeze had become a wind. She looked up at the sky. The storm would hit soon. Amy loved rain. She said it made people more willing to settle in and slower to leave. It seemed right that something, if only the weather, should go Amy's way this day.

Diana crossed the street, went inside the building, and climbed the stairs to Amy's apartment. She pressed the doorbell and waited. When Amy didn't answer, Diana actually felt light-headed with relief. Foolishly she knocked, just to be sure. This time Amy came to the door.

"I thought you were the pizza guy." She was plainly not happy to see Diana.

Except for the dark circles under her eyes, Amy looked the same as she had the week before. She had on jeans and a sweatshirt. Missing were the fishnet stockings and scarlet letter Diana only then realized she'd pictured in her mind. "I told you that you should have a peephole installed."

"Why are you here?"

"Since when do I need a reason?" She tried to keep the combativeness out of her voice. Amy was on the defensive and looking to be provoked.

"Since it's the middle of the day and you should be at work."

"Can I come in?"

Instead of moving out of the way so Diana could enter, Amy came forward and leaned her shoulder into the door frame. "I don't think that's a good idea. At least not today."

"Do you have company?" The question had taken on a new meaning, one Diana hadn't intended. The implication hung heavily between them. "If you let me come in, I can keep you from eating that pizza all by yourself. Think of the calories you'll save."

"Wow—you're willing to sacrifice that lean, mean body for me? What a sister."

"Don't do that, Amy."

"Don't do what?" she snapped.

"I didn't come to fight with you."

"No? That must mean you came to lecture. Thanks, but I believe I'll pass." She stepped back to close the door.

"Stop being a little shit and let me in," Diana said.

Despite an obvious attempt not to, Amy smiled. "Now there's the sister I know and love."

Unlike Diana's controlled expressions, when Amy smiled it involved her whole face. Her cheeks swelled and her eyes crinkled. It was almost impossible not to respond in kind. She and Diana were supposed to look alike, but despite Eileen Winchester's best efforts, they no more resembled each other than a Volvo and a Maserati painted the same color. Amy wore her dark brown hair short, pixie style, with bangs that looked as if they'd been cut with pinking shears. She favored oversize earrings, skirts that hit either midthigh or ankle, and heels that lifted her five feet eight inches to almost six feet. Diana's own dark hair was long, past her shoulders, and all one length. Her wardrobe ran to tailored suits and wool slacks with a couple of pairs of designer jeans for the occasional weekend in the country. Her earrings were conservative, some with gems, most plain gold.

It was a constant, well-vocalized puzzlement to Eileen how a child she had so carefully and personally chosen to be the sibling for her own dear daughter could have turned out to be so different. Anything Eileen couldn't understand, she didn't trust.

Before Diana could answer Amy, a man who looked to be well into his eighties came up behind her. He had on a blue shirt with a faded red stripe around the middle and was carrying a large insulated box tucked under his arm.

"You the lady that called for the pizza?" he asked Amy.

"That's me," she told him. "Hold on a minute, I'll get your money."

"I'll get it," Diana said. She dug twenty dollars out of her purse. "Keep the change."

"It comes to twenty-one eighty," he said, and handed her the bill.

Diana looked at Amy. "What did you order?"

"I don't remember."

She took another ten out of her wallet. He stuffed the money in his pocket before extracting a cardboard box out of the insulated one and handing it to Amy. He turned to leave.

"My change?" Diana prompted.

He gave her a puzzled look.

"Never mind," she said with a wave.

"My, aren't we generous?" Amy said when he was too far away to hear.

"How would you like to be that age and delivering pizzas for a living?"

She followed Amy inside. The blinds were closed and the drapes were drawn, making the normally cheerful-looking apartment with its mauves and greens and flowers and stripes seem dark and lifeless. Diana turned on a lamp as she passed through the living room. It didn't help. It was as if the spark that gave Amy's home its charm and made it feel inviting came from her. Without her enthusiasm the over-stuffed sofa and painted end tables seemed old instead of filled with character.

Normally Diana felt more comfortable here than she did in her own home. In keeping with his wishes, she and Stuart had surgically divided their financial responsibilities when they combined households. The condo, its upkeep, and all of the utilities were hers.

The rest, including the furnishing, was his responsibility.

He'd been quick to give his opinion about which condo she should buy but had purchased the furniture on his own, taking months to choose each classically minimalist piece. Everything was insanely expensive and made from leather, glass, or exotic woods. The effect was pure *Architectural Digest*, more exhibit than home.

Amy's apartment was the Snickers bar to Stuart's Godiva chocolate, filled with an eclectic assortment of things she'd picked up at garage sales, from estate auctions, and in newspaper ads. The pieces ranged from a fifties chrome-and-Formica kitchen set to a rococo clock that had belonged to their grandmother.

The clock was a family heirloom, one their mother unfailingly insisted rightfully belonged to her. Supposedly it had been a gift from Catherine the Great to one of their relatives and was worth a fortune. The money meant nothing to Amy; the value derived from the sense of belonging that came with being singled out by her grandmother to be the caretaker of the clock until it was passed on to the next generation. In the extended Boehm family, Grandmother Mary had been the one person besides Diana who had accepted and loved Amy without question or reservation.

"There's fresh lemonade in the refrigerator," Amy said as Diana followed her into the kitchen. "Or if you'd prefer beer, I think there's some in the crisper."

"What are you doing—" She stopped, but too late. When Amy left the clinic Diana had promised she wouldn't question or try to second-guess Amy's behavior. There had been times, especially when she knew Amy was going to a party where alcohol and drugs were as accepted as the chips and dips, when Diana had almost choked trying to swallow a warning. Somehow she'd always succeeded. Until now.

"With beer?" Amy finished for her.

"I'm sorry," Diana said. "It just slipped out."

"I suppose I should give you points for not trying to deny that's what you were going to say." She opened the cupboard and took out two plates.

"If you want to give me points, how about for all the times I've kept my mouth shut in the past?"

"And what do I get for all the times I would have killed for a drink and didn't?"

Diana thought about the question and asked mischievously, "Kill or drink?"

"Believe me," she said with a meaningful glance in Diana's direction, "there's been plenty of provocation for both." She popped the tabs on the pizza box and lifted the lid. For long seconds she stared at what she found inside. Finally she laughed. "You're not going to believe this."

Diana looked up from the silverware drawer. "What's wrong?"

"You have got to see for yourself." She stepped away from the box.

Diana peered inside and saw a round of naked bread. The far corner held a mound of cheese, pepperoni, mushrooms, olives, and other assorted vegetables. "Is this some new kind of pizza?"

"Yeah—right."

The sight was so bizarre, it took Diana a second to reason it out. She groaned. "We should have known. Did you see the way he had the box tucked under his arm?"

Amy picked out an olive, put her head back, and let the trailing cheese slip into her mouth.

"You're making me sick," Diana said.

"Hey, it's not bad. Try some."

Reluctantly Diana plucked off a mushroom and put it in her mouth. It was still a little crisp and had a wonderful woodsy taste. She tried a slice of pepper and then a piece of pepperoni. "Okay, so it doesn't taste as repulsive as it looks."

Amy reached overhead and pulled down a couple of bowls and handed one to Diana. "Dig in."

Diana took the bowl and gave Amy a fork. They each stabbed a corner and fought to separate a piece from the rapidly congealing whole. When the direct approach didn't work, they tried cutting, but that failed, too. Out of the corner of her eye Diana saw Amy's expression turn from eager anticipation to grim determination. The look caught her off guard and hit the section of her mind reserved for processing the sublime and ridiculous. She began to laugh.

Amy grinned. "We're acting like a couple of lions after the kill."

"Better yet, Uncle Pete and Aunt Rosy fighting over the last piece of pumpkin pie." The statement was all they needed to set them off. Soon it was one of those times when the laughter exceeded the humor, and the release was a gift. Minutes passed. Instead of lessening, the laughter built on itself. Soon they were gasping for breath and leaning against the counter to stay upright.

Almost blinded by tears, Diana grabbed a napkin. As she wiped her eyes she felt a band clamp around her chest. Without knowing when or how, the tears had become real. She looked up to see that Amy wasn't laughing anymore, either, but watching her. "I'm sorry," Diana said softly. "I didn't mean for this to happen."

"You always have to be so goddamned perfect." Amy slammed the lid on the pizza. "Why couldn't you have just come in here and screamed at me the way any normal person would?"

"I've never screamed at you."

"Well, maybe you should."

"Would it have made a difference?" At last Diana was angry. Her entire life she'd heard how "perfect" she was, from her parents, from her teachers, and from her friends. She sure as hell didn't need to hear it from Amy, the one person who knew better. "I don't understand what you want, Amy."

"To be left alone."

"Now?"

"All the time. Why can't I get that through your head?"

The accusation stung. "I don't interfere in your life."

"Then why do I feel as if you're always there looking over my shoulder?"

"That's not fair."

Amy put her hands against the counter and stared up at the ceiling. Thunder sounded in the distance. "No, it's not. I'm sorry. I have no right to take this out on you."

Diana had promised herself she wouldn't ask, but the word was out before she could stop it. "Why?"

"Why what?"

"Why would you sell yourself? And so cheaply? There isn't a man alive who could pay you what you're worth."

"You're not going to ask me if I did it first? Whatever happened to benefit of the doubt?"

Diana grabbed another napkin to finish wiping her eyes. "Darren Harris happened."

Amy recoiled. She hugged herself as if the oncoming storm had found its way inside. For a long time she stood perfectly still, saying nothing. Then, in a defeated voice, she asked, "Who told you?"

"I ran into Frank Pechacek at the jail this morning. He told me Darren Harris saw you at some hotel. You were with—"

"I should have known Mr. Harris would tell on me."

Amy's reaction was a hundred and eighty degrees from what Diana had expected. Instead of being angry or defensive or combative, it was as if she were still in school and her best friend's father had caught her stealing candy. "I don't know how many people he told, but Dad wasn't one of them. If he knew, he would have said something to me."

"It doesn't matter. He knows now."

"You sound as if you care."

She grabbed the pizza box and dumped it in the garbage. "Well, I don't. Why should I?"

When Amy dropped out of college for the second time Carl Winchester told her bluntly that he was through, that he wanted nothing more to do with his youngest daughter. Anxious to have her say, Eileen had called later that day to tell Amy that she was no longer a part of her and Carl's lives. Periodically Amy would go to charity functions or opening nights where she was certain to run into them. If Diana questioned the seemingly masochistic behavior, Amy claimed she got a kick out of seeing the looks on their faces when they first spotted her. Diana suspected what Amy was really looking for, but would never see, was their love.

"It's hard not to care," Diana said. "No matter what's happened, they're still your mother and father."

"They were never my mother and father."

It was a point Diana couldn't argue, a situation she had never understood. "Were you trying to get back at them? Is that why you started . . . why you became . . ."

"A prostitute?" she supplied.

"Don't do that, Amy. You know I don't think you're a prostitute."

"Oh, but I am. Not full-time, but I try to work as often as I can." There was a challenge to the answer, as if she were daring Diana to dig deeper.

Diana's stomach rolled, acid burned her throat. "Why? If you needed money, you could have come to me. You know I would have given you whatever I had. If that wasn't enough, we could have found a way to get more."

"I have plenty of money," Amy said coolly.

"Is someone forcing you to work for them? Are you being blackmailed?"

"Wouldn't that be wonderfully melodramatic? Sorry, but it's nothing like that."

Diana snapped. "Then why you would do something so stupid? How could you let yourself be used like that?"

The bravado was gone. Amy struggled for an answer. Finally she said, "I don't know."

"You have to know. Nobody prostitutes themselves for the fun of it."

"Do you want me to make something up?"

"If you don't know why"—Diana tried to sound reasonable—"then tell me how."

"What good would that do?"

"Damn it, I'm trying to understand. Give me that much."

"I met a guy in a bar." She unfolded her napkin and blew her nose. "He offered to pay." She shrugged. "I figured why not? After a while I discovered I liked it—no commitments, no expectations, no disappointments."

Diana didn't believe her. "What about diseases?"

"You read too much."

"AIDS is—"

Amy held up her hand. "Give it a rest. I'm not stupid. I protect myself."

In her entire life Diana had never felt as frustrated. She wanted to shout and pound her fists, create a scene Amy would never forget. But she was incapable of such behavior, shackled by lessons on deportment begun at her mother's breast. "How did you get out of jail?"

"A friend."

"Who?"

"It's none of your business."

"Your pimp?"

"I think you should leave," Amy said.

She couldn't; not like this. "I'm sorry."

Amy didn't say anything for a long time, just stood and stared at the floor. Finally she looked up at Diana. There were tears in her eyes. "Yeah, me too."

Diana didn't want to give up her anger; it gave her strength and focus. But she'd never been able to stay mad at Amy, not even when she took their father's brand-new Mercedes for a joyride and backed it into a tree. Amy was only thirteen at the time, and the potential punishment was so great, Diana had insisted on taking the blame.

With a sigh of release Diana put her arms around Amy. "I love you."

"I know you do," Amy said. "I just can't figure out why."

Diana stayed with Amy until almost ten that night, refusing to leave until she was reasonably sure the next time they saw each other, whether it was the following day or a week from then, there would be no lingering awkwardness. They talked, but not about the arrest or its possible consequences. Instead they dipped their toes in the pond of childhood memories and followed the drifting circles to known shores. The indulgence was one that, over the years and by tacit agreement, they had saved to heal only the most hurtful wounds. Like the time Amy was sixteen and late coming home from school because she'd had to stop to fix a flat. To teach her a lesson, their parents had left on their vacation without her. The housekeeper had called Diana at college, and she'd come home for the week to keep Amy company. Her mother had been furious when she found out.

The heaviest rain had come and gone by the time Diana drove home. She ran the windshield wipers intermittently to brush the mist aside and thought how nice it would be if there were a device that could do the same for her mind.

She said a silent prayer that Stuart would be asleep as she rode the elevator. She was barely awake herself, far too vulnerable to hold her own in a fight with him. It would be impossible to avoid a confrontation in the morning, but there were built-in parameters to any prework arguments. They might shout at each other over toast and coffee and continue through the roar of shower spray, but eventually their schedules would impose a limit. Stuart would sacrifice one of his lesser appendages before he would be late for work.

The elevator doors opened to a dim hallway. She'd told the super days ago that two of the lights were out, but changing bulbs obviously wasn't one of his high-priority jobs. If he still hadn't gotten around to it by that weekend, she'd probably do it herself. Better that than listening to Stuart complain.

The building was almost four years old and still only half-full. Supposedly the two other condos on their floor had bids on them, and with luck they would have neighbors in a couple of months. Without Stephanie Gorham, the one neighbor who had become a close friend, Diana would have felt as if she were living in a hotel.

Making as little noise as possible, Diana opened the door. It was completely black inside. Stuart must have been furious when he went to bed to leave her to stumble around in the dark and possibly awaken him. She ran her hand along the wall to the switch and flipped it up. The hall lamp should have come on, but it didn't. She stepped out of the doorway to let what little light was outside spill past her.

The lamp wasn't where it should have been; neither was the table it had sat on. Diana inched farther inside, feeling her way until she reached the switch that controlled the overhead lights in the living room. Nothing. She made her way to the window, opened the drapes, and looked around. The room was bare.

Not one piece of furniture sat on the floor, not one book or piece of artwork sat on the shelves beside the fireplace. Even the carpet Stuart had paid a fortune to have custom-made to match the Pollock-style painting was gone.

They'd been robbed.

She went into the kitchen. Cupboards and drawers hung open like grotesquely yawning mouths. Not even a box of cereal filled the cavities. She looked around again. Had she somehow gotten off on the wrong floor and wandered into a different apartment? Impossible. Only Stuart would hang green and gold wallpaper in the kitchen.

Her heart raced as she headed upstairs, but it wasn't fear that drove her anymore. When she hit the bedroom light switch she wasn't surprised when nothing happened. She opened the drapes just as the clouds split and let the full moon spill its light into the room. All that remained were the impressions in the carpet where the bed and chairs and dressers had been.

She went to the closets. Stuart's was bare, hers was as she'd left it that morning—except the floor. It was littered with the underwear, stockings, sweaters, and nightgowns that had been in her dresser that morning.

She went to the bathroom to confirm the obvious. Her toiletries were there, Stuart's were gone. The shampoo was missing from the shower as well as the half-used bar of French milled soap. She was on her way back out when she noticed a note taped to the mirror over the double sinks. She moved closer to make out the words in the dim light. I TRIED TO WARN YOU WHAT WOULD HAPPEN. YOU SHOULD HAVE LISTENED. I GUESS SOMETHING LIKE THIS IS WHAT I NEEDED TO PROVE HOW INCOMPATIBLE WE REALLY ARE.

At first she could only stand and stare at what looked like a stolen bit of melodrama from a grade B movie. Patiently she waited for a feeling of hurt, or disappointment, or loss to set in, but she was either too tired or too numb or possibly just didn't give a damn. She wasn't even all that angry. The one emotion she did feel was so unexpected, it took a while to recognize.

She was *relieved* Stuart was gone.

Instead of thoughts about how lonely she would feel at the breakfast table from then on, she was excited about the prospect of eating her cereal without having to listen to one of Stuart's tirades.

She wouldn't have to go to bed early anymore just because Stuart was tired and didn't want to be disturbed when she came up later. Not even the thought of coming home to an empty apartment night after night could dampen her growing enthusiasm.

She didn't know whether to laugh with pleasure at her newfound sense of freedom or cry for the years she'd wasted in the relationship.

Three

Diana had no idea how long she'd been sitting on the stair landing when she heard her name being called and remembered she'd left the front door open.

"Diana—are you home?" Stephanie Gorham called.

"Up here." Diana put her hand on a baluster with the intention of standing, but the result didn't seem worth the effort, so she stayed where she was.

Stephanie peered around the corner. She flipped the light switch for the stairs, the only one Diana hadn't tried. Naturally, it worked. Three recessed, sixty-watt bulbs lit the open stairwell.

"I would have been here sooner, but somehow you got by me," Stephanie said.

"I take it that means you already know what happened here?" She shouldn't have been surprised. Diana had come to believe Stephanie's job as a feature reporter on the *Star Tribune* had imbued her with some kind of mystic power to always be tuned in to whatever was going on. Very little got by her notice.

"I saw the movers when I came home for lunch. It wasn't hard to fill in the blanks." She stood at the bottom of the stairs and leaned against the railing. "I tried to reach you at work, but they said you were gone for the day."

"I didn't feel like talking to anyone." No other explanation was needed.

Stephanie looked around. "Did Stuart do this because of Amy?"

"I think Amy was just an excuse. We've been headed in this direction for a long time now."

"I'm sorry. . . ."

Diana gave her a reproving smile. Stephanie and Stuart had barely tolerated each other's company. "No, you're not."

"All right, so I'm not sorry he's gone. Next week you won't be, either. But that still leaves seven less than perfect days we've got to get you through."

"I don't think it's going to take near that long."

"Really?" She sounded doubtful.

"Stuart took everything, Stephanie, including a tube of half-used toothpaste. The only thing he left was my clothes and my makeup."

"Even all those exercise things he bought you last Christmas?"

She hadn't bothered to look in the gym. "I don't know—no, he wouldn't take that. It was a present."

Stephanie stepped around the corner to check the spare room for herself. "Wrong," she called out.

"Are you sure?" Her lethargy gone, Diana bounded down the stairs. Sure enough, the room was as bare as the day she and Stuart had moved in. The only thing left were the holes in the wall where the mirrors had hung. "The *bastard.*"

Stephanie laughed. "You've cursed that treadmill every day it's been here, and now you're cursing Stuart because he took it away?"

"It's the principle. Stuart might be able to lay claim

to everything else around here, but what was in this room belonged to me." She'd found a focus for her anger. Whirling around, she headed for the kitchen.

Stephanie followed. "What are you going to do?"

"Find out where Stuart went."

"How?"

"By calling every one of his friends."

"It's two o'clock in the morning, Diana."

"All the better to catch them off guard." She crossed the nook and closed a cupboard door to get to the phone. All she found were holes in the wall. "It just gets better and better."

"He even took the phone?" Stephanie came up behind her to see for herself. "How could he just come in here and clean the place out? Didn't some of this stuff belong to you?"

Diana shook her head. "When we decided to move in together, Stuart insisted we both get rid of everything we owned." She went around the kitchen closing the rest of the cupboards. "The deal was I would buy the condo and Stuart would take care of everything that went inside."

"So you wound up with the mortgage and taxes and insurance, and he got the food and furniture and toothpaste?"

"God, I can't believe I was so stupid."

"Me either," Stephanie mumbled.

"I heard that."

"You know, this would make a great article. There have to be other women out there who—"

"I think the Winchester name has been in the paper enough lately, don't you?"

Stephanie flinched. "Don't tell me that's how you found out about Amy."

"Not directly. Stuart saw it first. Finding it myself would have been easier."

"Say no more."

Diana liked that she never had to fill in the blanks for Stephanie. "I thought it was a mistake."

"I wouldn't want to believe something like that about my sister, either."

Diana's spurt of energy had peaked and was on a rapid downward slide. "I don't know what to do to help her," she said. "I used to think that once Amy got out on her own and built a life for herself away from our parents she would be all right. But after what happened yesterday, I just don't know anymore."

"Have you considered finding someone for her to talk to?"

"I assume you mean a psychiatrist." Diana walked over to the sliding glass door and checked the lock, forgetting for the moment there was nothing left to steal. "Amy was in counseling while she was at the hospital." She leaned her forehead against the cool glass and watched distant lightning as the storm moved east. "I thought it had helped."

"If not Amy, then what about you?"

Diana looked at Stephanie to see if she was serious. "What makes you think I need counseling?"

"Not counseling, necessarily, just someone to talk to."

"I don't have time for that now." She held her arms open to the emptiness surrounding her. "It seems I have some shopping to do."

"Well, I don't know any stores open this late, so you might as well come downstairs with me. The sofa's a little lumpy, but not as hard as the floor here."

"Thanks, but—"

"But what?"

Declining the invitation had been automatic; she

didn't impose on others easily. But it wasn't as if she had any real choice. Not only were there no towels for a shower in the morning, there was no toothpaste, or blow-dryer—and nothing to eat. She either stayed at Stephanie's or checked into a motel. "Give me a second. I'll get my clothes."

"Hey, I just remembered something. Last year I did an article about a guy who councils runaway kids. I think he might be able to help you."

One of the things Diana liked least about Stephanie was her dogged persistence when she got an idea. She sighed. There were times it was just easier to give in. "I don't know what good someone who works with runaway kids is going to do me, but get me his number and I'll call him tomorrow."

"Am I being too pushy about this? Would you rather I backed off?"

"What makes you say that?"

"You gave in too easily."

"I'm too tired to fight." Reluctantly she admitted, "And who knows, you may be right. Maybe I do need to talk to someone."

Stephanie put her arm around Diana's shoulders. "Come on, let's get out of here. There's a half gallon of ice cream and two spoons waiting for us downstairs."

Diana smiled at the irony. "Just what I need now that Stuart took off with my treadmill."

The next week Diana was at her desk at Sander's Food, reading a report from the sales department, when her assistant buzzed her. She swung her chair around and hit the intercom button. "Yes?"

"Mr. Kennedy is calling on line two."

Diana couldn't believe it. Five minutes ago she

would have bet half a year's salary that the message on the mirror was the last she would ever hear from him. She considered having her assistant tell him she was unavailable, but curiosity beat out one-upmanship. "Go ahead and put him through."

She picked up the receiver. "Forget something at the apartment?" she said sweetly.

He skipped both greeting and response. "Call her off. You can have whatever you want, just make her stay away from me."

Stuart's forte was intimidation. She'd never heard this desperate tone in his voice and was intrigued. "I don't know what you're talking about. Call who off?"

"Don't try to snow me, Diana." His voice rose from a strained whisper but still came through muffled, as if he had his hand cupped around the receiver. "Amy wouldn't pull this shit without telling you first."

Diana made a conscious effort to ignore the bubble of fear that came with the mention of Amy's name. "I'm not my sister's keeper. Whatever she's—"

"I don't care what it takes, I want you to get her out of here, and I want you to do it now."

"Are you going to tell me where 'here' is, or am I supposed to guess?"

"I'm warning you, Diana, I—" He stopped. His voice became artificially cheerful as he directed his attention to someone else. Several seconds of silence passed before he spoke to her again. "She's been showing up at my office every day since I moved out. I've tried to reason with her, but she won't listen. I'm through being nice. You either get her away from me or I swear I'll—"

"Don't threaten me, Stuart. I don't have to put up with that crap from you anymore." Wow, she couldn't believe how good it felt to fight back. She should have tried it a long time ago.

"I'm sorry if that's the way you see it. It's not what I meant."

It was exactly what he'd meant, and she didn't believe for a minute that he was sorry, but she liked that he'd felt it necessary to tell her. "I take it you're calling from work?"

"Yes."

"Amy's there with you?"

"Yes."

Diana didn't know what to say next. She didn't have a clue what Amy was doing at Stuart's office. "Let me talk to her."

"You're missing the point, Diana. I don't want anyone to know she's here because of me."

Despite acknowledging she had the upper hand, he still couldn't keep his sarcasm in check. "You're not making sense. How am I supposed to ask Amy to leave you alone if I can't talk to her?"

"Tell her when you see her tonight."

"I can't promise my talking to her will do any good. You know as well as I do Amy only listens when she wants to."

"What is this? Now you're trying to threaten me?"

"I wouldn't dream of it." His paranoid act was wearing thin. "You've gone off the deep end about this. Are you on something?"

"What do you want? The bedroom set? I can have it sent over next week."

"God, no." The last thing she wanted was the bed, a physical reminder of the times they'd made love.

"You never liked the living room furniture. Why would you want it now? Are you doing this to punish me? Is that it? You want to take what I value above everything else just to get even?"

"I've got too much work to do to listen to this."

"What do you want, Diana? Just tell me. I'll do it."

Good God, was it possible he wasn't acting? Could the paranoia be real? "Talk to Amy. Find out why she's there and what she wants. Make her happy and I will be, too."

"I did warn you, Diana. It wasn't as if I took off without saying anything."

He was actually trying to justify his behavior. She had an insane urge to laugh. "Did I forget to thank you?"

"You can be such a bitch."

"Good-bye, Stuart." She hung up before he had a chance to say anything more.

Diana tried to reach Amy the rest of the afternoon but kept getting her machine. On the way home she swung by the apartment to see if Amy's car was there. It wasn't. And, as usual, Amy's cell phone wasn't working—which meant she didn't have it with her or had forgotten to charge the battery.

After talking to Stuart, she'd been unable to concentrate on anything at work. She'd been mentally absent most of the meeting she'd set up with her staff for the launch of Sander's Foods' new line of low-fat muffin and cake mixes. They were playing catch-up with the other manufacturers and were highly cognizant that they had to come out bigger and better if they hoped to make an impact on the marketplace. The campaign would start in eight months, timed to take advantage of the annual diet craze that hit after the holidays. Diana's team had been responsible for the market research and would be peripherally involved until the product was established.

She was fortunate to be surrounded by a group of self-starters, men and women who required little hands-on guidance, something they hadn't had much of the past week. Her physical and mental absence couldn't go on much longer. She had to find a way to get her life back in order—not only her life, but her apartment as well. She'd been sleeping on a futon Stephanie had dug out of her storeroom and eating frozen dinners standing at the kitchen counter.

She hated shopping, hated everything about it. There were times she'd wondered if she lacked some female gene that gave every other woman she knew the ability to mix colors and stripes and checks and flowers and come up with something that not only looked good, but actually looked as if it belonged together. Whenever she tried, the result was as discordant as a third-grade band class.

Diana pulled into the garage of her building, got out of the car, and glanced up to see Amy's red Pinto in a visitor's parking space. Not until that moment was she aware how worried she'd been. Just to be sure, she checked to see the car was indeed Amy's—as if there actually could be two identical rusted-out pieces of uninsurable junk in all of Minnesota.

Peering inside, she saw empty water bottles and Grateful Dead CDs littering the floor. It was Amy's car all right. For some bizarre reason, Amy kept her apartment spotless and her car a rolling garbage can.

Arriving at her apartment, she had to sidestep to avoid a phalanx of boxes and bags lining the hallway.

"We're in the kitchen," Amy hollered.

Diana glanced in the bags as she passed. Some were filled with groceries, others pots and pans, and still others towels and sheets. She found Amy sitting on the kitchen floor surrounded by lengths of shelf paper and Stephanie standing at the counter, a piece of crumpled newspaper in her hand. "Where did all this stuff come from?"

Amy gave Stephanie a conspiratorial wink. "We bought it. We talked about waiting until you could go with us, but picking out everyday stuff is such a no-brainer, we didn't think you'd mind missing out."

"You don't, do you?" Stephanie asked.

"Hardly," Diana said. She looked around at the mixing bowls, glasses, and a shiny new toaster still waiting to be put away. Stephanie reached in a box and pulled out a plate. "I've always loved that Lenox pattern. I used to have—"

"Not used to," Amy corrected, obviously pleased with herself. "You still do. I saved them for you."

She'd forgotten that she'd given her china to Amy. "Did you save the sterling, too?"

"Yep." Amy grinned. "Pretty much everything else is fresh out of the store, though. Courtesy of Stuart Layton Kennedy."

Diana didn't share Amy's obvious delight. "Stuart paid for all of this?"

"And a whole lot more," Amy said. "You get to pick out a new bedroom and dining room set tomorrow, and then either a new sofa and love seat, or new gym equipment."

"How did you—" Diana stopped herself. The questions would have to wait until she and Amy were alone. For all of her outlandish behavior, Amy was an intensely private person. "Never mind. I don't think I want to know."

Stephanie moved the dishes to the sink. "You have to let Amy tell you about it. I've never heard a finer example of poetic justice."

Diana shot Amy a questioning look.

Amy's smile had disappeared. "Have a little faith, big sister."

"I'm sorry." She didn't know what else to say.

Picking up on the strained moment, Stephanie jumped in. "I have a great idea," she said to Diana. "Go upstairs and get changed. When you come down we'll have a surprise for you."

"Another surprise." She laughed. "I don't know how many more I can handle."

Stephanie took Diana's shoulders and turned her toward the stairs. "When Amy and I get through with you, you're going to think that Stuart walking out was the best thing that ever happened."

"You're too late," Diana said. "I decided that the night he left."

"I did notice you got rid of the ring. Did you send it back?"

"It's in my car ashtray. I haven't decided what I'm going to do with it yet."

Stephanie gave her a little shove. "Give us ten minutes."

Diana checked her watch and looked at Amy. "Ten minutes okay with you?"

Amy shrugged. "Whatever Stephanie says."

By the time Diana had changed into jeans and a T-shirt, washed her makeup off, and pulled her hair back in a ponytail, it was time to go downstairs again. "Ready or not, I'm coming down," she called from the landing.

She found Amy in the kitchen, putting dishes and silverware on a tray. "Where's Stephanie?"

"Her editor called in a panic because a story he was going to run in tomorrow's paper didn't work out—or something like that. He wanted Stephanie to E-mail him the one she'd been working on at home.

She said that unless he wanted changes, it wouldn't take long."

"Can I help?" She had no idea with what, but it was something to say that had nothing to do with Stuart.

"There's champagne and sparkling cider in the fridge. You can put them on ice and bring them outside."

"We're celebrating, I take it?"

"It was Stephanie's idea." Amy opened the sliding glass door with her elbow and went out onto the balcony.

Diana grabbed a stainless-steel bowl off the counter, stuck the bottles of champagne and cider inside, dumped ice and water around them, and then followed Amy outside. A checkered tablecloth covered several cardboard boxes that had been put together to form a makeshift table. A potted geranium served as centerpiece; votive candles nestled in wineglasses provided utilitarian elegance. "My first dinner party as a free woman. And I didn't have to do any of the work or planning."

Amy distributed the plates. "Are you really as okay with Stuart walking out as you want everyone to think?"

"Pretty amazing, huh? After all the time we were together, all I felt was relief when it was finally over. I think my reaction surprises me even more than it does you and Stephanie."

"I thought you were so crazy about him." A trace of doubt lingered in her voice.

"Maybe I finally saw him for what he was."

Amy moved around the table, setting the napkins and silver as carefully as if she were preparing a formal dinner party. "How can you not be hurt, or at least mad at him for leaving the way he did?"

"What's up, Amy? Why do you think I'm trying to hide something from you?"

"Because it was my fault he moved out."

"What makes you say that?" Diana asked carefully.

"Come on, Diana. I make the front page of the paper the same day Stuart dumps you. I'd have to be pretty dense not to figure that one out."

Diana put the bowl in the shade. "If you're looking for a reason to feel guilty, I can come up with a hell of a lot better one. Why didn't you find a way to get me out of the relationship sooner?"

"I figured we're all entitled to a few mistakes. Stuart was yours." She picked up the empty tray and tucked it under her arm. "Of course staying with him for almost four years used up a lot of your credit in the mistake department. You're going to have to tread carefully from now on."

"What did you do, Amy?" She'd sworn she wouldn't ask until they had more time, but the question was like a fishbone: she either spat it out or it became lodged in her throat. "How did you get him to agree to pay for all this stuff?"

"I sat in one of those chairs in front of that board with the stock quotes and stared at him."

There was something missing, something Diana wasn't picking up on. "You never said a word?"

She shook her head. "Not until the end. I didn't have to."

"Then what made him—"

"Think about it, Diana." There was a catch in her voice. She coughed to clear her throat. "What could get to Stuart faster than having a known prostitute hang around his office pretending she was his friend?"

Finally Diana felt the pain that had been missing. But it had nothing to do with Stuart or the tumul-

tuous changes in her own life. Her heart broke for
Amy. She'd used her own shame as a weapon to right
a wrong. Diana had always believed herself the
strong one in their relationship, the one who fought
the battles and cared for the wounded.

She couldn't have been more wrong.

Four

"*I had a great time today,*" Amy said as Diana pulled into the garage at Amy's apartment house. "I'm really glad you asked me to go with you." She'd intended the statements to sound casual, the way any two friends who hadn't seen each other for a while might end their shopping trip. Instead she sounded needy. Worse was the way her neediness made her feel, like a puppy trying to force its nose under a disinterested hand.

"It seems like forever since we've done anything together," Amy went on. Terrific—just what Diana needed, a guilt trip for not paying more attention to her little sister. "But then I can't blame you for that. It's my fault that we didn't see much of each other the past couple of years. I should have tried harder to get along with Stuart. You were caught in the middle, and I didn't do anything to make it any easier. Next time—"

"There isn't going to be a next time, at least not one you have to worry about." Diana parked her Volvo next to Amy's Pinto, switched off the ignition, and turned sideways to look at Amy. "From now on, where men are concerned, we're a package deal. Love me, love my sister."

Amy busied herself gathering her purse and packages to keep Diana from seeing how much her caring meant. "Sounds a little kinky to me."

Diana laughed. "You know what I mean."

"You don't have to worry," Amy said. "I won't ever put you in the middle again. The next time you find someone I'll do whatever it takes to make sure he likes me, too. We'll be a real family, we'll get together for Thanksgiving and Christmas, the whole thing." She was rambling but couldn't stop. "Of course I know you'll have to go to Mom and Dad's on the real days, but that's okay. The time someone actually celebrates isn't what matters, it's the people you celebrate with. And someday, when you have kids, I'm going to be the best aunt they could ever have."

"If I do get involved with someone again—and the way I feel now, that's a mighty big if—you won't have to do anything."

Amy shook her head in protest.

"I'm serious," Diana went on. "I meant what I said before. Any man I bring home will either like you for the person you are, or he's out the door."

"You might want to rethink that idea. You can't expect the kind of man you deserve to be thrilled knowing someone like me is his prospective sister-in-law."

"Speaking of sisters-in-law," Diana said, "I've been meaning to ask you whatever happened to Larry. I kind of liked him."

"We broke up months ago." There had been two guys since then whom Diana knew nothing about. "You and I haven't seen a lot of each other this past year."

Diana put her hand on Amy's arm. "I'm sorry. All I can do is promise it won't happen again."

What was it about her that the most casual touch could make her feel loved, even when it came from a guy she picked up in a bar? "If I'd known getting arrested would turn out like this, I would have tried it a long time ago."

Diana's hand tightened on Amy's arm. "I don't ever want to hear you say something like that again."

"God, Diana, you're so easy it's almost embarrassing."

The silence grew heavy between them before Diana said, "I know you don't want to talk about this, Amy, and I promised you last night that I'd leave it alone, but I can't. Have you thought about what might happen to you? Tell me you've at least gotten an attorney."

Amy gave her a warning look.

Diana exploded. "Damn it, I'm worried about you."

"Well, don't be." When would she learn to keep her mouth shut? "You should know by now that I can take care of myself. If the story hadn't made the newspaper, you wouldn't even know anything had happened."

"Is that supposed to make me feel better?"

"You aren't my keeper, Diana. I'm a big girl now."

"And that means I should stop caring?" She put her hands on the steering wheel. "If that's what you want, fine. But you're going to have to tell me how."

"You can care, you just can't tell me what to do."

"Even if I see you doing something that I know is wrong, something that will hurt you?"

Amy stared at the packages in her lap. "Did I tell you Stuart was wrong for you?"

"That was different."

"Oh? Why?"

"You can't tell someone they're in a bad relationship, they have to discover it for themselves."

"Since when? Weren't you the one who told me Bobby Fender was using me and that I should break up with him?"

"For cryin' out loud, Amy, that was when you were in the eighth grade."

"Sometimes I think that's how you still see me. I don't want you to take care of me, Diana, I want to be your friend."

"I don't know what I would do if anything happened to you. For my own peace of mind I need to know you're all right."

They'd come full circle. "I told you I wouldn't talk about the night I got arrested." She opened the door and started to get out. "It's behind me."

"How can it be behind you when—"

"Give it up, Diana."

"Damn it, some things don't just go away. They need to be talked about first."

"Fine. Go home and talk to Stephanie about it. Better yet, call Stuart. I'm sure he's got plenty to say." Until now the day had been one Amy had wanted to wrap in a ribbon and keep forever. She got out of the car, slammed the door, and headed for the stairs.

Diana rolled down the window and called after her, "Do you still want to go with me tomorrow?"

How typical of her sister. No matter how justified Diana's anger or how righteous her indignation, she wore the mantle of peacemaker. If there was rough water, Diana tried to calm it—even if she chanced drowning in the process. Thank God Stuart had finally walked out on her. "I don't know. Call me in the morning."

"I love you, Amy."

The words stopped her cold. They always did. Her defenses shattered, she turned. "I love you, too." She came back to the car and braced her hands on the door. "I did hire an attorney. He convinced them to drop the charges."

"How?"

"By pointing out how close to entrapment their case was."

"Why didn't you tell me?"

"I'm sick to death of the whole thing. I just want it to go away."

"But you knew how worried I was. All you had to do was—" She suddenly understood what Amy had been trying to tell her. "Enough said. You're okay, that's all that matters." Diana smiled. "See you tomorrow."

"Yeah, I guess. Just not too early."

Once inside her apartment, Amy dumped her packages and purse on the sofa and went into the kitchen to get a bottle of flavored tea out of the refrigerator.

She was exhausted, an unfamiliar but not unwelcome feeling. Normally she searched for something to fill her days. The last two she'd been on the run constantly. Stocking Diana's cupboards with staples had been easy compared to the search for new furniture. Shopping wasn't Diana's thing. Not only didn't she know what style sofa she wanted, she was light-years from settling on a fabric. The only opinion she'd expressed was a negative—if the sofa or chair or bedroom set was something Stuart would like, she wanted nothing to do with it.

After sticking a frozen dinner in the microwave, Amy went back into the living room to check her answering machine. She was expecting a call from the English professor she'd had in college. He'd once offered to write a letter of recommendation if she ever decided to go on to graduate school. Not that she'd made up her mind for sure about going back to school, but if and when the day actually arrived, the news would make a nice present for Diana. Maybe then she could start worrying about herself a little instead of her ne'er-do-well sister.

The message light was flashing. She counted the number of calls—five—but before she could hit the playback button there was a knock on the door.

Amy grew excited at the prospect that Diana had decided to spend the night after all. They could order Chinese and rent a couple of movies or just talk all night the way they had when they were kids.

She flipped the dead bolt. "Forget something?" she asked before the door had swung all the way open.

It wasn't Diana. Amy's hand tightened on the knob. She took an instinctive step behind the wooden barrier, as if it could protect her. "Mom—what are you doing here?"

Eileen looked past Amy into the apartment. It seemed a long time before she finally asked, "Are you expecting someone?"

"Diana just left. I thought maybe she'd . . . Never mind. It isn't important." Reason dictated Eileen hadn't come for a reconciliation. Still, there was a spark of hope in Amy that refused to be extinguished by logic.

"Would it be all right if I came in?" It wasn't so much a question as a subtle criticism of Amy's social manners.

"Yes, of course. You caught me off guard." She had every right to be flustered. In the six years she'd been living on her own, this was the first time her mother had come to see her. Amy opened the door wider and motioned her mother to enter.

Eileen went into the living room, where she selected the only occupied seat in the entire apartment, standing there until Amy came over to move her purse and the packages she'd left only moments earlier. "Can I get you something to drink?"

"I thought Diana told us you didn't drink anymore." Eileen sat down, her back rigid, her narrow hips barely taking up half the cushion. Her linen jacket appeared freshly pressed, the matching slacks as unblemished. Eileen Winchester didn't sweat, she glowed. When the wind blew her hair, every strand returned to its designated place. These things were seemingly inbred, as natural to her as her blue eyes. She had no understanding or patience for anyone less fortunate.

"I was offering you coffee. The last time I checked it was still considered something to drink." Amy didn't know whether she was angry or pleased that Diana had told their parents about her progress.

"That won't be necessary. I don't intend to be here long."

"Now why doesn't that surprise me?" Amy sat on the arm of the sofa, knowing full well it would rankle her mother. Ladies sat *in* chairs, not *on* them.

"I suppose I should get to why I came. There's no sense delaying this." Her hands gripped the smooth lizard skin covering the designer clutch on her lap. She looked at Amy for only a fraction of a second before her gaze shifted to the Monet print on the opposite wall.

"I'm fine, Mother. Thanks for asking."

"Are you really?" Eileen snapped irritably. "It certainly doesn't appear that way to me or Carl."

Carl? Amy wondered. What had happened to

"Father"? They weren't playing their usual game, or the rules had been changed. Her bravado slipped. "You look well," she said as a peace offering. "Are you still playing tennis?" It bothered her to admit she didn't know something so inconsequential about her own mother, but there was no use pretending an intimacy that didn't exist.

"Why do you ask?"

"No reason. It's just that— It isn't important."

Eileen glanced around the room, her gaze lingering on the rococo clock as she said, "This isn't a visit, Amy. I didn't come here to see how you are, or to answer questions about myself or your fath—about Carl."

Amy had a sudden, desperate urge to tell her mother that she was going back to school, that she was finally going to become someone Eileen and Carl Winchester would be proud to call their daughter. "All right, we'll skip the social pleasantries. Why don't you tell me why you did come so we can get this over with?"

For the first time Eileen exhibited signs of nervousness. She touched her hair and cleared her throat. "I have a proposition for you—a very lucrative one, I should add." She paused to clear her throat again. "And I would guess, judging from the way you're living, that you could use some additional money."

Amy ignored the insult. To draw attention to such declarations was tantamount to pointing out that it snowed in Minnesota in the winter. "You want to give me money? Why?"

"I—we—that is, Carl and I, think it would be better for everyone if you left the Twin Cities. You can live anywhere you want, as long as it's at least a thousand miles from here. We'll pay all of your moving expenses, of course, in addition to the rest."

"The rest?" Amy said carefully. The disappointment and pain shouldn't have been so overwhelming. Eileen had said and done things lots of times when Amy was growing up that had hurt almost as much.

"We are prepared to give you a very generous lump sum payment—half now and half when you're settled wherever it is you decide to go. Thereafter, you'll receive additional payments every January. The one stipulation—and I was told to make it perfectly clear to you that this was not negotiable—is that you must agree never to come back, not even for a visit."

When Amy said nothing, Eileen went on. "I realize you weren't expecting anything like this. You probably want a couple of days to think it over. But it is a great deal of money, more than you could ever hope to earn doing . . . whatever it is you do." She opened her purse and took out a check.

"I don't want it," Amy said.

Eileen put the check on the coffee table and stood. "I'm sure that as soon as I leave and you've looked at the amount, you'll change your mind." Her voice changed, becoming soft and saccharine. "It isn't just for me and your father I'm asking this, Amy, it's for Diana, too. With you gone she'll be able to give Stuart and her job the attention they deserve. She should have started a family years ago, but she feels she can't, not and take care of you, too. She gives you everything she should be saving for her own children."

"Diana doesn't want kids," Amy said. Too late she realized that in trying to defend herself, she'd handed her mother a weapon.

"Of course she doesn't. She's seen the heartache they can bring to their parents. Which is why it's so important that you leave now. Diana needs time to be around normal people. She needs to see her friends with their children and understand how wonderful a real child, one she gives birth to herself, could be."

Not even at her strongest could Amy withstand such an attack. "I want you to go now."

"When you decide, give Frank Pechacek a call. We've had him draw up some papers for you to sign."

"What kind of papers?"

Eileen adjusted her jacket, smoothing invisible wrinkles. "I'm not sure of the exact wording."

"I don't need the exact wording."

"It says that by accepting this settlement, you give up all future claims." She moved to the hallway.

"Claims to what?"

"To the Winchester name. To me and Carl—and to Diana." The last was said with steely determination.

"So I shouldn't look at this as a bribe to get rid of me? This is merely a way to give me my inheritance early? How thoughtful."

"What it is, Amy, is a way for us to look out for our own. Carl and I figured if you were taken care of now, you couldn't try to take what rightfully belongs to Diana when we aren't here to protect her."

Amy was desperate for her mother to be gone. She opened the door and stepped back to clear the way. "You should get out of here now."

"There's one more thing. I want my mother's clock back before you move."

Amy stared at her. "No."

"You're just doing this to hurt me. That clock can't possibly mean anything to you."

"Oh, but it does." She would never believe the truth, so instead Amy simply confirmed what her mother already believed. "I had it appraised."

Eileen stiffened. "Of course you did. It's precisely what I would have expected."

"Good night, Mother."

"How much do you want?" When Amy didn't answer, Eileen added, "I'll top the appraisal by ten percent."

Amy stepped back and closed the door without saying anything more. She waited, letting herself believe for several idiotic seconds that her mother would call out, that she would say she'd made a terrible mistake and beg Amy's forgiveness. Even when so much time had passed that it became impossible to sustain the fantasy any longer, Amy didn't let go easily. All the way to the bedroom she rehearsed the words she would say when Eileen came back.

She refused to believe her mother and father didn't love her. Somewhere in their hearts there had to be a place reserved for the daughter they had chosen. Despite everything that had happened between them, she was theirs in every way that counted. Wasn't that the way people who adopted children were supposed to feel? The connection couldn't go just one way—her grandmother had felt it, so did Diana. Someday Carl and Eileen would, too. Maybe when she was in school again. Or when she got married and started a family of her own. Amy only had to wait a little longer. Something would happen to change their minds.

But not here, not tonight. If she stayed home, she'd go crazy thinking about what her mother had said. She needed people and noise to help her forget, if only for a while.

Most of all she needed to be away from the phone. How else could she convince herself her mother had had a change of heart and tried to call to apologize?

* * *

"The usual?" the tall African American bartender asked.

Amy nodded. "Only with lemon instead of lime."

"Change is good once in a while." He grinned. Without looking he grabbed a glass, filled it with ice, and poured her soft drink from a nozzle attached to a long hose. "Haven't seen you around lately."

"I've been helping my sister." The man seated next to her slapped a dollar bill on the counter and got up to leave. Amy moved to take his stool, sitting with her back to the wall to give her an unobstructed view of the room.

"I thought maybe you were through with this place after what happened last time." He squeezed a wedge of lemon into her soda and slid the glass across the bar.

"I can't believe I was so dumb. That guy had cop written all over him." In reality she couldn't tell a cop from an accountant, but the regulars at Dimwitty's believed she was a pro and she did nothing to dissuade them. In the beginning she'd played the role as a lark, even going along with one of the real pros she'd met at the bar the night she'd been spotted by Darren Harris at the hotel. What Mr. Harris hadn't seen was when Amy had slipped out the back door ten minutes after she arrived. She didn't mind having the name, she just didn't want to play the game.

Her act gave her a reason for being at Dimwitty's that hid the fact that she had nowhere else to be. She slept with some of the guys she picked up, but most were left at the corner. The cop had been a challenge. She'd let herself get sucked into a game of words. He'd won. Big time.

The bartender went back to washing glasses. "Did

the reporter get it right? Those people really your parents?"

She grinned and winked. "If I really had a rich daddy like that, would I be doing this for a living?"

"Whew—I'll bet they were pissed when they saw their names in the paper. They'll probably sue."

"Yeah, and wind up with even more money." She swung around to look at the crowd. There were several regulars—the aging former yuppies who nursed a glass of wine all night and hit on anything that didn't shave, and the young guns who sat back and waited for the girls to come to them. She specialized in the businessmen who stayed at the hotels in the downtown area, the ones who would only be in the Cities for a couple of days. She liked knowing that no matter how she felt about a guy she picked up, the relationship wasn't going anywhere. It saved a lot of wear and tear on her emotions. If she never expected a call, she couldn't be disappointed when it didn't come. "Who's the guy in the blue sport coat?"

"Never saw him before."

"He alone?"

"So far."

Stretching to check her makeup in the mirror behind the bar, she said, "Well, not anymore."

She walked to the man's table slowly, her movements calculated to make sure he noticed her before she arrived. As she approached, she imagined her mother watching the performance. "Hi . . . my friend tells me you're here alone." She met his questioning gaze with a direct, open look. "Like some company?"

"Yeah, sure. That would be great." He stood and pulled out a chair for her to join him. "I hate drinking alone."

She held out her hand. "Amy Winchester."

"Matt Carpenter."

She tilted her head at a coquettish angle and pretended to study him. "If I had to guess, I'd say you weren't from around here. We don't get enough sun all summer to produce a tan like yours."

"I play a lot of handball." He patted his stomach. "Keeps me fit, if you know what I mean."

"And where is it you play this handball?"

"Abilene." When she didn't respond, he added, "Kansas."

She purposely turned her chair to face his before she sat down. What good was it to wear short skirts if her legs were hidden under the table? "Here on business?"

He nodded. "Insurance."

"Buying or selling?" She guessed him to be either a tired forty or a well-preserved fifty. He'd accepted his thinning hair, wore bifocals with lines, and made no attempt to hide his excitement at having a young woman approach him.

"Actually, neither. I'm here recruiting agents for my company."

"Any luck?" She purposely turned her head to watch someone come in. When she looked at him again, he was staring at her legs. She answered with a smile, slow and encouraging.

"I'm sorry—what did you say?" he asked.

"I wondered if you'd had any luck."

He still seemed confused.

"With the recruiting?" she prompted.

"Oh. No, not really. No one seems to want to relocate. Not that I can blame them. From what I've seen, I don't think I'd want to leave this place, either."

"Come back next winter when it's fifty below. You might have an easier time convincing them." She took a piece of popcorn from the bowl on the table and put it on the tip of her tongue.

"Can I get you a drink?" He already had his arm in the air to wave at the cocktail waitress.

Amy put her hand on his arm. "It's a little noisy in here, don't you think? Makes getting to know someone kind of difficult."

"Uh, yeah, now that you mention it, I can see that it would." He looked at her but as quickly looked away again. "If the noise is bothering you, we could go someplace else."

"I think I'd like that—somewhere quiet so we can talk."

He swallowed nervously. "There's a bar at the hotel where I'm staying. It didn't look too busy when I left."

Amy stood and ran her hand over the front of her skirt to smooth the wrinkles. A picture of her mother doing the same thing flashed through her mind. Like mother, like daughter. Somehow Amy didn't think Eileen would be pleased. "I was hoping we could find someplace *really* quiet."

His entire demeanor changed. Her intentions had finally gotten through to him. He threw back the last of his drink and stood. Almost as an afterthought, he shoved his hand in his pocket, pulled out a crumpled bill, and dropped it on the table. "You need to work on your delivery, sweetheart," he said to Amy. "You're sending mixed signals." He put his arm around her waist and guided her toward the door. "If I'd known up front you were a professional, we could have saved us some time."

They walked through the double doors together. When they were outside he moved his hand up to cup her breast, kneading his fingers into the soft flesh. "I never would have guessed just looking at

you," he said, his excitement growing. "Somehow
you don't fit the part." He stopped abruptly and
looked down at her.

"What's the matter?" Amy demanded. Oh, God,
he couldn't be a cop. Not again. She hadn't done anything, hadn't named a price or said what they would
do when they got to his hotel room. She tried to jerk
her arm free. He tightened his grip until the pain
made her gasp.

"Settle down," he said. "I just want to make sure
you're not really a guy."

Amy almost laughed aloud. Her relief was like a
hit of coke. She moved in close and rubbed herself
against him. "Feel anything that shouldn't be there?"
she said in a husky voice.

"I don't know. I've heard some pretty wild stories." After a quick look around to make sure no one
was watching them, he grabbed the hem of her knit
top, pulled it up, and exposed her breasts. "Jesus H.
Christ." He sucked in a breath and actually licked his
lips. "There's no way these belong to a man."

Amy twisted away from him and yanked her top
back down. When he reached for her again, she
slapped his hands away.

"Just a quick feel," he protested.

"I don't work in public."

He laughed. "What a joke. A hooker with
standards."

Amy put her arm through his and wondered if
her mother would appreciate the irony.

Five

If the accommodations were any indication of the status Matt Carpenter had with his company, the main office was getting along just fine without him. The room had the standard double bed, a small, round table with a single chair in the far corner, and a Formica dresser with a nineteen-inch television perched on the corner. Several hooks were missing from the orange-and-green-striped curtains that had been permanently closed by someone with a stapler and a desire for privacy. The carpet looked tweed in the corners and brown in the middle. Two shirts and a pair of slacks hung inside the open closet; a molded plastic briefcase sat on the table.

Amy had seen hotels like this one in movies, but never in real life. This was a world she didn't know, a game with new rules. She didn't like being there. She took a hard look at Matt Carpenter and decided she didn't like him, either.

"It's not much," he said, yanking the knot on his tie. "But I never did see the sense in paying what they ask at places like the Hilton just for a place to sleep."

"Especially if your company lets you pocket the difference."

"You got that right. They don't give a damn what we do with their tightfisted per diem as long as we get the job done." He hesitated. "That reminds me, we never did settle on a price."

This was her chance. All she had to do was name a figure so high that he would refuse to pay, and she could walk. "Two hundred dollars."

He didn't flinch. "Say I pay what you're asking. What do I get for my money?"

"You get it straight, and you wear a rubber. Anything else costs extra."

"Why would I pay two hundred dollars for something I could get free at home?"

"The price isn't negotiable. Take it or leave it."

"You're new at this. I can tell."

Before she could stop him, he'd shoved his free hand up her top and kneaded her breast, squeezing hard enough to hurt. Outraged, she pushed him away. He retaliated by grabbing a handful of the silk knit and twisting his fist until the material was a knot at her throat. Her worry turned to a quick, sickening fear. Instinctively she knew it would be a mistake to let him see that she was afraid. She stuck her chin out and glared at him. "The price just went up a hundred dollars."

He moved in so close, his breath mingled with hers. "Once you see what I got waiting for you, you're gonna want to pay me."

"Let go of me, you son of a bitch."

"Keep it up, baby." He tried to kiss her. "I like a gal with spunk." She wrenched her head away, and he stuck his tongue in her ear. "Yes sir, I do enjoy a challenge. Might as well be fuckin' a board as the ones who just lay there."

"How about the ones who scream?"

"Go right ahead. Yell all you want. When the cops get here whose ass do you think they're gonna haul off?"

"You were right," Amy said, trying a different tack. "I am new at this. And I've changed my mind." He didn't say anything. She fought to keep the high pitch of panic from her voice. "You want someone who knows what they're doing. It's early. There's still time for you to find a girl who will do whatever you want, one who's really good, someone cheaper. I'll even help you find her. I know where a lot of the pros hang out."

"I don't want someone who's old and used up. I like my women fresh—like you." He took her hand and rubbed it up and down against the front of his pants. "Besides, Junior here is ready, and he doesn't like to be kept waiting."

This was a game to him. The more she fought, the more it aroused him. From somewhere deep inside, a voice she didn't recognize said, "Please, don't hurt me."

"Oh, it ain't that big," he said, misinterpreting her fear. "But I can guarantee once you had Junior, he's gonna spoil you for any other man's dick."

Her stomach convulsed. She had to get out of there. "I have to use the bathroom."

"What for?" he asked suspiciously.

"What do you think?"

"Give me your purse," he demanded.

"I need it."

"Take what you need—the rest stays with me."

He'd called her bluff. She opened the small bag and took out a gold pill case, resisting the temptation to try to palm her driver's license. She didn't care about the credit cards, she just didn't want him to know where she lived. "I'll be right back."

"What's in there?"

It was aspirin, but on impulse she said, "Ampicillin."

"That's an antibiotic. What's wrong with you?"

"Clap." She had no idea where the word had come from or what it meant, only that it was a disease and sexually transmitted.

"No one gets that anymore."

"That's what I thought, too." He wasn't as confident as he wanted her to believe.

"Let me see."

Her mouth went dry. "What?"

"Give me the box." Before she could respond, he snatched the container and looked inside. "What do you think I am, stupid? There's nothing in here but aspirin."

Amy had never experienced the kind of fear that came over her at that moment. The game had changed. There were new rules, only she had no idea what they were. "Please . . . just let me go." *No*, it was wrong to beg. It made her look weak.

He flung the pill box across the room. "Nobody forced you to come here."

Maybe she could reason with him. "And I shouldn't be forced to stay."

"That's not the way it works, baby. You started something that I'm going to see you finish. There's nothing in this world I hate more than a cock tease."

Her options had narrowed to fight or flight. She bolted for the door. He was on her before she had the safety lock half-undone. She was utterly unprepared for what happened next. The first blow slammed her head against the wall. The second felt as if an explosion had gone off in her head. Glass-sharp shards of pain pierced her eyes and jaw. With the third blow, his open hand became a fist. Blood slid down the back of her throat.

Foolishly she fought to stay upright.

Nothing she did seemed to have any effect on him. It was as if he were some macabre wind-up toy that couldn't stop until it had wound itself down. With mechanical precision, he hit her again and again. Instead of closing her eyes to the onslaught, she struggled to see through the blinding dizziness.

Finally it didn't matter how grim her determination, her legs could no longer hold her upright. Slowly she sank to the floor. Her pain receded. She felt as if she were floating. Someone said something, but the words were jumbled, meaningless.

"Get back here, you bitch. I didn't hit you that hard. Stand up, goddamn it."

Amy's head hurt, a terrible throbbing pain that made her wince with every heartbeat. She put her hand to her temple the way she did when she had a headache. Her fingers touched an unfamiliar surface, round instead of flat, taut instead of yielding. She tried to open her eyes. The pain stole her breath. Her heart beat harder at the smallest effort. For a terrifying minute she believed her head would burst with its unrelenting force.

She sat perfectly still, afraid even to move her hand from her face. It seemed forever before the pulsing red flashes behind her eyelids began to slow and the knives were put back in their sheaths. She stayed motionless for a long time before she experimented with movement again, making small bargains with the pain, yielding instantly to its warning when she attempted too much, too fast.

She was thirsty, the kind that when you were a kid you stuck your mouth under the faucet and took in gulp after gulp of water until your stomach couldn't hold any more, and still you weren't satisfied. Concentrating, she tried to lick her lips with a tongue that had grown too big for her mouth. Her lips were swollen and cracked and covered with something hard and crusty.

It was blood. There was more blood under her nose and around her eyes.

Slowly pieces of memory drifted back, like unconnected clips from a movie. She worked to fit them together. Finally, with concentrated effort, only blinks of time remained missing. What she didn't know, she guessed. The piecemeal mental process wasn't alien to her; she'd honed the skill when she'd been drinking.

Despite the pain, she forced her eyes open and looked around. She was in an alley, wedged between a Dumpster and a brick wall, abandoned like a piece of carelessly discarded garbage. Her legs were folded under her, numb to the touch yet filled with a deep ache. Rocking from side to side, she moved until she'd freed one leg and then the other. The circulation returned with a vengeance, the muscles tingling and then roaring with pain. That he'd beaten her was obvious, but what else had he done? She purposely catalogued the pain, assigning reason to every sore muscle. With a perverse feeling of gratitude, she realized she hurt everywhere but where she had expected. He hadn't raped her. Maybe the beating itself had been his goal. Standing took several attempts, with long minutes in between as she waited for the pain to subside enough to try again. Upright at last, she crossed one hand over the other until she'd worked her way around the Dumpster. When she gained an unobstructed view, she stared intently down the alley, first one way and then the other. She thought she recognized an antique shop a couple of blocks up from Dimwitty's but wasn't sure.

She took another step. Her foot landed on something sharp. She wasn't wearing her shoes.

She made her way back to where she'd been sitting to search for her shoes. They were there; so was her purse. She looked inside the small leather bag. Her money was gone, but she didn't care. She was pathetically grateful that he'd left her keys. She would have crawled home on her hands and knees before she asked anyone for help. No one could see her like this. No one.

She stepped into her shoes and slowly made her way to the end of the alley. When she stopped to rest, she thought about her mother. If she were there now, would she feel sad and try to help, or would she walk away in disgust? And Diana? Amy had seen disappointment reflected in her sister's eyes too many times to have to guess how she would react. The road was so familiar, she knew every hill, curve, and landmark.

Maybe her mother was right. She would be doing them all a kindness if she just disappeared.

Diana would be upset at first, but after a while, when her life was her own again, she would see that it was for the best. She might even be grateful. A month, even a week ago, Amy would have recoiled at the idea of leaving the cities. Now she couldn't think of a better way to tell Diana how much she cared.

Six

Diana knocked on Amy's door and waited. When there was no answer, she knocked again and stepped closer to listen for a sound that would indicate Amy was up or that she was even home. Nothing.

She'd called earlier to tell Amy she was running a little late and assumed she was in the shower when the machine picked up. Even though they hadn't made definite plans, it wasn't like Amy to just take off; that she could have forgotten wasn't even a possibility. A dentist's appointment might slip Amy's mind, but not shopping, especially not when it involved rummaging through her favorite thrift and antique stores.

Diana had a key to Amy's apartment, but she'd used it only twice, the first time when Amy was out of town and thought she'd left her curling iron plugged in, the second when she'd dropped by to pick up a birthday present. Amy was supposed to be gone but had come back unexpectedly and was in the shower with a man Diana hadn't seen before or since. Amy still laughed about it; Diana never had.

She glanced at her watch. The stores wouldn't

open for another half hour—enough time to hit Rico's and pick up rolls and coffee for their breakfast. If there was still no answer when she got back, she would use her key then.

Not until Diana was inside her car and ready to pull into traffic did it occur to her that she should have checked the garage for Amy's car. She grabbed her purse and made a dash across the street, ignoring the glare from the woman who'd been waiting for her parking spot.

Amy's Pinto was in its assigned place, but sitting at a crazy angle, as if she'd been half-asleep when she drove home or half— Diana shoved the thought from her mind. She refused even to consider the possibility Amy might be drinking again.

The idea of walking in on Amy with some guy no longer seemed so horrible.

Diana had her keys in her hand by the time she hit the stairs. Before she'd climbed the single flight, she'd sorted through the ring and singled out the right one. Yielding to a lifetime of ingrained social behavior, she had to knock one last time before she let herself in. There was still no answer.

As she entered the hallway she stopped to listen, clinging to the seductive hope that she would hear voices, or the shower, or Amy moving around in the kitchen. The silence was complete, as strange and alien as a forest stilled by an intruder's footfall. A sudden overwhelming urge to leave hit Diana. She felt a compulsion to retrace her steps to the hallway, close the door, walk away, and let Amy make contact when she was ready. Call it intuition, gut feeling, the name didn't matter; all she knew for sure was that there was something inside she did not want to see.

A surge of anger swept through her. *Damn it,*

Amy, your timing really stinks. You could have at least let me get my own problems out of the way before you handed me yours.

The fit of pique was gone before she could act on it, a funnel cloud that never touched ground.

Finally Diana called out, "Amy, it's me. Are you here?" She hung her purse on the antique coat rack and waited for an answer. When none came, she started toward the bedroom but was distracted by a lamp that had been left on in the living room.

Her gaze drifted from the lamp to the sofa and a prone Amy still dressed in her bathrobe, her hair slicked back as if she'd just washed it, her arm flung over her face, as if purposely closing herself off from the world. With a giddy sense of relief, Diana came into the room and leaned over the coffee table, touching Amy's shoulder. "Hey, sleepyhead—time to get up. We've got places to go, people to see, and money to spend."

Amy didn't respond, not even to moan in protest at having her sleep disturbed. Diana shook her again, a little harder this time. Again, nothing. She moved closer. Her foot hit something. Looking down, she saw that it was an empty pint bottle of vodka. A dozen emotions scrambled for position, each demanding to be thought and heard and felt first. Diana didn't know whether to cry with disappointment or scream with rage and frustration.

Damn it, damn it to hell.

What could have happened since last night that was so terrible it would make Amy start drinking again? She shook her sister's shoulder again, harder this time. "Wake up. I want to talk to you."

Amy's arm slipped from her face. Diana gasped in shock and surprise. Logic dictated the bruised and battered woman in front of her was her sister. Never mind that she looked nothing like the Amy that Diana knew. "Amy?" she said, her voice a choked, frightened whisper. "Is it you?"

Interminable seconds passed while Diana stood frozen, her mind mired in confusion. In the safe, protected world she inhabited, violence was a province of movies and television. Blood was syrup, and bruises washed away with soap. Actors didn't look the way Amy did now; the reality would have been unbearable even at a safe distance in a theater.

An urgency broke through the protective shell of observation. The woman lying on the sofa wasn't an actor, or a stranger; it was Amy.

Diana dropped to her knees. "Who did this to you?" she demanded. Amy's unresponsiveness went beyond a drunken stupor. Not only wasn't she moving, she was barely breathing.

Concern became panic. Diana grabbed Amy's wrist to feel for a pulse. Something dropped out of Amy's hand and rolled onto the floor. A prescription bottle, capless and empty. Diana picked it up and read the label.

Cloridate.

What in the hell was cloridate?

She tossed the bottle on the table and pressed her fingers against the pulse point on Amy's wrist. After several seconds she tried another spot and then another. Finally she tried Amy's throat and found a beat, slow and weak, but enough to make Diana cry out in relief.

She got up, hitting her shin against the coffee table as she scrambled for the phone.

The fire department arrived first. After showing them the prescription and vodka bottles and answering questions she immediately forgot, Diana stood in a corner and watched as the strangers in blue uniforms took over the care and handling of her sister. She pleaded with them to be careful, to go to extraordinary lengths, to do whatever was necessary to save Amy's life.

A short time later two ambulance attendants came into the already crowded room. When one of the firefighters moved to help lift Amy onto a gurney, Diana saw there were wires leading from her chest to a small box and a rebreather covering her mouth.

She followed them outside and down the stairs, swallowing a dozen questions she was afraid to ask for fear the precious seconds it would take to get an answer would be the ones Amy needed to save her life. Diana rode in the front seat of the ambulance, reciting a litany of prayers she had learned as a child in catechism and had rarely had used since. She was tempted to bargain, to offer the God she had come to doubt more often than she believed whatever He wanted in exchange for her sister's life.

The hospital was more organized chaos as Amy was taken into a curtained-off room and Diana was asked more questions. Finally, when the last of the papers had been filled out, she was directed to wait in an area with institutional chairs, two-year-old magazines, and a television mounted on the wall.

All Diana's life she had done whatever she was told, taking her cue from Amy, whose perversity made every road she traveled twice as difficult to navigate. At times her malleability seemed more cowardice than wisdom, an excuse to avoid confrontation cloaked in social mores. She tried to imagine what Amy would do if their positions were reversed. Would she sit quietly by and wait for information, or would she be in the heat of battle demanding her sister be given immediate and intensive care?

The answer was painfully obvious. Before her

judgment could overrule her instincts, Diana got up and walked past the reception desk and into the treatment room. It might not be her father's hospital, but his name would still carry weight. Dr. Carl Winchester was a powerful force in the medical profession in the Cities, and whether he would approve or not, he was about to become a loud and insistent advocate for the daughter he no longer claimed.

Later that afternoon, Diana watched the rhythmic jumps on the monitor as it recorded Amy's heartbeat. She was hungry but reluctant to leave to get something to eat. According to the nurse, Amy could come out of the coma at any time, and Diana wanted to be there when she did.

A soft knock sounded on the door. Before Diana could get up to answer, Stephanie stuck her head inside.

"How's it going?" she asked in a whisper.

"The same." Her gratitude at seeing Stephanie was tempered by disappointment that it wasn't her mother or father. She'd called both Stephanie and her parents hours ago, only minutes apart, reaching Stephanie's answering machine and Glenda, her father's secretary. Glenda had promised to find her parents and tell them to call Diana at the hospital as soon as possible.

Stephanie came into the room, carrying a green vase filled with flowers in one hand, a stuffed animal in the other. "I'm sorry I didn't get here sooner, but I didn't get your message until about a half hour ago. I had this boring interview with a guy who juggles chain saws and . . ." The words died in her throat when she saw Amy. She moved closer to the bed. "Jesus, you didn't say she'd been in an accident."

Diana hadn't known what to say, so she'd kept it short and simple, telling Stephanie she couldn't keep their dinner date because Amy was in the hospital. "It wasn't an accident."

Stephanie put the flowers and stuffed animal on the nightstand. "Then what was it?"

"Someone beat her up."

It took a while for the idea to sink in. When it did, Stephanie became enraged. "Who?"

"I don't know."

"You mean the son of a bitch is still out there?" Stephanie stared at Amy. "Who found her?"

"I did." Diana led Stephanie away from the bed, filling her in on what little she knew.

"You don't think . . ." Stephanie struggled with what she would say next. "You don't think she . . . Never mind."

"That she tried to kill herself after the guy left?" Diana finished for her.

"I know you've already got enough to worry about, Diana, but if it were just the alcohol, or just the pills, it would be a lot easier to believe this was an accident."

"You're not saying anything I haven't already considered." Diana rubbed the back of her neck as she looked at Amy. "According to the lab report she only took five or six pills."

"I thought you said the bottle was empty."

"That must have been all she had." Diana had gone over and over everything that had happened that morning, analyzing every clue, giving purpose and meaning to every detail no matter how small or seemingly inconsequential. What she didn't know, she guessed. If the resulting conclusions didn't make sense or weren't to her liking, she guessed again.

"I didn't know she was drinking again."

"She isn't. At least not before last night." Diana

folded her arms across her chest and leaned her shoulder into the wall. "It was only a pint. If she were really trying to kill herself, don't you think it would have been more? And if there were only five or six pills left in the bottle, wouldn't she have taken something else, too?"

Diana could see she hadn't convinced Stephanie. "Amy has never done anything halfway. If she'd really wanted to kill herself, she would have succeeded."

"I understand why you need an answer," Stephanie said gently, "but you're trying to apply logic to an irrational act. It doesn't work." She took off her jacket and laid it at the foot of the bed. "What did your parents say when you told them?"

With anyone else, Diana would have tried to pretty up the truth, to make it something it wasn't. "I left a message, but they haven't called back."

Stephanie cocked an eyebrow in surprise. "I would have thought at the very least they'd be out there doing damage control by now. From what I hear, the hospital grapevine is almost as good as the newspaper's."

"Maybe Glenda couldn't find them." She was making excuses. "I was hoping . . ." To say the words out loud would force her to face the truth. Her call hadn't been returned because they didn't care.

Stephanie glanced at Amy. "I know what you were hoping, but it's not going to happen. At least not in this lifetime."

"It would mean so much to Amy if they came through for her just one time."

"You've got to stop doing this to yourself—and to her. From what you've told me, I don't think your mother and father would have been all that upset if Amy had succeeded."

Diana flinched at the harshness but didn't try to

deny Stephanie's assessment. "They never really loved Amy. It's always been a mystery to me why they adopted her."

"Did you ever ask them?"

"No." She'd been raised not to question her parents' actions or decisions. Like the good little girl she was, Diana had believed what she was told. No matter how many nights she had heard Amy cry herself to sleep, or how many nights Diana had brought Amy into her own room to stop the tears, she had never questioned her parents' actions. If they treated Amy with thoughtless neglect, they had a good, if mysterious, reason. If they constantly criticized, it was for her own benefit. If they refused to forgive, it was to teach a much needed lesson.

"Don't you think it's time you did?"

"I don't know what good it would do now." It was the easy, automatic answer, the kind of response ingrained in an impressionable child and clung to by a peace-at-any-price adult.

"Whether it does any good or not, don't you think Amy has a right to know why she was adopted?"

"I suppose you're right. Someday I'll—"

"What's wrong with right now?"

Diana didn't have an answer. Stephanie was right about this, too. If she waited, the anger she needed for fuel would no longer be strong enough to see her through. "Can you stay with Amy for a while?"

"For as long as you need me."

Diana went over to the bed and took Amy's hand. She searched for a place to kiss her sister where there were no cuts or bruises and settled for a spot on her forehead less damaged than anywhere else. "Wish me luck," she whispered.

"Do you want me to call you if she wakes up?" Stephanie asked.

Diana considered her answer. She didn't want any distractions when she faced her mother or any excuse to back down. "Only if she gets worse."

She might not be able to give Amy the answers she wanted or needed, but from now on she would have the truth.

Seven

Diana pulled up to the stop sign, leaned over the console in her car, took out the remote control that operated the front gate to her parents' house, and watched the enormous *W* on the metal bars split backward to allow her entrance. As a child she'd accepted the eight-foot-high iron fencing as normal. Not until she was old enough to venture farther out into the world did she begin to question the seemingly extraordinary security methods used by her parents to protect their home. True understanding didn't come until she had been gone from the compound long enough to be able to look at it and her parents with a modicum of detachment.

The aura of success could be gained in two ways, by earning it or creating it. When Eileen agreed to become a Winchester—an old and respected name in Minnesota despite the fact that the family no longer wielded the enormous influence or fortune it once had—she wasn't so blinded by love and confidence that her new husband would someday be a man of power that she was willing to put her fate completely in his hands. To aid the process she purposely and calculatingly set about creating the illusion of importance. The first, and most important, step was to live in the "right" neighborhood—and not just in any house, but one that bespoke the social status she would one day have in reality as well as perception. It was of little consequence that she'd nearly depleted her own trust fund before Carl's income was high enough to contribute more than basic upkeep. As in all aspects of her life the end justified the means, and there was hell to pay for anyone or anything that stood in her way.

Rather than park under the portico and use the front door, Diana drove to the back of the house and went in through the kitchen. Helen, the housekeeper who had been with the family since Diana was a child, was at the sink, peeling carrots. She looked up and smiled. "You know your mother hates it when you come in this way," she said as she wiped her hands on a towel.

"Is she home?" Normally, when Diana came to the house she made a point of spending time with Helen, relishing the stories she told about her grandchildren, using them as an antidote to the relentless, vitriolic gossip her mother relayed. Today, despite the compelling need for escape, she couldn't allow herself the luxury.

Helen tossed the towel on the counter and came toward Diana. Her smile disappeared as she drew closer. "I took some tea to her in her office about fifteen minutes ago. She was working on something. My guess is that she's probably still there."

"And Dad?"

"He left about an hour ago."

"Damn—" Saying what she'd come there to say would be hard enough once; she didn't want to have to do it twice. "I wanted them both here."

"Are you all right?" Helen asked tentatively.

"Yes . . . no, I'm not." Why deny the obvious?

"Is there something I can do?"

Diana had been taught that problems, especially when they involved family, were private matters, to be handled discreetly, drawing as little attention as possible. Hold inside whatever pain you were feeling. Put a positive spin on everything. If you must cry, do it alone. It was a code designed to bring admiration from peers and a loneliness so desperate that, at times, alcohol and pills seemed logical answers.

"Not for me," Diana said. "But there is something you can do for Amy. You could call her in a couple of days when she gets home from the hospital. I know she'd love to hear from you."

"No one told me. . . . Why is she in the hospital? What happened? Is she all right?"

The depth of concern on Helen's face and in her voice was a gift to Diana. The kindness of strangers was ephemeral; friends provided building blocks. Her mother would be furious if she found out Helen knew the truth about Amy, but Diana couldn't find it in herself to care. "Someone beat her up. And then— I don't know what really happened then," she admitted. "All I know for sure is that she drank a pint of vodka and took half a dozen sleeping pills."

"God in heaven . . . that poor child." She crossed herself. "Is she going to be all right?"

"For now."

"Will they let me in to see her?"

The caring was almost Diana's undoing. "If you have the time, I know—"

"Of course I have the time." Helen put her arms around Diana and gave her a hug. "What could be more important?"

"I'll leave word at the nurses' station that you'll be visiting."

"Do you think she would like some homemade cookies? I could make chocolate-chip. They were always her favorite."

Diana would wager an entire year's salary that her mother couldn't name one favorite thing of Amy's. "She may not be able to eat them right away, but I know she would love to have them."

Helen grew animated at the prospect of something to do. "I'll bake them this afternoon."

"Thank you."

"For what?"

"For caring."

"Of course I care," she said with an impatient shake of her head. "You and Amy are like my own." She went to the pantry, opened the door, and tore a page out of the tablet that held her shopping list. "My memory's not what it used to be. If I don't write things down, I forget them as fast as I do the answers on *Jeopardy*. Now tell me Amy's room number and how I get to the hospital."

After jotting down the information, Diana reluctantly left to find her mother. The door to her office was closed. She tapped lightly and waited for an answer.

"Yes?" Eileen said. "What is it?"

"It's me, Mother." Diana opened the door and went inside. "I need to talk to you." Normally she would have added, "If you have a few minutes." Today she didn't care how busy her mother was or how important her latest crisis.

With a show of restrained impatience, Eileen removed her half-glasses, pushed her chair back from the Louis XIV desk, and stood. "I've been expecting you."

As always, Eileen Winchester looked the role she played. Today it was lady of the manor, which called for a classic, understated appearance—tan, light-weight wool slacks, ecru silk blouse, and Bruno Magli heels. The adornment was kept to a minimum: a gold necklace, simple gold earrings, and a Piaget watch.

"I left a message for you hours ago," Diana said. "Why didn't you return my call?"

Eileen fixed her daughter with an icy stare. "You'll use a civil tone when you are in this house."

Diana closed the door. Treating her like a way-ward child was Eileen's way of gaining the upper hand. But somewhere between the kitchen and the office Diana had stopped worrying about offending her mother or caring about winning her cooperation. "That's not going to work this time, Mother. You might as well save your breath."

Eileen could not hide her surprise. "You either control yourself or I'll—"

"You'll what? Have me thrown out? Disown me?"

The indignant pose turned to outrage. "She told you," Eileen seethed. "The little witch. I should have known she couldn't be trusted."

Diana froze at the attack. Something had just happened, but she had no idea what. It was every-thing she could do to keep her confusion from show-ing. Her only chance to find out what her mother was talking about was to play along. "Of course she told me." Diana automatically assumed the "she" was Amy. "We tell each other everything."

Eileen reached for the phone. "It's not too late. I can still have the check stopped."

"I wouldn't do that if I were you."

"Oh?" She had her hand poised over the auto-matic dial. "And why not?"

Her answer had to be perfect. Eileen Winchester

was a consummate game player. She would detect the slightest miscue. "Because you'll never get what you want if you do."

Eileen hesitated, a scavenger wary of a too easy meal. Finally, unable to detect an alien scent, she moved forward. "Are you telling me there's still a chance Amy will leave the Cities?"

The question was so unexpected, Diana was at a loss for an answer. Frantically she tried to fit the pieces together. At first she thought the logical conclusion too abhorrent, even for her mother. But nothing else made sense. "You offered Amy money to move away from here? How could you do that to your own daughter?"

"*She isn't my daughter.*" Eileen slammed down the phone.

Diana thought about what Amy had been through and what she had tried to do to herself. The pain she felt threatened to choke her. "I've never been as disappointed in anyone as I am in you right now. You make me sick."

"How dare you talk to me that way? I'm your mother. I deserve your respect."

"Respect is earned."

For the first time in Diana's memory, her mother seemed to be at a loss for words. Finally she said in a quieter voice, "This is all her fault. Amy's caused nothing but trouble from the first day we brought her into this house."

"Since the first day, Mother? She was a baby, not even a week old."

"She screamed constantly. She didn't shut up for six months."

"Lots of babies have colic. That was hardly her fault."

"Before she came you were a loving, happy child.

You changed the minute you saw her. You became secretive. You sneaked into her room at night to sleep with her even after I expressly forbade you to do so. There were times you even lied to your father and me because of her." She held up her hand to stop Diana before she could say anything in her own defense. "Oh, don't try to deny it. I know how many times you made up stories to cover something Amy had done. I'll never forgive her for turning you against me and your father."

Diana realized it was useless to argue the point. Instead she asked the question that had brought her there. "Why did you adopt Amy?"

Surprisingly, Eileen didn't try to evade answering. "It was your father's idea. He started in on me the minute we found out we weren't going to have any more children of our own."

Eileen often tried to deny culpability for something she considered a mistake—her memory could be amazingly selective when it suited her—but this time Diana believed her. "Why another daughter? Why not a son?"

"It had nothing to do with that. Your father just didn't want you to grow up the way he did. He said he used to beg his parents for a brother or sister, but they were too caught up in their own lives to see how lonely his was. He swore he would never do that to a child of his own."

"I've never known you to have trouble telling Dad no when you didn't want to do something. Why did you give in on this?"

"I was stupid enough to listen when he told me that she would be good for you, as a companion." She laughed at the irony. "Can you imagine?"

"You mean you never considered Amy your daughter? Not even in the beginning?"

"I already had a daughter, one I'd given birth to. How could I possibly feel the same about a stranger?"

"Amy wasn't a stranger when you brought her home, she was a brand-new human being, a clean slate."

Eileen sat back down and busied herself straightening the papers on her desk. She moved a Baccarat paperweight shaped like a golf club from one side to the other, replaced a Mont Blanc pen into its holder, and dropped a gold-plated paper clip into a drawer. "I don't expect you to understand now, but you will when you and Stuart have a child of your own. I don't care what all those books say. There's a bond between a mother and her own child that can't be duplicated. All those people who claim they love the child they adopted as much as the one they gave birth to are either deluding themselves or out-and-out lying."

So much made sense now. The favored treatment Diana had received the entire time she and Amy were growing up had nothing to do with being an acquiescing, easy child and nothing to do with anything Amy had or hadn't done. "You never loved her . . . you never even tried."

Eileen eased back in her chair as if it were a throne and she was the queen—ready to pass judgment on her hapless subjects. "I've heard enough whining about this from you. We gave that girl everything, including your father's name. She lived in a beautiful home, went to the best schools, had every opportunity to make something of herself. *And how did she repay us*? Your father will never tell you this, but he almost collapsed when he opened the newspaper and saw the Winchester name plastered all over the front page. He even considered resigning his position on the board. It was a humiliating experience. I will never forgive Amy for doing that to him."

Unbidden, memories came flooding back to Diana, small, painful moments she'd tried for years to deny or explain away. She could see her mother sitting on the sofa and Amy crawling up to sit next to her. No words were necessary, a frown was all it had taken to send Amy away. When Diana was old enough to learn to drive, her father taught her; Amy was sent to a driving school. Carl and Eileen had attended every play, every recital, every open house, when Diana was in school. Rarely had they found time for Amy, no matter how impressive the accomplishment.

All her life her parents had raised Diana with rules that they never even mentioned to Amy. Expectations, guidelines, and social mores were drilled into Diana from the breakfast table to bedtime. Nothing was ever required or asked of Amy beyond behaving in a way that wouldn't bring embarrassment to the family. It was as if she weren't important enough to care what happened to her once she was grown.

"When you decided to adopt, how did you find Amy?" Diana asked.

The question took Eileen off guard. "Why do you want to know that?"

Diana managed to rein in her anger. Further confrontation was not the way to get what she wanted from her mother. "Why did you offer Amy money to get her to leave the Cities?"

"I was doing it for your father—and for you."

"Amy is never going to leave here unless she has a reason to go somewhere else. What if I could find her real mother? Don't you think that might be reason enough?"

Eileen considered the idea. "What makes you think her real mother would want to see her?"

"It's been almost twenty-five years. Maybe she's had a change of heart. I understand a lot of women do."

"And if she hasn't?"

"Why are you fighting me on this? Do you have a better idea?"

"I don't understand why you feel you should put yourself out for Amy. What has she ever done for you?"

Eileen was testing her. Diana had to play along in order to win her mother's cooperation. "I'm not doing it for Amy—I'm doing it for you and Dad. It's time we had some lasting peace in this family. If that means finding another family for Amy, then that's what I'll do."

Remarkably, Eileen believed her. But then she'd lived her entire life seeing what she wanted to see, believing what she wanted to believe. "It was a private adoption," she said.

Before she could say anything more, the door opened and Carl Winchester stormed into the room. He turned on Diana. "When is this going to stop?"

The veins stood out on his neck, pulsing staccato with every heartbeat, as if keeping time for a heavy-metal band. She had never seen her father so angry. Instinctively she took a step away from him. "I don't know what you're talking about. When is what going to stop?"

"Don't play dumb with me, Diana. I've had it up to here." He made a slicing motion across his forehead with his hand.

"Is it Amy?" she asked, a sudden fear gripping her. "Did something happen to her?"

"You know very well what happened," he said, controlling his anger with obvious effort. "And you never even bothered to tell me. How do you think it felt to have some goddamned orderly come up and ask me about my own daughter, and me not know what in the hell he was talking about?"

Diana's fear turned to fury. "Is that all you care about? How it made *you* feel?"

Carl gave Diana an intimidating stare. "You expect me to care about some common whore when she gets beaten up by her john?"

The words hit like daggers. "You don't mean that."

"The hell I don't."

She had to get out of there. "Stay away from Amy," she warned her father. "I don't want you anywhere near her." To her mother she said, "You can take your check and shove it. Whatever Amy needs from now on, she gets from me."

Diana never saw what came next. She felt an explosion on the left side of her face, followed by a field of swirling stars. She staggered backward, her hand covering her cheek.

"You will not talk to your mother like that!" Carl roared.

He'd hit her. She was more stunned than hurt. Not once in all her years had he lifted a hand to her. For long seconds she stared at her father. "I can't believe you just did that. Tell me, Dad, how does it feel to hit a woman? Does it make you feel powerful? In control?" She waited until he started to answer before she cut him off. "Do you suppose that's the way the guy who beat up Amy felt?"

"I probably shouldn't have, but—"

"Probably?" she shot back.

"You're my daughter, I—"

"It doesn't matter." Diana moved to step around him. She had to get out of there.

He put an arm out to stop her. "Don't leave. Not until we've finished talking about this."

"There's nothing you have to say that I want to hear."

"Let her go, Carl," Eileen said. "She's just grandstanding."

Diana stopped to look at her mother. "Why don't you call Stuart? I'm sure you could get him to see your side of this."

"See?" Eileen said. She smiled at her husband. "I knew she wasn't serious. Stuart will take care of her for you."

Eight

———

Three strikes and you're out.

The metaphor wove itself into every thought as Diana drove back to the hospital. Only it didn't fit. Her parents had been given a season's chances at bat with Amy and they'd never once connected. They should have been called out a long time ago.

Baseball players had umpires to guarantee fair play; no one had assumed that role for Amy. Diana had tried, but she'd been ill equipped and sadly ignorant of the rules. Too often she'd been too caught up in her own battles to see or recognize what was happening to Amy.

Despite Diana's determination to make up for Amy's past, the pervasive question that had formed during the argument with her mother insinuated itself into every thought or plan or idea.

Was it possible for Amy to receive enough love and acceptance to undo a lifetime of parental neglect and rejection—or was it really too late? Could her biological mother repair the damage done by Eileen and Carl Winchester, or was the destruction so profound that it was irreversible? If so, where did that leave them? Could Amy make it through life without ever believing in herself?

The possibility haunted Diana. The human spirit might be wondrously resilient, but it was not indestructible.

She had to do something to help Amy, and she had to do it while there was still time.

A horn sounded behind Diana. She looked up and saw that the light had turned green. It was Saturday and the traffic was lighter than it would have been during the week, but if she didn't start paying attention to what she was doing, she was going to end up in the bed beside Amy's.

Fifteen minutes later, her plans no further along than they had been when she'd left her parents' house, Diana pulled into the parking lot at the hospital. She stopped by the gift shop to pick up flowers before she went to Amy's room. Considering the circumstances, it was an almost meaningless gesture, but if seeing yellow and pink and orange tulips spilling out of the back of a clown holding balloons brought even a moment's pleasure when Amy woke up, it was worth the effort.

Stephanie was standing at the window when Diana came in the room. "How is she?" Diana asked, keeping her voice low, as if Amy were merely sleeping.

"She's moaned a few times and moved around a little, but she hasn't opened her eyes yet. At least not that I've seen."

"Has the doctor been by?"

Stephanie shook her head. "How did it go with your mom?"

Before she answered, Diana put the flowers on the nightstand and checked Amy. It seemed as if the bruises and swelling had changed even in the short time she'd been gone. Some areas looked worse, others better. "I learned some things I'd just as soon not know."

"Such as?"

Revealing the underbelly of her family's character didn't come easily, even with someone she trusted as much as Stephanie. After several seconds she went over to the window, gently separated the blinds with her finger, and stared outside. Speaking so softly that Stephanie had to lean forward to hear, Diana told her, "You've heard of kids so spoiled they had their own pony? My parents got me a sister."

"I'm not sure I understand what you mean."

"Eileen and Carl Winchester didn't want their little girl to grow up all alone, so they bought her a playmate."

"Wait a minute. I'm getting some weird vibes here. Please tell me you're not looking for some way to blame yourself for what your parents did to Amy."

"If it weren't for me, they would never have—"

"Cut the bullshit, Diana. This mea culpa business isn't going to help you or Amy."

She thought about what Stephanie said. "You're right. It must be a real bore to listen to me at times." She shook herself. "Ugh."

"More painful than boring."

"Well, no more." She glanced at the bed to make sure Amy was still asleep. Satisfied, she said, "I need your help with something."

Distracted, Stephanie didn't respond right away. Instead she opened the blinds and looked closely at Diana's face. "What happened to your cheek?"

Instinctively Diana covered the side of her face with her hand. "My father decided I needed disciplining."

"He hit you?" she asked, stunned at the idea.

"Slapped me."

"It's semantics, Diana."

"I know." She became aware of her hand and brought it back down. Why had she tried to hide that she'd been hit? She was embarrassed about her appearance, but it was more than that. She was actually trying to protect her father, the very man who'd hit her. Jesus, was this the way battered women behaved? She looked at Amy. "Do you suppose Amy took the pills and vodka because she felt guilty? Could she have been trying to run away from what happened to her?"

"It makes a lot more sense than anything I've been able to come up with. Like I said before, it seems to me that if she was really trying to kill herself, she wouldn't have stopped at five or six sleeping pills, she would have popped every aspirin and cold remedy in the place." She lowered the blinds again, giving the room a softer, less sterile look. "You said there was something you wanted me to do for you."

"I want to find Amy's birth mother." The longer she thought about it, the more determined she became. "But I don't have the first idea how to go about it."

Stephanie's eyes narrowed in thought. "There was a story in one of the major magazines a couple of years ago about a woman somewhere in Chicago— no, I think it was Detroit—who did that kind of work. She almost never failed, but as it turned out, it was because her operation wasn't always on the up-and-up. It seems she used contacts in government agencies to sell her classified information. As I remember it, the story was written after she got out of prison and was about to start up business again. Supposedly this time around she was going to stick to legitimate channels."

"Do you remember her name?"

Stephanie smiled. "I'm good, but not that good. I'll give Mike Jones a call when I leave and have him look it up for us—and anything else he can dig up on the search for birth mothers."

"Who is Mike Jones?"

"He runs the newspaper library. Nobody is better at finding information. And he's fast."

Now that she'd decided on a direction, it was hard to put off getting started, even if only for as long as it took to come up with a name. "I don't want Amy to know about this. At least not right away."

"Do you think that's wise? She's going to suspect you're keeping something from her. That could be worse than telling her outright."

"I'll just have to be careful."

"I don't mean to be pushy about this, but—"

"I can't take the chance, Stephanie. What if I tell Amy what I'm doing and she gets her hopes up, only to find out her birth mother doesn't want to see her? How much rejection can one person handle?"

"I didn't think of that," Stephanie said. "All I ever hear about are mothers who want to find their kids. I guess it's only reasonable to assume there are some who don't."

"If not the majority."

Almost as if on cue, Amy moaned and brought the arm with the IV line up to her face. Diana went over to the bed to check the catheter and waited to see if Amy was going to wake up this time. Several seconds passed before her eyelids began to flutter. Finally, with effort, she kept them open long enough to focus.

"Welcome back," Diana said. "I was beginning to think you were going to sleep all day."

"What are you . . . doing here?"

"We had a date to go shopping, remember?"

Amy frowned. "Oh, yeah. I must have . . . must have overslept." She tried to sit up and immediately lay back down again. "God . . . my head is killing me."

"I'm not surprised." Diana adjusted the pillow.

When Diana moved, Amy caught sight of the IV bottle. "Where am I?"

"In the hospital."

She turned her head to get a better look, winced in pain, and returned slowly to her original position. "Why?" she asked a full minute later. "What happened?"

"All I know for sure is that someone beat you up, and that when you got home, you took some sleeping pills and washed them down with a pint of vodka. The who and why I'm waiting for you to fill in for me."

Amy closed her eyes. She was still so long, Diana thought she'd gone back to sleep.

"I don't want to talk about it," she finally said.

Diana had her mouth open to argue when she felt Stephanie's hand close on her arm. "All right," she said. "I'll wait until you do."

Amy seemed visibly to relax after that. Within minutes her breathing had changed to the rhythmic pattern of sleep. It was what the doctor had told Diana to expect. For the first day, and possibly the second, Amy would sleep more than she would be awake. When she was awake, she would be lethargic and confused.

"Do you think she'll change her mind?" Diana asked Stephanie.

"I wouldn't bet on it. My guess is that she'd just as soon you never found out what happened."

"Then how will I be able to keep it from happening again?"

Stephanie guided Diana back over to the window, where they could talk above a whisper. "You won't. Any more than you're going to be able to keep Amy from picking up another bottle or taking more pills. You can't live Amy's life for her."

"I know that here"—she tapped a finger against her temple—"but not here." She pressed her hand to her heart. "I'm just so damned scared."

"It's not going to help Amy if she thinks she's screwing up your life, too."

"I can get away with it for a while. I'm going to have her move in with me until she's on her feet again."

"Oh? And on which part of the floor do you plan to have her sleep? Or were you thinking the two of you could share the futon?"

It was far harder for Diana to ask for help than to give it. She rarely borrowed, but eagerly lent, took care of her friends' pets or their apartments when they vacationed, but had never asked to have the favor returned. She wouldn't have thought to impose on Stephanie now if not for the more desperate need to help Amy. "That brings me to the second favor. . . ."

"Something tells me I don't want to hear this."

"You can say no."

"Thanks."

Diana dug a credit card out of her wallet. "I'd like you to go to Dayton's before it closes tonight and pick out a couple of bedroom sets and some things for the living room."

Stephanie stared at the card and then at Diana. "You want me to buy furniture for you?"

"I'm sorry. I know I'm asking a lot, but I don't know what else to do. I really don't want to leave Amy again. Especially now that she's finally awake. And I really want to be here if she changes her mind about talking. It kills me to think the bastard who beat her up is going to get away with it."

"How am I supposed to know what to buy? This isn't like picking out a can opener. Furniture is expensive, and it lasts a long time."

"Get whatever appeals to you. And offer whatever they want to get someone to deliver it before ten tomorrow."

"Tomorrow's Sunday, Diana."

"I know. But if anyone can get them to do it, you can. I've seen you at work. You could talk a flock of geese into flying south for the summer."

Reluctantly Stephanie took the credit card. "At least give me some direction. I don't know the first thing about buying furniture."

"I don't care what you get. All I need is a couple of beds, dressers, and something to sit on. The important thing is that I'm able to convince Amy she can come to my place when she leaves here, and it won't be an imposition."

"What if you don't like what I pick out?"

Diana smiled. This was a side to Stephanie she'd never seen. Normally she radiated confidence. "Just stick to your basic avocado and orange and you can't go wrong."

Stephanie's eyes widened in horror. "You're not serious."

"I'll make you a deal. Whatever I don't like, I'll sell to you for half price as soon as I don't need it anymore."

Stephanie considered the offer. "I can live with that."

"Now get out of here before the store closes."

"Do you want me to drop by Amy's and pick up some things for her? What about her friends? Shouldn't we let them know she's in the hospital?"

Diana couldn't ask Stephanie to take on any more than she already had. "I'll go over myself as soon as Amy is settled at my place and I feel comfortable leaving her alone. Until then she can use my stuff."

"And her friends?"

"I don't know," Diana admitted. "I'm not sure she'd want them to find out about this. Why don't we wait and ask her?"

Stephanie lifted the strap of her purse over her shoulder. "I'll be back to let you know how the shopping went."

Diana was hit with a sudden overwhelming feeling of gratitude. She might not have been given the world's best parents, but no one had a better friend. She reached out and gave Stephanie a hug, not the quick, pat-on-the-back kind, but one that said what she was feeling. "Thank you—for everything."

Stephanie returned four hours later wearing a slinky black dress that negated any possibility of underwear, heels held to her feet with skinny silver straps, and shimmering earrings that brushed her shoulders. She had two white paper bags in her hands. "I figured there was no way I was going to get you to go out, so I did the next best thing."

Diana closed the magazine she'd been reading and got up from her chair. "I'm sure when Amy wakes up she will appreciate the effort, but you really didn't have to get dressed up for us."

Stephanie did a slow turn. "It's just something I found hanging in the back of the closet."

"Uh-huh—along with a couple of Judith Leiber purses you picked up at a thrift store?"

Stephanie grinned. "Like it?"

"Can you like something and be jealous at the same time?"

"What a nice thing to say."

"You should have told me you had plans."

"Why?"

"I wouldn't have asked you to—"

"Then I'm glad I didn't say anything. Once I got the hang of it, I *loved* buying all that furniture. You must have one hell of a credit limit on that card. After the salesman ran through the first bedroom set, he got all excited and started showing me the upscale stuff."

"I owe you—big time," Diana said.

"You're not even going to ask me how much I spent?"

"I don't care."

Stephanie dug Diana's card out of her purse. "I didn't go crazy, although there was a coffee table I fell in love with that cost as much as the sofa and love seat combined that really tempted me. Maybe we can go back there sometime, and . . . You're not interested in any of this, are you."

"If this hadn't happened to Amy, I probably would have spent the next six months on your futon. I am, however, interested in your date. Who's the lucky guy?"

"Stan Houghton. I met him when I was doing a story on the Vikings last season. We've been going out off and on since."

It was strange Stephanie hadn't mentioned him before now. "Player or management?"

"Please—I have better sense than to go out with a professional football player." Before Diana could say anything about the number of players Stephanie had dated, she added, "More than once."

Diana took the bags and inhaled deeply. "God, whatever this is, it smells wonderful. I had no idea I was so hungry."

"How's our girl?"

"Good. She's been drifting in and out since you left. The last time she stayed awake ten whole minutes."

"How long ago was that?"

"Just before you came in." It had been more than a casual question. "Why?"

Stephanie reached in her purse and pulled out an envelope. "I stopped by the newspaper."

"You got it?" Diana put the bags on the table beside the bed, then glanced at Amy to make sure she was still asleep before taking the envelope and going over to the window to read the list of names and phone numbers.

Stephanie came up to look over Diana's shoulder. "The woman on top, Margaret McCormick, is the one I told you about. Mike checked around and came up with other people who do the same thing in case she didn't work out."

"I had no idea finding people was such a thriving business," Diana said.

"He told me this was just a small sampling."

"I'm going to have to find a special way to thank him."

"Anything chocolate will do."

Diana stared at the names. "I wonder what she's like."

"Who?"

"Amy's mother."

"She could be anyone," Stephanie said. "It's kind of scary when you think about it."

"What if she's someone who was really young when she had Amy and went on to become famous? Think how hard it would be for Amy to fit into that kind of life."

"More important, what if she turns out to be someone you hate on sight? Would you still tell her about Amy?"

"I don't know."

"Well, you've got lots of time to think about it. Right now there's some Chinese food that needs our attention."

"Aren't you going out to eat?"

"Yes." Stephanie handed one of the bags on the table to Diana, reached in the other, and took out a small white box and a pair of chopsticks. "But not to a Chinese restaurant."

"Do you know what I like least about you?"

Stephanie took a bite of tempura shrimp and rolled her eyes in ecstasy. "This is just a guess, but I have a feeling it has something to do with my metabolism."

"Isn't there one knot in your family tree?"

"Rumor has it that a thrice-removed cousin of my great-great-uncle was hanged for being a horse thief."

"You're lying."

"Yeah, but it makes a good story, don't you think?"

Diana took a bite of egg roll and said a quick prayer that someday Amy would have good stories to tell about her own family.

Nine

Amy rolled to her side, swung her legs over the edge of the bed, and carefully pushed herself up to a sitting position. She'd discovered that if she did anything but lie perfectly still, her head would throb with every heartbeat. Her short-term goal since first being allowed to get up two days ago had focused on traveling from the bed to the bathroom while maintaining her heart rate at a steady sixty-five beats. Sometimes she succeeded, sometimes she didn't.

Which, all things considered, was pretty much the way she would have described her life.

She glanced at the window and tried to guess the time by the angle of light stealing through the blinds. The nurse had promised Amy that she could go home after lunch. Only she wasn't going home, exactly. Diana had insisted she stay with her for a few days. She would have preferred being alone—she had a lot of thinking to do—but it was obvious Diana wasn't up to the separation. Amy had to give her sister credit. She was walking a mental tightrope, but she never let it show. Her willingness to back off questions was another surprise. Not that Amy expected any changes to last much past her recovery.

Thank God she'd gotten rid of her clothes before she started drinking. Diana had never seen her dressed that way, and Amy preferred she never did. And thank God she'd gotten rid of the check. Amy didn't give a damn about protecting her mother, but she didn't want Diana to feel she had to take sides. Eileen would never forgive Diana if she chose Amy over her. One estranged daughter per family was enough.

She had gotten rid of the check, hadn't she? It bothered her that the memory wasn't as clear as that of gathering her clothes and throwing them away. But then there were a lot of missing pieces, some she hoped would never return.

Amy looked up when the door opened and the doctor who'd been checking on her for the past two days came into the room. He was on the short side of thirty, with California blond hair, horn-rimmed glasses, and a sexy all-the-way smile. Under other circumstances Amy might have been interested in seeing him outside the hospital. As it was, she hoped they never ran into each other again.

"I see you're up. How's it feel?"

"As if my head were about to explode."

"I'm not surprised. You took a hell of a beating. It's going to be a while before you're back to normal." He came up to the bed, took a small penlight out of his pocket, and flashed it into her eyes. "Have the police been in to see you yet? They've been by several times, but you were always asleep, and your sister refused to let them wake you."

Amy went rigid. "Why do the police want to see me?"

"It's obvious you didn't do this to yourself."

"I don't know what happened," she said too quickly to be convincing. "Or how. There's nothing I can tell anyone."

"Now why do I find that hard to believe?"

"Now what makes you think I care?" she mimicked.

He smiled. "You really are feeling better."

Amy was long past the girl who could be taken in by a charming bedside manner. She didn't mean to antagonize the doctor; it was simply a matter of self-preservation. Her days of caring what men said, or did, or felt, were over. "Look, all I need or want from you is a signed release from this place. You can take your—"

He held up his hand. "And you can stop right there. Your father warned me what I was in for if I was dumb enough to let myself get involved with you. I'm not, so you can save whatever it is you were going to say for the next person on your list." He stuck the penlight back in his pocket.

She shouldn't have been surprised, and she sure as hell shouldn't have been hurt that her father had talked to the staff about her. "The release?" she prompted.

"As far as I'm concerned, your regular physician can take over now. You should make an appointment to see him in a couple of days." He started to leave, then turned back as if he'd just remembered something. "You might want to ask him about seeing a counselor. I don't know that it would help, but it sure as hell wouldn't hurt."

"Thanks for caring," Amy said.

"You're welcome," he said, and smiled.

Amy stared at the door after he'd gone. She was going to have to work on her delivery. He'd completely missed the sarcastic tone.

Diana flipped through her key ring to find the key to Amy's apartment. That morning at the hospital she'd been prepared to go to battle to convince Amy to move in with her, but Amy hadn't even attempted an argument. While it made the preparations easier, Diana would have felt more comfortable if she'd encountered at least some token resistance. Amy liked to sail in rough water. It was as much a part of who she was as her brown eyes and flashy jewelry.

The physical changes were almost easier to accept. It was amazing how quickly she'd grown accustomed to seeing the broken blood vessels that made Amy's eyes more red than brown, or the swollen flesh and damaged cartilage that made her nose look as if it belonged on a punch-drunk fighter.

What she couldn't accept, what scared her more than she wanted to admit, even to herself, was Amy's unresponsiveness. No one carried a bigger chip on her shoulder or fought harder against a perceived injustice. Diana had tried for days to understand why Amy was willing to let the man who'd beaten her up go free. She was no closer now than she had been in the beginning.

Diana let herself into Amy's apartment, determined to pick up the things Amy had requested and then get back to the hospital.

That was before she saw the living room. When Amy eventually came home, it couldn't be to this— the silent testimony to the chaos that had come with trying to save a life. Furniture stood in corners, shoved aside to make room for firemen and paramedics. A lamp shade hung at an odd angle. The magazine rack knocked over by the gurney had spilled its contents on the floor. Only Amy's precious clock remained untouched, sitting on the mantel, placed precisely so that everyone who came to visit could see it in its glory.

Diana went after the room with determined haste until only the coffee table needed to be moved back into place. As she lifted one corner and then the other, she almost missed seeing the piece of paper that had stuck under one leg. It was a check, made out to Amy and signed by Eileen Winchester.

So this was the infamous—

Her gaze fixed on the date in the upper-right-hand corner. Her mother had been at Amy's apartment that past Friday night. She was the link between the time Diana had dropped Amy off and the way she'd found her the next morning. Eileen hadn't inflicted the beating, of course; her methods of destruction were mental, not physical. But Diana was willing to wager her trust fund that Eileen had been the catalyst for whatever happened later.

Then she looked at the amount, to see how much her mother had been willing to pay to get rid of her own daughter.

Two hundred and fifty thousand dollars.

It was nowhere near what Amy would be entitled to as heir to half the Winchester fortune, but a nice sum nevertheless. Diana tapped the check against her opposite hand as she considered her options. She imagined the satisfaction that would come from destroying so grand an amount, but it paled in comparison with the thought of her mother's reaction when she discovered the money missing from her account.

At last Diana had something that made her smile. She would come back for Amy's things later. First she had to make a trip to the bank.

The transaction proved far easier than Diana had thought possible, even with being a member of a family who'd banked at the same branch for over thirty years. She was as well known by the officers as the tellers. And, luckily, so was Amy.

After the brief formality of verifying she was

indeed a signatory on her sister's account and entitled to participate in any and all activity concerning the account, Diana asked a series of innocuous questions that revealed her mother had not stopped payment on the check as she'd threatened. Undoubtedly she'd felt she had plenty of time with Amy still in the hospital, or perhaps she was clinging to the hope that once Amy was out, she would take the money and disappear.

With a show of reluctance, Diana confided the money was a desperately needed loan. She hoped it would be enough to explain the request for an immediate transfer of funds from her parents' account and the drawing of a cashier's check for the full amount. She went one step further by hinting the money was a loan for a house and that the deal would fall through if not consummated that afternoon.

The last thing Diana did before leaving the bank was visit her safe-deposit box. In the privacy of the room beside the vault she took the cashier's check out of her purse and put it into her drawer. She had no idea what she would eventually do with the money, only that Eileen Winchester would never see a dime of it again.

Before heading back to the hospital, Diana stopped by her office to pick up the work she would be doing at home while Amy was there. On her way out she ran into Bill Summersby in the hallway. Four months earlier Bill had been brought in from Pillsbury to be Sander's Foods' vice president in charge of marketing.

"I heard about your sister," he said. "I want you to know how sorry I am. If there's anything I can do, I'd consider it a compliment if you'd ask."

"I know that you personally arranged for me to have this next week off. It means a lot to me that I'll be able to stay home with Amy. Thank you."

He pointedly looked down at her bulging briefcase. "It looks as if you plan to spend the time working. We'll miss your input at meetings. If you get a chance, stop by."

"I'll try, but don't look for me. Amy is still in pretty bad shape."

"Did they catch the guy yet?"

She knew she had to get used to the question; it was going to be asked a hundred times in a hundred different ways. "No," she said simply. "And I'm not sure they ever will. Amy doesn't remember much about that night."

"Maybe it's for the best."

He was letting her off easy, and she could have hugged him for the kindness. "I appreciate your concern."

He put a comforting hand on her shoulder. "Like I said, anything I can do . . ."

The files Diana had tucked under her arm began to slip. She hiked them back up. "Amy's waiting for me. I'd better get going."

"I'll walk you out." He carried her briefcase to her car and stood on the sidewalk as she drove away, giving a final wave as she turned the corner.

Amy looked a lot worse before she started looking better. After a week of avoiding mirrors and shiny surfaces, she walked into the bathroom one morning while Diana was fixing her hair and stared at herself in the mirror.

"I don't think green is my color," she said.

"Me either," Diana said to Amy's reflection. "Personally, I've always thought peaches and cream suited you best."

Amy leaned over the sink for a closer inspection. "I must have been pretty messed up."

"You've never once looked to see what he did to you?"

"I felt it, I didn't need to see it."

"Does he live here?" The question was out before Diana realized what she'd done. Not only had she asked something she'd promised she wouldn't, she'd let Amy know she didn't believe the story she'd told everyone, including the police, about not remembering. "I'm sorry. Forget I said anything."

"No."

"No you won't forget?"

"No he doesn't live in the Cities."

"Does he— Damn it, there I go again." She put down the curling iron and turned to face Amy. "You're going to have to lay this out for me. I need to know exactly where we stand. Can I talk about what happened or not?"

"I guess with me still walking around looking like this"—she leaned toward the mirror again and touched her cheek—"it's pretty hard not to say anything."

"At times I'm so angry, I can't think about anything else." On impulse, she adjusted the collar on Amy's knit shirt, reassuring herself with the simple gesture. "I almost lost you, Amy. Do you have any idea what it would do to me if that happened?"

"How would you feel if I moved away from here?"

Diana had to be careful she didn't reveal anything she wasn't supposed to know. "What brought that up?"

"It's something I've been thinking about lately."

"Any particular reason?"

"Don't you ever get the feeling there's something out there waiting for you? We've lived in Minnesota our whole lives, Diana."

"I like Minnesota. Why would I want to live anywhere else?"

"If you don't look, how will you know if there isn't someplace you would like better?"

"This isn't about me," Diana reminded her. "You're the one with itchy feet."

"Where's your spirit of adventure?"

The doorbell rang before Diana had to come up with an answer. "Would you get that?" It was a test.

Amy didn't move. "Are you expecting someone?"

Diana didn't have the heart to push Amy into doing something she wasn't ready to do. "It's probably a delivery from the office. I have to sign. I might as well go down myself."

Amy combed her hand through her hair and picked up the curling iron. "I'm going to see what I can do with this mess."

The doorbell rang again before Diana was halfway down the stairs. "I'm coming," she shouted.

It was Stephanie. She mouthed, "Where's Amy?"

"Fixing her hair. What's up?"

"I heard from Margaret McCormick."

"Already? It's only been three days since your meeting." Afraid she would change her mind about finding Amy's birth mother after Amy came home from the hospital, Diana had taken Stephanie up on her offer to make the initial contact with Margaret McCormick. The only information they'd been able to give her had come from Helen, and was so sketchy neither she nor Stephanie had given it much chance.

"Margaret said this was one of the easiest cases she'd ever worked on."

"Then it's done?" Diana had thought she would have more time to consider and weigh the consequences of what she was doing. It was one thing to pursue, another to discover. "She's actually found Amy's mother?"

Stephanie nodded. "She lives in Wyoming."

"Wyoming?" Diana had imagined Amy coming from an exotic background, her mother a struggling artist or Rhodes scholar forced to make a choice between education and motherhood. She knew less about Wyoming than Outer Mongolia; the people who lived there were as big a mystery to her as purple lipstick. How could her sister have come from such a place?

"She has a brother and three sisters. Two of them, the brother and one sister, are older, the other two, younger."

"Amy's mother?"

"No—Amy."

It took a minute for the news to sink in. Diana had never considered the possibility Amy would be part of a family. "Good grief—how many times has this woman been married?"

"That's the strange part. According to—" Stephanie looked up and pasted on a quick smile. "Hey," she called over Diana's shoulder. "We were just talking about you."

"I figured as much," Amy said. "Want me to go away again?"

"Don't be silly," Diana told her. "We were trying to come up with a way to get you to make some more of those pork tamales you made last year." The lie came too easily. What came next? Cheating?

Amy seemed pleased at the request. "I don't know if I remember how."

"I could go over to your place to get the recipe for you," Stephanie offered.

"No, you stay here and I'll go," Diana said. "That way I can stop by the store and pick up what we need." She didn't want to go to Amy's apartment, she didn't want to go to the store, and she didn't want tamales for dinner. But there was no way she could dump anything more on Stephanie.

"Wait a minute," Amy said. "Are you two sure it's *my* tamales you're remembering? Last year was the first and last time I ever made them. I don't remember anyone making a fuss about them then."

Diana jumped at the chance. "Now that you mention it, maybe—"

"I'm absolutely sure," Stephanie chimed in. "They were the best I've ever eaten, and remember I lived in Texas for two years. I even told the food editor at the paper how good they were."

"All right," Amy said with a shrug. "If you're sure you know what you're talking about."

"We'll help." Stephanie hooked her arm through Amy's. "As soon as Diana gets back from the store, you tell us what you want us to do, and we'll do it." Stephanie did a double take as she passed the living room. "Wow, I just can't get used to seeing that stuff in there. I did one heck of a job, even if I do say so myself."

"That you did," Diana said as she looked at her new furniture. Where there had been beige and white and brown there was now green and mauve and lavender. The wood was cherry, stained dark and polished to a lustrous shine. The limited-edition print over the fireplace was a Charles Wysocki, a cat asleep in a gardener's shed, surrounded by mounds of junk and the warm light of summer. Stuart would be horrified at the change. All those trips to furniture studios and art galleries had been wasted on her. She remained with the hoi polloi. There's not one thing I would change."

"I suppose that means the half-price sale is off?"

Diana laughed. "Are you crazy? You're talking to the lady who was willing to live out of packing crates."

"I've been thinking how nice Grandma's clock would look in here," Amy said.

A cold chill climbed Diana's spine. She turned to face Amy. "Only if you came with it."

Amy was the first to break eye contact. "It was just a thought."

Any hope Diana had harbored that she had time to think about her decision to contact Amy's mother abruptly died. If she didn't do something, and soon, she was liable to wake up one morning and find Amy gone.

Ten

"Welcome to Jackson," the hotel clerk said. "How can I help you?"

"I have a reservation."

"And the name?"

"Diana Winchester." She handed him her Visa card.

He checked a computer monitor as he ran the card through a machine and handed it back to her. "You'll be staying with us a week?"

She'd told Amy not to expect her back home before then, but if everything went the way she hoped, she could be on her way back to Minneapolis in as little as three days. If not, there was no telling how much longer she might have to stay. "Will there be a problem if I have to leave early or extend an extra day or two?"

"Not at all. Why don't I just leave the departure date open? That way we won't run into any problems later."

"As soon as I know something, I'll get back to you."

"Enjoy your stay." He handed her a key in a folder

that listed the hotel's services. "If you'll wait over there by the bison, I'll ring for someone to help with your bags."

She glanced back at the enormous stuffed buffalo she'd passed on the way in. As offensive as she found the small stuffed animals scattered around the cavernous lobby, the large ones actually gave her the creeps. "Thanks, but I can handle them myself."

She started toward the elevator and then remembered there was something else she'd meant to ask him. "Could you tell me how to get to Martell Outfitters?"

"The store or the guide office?"

The question threw her. The report hadn't mentioned anything about a guide service. "The store."

"Go out the front door, turn left, and then up two blocks. It's on the corner across from the Barbecue Hole. You can't miss it."

She smiled her thanks, picked up her bags, and headed for the elevator. Her room was on the second floor in the back corner. It was large and comfortable and decorated in the same western motif as the lobby, minus the assortment of wildlife. She opened the curtains to let in the late afternoon light and stood mesmerized at the expansive sight that greeted her. For the first time in her life she understood the true meaning of majestic and how something could be intimidating and awe-inspiring at the same time.

She'd never seen real mountains, at least not what Wyoming considered mountains. On the drive in from the airport, she'd almost run her rental car off the road staring out the window. Minnesota was nothing like this place. The wilderness there had a comfortable, welcoming feel to it. A trip into the woods held implied promise that the explorer would be safe, the experience rejuvenating.

The mountains and forests that surrounded Jackson Hole seemed to shout a warning—trespass at your own peril. There was nothing gentle or forgiving in the sheer rock faces that projected above the timberline or in the dense verdant growth that hugged the hillsides. The raw beauty was unlike any Diana had ever known and inspired as much fear as awe.

What kind of people purposely chose to live in a place that daily reminded them of their insignificance? Did they develop egos to match their mountains or were they boringly humble? Diana had a page of clinical details about Amy's family, but nothing about who they really were. There were clues: the Martells were one of the original homesteaders in Jackson and, unlike many of the early settlers, had survived and prospered both through impossibly harsh winters and, later, the endless waves of tourists. They still owned their original ranch as well as a thriving business in Jackson. In a city with less than six thousand permanent residences, a place that was as much tourist attraction as real town, the Martells wielded a disproportionate share of influence. They were pillars in a small, incredibly lucrative community and, if the report was reliable, uncommonly close-knit.

Diana couldn't understand how Amy fit in the picture, but there was no question she did. She might not be a Martell, but she was Dorothy Martell's daughter. For a woman who'd gone to all the trouble to have her baby in another state and then give it up for adoption, Dorothy had left a remarkably wide trail. Not only had she used her real name at the hospital, she'd sent a thank-you note to one of the nurses with her mother's return address on the envelope. The nurse still had the letter, pasted in a scrapbook, the ink a little faded but readable.

Either Dorothy Martell had believed adoption records couldn't be breached or she'd secretly hoped her daughter would want to find her someday. Diana prayed it was the latter.

The telephone rang, something routine at home, startling in a motel room. Diana rounded the bed and picked up the receiver. "Yes?"

"Hi," Amy said cheerfully. "I thought I'd try to catch you before you left for one of your meetings."

"What's up?" Diana had known there was no way Amy would believe she was going to Jackson Hole for a vacation, so she'd created a story about attending a food industry conference in the town of Jackson. Bill Summersby had agreed to give her time off work and to cover for her should anyone start asking questions, but he'd made it clear he wasn't pleased with her timing. They were coming down to the final phase of the marketing project for the new cereal and needed everyone involved to be available for last-minute changes. She'd arranged for her assistant to sit in on the meetings and to E-mail her the minutes, but the communication was necessarily one way. She was paid for her ideas.

"I was just checking to make sure you got there all right."

She wasn't used to having Amy worry about her. It was both sweet and annoying. "I had my assistant call ahead and tell them I was traveling without my parents. They had this really cute guy waiting to help me make the connection."

"Smart-ass."

Diana laughed. "How are you doing?"

"Oh, so it's all right for you to worry about me," Amy said, mustering an indignant tone, "but I'm not supposed—"

"You can worry about me all you want," Diana conceded. "Especially if I'm dumb enough to let someone talk me into going white-water rafting."

"Are you?"

"Remember who you're talking to, Amy."

"Just last week you said you couldn't come up with a reason to leave Minnesota, and now look where you are."

"That's different. This is business." Diana flinched at yet another retelling of the same lie. Amy was going to be a long time forgiving the deception, no matter how compelling the reason.

"I should have come with you."

"Next time." She'd purposely left for Wyoming as soon as she could get away, knowing Amy wouldn't ask to come with her until all signs of the bruises were gone.

"What's it like there?"

"Amazing—too beautiful for words. And really different. The town sits at the end of a valley, and it's surrounded by mountains that look like giant canine teeth. On the way to the hotel we passed a park with four enormous arches made out of interlocking elk horns." Suddenly, with a rush of love and fear at what lay ahead for them, she desperately wished Amy were there to share it all with her. "You'd love the shops . . . and the galleries."

"Have you seen any cowboys?"

"I don't think so. I've seen a lot of store-fresh cowboy hats, but not any bow legs to go with them."

"Well, don't go bellying up to some bar and let the guy next to you talk you into staying. I miss you already."

"I just left this morning."

"It's probably because you're so far away."

Diana couldn't shake the feeling that what they were saying was a preview of things to come. "Are you having dinner with Stephanie?"

"She has a date."

"Why don't you give Lu-Ann or Karol a call. I'm sure one of them would—"

"Give it a rest, Diana. It's not going to hurt me to spend a night alone. As a matter of fact, I'm looking forward to it."

"I thought you said you missed me."

"So, I lied."

She glanced at the window and saw how deep the shadows had grown in the mountains. If she was going to make it to the Martells' store that evening, she was going to have to get moving. "I'm hanging up on you now," she said. "I've got places to go and people to see." At last something that at least resembled the truth, even if the implication was misleading.

"I'll wait for you to call me tomorrow. No telling when you'll get back to your room."

"I love you, Amy."

"Me too," she said cheerfully. "Now get out there and do a little sightseeing. I want you to tell me what it looks like *outside* the motel when you get home."

Diana was smiling when she hung up the phone, but the smile was as transitory as her confidence. She wanted a guarantee that her meddling wouldn't make Amy's life more complicated than it already was. Once the curtain opened on this new cast of characters, she would lose her job as director. She might insist they take a bow or leave the stage, but it was unlikely they would follow her instructions. All the more reason to find out as much as she could about the Martells before actually making contact with them.

Martell Outfitters turned out to be a much bigger enterprise than Diana had thought. She'd pictured it as one of the small fishing and hunting shops she'd passed on her way to the hotel, certainly not something that took up half a block. The windows were works of art, with animated figures that displayed the variety of products to be found inside. Each focused on an individual sport—fishing, mountain climbing, backpacking, and white-water rafting—and contained everything anyone could possibly want to know or take with them on their adventure, from clothing, to books, to custom-made equipment, to specially prepared, vacuum-packed foods.

If the amount spent on the windows was in proportion to the profit made on the business, the Martells were even wealthier than the report had indicated. Diana would have preferred the family be less affluent. With so many personalities involved, one of them was bound to play the skeptic and question Amy's motive for wanting to return to the fold.

As far as Diana was concerned, the more interesting question would be why Amy had been allowed to become the outsider in the first place.

She came to the corner and the front door. It was massive and intricately carved with scenes of mountains and wild animals and, she noted, cleverly angled to draw in foot traffic from both directions. The door had been hung perfectly and, despite its weight, opened with minimum effort. Diana considered taking her ease of entry as a sign of things to come, then laughed at her own naiveté. Even if it turned out Dorothy Martell was eager to have Amy back in her life again, nothing about the meeting would be easy for either of them.

The store was as impressive on the inside as it was on the outside. Dozens of customers filled the aisles, all carrying purchases, yet the shelves and racks looked as if they'd just been faced. The lighting was subdued, and "feel good" music played in the background. She spot-checked prices as she went along. She had no idea how much fishing poles and vests should cost but was willing to bet this was not the place to come for bargains.

Diana had a coffee table book on wildflowers open in her hands when a woman came up to her and said, "The photography is extraordinary, don't you think?"

"Yes, it . . ." The rest died in her throat. It was as if Amy had suddenly appeared, altered slightly by the process of instant transport, but Amy nevertheless.

"I'm sorry, I didn't mean to startle you," the woman said.

"No—you didn't." Diana put the book back on the shelf, stalling for time to regain her equilibrium. She realized she hadn't expected familial resemblances, at least not like this.

Without giving it conscious thought, she'd simply assumed Amy would be half-sister to Dorothy Martell's other children, that her pregnancy had been the result of an affair or possibly even rape. But it was obvious Amy shared the same genetic background with this woman. Which made it all the more puzzling that Dorothy Martell had given up one child while she kept four others. "It's just that you look like someone I know."

She smiled. "You must be a friend of Judy's."

Dear God, they even smiled alike. Diana knew she was staring, but was so caught up in the search for details that would set Amy apart from this person, that she simply couldn't look away. "Judy?"

"My sister."

Of course. The youngest sibling. Her name had been in the report along with the other two sisters, Sharon and Faith. The brother was Trent . . . no, *Travis*. The report had said Faith and Judy were gone for the summer, so the woman in front of her had to be Sharon Martell Williams, the only married sibling. "Actually, the woman I know lives in Minneapolis."

"Then she can't be one of us. The Martells have been in Wyoming so long, we're considered a native species." She patted her belly and grinned. "Obviously not one on the endangered list."

Diana looked at Sharon's softly rounded stomach. The pregnancy wasn't far along, and had she not pointed it out herself, it would have been easy to miss.

Amy was about to become an aunt. The thought was so bizarre, it was almost incomprehensible. For her and Amy's entire lives, whatever had happened to one had happened to the other. Now this wondrous event was about to take place in Amy's life, and Diana was excluded. "You look so much alike," Diana murmured, her thought finding voice.

"I once read that we all have a double somewhere in the world. I guess mine must be in Minnesota. It would be fun to meet her someday." She laughed. "Although something tells me we'd pass right by each other without a backward glance. I can't even see the likeness in my own family."

What had she expected—some kind of reaction, an indication this Sharon knew she had a sister she'd never seen? "Her name is Amy."

Again there was the quick smile, only this time it was more perfunctory than engaging. "You'd probably like to get back to your shopping. Let me know if there's anything I can help you with."

"Yes . . . I will. Thank you."

Diana watched Sharon as she approached a customer, talked for several seconds, and then stepped behind the counter to ring up a sale. She even tilted her head the way Amy did when she was talking to someone. Did the other sister, Judy, share their mannerisms, too? What about Faith?

For the first time the full impact of what she'd come to Wyoming to do hit home. Fifteen minutes ago Amy's family had been names without faces, characters without personalities. Now at least one of them was as real as Amy herself. A complete stranger could pick Amy and Sharon out of crowd and know they belonged together.

Why not? Sharon was Amy's real sister. The thought sickened Diana. She'd come there thinking no matter what happened her position in Amy's life was secure. No one could take away the years they'd spent together or the love that bound them. But with the ease of a north wind scooting a cloud across the sky, Diana had seen that belief swept away.

She was afraid. To her shame, it wasn't for Amy anymore, it was for herself.

Eleven

—

Diana gave up trying to sleep when it was still dark the next morning. She stayed in her room, surfing through a dozen infomercials on television and then reading everything and anything she could find on the tables and in the drawers. High on her list of things to do that day was to find a bookstore.

After her second reading of the back of a map that described all the things to see and do in Jackson Hole and all the restaurants and hotels in the town of Jackson, she got up and opened the curtain. False dawn outlined the mountains to the east. It would be light soon and safe to go outside. A month ago she might have gone to the park to witness the sunrise outside in the crisp morning air, but to do so now would take a trust and innocence she no longer possessed. She should be angry and less accepting of the loss, and maybe someday she would be. But right now she had other things on her mind.

When it grew light enough to see details on the buildings across the street, Diana slipped into her clothes, went outside, and walked through town, looking for an open restaurant.

"Mornin'," the waitress called when she looked up and saw Diana standing in the doorway. "Just have a seat anywhere. I'll be right with you."

The restaurant had a fifties look, with chrome-and-Formica tables and tuck-and-roll seats in the booths, all too new to be original. Amy would feel at home here. Diana sat in the back by a window, where she could watch the town come to life. She was barely seated before the waitress appeared, a steaming pot of coffee in one hand, a menu in the other. "Patty" was stamped on the plastic pin fastened to the breast pocket of her pink-and-white uniform.

"Coffee?"

"Please—and an English muffin."

"You beat the regulars this morning." Patty stifled a yawn as she poured the coffee. "Got a big day ahead of you?"

"Yes."

"Going rafting?"

"Meeting someone—for the first time," Diana said. She smiled automatically. "Well, it looks like you'll have the weather on your side. I heard on the radio it's supposed to hit eighty this afternoon."

Just as automatically, Diana returned the smile. She was grateful for any distraction, even superficial conversation. "It was raining when I left home yesterday."

"We could use some rain around here. Muffin all you're having?"

Diana nodded.

"There's some great-lookin' cinnamon rolls back in the kitchen. Baked fresh this morning."

She was tempted. Food was only a temporary fix, but there were times an indulgent bridge over a short crisis was all she needed. Now if she could only come up with a way to make the calories temporary, too. "I'd better not."

The waitress nodded knowingly. "I'll be right back with that muffin."

When Diana was alone again, she turned to look outside. It wasn't just second thoughts that had taken chunks out of her confidence since seeing Sharon Martell Williams; she'd moved on to real and compelling doubts. On one level she could still picture Amy in the midst of an extensive, loving family. But there was another level, one ruled by pragmatism, that insisted she take a more realistic approach and recognize how disruptive Amy's sudden appearance could be and how potentially divisive.

Diana tried to put herself in Sharon's place and to imagine how she would feel if presented with a grown sister, someone who was close to a mirror image on the outside but lacked even the most basic shared experience on the inside.

Sharon was June; Amy, December.

A bell sounded, drawing Diana's attention to the front door. A tall man wearing a battered cowboy hat came in. He was dressed in jeans and a plaid shirt and looked more as if he were ready for bed than just from it. He took off his hat, hung it on the rack by the door, and ran both hands through his dark brown hair. The distinct trails his fingers left behind did nothing to improve his appearance. What seemed a week's worth of beard added to his unkempt look. Diana knew she was staring but was mesmerized. If this guy was a typical cowboy, the ad agencies had sold the rest of the country a real bill of goods.

After glancing toward the kitchen, the man walked past several tables and took the booth opposite hers. When he was seated he looked up, directly into her eyes. She immediately looked away, but not before she'd seen a smile form. It brought a hint of invitation to his dark brown, bloodshot eyes. The effect was magnetic. Almost as if she had no control over her own actions, she looked at him again. He was still staring and still smiling. Her heart did a peculiar little skipping thing that set off an alarm in her mind.

She knew this man.

They had met somewhere. She didn't know where, or when, or how, or under what circumstances, but she was absolutely certain their paths had crossed. To give herself something to do while she sifted through all the planned and chance meetings she'd had with men who'd made more than transitory impressions, she picked up her cup and took a drink of the strong black liquid. She neither tasted its acidic bite nor felt its heat as it slid over her tongue and down her throat.

The waitress came out of the kitchen, this time carrying a plate in one hand and the coffeepot in the other. "Hey, Travis . . ." The smile in her voice was as big as the one on her face. "Where you been keeping yourself?"

Travis? The coffee Diana had just swallowed hit her stomach with a wrench. No wonder she'd thought she knew him. What was it with her and the Martells? Was she destined to run into one of them everywhere she went?

"Here and there," he said.

"From the looks of you, I'd say more 'there' than 'here.'" Without taking her eyes from her new customer, Patty sat the plate in front of Diana, topped off her coffee, and went over to pour a cup for Travis.

"I took some horses up to Miller Butte," he answered cryptically.

"Lookin' for that hiker?"

"Me and about a hundred others."

"They find him yet?"

"Last night." Travis grinned and shook his head, a disbelieving look in his eyes. "All that searching and not a trace, then when we're about to give up, he sees our fire and comes wandering into camp."

"He say how he got lost?"

"If he did, I didn't stick around to hear."

She put the pot on the table and used both hands to adjust her apron. "Whatcha gonna have this morning?"

"That depends. . . ." He waited for her.

"Yeah, we got 'em," she said with a hint of disapproval. "You want one or two?"

"Give me one to start, with a big slab of butter on the side."

She frowned. "You mark my word, Travis Martell. One of these days all your high livin' and reckless eatin' are gonna catch up with you."

"If it does, I promise I'll die a happy man."

"And have half the women in town wearing black."

He gave her a playful wink. "Only half?"

Her frown turned into a reluctant grin. "You know, it just might be that all the garbage you eat could settle around your belly instead of just outright killin' you. Did you ever consider that?"

"There's a reason they call 'em love handles, Patty."

"I don't care what they call 'em. All I know is that the mornin' you get out of bed and can't see your toes, you can bet there won't be no one lookin' at your backside, neither."

She'd bested him. Travis held up his hands in defeat. "I promise I'll have something green and crunchy for lunch."

"How about I leave off the butter now?"

"Next time."

She sighed in resignation and left for the kitchen.

Caught up in the exchange, Diana had been watching them openly. Now, afraid Travis would notice her intense interest, Diana turned to stare out the window.

She could actually feel him looking at her. She took a bite of her English muffin, but her appetite was gone. Dropping it back on the plate, she reached for her coffee.

It was stupid to stay. What possible good would it do to spy on Amy's brother? What could she learn from him that would make any difference with his mother? She took a five-dollar bill out of her purse, laid it on the table, and got up to leave.

Deciding it would be less obvious to acknowledge Travis on her way out than to purposely ignore him, she glanced in his direction as she passed. He was sitting with his elbows on the table, his hands covering his face. Long, work-roughened fingers worked the skin on his forehead and temples. Instead of relief that she could escape unnoticed, Diana felt an inexplicable twinge of disappointment.

Travis heard the woman in the booth next to his preparing to leave, even smelled a faint hint of something flowery as she got up, but when he stopped trying to work the fatigue from around his eyes to look over his shoulder, she was already gone. She'd left without finishing her breakfast. Not that he could blame her. He'd been around hunters who'd come out of the backcountry after a three-week stay who looked and smelled better than he did this morning. If he weren't such a creature of habit, he would have given her some space and parked himself at the counter, but the thought hadn't even occurred to him until he saw the look she gave him when he sat down.

"What'd you do, chase her away?" Patty slid a plate in front of him. The cinnamon roll was still warm, with icing dripping down the sides in decadent cascades. The butter was there—if not in the quantity he'd requested, still a generous amount.

"I guess she must have been sitting downwind."

"Truth be told, I've seen you lookin' and smellin' prettier myself."

"As soon as I finish here it's home to a long, hot shower." He would have liked to add, "And then to bed," but he had an appointment with a mechanic who was flying in from Ohio to work out some equipment problems they'd been having at the ranch. It was a last-ditch effort by the tractor company to repair a piece of machinery that was down more than operational. Failing that, they would either replace a quarter million dollars' worth of two-year-old equipment with brand new or lose the ranch as a customer.

"Sandy Pitcher was in here looking for you last week," Patty said. "She wanted to know if you'd been talkin' about her or if I'd seen you around town lately. She didn't come right out and ask had I seen you with anyone, but you could tell that's what she was after."

Travis cut a wedge of roll, dipped a corner in the butter, and stuck the piece in his mouth. To outsiders Jackson looked like a busy, expanding city, but in reality it was a small town where everyone knew each other and no one minded their own business. "What did you tell her?" he asked before taking another bite.

"That you come here for the food, not conversation, and that you're always alone."

"Did she believe you?"

"No."

"She's a hard one to convince of anything." Damn, he was slow this morning. Given that kind of opening, Patty would be on him like a sunburn.

"So it's true?" She leaned her hip against the table. "You two really are finished?"

"What was that you just said about food and conversation?"

"Tell me this one thing, and I'll leave you alone."

Travis chuckled. "And the sun will come up in the west tomorrow morning." He hated gossip, even when he wasn't the one being talked about. He'd never understood the need to know, or meddle, in someone else's business. Give him a good horse, a mountain, and a bedroll, and he was content to let the rest of the world be.

"You know I can keep a secret. Didn't I—"

"Talk to Sandy. She'll tell you all about it."

The bell over the door sounded, announcing the first of what would soon be a stream of early morning white-water rafters stopping by for breakfast. The logo on the guide's jacket indicated this group was with Snake River Runners, the company Travis had joined when he'd first considered going into the business himself. His enthusiasm for running the same stretch of river day after day had run out long before the season. The next year he'd worked as a guide for out-of-state hunters. He loved the backcountry, hated the clients, most of whom came to drink and kill with little regard for excesses in either.

He settled on starting a company that provided small, personalized trips into the wilderness. The groups went by foot or horseback, to fish or sightsee or simply lie back and count stars. In eight years, with only word of mouth as advertisement, TMO, Travis Martell Outfitter, had grown from a one-man operation to fifteen guides and two full-time people to run the office. Travis rarely got to lead any of the trips himself anymore; about the time the company had taken off, his father's health had begun to degenerate.

The past year Travis had spent nearly as much time at the ranch as he had at TMO.

Patty made a face as she watched the influx of customers. Before leaving to take care of them, she put her hand on Travis's shoulder, leaned over, and refilled his cup. "Don't you go anywhere. I'm not through with you."

"I hate to disappoint you," he said, knowing she didn't believe him, "but as soon as this cinnamon roll is gone, so am I."

"You rat—" She gave him a playful punch on the shoulder. "People count on me to know what's going on around here. What are they going to say when they ask me about you and I have to tell them I don't know anything?"

"You can tell them we're still looking for someone to help with the haying this fall."

Fortunately Patty was still running orders when Travis finished his breakfast. He left enough to cover the bill and tip on the table and gave her a quick wave before heading out the door. She returned the wave, reluctantly.

If he could find a way to control that damned sweet tooth of his, he'd eat somewhere else until the town's attention had shifted to the next hot story. He and Sandy hadn't gone together long enough to warrant the talk their breakup had started. When he'd said as much to Sharon, she'd given him one of her insufferable sisterly grins and said there was a way to get the gossips off his back—get married. Which, as far as he was concerned, was a little like the old joke about the operation being a success but the patient dying.

Travis got inside his truck, picked up the phone, and called home, punching in a combination of numbers when the answering machine picked up. Knowing he'd be gone for several days, he'd shut the house down, including the water heater. The coded message would start everything up again.

He'd built his house himself, measuring every board, hammering every nail, placing every window. The land had been his great-grandfather's, won in a poker game before the turn of the century. Twenty acres were all that was left from the original six hundred; the rest had been sold to pay taxes on the main ranch during the Depression. Now Travis was surrounded by national park and elk refuge land, insulating him from the vacation homes that relentlessly consumed the mountainsides ringing Jackson. He never tired of the beauty around him or took it for granted.

Knowing he had a place to go where he could live life on his own terms gave him the ability to cope with the outside world. His isolation was his strength, something he needed now more than ever before and something that seemed to be in shorter and shorter supply lately. He was needed by too many people and unable to say no to any of them. He'd never intended to follow in his father's footsteps, had no desire to take over the ranch. Yet he found himself slowly assuming the role. His father was still a relatively young man at fifty-five, but with a failing body—one he refused to accept or even acknowledge. In August Martell's mind, Travis was only helping out temporarily. He was confident he would feel better in another day or week or month.

Travis clung to the hope that Judy or Faith would marry someone who wanted to take over. He'd even tried to introduce them to a couple of his fraternity brothers who'd majored in agriculture, but his sisters were suspicious and had balked at the idea.

Travis turned off the main road onto the rutted

dirt one that led to his house. If he didn't get the scraper and take down some of the high spots, he was going to be putting dents in the roof of the cab with his head and cracking teeth before long. It seemed such a simple thing, half a day, no more. He'd had it on his list of things to do for months, and it seemed something always got in the way. A few more months and he'd have to give in and hire it done.

A rabbit broke out of the brush and ran across the road, a coyote hot on its trail. Both looked sleek and well fed, making it a contest that would be won by the smarter or the luckier.

He'd always considered himself blessed with a healthy dose of each, yet he was running like hell and still going to bed feeling hungry and hunted.

Twelve

Diana paced the motel room, trying to decide whether to call Amy's mother before going to see her or to just show up. Each introduction had its advantages and drawbacks. If she called first and Dorothy Martell said she didn't want to see her, there was sure to be an unpleasant confrontation when she arrived at her front door anyway. If, on the other hand, she came unannounced, there was no telling what might happen.

She'd already used up half the morning vacillating between fair and expedient and was no closer to a decision than she had been before she'd left Minneapolis. It was time to make up her mind and get on with it.

Her hand was poised to dial when something stopped her. It might be kinder to break the news over the phone, but all Dorothy Martell would have to do to get rid of her was hang up. Besides, Diana wanted to be able to gauge the woman's reaction, to know whether it was joy or fear or anger that lit her eyes when she learned her daughter was about to become a part of her life again.

Before the renewed mental debate could go any

further, Diana grabbed her purse, left the motel, and headed north. Once she left town, the directions changed to miles rather than streets, with a couple of landmarks thrown in. Finally, when she was sure she'd gone too far, she came to a gravel road with a metal arch spanning the entrance. A circled, stylized *M* marked the center.

The tires of her rented Jeep crunched onto the gravel as she left the main road. Her heart in her throat in anticipation, she glanced at the odometer. Three more miles—five, ten minutes at the most. Damn, what she wouldn't give for a crystal ball, a premonition, a guardian angel sitting on her shoulder, telling her that what she was about to do was not only right, it was predestined.

Instead her thoughts kept returning to her high school mythology class and Pandora's box. She had a mental image of herself lifting the lid to a world of trouble. Knowing distance protected Amy from whatever might happen kept Diana from turning around and going home, but it did nothing to untie the knot in her stomach.

Diana searched the road ahead, looking for signs of activity. According to the report, the Martells' was a working ranch. She wasn't sure what that meant, but in her world working meant people. A field of some kind of grass or grain was off to her left, cows grazed in the one to her right, but not one human anywhere.

The road that had run as straight as her hair without a perm suddenly curved to the left. As soon as she was pointed in the new direction, she caught sight of the house. She'd expected something like the Minnesota farmhouses she was used to seeing at home; this looked more like a mountain lodge with log walls and a green metal roof to shed the snow.

The outbuildings were made from rough-hewn lumber, the fencing split rail. The effect was solid and permanent and timeless, as if the owners had always been there and always would be.

Why had Amy been singled out to be denied this heritage?

Drawing closer, Diana saw the signs of life she'd missed before. Several trucks and utility vehicles were parked around the yard, and a pair of black-and-white dogs sat under a tree, prepared to announce her arrival. A group of men stood around a tractor, staring into the engine compartment.

Diana pulled her Jeep into the compound. The dogs barked dutifully; a couple of the men looked up, but no one came out of the house. By not phoning first, she'd taken the chance Dorothy wouldn't be home. It was either that or try to explain why she wanted the schedule of someone she'd never met.

She took a deep breath before she got out of the Jeep and then another. By the time she got to the front door she was hyperventilating. She rang the doorbell and it was answered by a young woman wearing jeans and a T-shirt who had a rag flung over one shoulder.

"Can I help you?" the woman asked, wondering openly at finding a stranger at the front door.

"I'm looking for Dorothy Martell."

"Is she expecting you?"

"Not exactly. I was hoping—"

A female voice intruded from a room off the hallway. "Who is it, Felicia?"

"Someone to see you."

Several seconds passed before a small, trim woman appeared in the doorway. She sent a questioning look in Diana's direction. "Yes?"

Diana was too stunned to answer immediately. Looking at Amy's mother was like seeing the woman she imagined Amy would be at fifty. Everything about her, from the pixie haircut and clipped fingernails to the broad, stubborn jaw and questioning brown eyes, created an undeniable tie to Amy. She didn't know how to react or what to say. She was looking at an older version of her sister, her best friend, and the woman was a total stranger.

Dorothy turned to Felicia. "Did she say what she wanted?"

"I didn't ask."

"We have a mutual friend," Diana said, finding her voice.

"Oh?" Dorothy's eyebrows rose in curiosity. "And who is that?"

"If we could talk in private?"

She studied Diana as if taking her measure. "I'll take care of this, Felicia. You can go back to what you were doing."

"I'll be in the kitchen if you need me."

When Felicia was gone Dorothy said, "Would you like to come in?"

"Yes, thank you."

"Why don't we talk in my office?" She held out her hand to indicate the way.

Diana cast a quick glance past the entrance and into the living room. It was large and open, with a wall of windows framing an incredible view of the mountains. The furniture was casual and understated and wildly expensive. Stuart would have felt right at home. Diana was puzzled. It wasn't that she questioned a rancher's wife having such things, more that she wondered why she would want them. This kind of furniture was a status thing, made to impress people who liked swimming in little ponds. How, why, had Dorothy Martell allowed herself to get caught up in that world in the wilds of Wyoming?

"I'm sorry, I don't think I caught your name," Dorothy said when they were inside her office.

"Diana." She held out her hand. "Diana Winchester."

"And this mutual friend?" She waited for Diana to sit down before she took the chair behind the desk.

Diana swallowed. There was no easy or gentle way to lead into what she'd come there to say. "Her name is Amy. It's probably not what you would have called her, but it was the name my parents chose for your daughter."

Dorothy didn't move, not even to blink. "I'm afraid you've made a mistake." Her face betrayed no emotion, not even a spark of interest.

"I know what a shock this must be for you after all this time, but please hear me out." Diana came forward in her seat. "Amy needs you. She's—"

"Who are you?" Dorothy said coolly.

"I'm Amy's sister—my parents adopted her."

Dorothy got up and closed the door, then sat down behind her desk again. "Why are you here instead of this Amy person?"

"She doesn't know I found you. I thought it—"

"What do you really want? Money?"

The question stunned Diana. It hadn't occurred to her that her motives might be suspect. "I just want Amy to have a chance to know her real family."

"Why should I believe you?" She held up her hand to stop Diana from answering. "Never mind. It doesn't matter. I'm not this girl's mother." Dorothy shot Diana a piercing stare. "And I want nothing to do with her. *Do you understand?*"

"No, I don't. Whatever happened to you twenty-six years ago that made you give Amy away is your business. I don't want to know—I don't even care. But I do care what happens to Amy now. You assumed a responsibility when you decided to carry her full term—you either loved her yourself, or you found someone who could do it for you."

"I told you, I'm not your sister's mother. You're wasting your time here—and mine." She started to get up. "Now if that's all, I have work to do."

Diana couldn't leave. Instinct told her she would get only one chance with this woman. "There isn't anyone in this town who couldn't pick the two of you out of a crowd. Whoever saw Amy and Sharon together would know they were sisters. I understand Judy looks a lot like they do, too. At least three children out of five had the same father. Why did you give one of them away?"

"You saw Sharon?"

"I wasn't looking for her. I went into your store and she was there."

Dorothy became a lion protecting one of her cubs. "You stay away from my daughter."

If only Diana could find a way to put Amy inside Dorothy's protective circle. "Does Sharon know she has another sister?"

"How could she? It isn't true."

Diana reached for the envelope inside her purse. She'd imagined showing Amy's mother the photographs under different circumstances, but she needed something to stop their going around in circles. She placed the top three pictures in a line across the desk. They were all of Amy as a grown woman. The others, when she was a child, would come later.

At first Dorothy refused to look, fixing her gaze on Diana instead. The glare she sent was meant to intimidate, but it didn't faze Diana. She was experienced in such things; her entire life had been spent with an expert at browbeating. Dorothy and Eileen were a perfectly matched pair in that department.

Finally Dorothy could hold out no longer and

cast a dismissive glance at the photographs. She almost pulled it off, but before she looked up at Diana again, a flicker of recognition gave her away.

"She's really beautiful, don't you think?" Diana asked gently.

"You're wasting your time here." Dorothy gathered up the pictures and handed them to Diana. "This girl has nothing to do with me or my family."

Despite logic and evidence, Diana couldn't shake the feeling she was talking to Amy. They were so much alike, even in anger. An irrational voice in Diana's head kept insisting that if she could only find a way to chip through Dorothy's shell, she would find the same tender and understanding soul that was inside Amy. Once there, everything else would fall into place.

"I wish I could respect your privacy," Diana said. "I would leave and not say another word to anyone if this weren't so important to Amy."

Dorothy drew herself up in her chair. "Are you threatening me?"

"What?" The question startled Diana.

"You have no idea how much trouble I can cause you. The Martells are a power to be reckoned with in this community. You might think you can force this girl down our throats, but to try would be the biggest mistake of your life. If she comes anywhere near me, or anyone in my family, I promise you I will make her life a living hell."

Diana leaned back in her chair. "I'll bet you're the one who castrates the bulls around here."

"Listen to me, you little bitch, I've spent my entire life protecting what was mine. There's no way I'm going to let you come in here and ruin everything for me."

"I had no idea I had such power," Diana said

carefully, letting the idea take root. "You want to tell me how I could destroy you, or should I guess?"

"I'm warning you, I'm the last person you want to mess with."

"I guess I should be scared? Is that it?"

She might as well have dragged a carcass in front of a starving dog. Dorothy jumped up and leaned over the desk. "Get out of here."

Diana felt more disappointment than fear. She couldn't have made a bigger mess out of coming there, yet she had no idea where she'd gone wrong. How could she initiate repairs when her strongest inclination was to strike back? She might not have the mother role in protecting a cub, but she would take on anything and anyone who threatened her sister.

"I'll leave for now. I'm sure you'd like a couple of days to think things through. When you do, why don't you call me? I'm staying at the Manderly Inn."

"There's no way in hell you will ever hear from me. You might as well go back to wherever you came from."

"Minneapolis," Diana supplied.

Dorothy came around the desk, opened the door, and stood to the side. She started to say something when the sound of a male voice coming from the hallway distracted her. Instantly her anger turned to something else. She seemed torn between closing the door or hurrying Diana outside.

"Mom," Travis called. "Are you in here?"

Dorothy turned to Diana. "I want you to leave— *now*."

"Will you call me?"

If looks could maim, Diana would leave limping. "It won't do any good."

"Will you?"

"Yes, damn it. Now get out of here."

Diana moved past Dorothy into the hallway and was at the front door when Travis came out of the living room. She almost didn't recognize him without the beard and dressed in clean clothes. There was a moment of question and then recognition before he smiled and said, "We meet again."

Diana glanced back at Dorothy. She had put a smile in place, as if delighted that Travis had arrived in time to meet her guest. It was one of the most remarkable performances Diana had ever witnessed.

Travis held out his hand. "Travis Martell."

Diana didn't know what else to do except take his hand and introduce herself. "Diana Winchester."

"Ms. Winchester was just leaving," Dorothy said. "She's late for another appointment."

"Don't let me keep you," Travis said.

Diana turned to Dorothy. "Remember, that's the Manderly Inn. I'll be waiting to hear from you." To Travis she said, "Maybe we'll run into each other in town again." She was taking a chance but knew Dorothy wouldn't call unless goaded.

Travis studied Diana for several seconds. "I'll keep an eye out for you." He walked her outside and stood on the porch until she'd driven away.

Dorothy came up beside him. "You were looking for me?"

"Who is she?"

"Didn't you just say the two of you had already met?" she asked evasively.

"Not met, exactly. We sat across from each other at Rosy's this morning."

"She's a beautiful young woman. I'm not surprised you remembered her."

"So, who is she?" Travis repeated.

"Just someone trying to sell something."

"When did you start having salespeople come out

here? I thought you had a hard and fast rule that you always met them in town." Travis knew his mother too well to miss the tension in her voice.

"She was only going to be here a couple of days, so I made an exception. I doubt I'll ever do it again." She locked her arm through his. "Now come inside and let me fix you something to drink."

"What was she selling?"

She tugged on his arm and led him into the house. "It isn't important."

"Indulge me." Something was bothering her, something she wasn't telling him.

"It was a new line of fishing gear."

An edge had developed in her voice that was a clear warning she didn't want to be pressed any further. As he had all his life, Travis ignored it. "Don't you think it's kind of strange she showed up here without samples or even a catalog?"

"Why are you making such a big deal out of this?"

"I don't know," Travis said. "Why are you?"

"Do you want something to drink or not?" she snapped irritably.

"First tell me what's bothering you."

"Nothing." In a calmer voice she went on, "No, let me take that back. You made such a big production about needing your privacy when you moved out of here, and yet you refuse to grant me mine."

Travis was more convinced now than before that something was going on. His mother rarely lost her temper. "All of this over a visit from a woman trying to sell you fishing gear?"

Dorothy stood very still, closed her eyes, and took a deep, calming breath. Seconds later a smile appeared. "Diana Winchester is a disagreeable young woman I would just as soon forget I ever met. She's taken the approach that to succeed in a man's world she has to outtalk, outswear, and outdeal her competition." She shuddered, as if trying to shake off the memory of the encounter. "You can see how even talking about her upsets me."

"Are you going to report her to the company?"

"Of course. It's important they know who's out here representing them."

"Maybe you should talk to Sharon about her." He was testing to see how far she would go.

"Yes—that's a good idea."

He heard the tractor start up and remembered why he'd come in the house. "Dad thinks you should talk to this guy before he leaves."

"Why? I thought he was just a mechanic."

"He mentioned something about a long-term repair policy Dad thought you might be interested in getting."

"Tell your father the only thing I'm interested in is a tractor that runs more than two weeks out of four."

Dorothy handled the money side of the ranch, Gus everything else. They were always at odds about something. For years, whenever she thought she could get away with it, Dorothy would put Travis in the middle. Once he recognized what was happening, he refused to let himself be manipulated into that position. "You're going to have to tell him yourself. I've got to get back to town."

"You know how your father hates it when he thinks I'm being unfair with one of our accounts. If it were up to him, those people would walk all over us." She was on a roll, the encounter with Diana Winchester seemingly forgotten. "Who do you think got the company to fly that mechanic out here? But will I get the credit when your father brags to his friends about all the special attention? I'll bet you that by tomorrow he'll have convinced himself the whole thing was his idea."

He couldn't contradict her. He'd sat in on a lot of bull sessions with his father and his cronies. Sharing accomplishments wasn't something any of them did well. "Does it really matter whose idea it was?"

"Why do you always stick up for him?"

Travis groaned. It was the same old argument. "I've got to get going. Would you mind telling Dad to stop by the office after he takes the mechanic to the airport? He said he'd look over the new saddles that came in last week. I don't want to uncrate any more of them if I'm going to send them back."

"I thought you weren't going to do any more pack trips after this year." She followed him out to the porch.

"I wasn't, but then we started getting so many reservations, I decided to keep it on the schedule for another season."

"Wouldn't it be better to put off buying new saddles until you're sure?"

"Perhaps, but that's not what I'm going to do." Travis had tried, but he'd never been able to convince his mother that when he wanted help or advice on running his company, he would ask. If there were mistakes to be made, he wanted to be the one making them. And if he succeeded, he wanted to know it was because of his efforts. Luck, he was willing to accept any way it came.

"If you really feel it's necessary to have new equipment, you could rent it a lot cheaper than—"

"Give it a rest, Mom." Travis leaned over and gave her a quick kiss on the cheek. He was halfway down the steps when he remembered the second reason he'd come to see her. "Don't let Dad move that hay all by himself. I'll send someone out to give him a hand."

"You know he doesn't listen to me about things like that."

"Well, try, would you? There's no way I can get a guy out here before Wednesday."

She made a helpless gesture with outstretched hands. "I'll do my best."

Travis skipped the last two steps in his rush to get going. It wasn't until he hit the main road that his thoughts drifted back to Diana Winchester. He was inclined to put their second meeting off to coincidence, but he'd never believed in coincidence. Especially not where his mother was concerned.

Something was going on. If he weren't so damned busy, he'd be tempted to investigate.

The thought brought him up short. What possible business did he have snooping into his mother's affairs? Maybe there was more of her in him than he'd thought. The possibility didn't please him.

Thirteen

Twenty-six years and not a word, and then, with no warning, the unthinkable had happened. Dorothy sat down heavily in her chair, leaned her elbows on the desk, and covered her face with her hands.

She couldn't remember ever being so angry, or so scared. Goddamn it, if she'd wanted that girl in her life, she wouldn't have given her away. What right did Diana Winchester have showing up after all these years to plead this Amy's case?

Articles were always being written about the rights of the adopted child. What about the rights of the mother? Nothing on the release form she'd signed said anything about the child having the option to look her up someday and ruin her life. It wasn't fair, and she wasn't going to stand for it.

But what to do? So far she'd handled it all wrong. She should never have lost her temper. To do so was stupid and dangerous. Determined people fought back when they were threatened. Diana Winchester might not be the smartest or most clever person Dorothy had ever met, but it was obvious she was determined.

Dorothy had prepared herself for the possibility that when the girl turned eighteen or twenty-one she might want to look for her mother. Then those years came and went without contact, and Dorothy had finally been able to put the worrisome problem behind her. Now this Diana person had shown up.

How was Dorothy supposed to deal with someone she couldn't appeal to on a basic parent-child level? All of her arguments had been created with that bond in mind. She was prepared to show her daughter that she'd given her up out of love and that it would be an act of love for her not to try to come back into her mother's life.

Diana Winchester wouldn't buy it for a minute.

Dorothy had to come up with another plan. She had to do it fast, or she could lose everything she'd worked so hard to gain.

First on the list was making sure Travis and that woman didn't run into each other again. He'd been five years old when his sister was born, old enough to remember details that didn't mesh with the story she'd told everyone later. Dorothy couldn't let those memories surface and have him start asking questions she couldn't answer.

In the meantime she had to act as if everything were normal. And that meant going outside and talking to Gus.

She found him in the barn with the mechanic. "Travis said you wanted to see me."

August Martell was in the middle of showing his prized antique John Deere tractor to his visitor. Despite inches lost in the spinal fusions he'd undergone since coming home from Vietnam, Gus was still able to look over the tractor engine to where Dorothy was standing.

"It's been taken care of. I told Walt here to have

the insurance people send us the papers as soon as he got back to the office."

Dorothy bristled. It was her job to take care of such things. When necessary she would consult with Gus; otherwise she made whatever decisions had to be made based on the ranch's need and their personal economics. With Judy and Faith still in college, and Martell Outfitters a separate corporation now, there were some months she had to loan the ranch money from their savings to meet payroll. Gus had no idea how much they paid for diesel every year, let alone whether they could fit another insurance policy into the budget.

"That's fine, honey," she said. "I'll go over them as soon as they get here." Go over and then round-file.

Gus motioned for her to come closer. "I was just showing Walt our collection. He seems to think we've got ourselves some pretty valuable pieces here."

"I've been to a number of farm auctions," Walt said. "It's amazing what some of these things bring from collectors."

Dorothy covered her anger with a smile. "Most of what we have has been in the family since it was new. I'm sure Gus told you that the ranch has been in the Martell family for four generations." If Gus hadn't told him, Walt would be the first who'd escaped the story. Gus bragged about his family to anyone and everyone who would listen. It was as if he thought someone might actually care.

"That's what Gus was telling me."

"I'm afraid it's gonna end with me," Gus said. He put his arm around Dorothy and gave her shoulders a squeeze. "Unless we can talk one of our younger daughters into taking over or marrying someone interested in the ranching business."

"I'm not ready to give up on Travis yet," Dorothy said. "Every now and then I see signs that he's coming around. We just need to give him a little more time."

"I think you're imagining those signs," Gus said. "But you go right on ahead. I'd die a happy man knowing Travis would take over when I was gone."

"Sometimes these kids just need to get away to see how good they had it at home," Walt said. "I've seen it happen time and time again. There's nothing can take the place of family. It don't matter how good it looks from the other side of the fence, once they go out there and graze a while, they see it's not anything but the same old grass with newfangled barbed wire."

Dorothy mentally took Walt's homespun rambling a step further. A rolling wave of fear left her sick to her stomach as she thought how easily all she loved could be taken away from her. She had to get rid of Diana Winchester, and she had to do it as quickly as possible.

"I have some things to do in town," she said to Gus. "Do you still want to go by Sidney's?"

"I'll be heading in later to drop Walt off at the airport. How about if I meet you in town? We can get something to eat and take in a movie."

She didn't want him anywhere near town until Diana Winchester was gone, but he was sure to ask questions if she told him no. "Meet me at the store. Maybe we can talk Sharon and Davis into going with us." She was counting on safety in numbers and that Diana Winchester wasn't the type to make a scene in public.

"Sounds good to me." He took his arm from around her shoulders. "Why don't you see if you can round up Travis, too? We'll make it a family night out. Haven't had one of those since the girls took off on their tour."

Dorothy turned to Walt. "You're welcome to join us if—"

"I appreciate the invitation, but my plane leaves at four."

Dorothy surreptitiously glanced at his hands before extending hers. They were surprisingly clean for a mechanic's. "It was nice meeting you, Walt."

"And you," he said.

Forty-five minutes later Dorothy was in the middle of an argument with the clerk at the front desk at the Manderly Inn.

"I'm sorry, Mrs. Martell, there's no way I can give you Miss Winchester's room number. I'd be happy to put you through to her on the house phone, but that's all I'm allowed to do."

"Where are they?"

"Over there." He pointed to a table under a mounted elk head.

The operator put her through to Diana's room, but there was no answer. On her way out the clerk called, "Would you like to leave a message?"

From somewhere she summoned a breezy smile. She didn't want him giving her visit too much importance. "That won't be necessary. I'll check back later."

Travis drove by as his mother came out of the hotel. He waved, but she was preoccupied and didn't see him. At the stoplight he looked back in his rearview mirror and watched her hurry across the parking lot and get in her car. In her rush to leave she hit the elevated curb so hard that the front of her car bounced in the air.

What in the hell was his mother doing at the Manderly?

The question no sooner formed than he had his answer. The woman who'd been at the house that morning had said she was staying there. The connection brought an uneasy feeling. In his memory, no one had ever made Dorothy Martell feel ill at ease in her own home. No one until Diana Winchester, that is. Something was going on his mother didn't want him to know. But what? Secrets were alien things among the members of his family, impossible to keep, therefore rarely attempted.

He glanced at the dashboard clock. He had an hour before he was scheduled to meet a group of returning backpackers and ride back to the main office with them on the company bus. The effort was strictly goodwill, a chance to find out what his customers had liked about the trip and what they would change next time out. Travis was convinced that more than anything else he did for his clients, actually listening to them brought the referrals and return customers. In less than seven years TMO had become the leading guide company in Jackson.

A horn honked behind him. He looked up and saw the light had turned green. With a quick wave to the other driver he started across the intersection. Halfway through he changed his mind and turned left. The last-minute maneuver earned him another honk.

He picked up his cell phone and called the office to arrange for someone else to meet the backpackers. Three more left turns brought him back to the Manderly.

Diana bent over, braced her hands on her knees, sucked in air as if it were the coin of the realm and she were facing bankruptcy. She should have been mortified to let anyone see her in this state instead of praying some kind soul would come by and rescue her.

She tried to remember what had made her think jogging at six thousand feet would be a good way to work off her frustration. For the first couple of miles she'd been so completely focused on Dorothy Martell that she hadn't even realized what was happening to her own body. Not until little black spots started dancing before her eyes and a big brass drum started playing in her head did it even occur to her to slow down.

Maybe incapacitating herself had a positive side. She'd never been good at waiting, and now she wouldn't be tempted to drive back out to the Martell ranch and have another useless encounter with Amy's mother.

Basic common sense told Diana that Dorothy had to come to her the next time they met. It would be a mistake to try to rush her into a decision. Amy's mother had a lot to think about, including how to break the news to her family.

With time and distance between them, Diana wasn't as upset about Dorothy's negative reaction as she had been at first. People responded to stressful situations differently. Judged by her actions and not her words, Dorothy couldn't be the harridan she seemed. It was obvious she had a strong maternal instinct. She'd given birth to four other children in addition to Amy, two of them after she'd given Amy away.

At last she could see the hotel. She used an image of herself sinking into a tub filled with hot water to goad her the final hundred yards.

She'd made it to the parking lot when, out of the corner of her eye, she saw someone approaching from the opposite direction. It was a man . . . a very tall man . . . wearing a green knit shirt and jeans. She let out a weary groan.

What was it with her and Travis Martell? Was there some mystical chart that dictated their paths were destined to cross a certain number of times every day?

Travis reached the door first. He smiled and held it open for her. "Just the person I was looking for."

She glanced over her shoulder. "Are you talking to me?" That the meeting had been planned was the last thing she'd expected. She brushed back the hair that had come loose from her ponytail.

"I was hoping you might have a minute to show me your company's new line of fishing equipment."

The fishing equipment thing must have come from his mother, an explanation to cover her being at the ranch that morning. She didn't dare respond without more information. "Uh, would you mind giving me an hour or so?" She tugged on the hem of her sweaty top. "As you can see, I'm not exactly at my best."

"No problem."

She smiled and moved to go around him. "Why don't you call me in—"

"What I meant is that you don't have to clean up for me. You're fine just the way you are."

He knew damn well her being in Jackson had nothing to do with fishing equipment. "What is it you really want, Mr. Martell?"

"Travis—please."

"Well?"

"Can we go somewhere else to talk?"

"I don't—" What good would it do to put him off? He was going to find out why she was there sooner or later. "All right, but I really would like a chance to clean up first."

"How long will that take?"

For some reason the question, and the almost

condescending way he'd asked, hit her wrong. "You have four sisters. Figure it out for yourself."

"I have three sisters."

Diana stared at him. The slip had been genuine. The temptation to correct his mistake was like a gremlin dancing on the tip of her tongue. "Give me a half hour."

"I'll wait for you here in the lobby."

What did he think she was going to do, sneak out the back door? "Surely you have something better to do with your time."

"Nothing that I could get done in half an hour."

"Suit yourself." She left determined not to rush but was back in twenty-five minutes.

He stood when he saw her get out of the elevator. "You clean up real good," he said with a drawl.

She'd put on the navy blue silk-blend slacks and jacket Amy had given her for Christmas. "Thanks— you do, too."

"So it *was* my fault you left the restaurant in such a rush this morning."

"I don't understand." Her purse strap slid off her shoulder. She reached up to put it back.

"You left in such a hurry, I figured it had to be either the way I looked or the way I smelled that drove you away." He took the sting out of the words with an easy grin. "Most likely it was a whole lot of both."

She realized she could like this man and that he was someone Amy would like, too. "Heroes are allowed latitude about such things," she teased.

He frowned. "I'm no hero."

"What else would you call someone who gives up a whole week to look for a lost hiker?"

"That happens here all the time. It's just something you do."

Had it been Stuart, he would have taken an ad out in the paper to puff himself up. "You said you wanted to talk to me."

"Have you had lunch?"

"Yes, but you could tempt me with something chocolate and high calorie."

"So you're one of those people who run to eat."

She laughed. "Is there any other reason?"

They walked to a quiet restaurant two blocks from the hotel where the waiter called Travis by name and looked genuinely pleased to see him.

"Chocolate isn't my thing," he said when they were seated. "But I've seen longtime feuds settled over the apple tarts they serve in this place."

Diana studied him over the top of the menu. He was trying hard to make her think he was just a good old country boy, ingenuous and nonthreatening. She didn't believe it for a minute. "Is there a set amount of time we have to spend on idle conversation before you get to the real reason you wanted to talk to me?"

He picked up his water, took a drink, and returned the glass to the table in slow, deliberate movements. "Am I keeping you from something?"

"Answer my question first."

"No—there isn't a set time. I just wanted to find out what I could about you."

"Why?"

"I'm always suspicious when people lie to me."

She laid the menu on the table. "I haven't lied to you."

"To my mother, then."

"I didn't lie to her, either," she said carefully. How much did he know?

"If you're here selling fishing equipment, I'm on leave from the New York City Ballet."

She had tried to reach Dorothy at home to find

out what she'd told Travis, but Felicia had said she was out for the day. Diana was on her own. "I don't know who told you that, but—" Now she had told a lie. "Yes, I do. It had to have been your mother."

"Are you saying she got it wrong?"

"I never said I was selling anything."

"Then what did you say to her?"

"Why aren't you asking her these questions?"

"Because she would never tell me if someone was threatening her. I would have to find that out on my own."

"Threatening her?" Diana repeated too loudly. She glanced around to see if she'd attracted anyone's attention before she added in a lower voice, "Just what did she tell you about me?"

He hesitated. "It wasn't what she said, so much as the way she said it. Something is going on between you two and I want to know what it is."

Diana shoved her chair back and stood. "Did it ever occur to you that it was none of your business?" As soon as she asked the question, she realized how wrong she was. Amy was Travis's sister. He had every right to know about her.

"Sit down," Travis said.

"Don't tell me what to do."

"Please."

She'd made her point; nothing would be gained by carrying it further. The waiter arrived at the same time as she sat down again.

"Have you decided?" he asked pleasantly.

"I'll have the apple tart and coffee," Diana told him.

"Make that two," Travis said. When the waiter was gone again, he asked Diana, "So, if you're not in sales, what do you do?"

"I'm the public relations director for Sander's Food."

"The cereal company?"

"We're more diversified than that, but cereal is how most people think of us."

"What has Sander's Food got to do with my mother?"

"Nothing." Why was she protecting Dorothy Martell? Travis was a grown man. Didn't he have a right to know he had another sister even if his mother refused to claim her? "I came here on my own."

He didn't say anything, waiting for her to go on.

She had no idea where to begin. After making such a mess of her meeting with Dorothy, she knew there had to be a better way to lead into such potentially life-altering news; she just had to figure out what it was. "Have you ever wondered why there are so many years between your sisters Sharon and Faith?"

He stared at her as if she'd just asked him if he knew the moon was an optical illusion. "Listen, I'm not someone who likes coming at things from obtuse angles. Why don't you just say whatever it is you have to say?"

She believed him, but doubted he'd feel the same five minutes from then. "You have another sister."

"I *had* another sister," he said. "She died at birth."

Now it was Diana's turn to be confused. Was he talking about Amy or yet another sister? "When?"

"Twenty-six years ago."

He was talking about Amy. "She didn't die. Your mother gave her up for adoption."

Travis sat back and planted his hands on the arms of the chair. "You don't know what you're talking about."

"I understand why it might be hard to—"

"What kind of scam are you running?"

She could go along with him questioning whether

she might have made a mistake, but not the instant assumption she was a criminal. "You know, I'm getting a little tired of this. What possible reason could I have for coming here if I wasn't telling the truth? Do you honestly think your family is such a prize that someone would cook up a scheme just to get into it?"

"If you really believe that, why bother at all? Why not just go back to wherever you came from and forget all about us?"

"Because what I came here to do is too important."

"All right, I'll bite. Why is it so important?"

Before she could answer, the waiter came back with their tarts and coffee. She waited until he was gone again and then said, "Amy needs to feel she belongs somewhere."

He threw up his arms. "Now what are you talking about? Who the hell is this Amy person?"

How had she convinced herself telling him was a good idea? "Amy is your sister."

"Wait a minute, I thought . . ." His eyes narrowed as he looked at her. "If you're not . . . who are you?"

"Amy is my adopted sister."

"Where was this Amy supposed to have been born?"

"Ohio."

"When?"

"June. She'll be twenty-six her next birthday." It was only weeks away, and Diana still hadn't decided what to get her.

"Jesus," he said in a harsh whisper, a stricken expression on his face. "Do you have a picture of her?"

"What is this? All of a sudden you believe me? Why?"

Travis swallowed, hard. "I can't tell you, not yet."

Diana hesitated. Travis looked as if she'd told him that a sister he thought was alive had died instead of the other way around. There wasn't a flicker of happiness or even hope that what she'd told him was possible. Instead he projected a grim resignation.

She reached in her purse, brought out the three pictures she'd shown Dorothy earlier that morning, and handed them to Travis. "These are the most recent I have. I brought others, but I think this is enough to tell you what you want to know."

Travis handled them as if they were made out of plastic explosive. Seconds turned into minutes as he intently studied each picture in turn. Finally he said, "She looks sad."

Diana had purposely brought pictures of Amy smiling. "Why do you say that?"

"I don't know." He thought about it some more. "I guess it's because Sharon smiles that way when something's bothering her."

"Then you believe me?" she asked carefully.

A profound weariness settled over his features. "I wish to hell I didn't."

Diana felt as if she'd finally crested the mountain. The descent might be bumpy, but at least it would be downhill from then on. "Then you'll help me with your mother?"

He handed her the photographs. "The only thing I'll help you do is leave town."

Fourteen

Travis flinched at the look of disappointment Diana gave him. It was easier to deal with the anger that appeared seconds later. "I'm sorry," he said.

"What is it with you and your mother?" Diana threw her napkin on the table. "Amy is her daughter. She's your sister—every bit as much as Sharon or Judy or Faith. How can you turn your back on her?"

"You're making a scene."

"You think this is a scene? Just wait."

Travis glared at her. "You're a little old to be throwing tantrums because you didn't get what you wanted."

"Don't you talk to me like that, you son of a—"

"Bitch?" he finished for her. "I might be offended under different circumstances."

The statement was like water to her fire. She leaned back in her chair again "Why?"

Travis wiped his hand across his face. He couldn't remember ever feeling as tired. "A hundred reasons."

"Give me one."

They were like a couple of managers trying to win the best deal for their fighters. Travis would do whatever it took to protect his father; Diana cared only about Amy. "Everyone in my family—except my mother, obviously—believes Amy is dead. That includes my father."

"That's a fact, not a reason."

"Think about it, Diana," he said impatiently. "Lies are told to protect someone, or to cover something up. If this comes out, it will destroy my father. I can't let that happen."

"Where was he when Amy was born?"

"In Vietnam. He'd been reported dead."

Diana's mouth opened in surprise. "And your mother still gave his baby away?"

"I don't understand it, either." The obvious answer was too terrible even to contemplate. "Maybe she was in such deep shock that she didn't realize what she was doing." Why was he making excuses for her when he knew damn well shock had nothing to do with what she'd done? He'd only been five when they got the news that his father had died, but he could remember that day and the months that followed as clearly as he could remember the day his father came home.

Less than a month after the soldier arrived at their door to tell them August Martell had been reported dead when his helicopter was downed on a routine rescue mission, his mother moved back to Ohio with her parents, taking him and Sharon with her. His grandparents had begged her to stay at the ranch. Distraught at losing their son, they told her they couldn't bear the thought of losing their grandchildren, too.

The day his mother went to the hospital with labor pains, Travis sat on the front porch and waited for her to come home with his new brother. She'd promised him a brother before his father died, and he had clung to that promise. She came home alone.

Days later she told him he'd had a sister, but that the baby had died because she didn't have a father.

He had lived in secret terror that he, too, was destined to die, until news that August Martell was alive arrived several months later. Gus was scheduled to come home the week before Christmas. Dorothy loaded them all in the car and headed back to Wyoming, braving blizzards and holiday travelers to be at the ranch to greet her husband with the news that she'd lost their child. Gus blamed himself and had carried the burden all these years, as if it were his punishment for not getting back to them sooner.

"Travis?" Diana reached across the table to touch him gently.

He looked down to where her hand rested on his. Her fingers felt warm against his skin and unexpectedly solicitous. In the back of his mind, he noted she wasn't wearing a ring. "What?"

"You went someplace without me."

"I was remembering what it was like when my father came home."

"Was he a prisoner?"

How much should he tell her? Would it make a difference? "He was captured, but escaped before they could get him to one of the main camps."

"Did he get to come home right away?"

"After a couple of weeks in the hospital. He was in pretty bad shape when they found him."

"Don't you think he would want to know about Amy?" She removed her hand. "More important, don't you think he has a right to know?"

"It would destroy him," Travis said. "He would lose everything he believes in."

"So it's Amy who winds up paying for everyone's mistakes. She's the real loser in all of this—and the most innocent. It just isn't fair."

"Has her life been so bad?"

"Have you ever read the studies about babies who failed to thrive because no one touched or loved them? Imagine a lifetime of . . ." She stopped to take a breath, blinked several times, tried to go on, and then gave up.

Travis didn't know what to say. Dorothy had been a caring, if domineering, mother to the children she had kept. The confidence he had as a man was a direct result of the unequivocal love he had received as a child. "Were you treated the same way?"

"No—I was their natural child. They adopted Amy so I wouldn't grow up alone."

If he hadn't been so damned eager to meddle in something he should have stayed out of, he wouldn't be in this mess. "I can't help you, Diana."

"Can't or won't?"

"Both. My father doesn't deserve what this would do to him."

"And Amy does?"

"Think about what you're asking. I don't even know Amy. I love my father. Why would I sacrifice him for her?"

"What's to keep me from going to him myself?"

He'd known it would come down to this. Bottom line, she was the one in control. "How is it going to help Amy to know she destroyed her family by coming back to them?"

Diana stared at him, long and hard. "Little by little, she's dying, Travis. Every day she loses another piece of herself. Pretty soon there won't be anything left."

Without saying more, she got up and walked out.

Travis felt as if she'd gut-punched him. Still, he didn't go after her. He couldn't.

But there was one thing he could do for this sister

he would never meet. He could give her answers. She had a right to know why she'd been given away.

He paid the bill for desserts neither he nor Diana had touched, got in his truck, and headed for the store. On the way he tried reaching his mother at the ranch on his cell phone. She wasn't there. She wasn't at the store, either. Sharon told him she'd stopped by earlier to invite her and Davis to go out to dinner that night but that they'd already made other plans.

Travis drove around town for another hour and made one last phone call to the ranch before giving up. He was afraid Diana would be gone if he waited any longer, and he wanted to tell her good-bye.

He used the house phone at the Manderly to call her room. She answered on the second ring, sounding nasal, as if she'd been sleeping. "It's Travis. Are you all right?"

"What do you want?"

"A minute—that's all."

"I don't have a minute. Would you please get off the phone so I can call the airport?"

Something had happened in the two hours they'd been apart. It wasn't anger he heard—it was fear. "What's going on, Diana?"

"It's none of your—" She made a choking sound. And then, "Amy's in the hospital."

"Why?"

"What possible difference does it make to you?" She hung up on him.

Travis glanced at the clerk behind the desk. He was the younger brother of one of his guides. "Hey, Roger, how's it going?"

Roger looked up and smiled. "Good. How about you?"

The smile was eager; Roger had plans to follow in his brother's footsteps. "I was just talking to one of your guests—Diana Winchester," he said. "We were cut off, and now I can't get her back. Could you check the line for me?"

"Sure thing." He checked the register, picked up the phone, and punched in a series of numbers. "It's busy."

"She's probably trying to get me. Maybe I should just go up there instead." He frowned. "I can't remember whether her room number was 207 or 208." He hadn't been able to see the last number Roger had hit when he'd tried to call.

"It's 207," Roger supplied.

"Thanks. I owe you one."

"No problem."

Travis took the stairs rather than wait for the elevator. Diana's room was near the end of the hall. He could hear her talking but couldn't make out what she was saying. He knocked and waited. Seconds later she opened the door. "I was afraid you wouldn't answer," he said.

"I wouldn't if I'd known it was you."

It was obvious she'd been crying. "Can I come in?"

"No. I'm busy." She started to close the door.

He put out his hand to stop her. "Please."

"I'm on the phone."

"I can wait."

She hesitated and then gave in, walking away and leaving him to take care of himself.

Her suitcase stood open on the bed, empty. He pulled the chair out from the desk and sat down. Her back was to him, her hand holding her hair from her face in an impatient gesture.

"When is your next flight?" she asked. "I'll take anything, I have to get to Minneapolis tonight." She sat down on the bed. "Standby is all you have? Until when?" She waited. "No, that's too late." She hung up and reached for the phone book.

"Why don't you let me do that while you pack?" Travis said.

She seemed unsure whether to trust him with the task but then yielded the phone. "I don't care what it is, or who it's with. Just get me out of here as fast as you can."

He dialed a number without looking in the book. A minute later he was put through to an old friend who owed him a favor. When he hung up, he turned to Diana. "You leave in an hour."

She swept up a drawer full of clothes and dumped them in the suitcase. "When do I get in?"

"I didn't ask, but it's a direct flight."

She looked at him over the suitcase. "I suppose I should thank you. Or maybe you should thank me. You wanted me to leave, and now I am."

He ignored the jab. "What happened to Amy?"

"Please, don't pretend you care."

"Goddamn it, would you stop treating me like the enemy and tell me what happened?"

"A blood vessel ruptured in her brain. They had to operate to relieve the pressure."

"Is she all right?" He grabbed something pink and silky that had fallen out of the suitcase.

Diana started to answer, but the words wouldn't come. She put her hands over her face and turned her back to Travis.

He watched her lose her battle for composure. The stiffness left her spine, her breathing became hiccuped. Her fear infected him, drawing him in, making him feel something he would have sworn was impossible. The fierce protectiveness he felt for the family he'd always known spread to encompass a sister he'd never met. "What can I do?"

Diana sat back down on the bed. "Nothing."

If he'd known her longer or better, he would

have taken her in his arms and held her until her tears were spent. Instead he took her clothes out of the closet, folded them, and put them in the suitcase. When he was through with the closet, he went into the bathroom and gathered her hair dryer and make-up and everything else that looked as if it belonged to her and not the hotel. He stuffed it all in a corner of the suitcase and started to close the lid.

"My shoes." She got up and went to the closet.

Travis took them from her and crammed them into the other corner. "Is that everything?"

"I think so."

"Stay here. I'll check you out and be right back."

"I can do it."

"Do you really want to go down there feeling and looking the way you do, or are you just being stubborn?"

She reached for another tissue from the nightstand. "I'll be ready to leave when you get back." She dug into a side pocket of her purse. "Here, take this." She handed him her credit card.

Rather than argue that her card was useless without her there to sign, he stuck it in his pocket and went down to the lobby. He was back in ten minutes.

She'd combed her hair and fixed her makeup while he was gone. Except for her red eyes, it would have been hard for anyone to guess what she'd been through.

"Ready?" he asked.

She nodded. When he went to get her suitcase, she said, "I can get out to the airport by myself. You don't have to go with me."

"How do you plan to return your rental car and get to your plane?"

"I'll take the shuttle, or ask someone at the agency to drop me off."

"It's a waste of time to stand here arguing with me about this. You have two choices—you can either let me drive your car, or you can come with me in my truck."

She handed him the key. "Now I know where Amy gets her stubbornness."

"It's a Martell family trait."

She stared at him. Slowly her eyes filled with tears again. "She has a right to know her family, Travis, especially you. She always wanted a brother."

"I'm sorry, Diana."

"Yeah, me too."

The thought that he might run into his father at the airport didn't even occur to Travis until he pulled to a stop in front of the private plane terminal. He started to move the Jeep when he saw Gus waving to him and realized it was too late.

"Someone's trying to get your attention," Diana said.

He turned to her. "That's my father. I know you don't feel you owe anything to me or my family, but I'm begging you not to say anything to him."

A dozen emotions played across her face. "There's only one thing I care about anymore, and that's getting back to Amy."

"Thank you." Travis got out of the car to greet his father.

"You're the last person I expected to see out here," Gus said, giving Travis a huge smile. "Did your mom send you out to find me?"

"I'm doing a favor for a friend," he said. "I haven't seen Mom since this morning."

Gus looked up as Diana got out of the car. "Sorry," he said. He took off his hat and extended his hand. "I didn't see you in there."

"Dad, this is Diana Winchester. Diana, this is my father, August Martell."

"Gus," he corrected Travis.

She stared at him hungrily, as if memorizing every line of his weathered face. "I'm pleased to meet you, Gus."

"You coming or going?" he asked.

Travis took the suitcase out of the back. "She's on her way to Minneapolis."

"Too bad. I would have asked you to join us for supper if it was the other way around. You could have met the rest of the family." He smiled. "At least all of us that are here."

Travis had a knot in his throat as he waited for Diana to say something.

"I would have enjoyed that," she said. "Maybe next time."

"It looks like Brendan's ready to go," Travis said.

"So, she's going out with him, is she?" To Diana he said, "Brendan's a hell of a pilot, but he doesn't know anything but full speed and stop. If I were you, I wouldn't take my seat belt off until the plane was on the ground again."

Diana shot Travis a questioning look. "I'll explain later," he said.

"It was nice meeting you," Gus said.

"If you wouldn't mind waiting, I could use a ride back to town," Travis told him. "Why don't you meet me at the rental desk."

"I'll be there." Gus headed back to his truck.

Travis picked up Diana's suitcase with one hand and took her elbow with the other, steering her to an open gate.

"What's going on?" she demanded. "I thought you—"

"There was no way you were going to get out of

here tonight on a commercial flight, so I asked a friend if he would take you." He let go of her arm and pointed to a private jet sitting on the tarmac. "That's his plane."

"I . . . I don't know what to say."

"Then don't say anything."

Brendan must have been watching for their arrival, because he left the cockpit to greet them as they came up to the plane. He leaned out the door and grinned. "Next stop Minneapolis."

"I owe you one," Travis said to him.

"As I see it, you've got a dozen more trips coming before we're even close to being even."

Travis handed him Diana's suitcase. When he was alone with her again, he said, "I hope everything is all right when you get there."

"Do you want me to call you?"

He was tempted, but reason prevailed. "It would be better if you didn't."

She nodded. "I like your father."

"He's one of a kind." A thought struck him that made him smile. "Can you imagine my mother's expression if the three of us had walked into the restaurant together?"

She smiled in return, but it was more gift than good humor. "If anything happens to make you change your mind, you'll let me know?"

She knew as well as he did that nothing would ever change. It couldn't. Still, he asked, "How do I reach you?"

She thought a minute. "Forget what I said. I know nothing is ever going to change, and I don't want to wait for you to call."

Brendan came to the door again. "I'm ready when you are."

Diana climbed halfway up the stairs, turned, and

looked into Travis's eyes. "I shouldn't like you . . . but I do."

She disappeared before Travis could say anything back.

He waited until the plane was in the air before returning the Jeep.

On the trip into town with his father, Travis rolled down the window and leaned his head back, letting the warm summer air wash over him as he gazed at his beloved mountains. With an ache that stole his breath he wished he were there, alone, with only the wind and trees for company.

"She seems like a nice girl," Gus said. "How come you didn't try talking her into staying a little longer?"

Travis put his hand to his forehead to shield his eyes from the sun. He wanted to forget Diana . . . her deep brown eyes, her incredible legs, the way she smiled, her willingness to go to battle for something she believed in—the reason she'd come to Jackson.

"She wasn't my type, Dad," he said, only then realizing it was a lie.

Fifteen

Hospitals weren't the mysterious, frightening places to Diana that they were to a lot of her friends. While she'd never been a patient, she'd been in or around the environment her entire life. Still, when she'd brought Amy home two weeks ago, she'd decided she'd had enough of green walls, linoleum floors, and antiseptic smells for the rest of her life.

As a volunteer she'd visited patients whose pain had touched her, even made her cry at times. But not until she'd found Amy unconscious had she understood what it was like to be scared for someone. Worst of all was the complete and utter sense of helplessness that came with knowing there was nothing she could do to help.

Only one thing truly terrified Diana—the unknown. She could deal with anything as long as she knew what it was. At work bad news never threw her; she simply studied what had gone wrong and either started again or found a way around the problem. It was the waiting that drove her crazy, that sapped her strength and confidence.

She'd called the hospital from the plane. No one

would tell her anything that she could hang on to. First the nurses, and then the doctor, and finally even Stephanie had said that Amy was doing as well as could be expected. What the hell was that supposed to mean—as well as someone who was going to wake up at any moment or someone who might never wake up again?

The taxi ride from the airport to the hospital felt as long as the flight from Jackson. She had the driver drop her off at the emergency entrance, knowing there would be someone at the desk after hours. The male nurse directed her to surgical intensive care.

"My God . . ." Diana stood frozen in the doorway. All she could do was stare. She'd tried to imagine the worst, but she hadn't come close.

The room Amy occupied this time was nothing like the one she had been in before. Here there were no windows to the outside, or pictures, or even a rolling tray to hold personal belongings. Instead the bed was flanked with half a dozen machines that monitored her breathing, her blood pressure, and her heart rate. One kept track of internal cranial pressure, the others Diana didn't recognize. Beside the monitors were IVs that fed and medicated and metal rails that kept Amy's inert body confined to the bed. No television or radio cut the silence, only the constant, rhythmic hiss and thump of the machine that pumped air into Amy's lungs.

Her face was nearly lost behind the tube attached to her mouth and the enormous white bandage encasing her head. She looked impossibly small and pale, the few remaining bruises the only color on her cheeks.

After several seconds, a movement in the corner of the room caught Diana's eye. Stephanie got up from the chair she'd been sitting in and came to give her a hug.

"Luckily, before I'd opened my mouth about who I really am, one of the nurses told me they had a rule that only members of the immediate family could stay with intensive care patients. I told them I was Amy's sister." She took Diana's suitcase and purse and put them beside the chair. "I don't think they believed me, but I was the only one here, so they let me stay."

"How is she?" Diana couldn't move, not even to cross the room to Amy's bed.

"The same. At least as far as I can tell. The numbers on the monitors change every once in a while, but just when I start to panic, they go back to where they were."

"Do they know why this happened?"

"The doctor thinks it's a delayed reaction to the beating."

"I'm so glad you were with her." Stephanie had told her on the phone that Amy had been complaining of a headache since the night before. She'd come downstairs—Stephanie thought to borrow aspirin—and had collapsed before saying anything.

"Me too."

"Did you call my parents?"

"I didn't, but someone must have. I know your dad was around for a while."

"In here?"

Stephanie shifted her weight nervously and looked away. "No, one of the doctors told me they talked to him before they operated."

Diana put her hand to her throat, fighting a feeling that she was choking. "When is she supposed to wake up?"

Stephanie didn't answer right away. Finally, as if realizing how ominous her silence would appear, she said, "Any time."

Diana hugged herself, suddenly intensely cold. "What you're saying is that she should have been awake by now."

"I'm just repeating what the doctor told me," Stephanie said carefully.

"Please don't do that. You're the best person I know at reading between the lines. Tell me what you think is going on."

"All right. From everything I've seen and overheard, the best-case scenario would have been for Amy to wake up out of the anesthesia, although no one seemed surprised when she didn't, or even all that upset. To me that means what's happening now isn't all that uncommon. It's important for you to keep reminding yourself that what they're doing for Amy is treatment, not maintenance."

"I'm going to see if I can find her doctor."

Stephanie glanced at her watch. "She said she'd be back in about a half hour."

"I can't wait that long."

Stephanie grabbed Diana's arm as she started to leave. "Tell Amy you're here."

Diana frowned in confusion. "I thought you said she was—"

"It doesn't matter." When Diana still held back, Stephanie said, "I did a Christmas story a couple of years ago about some kids who almost lost their mother in a car wreck. They took turns staying with her, talking and reading and singing until she was out of her coma. I went to interview them, thinking it was just another one of those 'miracle' stories we run for the holidays. But then I talked to the doctor and he changed my mind. He said no one believed the mother would ever wake up again, but the kids wouldn't listen. They refused to stop hoping. It's up to us to convince Amy this world is worth coming back to."

Only then did Diana realize that mixed with the need for more information was a need to protect herself from Amy. She was scared, more scared than she'd ever been in her life. She didn't know how to keep the fear from overwhelming her except to do something, anything, to keep busy. She was desperate to find a way to stop herself from thinking, to stop herself from feeling.

Not even finding Amy unconscious and barely breathing had been like this. Then she'd still been protected by a life free from things that couldn't be controlled. She'd known that tragedies happened—she saw them every day on television and read about them every day in the newspaper—but they happened to other people. Now she was forced to face that what she'd believed wasn't true.

Taking a deep breath to steady herself, Diana went over to the bed. She looked hard and long but couldn't see the Amy she knew. This was not the spirited sister who had glued all the shoes in their parents' closet to the floor after they took her cat to the animal shelter for clawing a chair. The shell was there—the tiny mole at the corner of her mouth, the one eyebrow that arched higher than the other—but the essence was gone. For a horrifying instant Diana was sure that Amy had died, that the machines were lying.

A sob caught in Diana's throat. She didn't want to live in a world without her sister.

Stephanie moved to stand beside Diana. She laid her hand on Amy's knee. "Hey, babe, if you knew how awful you looked, you'd be up and out of here in a flash. Now don't take this wrong, but I've seen fish two days out of the water that look better than you do right now. It's time to wake up and go home."

Something hit the crisp white sheet beside Amy's arm. Diana looked down at a small damp circle.

Another appeared, and then another. It was then that Diana realized she was crying. Her fear, her sorrow, demanded to be heard. She could be brave again tomorrow. Tonight her heart was breaking. She bent to brush a kiss on Amy's pale cheek. "I'm sorry I wasn't here for you."

Stephanie nudged Diana with her elbow. "That is not the kind of thing she needs to hear." She reached over to wipe the tears from Diana's cheeks. "Give her hell for not waking up, or promise her you'll have Helen make her another batch of chocolate-chip cookies. Tell her anything except that it's okay to give up."

"Did you hear that?" Diana looked directly at Amy, as if she expected an answer. "Chocolate-chip cookies. I'll bet I could get Helen to make a double batch. I'll even have her put in twice as many pecans as she did last time."

"I like them better without the nuts," Stephanie said.

Diana reached for Amy's hand. It was soft and familiar, even if there was no response. "Don't you dare leave me, Amy. If you do . . . I swear I'll give Mother your clock."

Stephanie smiled. "Oh, that's good. I know I always respond well to threats."

On impulse Diana turned and put her arms around Stephanie. "You're the greatest."

"You too." She hugged her back.

Stephanie left an hour later. She made sure Diana had eaten and had elicited a promise that she would call if there were any changes. "I'll stop by on my way to work," she said as Diana walked her to the elevator. "I have that story on firehouse cooking I have to turn in tomorrow and an interview with a decoy carver at eleven. I should be back here by one at the latest."

"You don't have to—"

She gave Diana a stern look. "I don't want to hear any more of that. Understand?"

Diana nodded. "I'll see you in the morning."

"That's more like it." The elevator arrived. Stephanie got in. "You'll call me if anything happens," she said as the doors began to close.

"I promise," Diana said. She turned and saw her father headed in her direction. It was the first time she'd seen him since their fight.

"Don't you think it's time you went home?" he said. He was wearing surgical greens and looked exhausted.

"I just got here an hour ago."

He frowned. "The nurse told me you were the one who brought her in."

He hadn't even bothered to find out for himself. "Why don't you walk me back?"

"It's stupid for you to stay here, Diana. It could be days before Amy wakes up. Someone will call you if there are any changes."

Carl Winchester was known for his surgical skills, not his bedside manner. She tried to tell herself he was being practical, looking at things through a doctor's eyes and not a father's. "Don't you want to see her?"

"I looked at her chart."

If she said what she was feeling, she would alienate him, and she needed to have him on her side if at all possible. He could cut through mounds of red tape with a phone call. Amy might need him yet. "What did it say?"

"She's doing as well as can be expected."

Diana turned and leaned her back into the wall. She was beginning to feel the effect of two nights without sleep. "I could get that line from anyone."

"What do you want me to say?"

"That she's going to be all right."

"I don't know that she is. At this point no one can tell you something like that. At least they shouldn't. A hundred things could still happen."

"What harm would it do to give me hope?"

"Would you prefer false hope over the truth?"

"Yes."

"Well, you're going to have to get it somewhere else." He went over to the elevator and pressed the down button.

"Say hello to Mom for me."

"I'm not going to act as go-between for you and your mother. If you have something to say to her, pick up the phone and say it." Impatiently he tapped the button several more times.

"I take it she's still mad at me."

"My guess is she's more hurt than mad." The elevator arrived. "Don't wait too long before you go over to see her, Diana. You know how she can get."

Just before the doors closed, Diana said, "Tell her I'd like to take her to breakfast tomorrow—she can meet me in Amy's room."

Carl answered, as Diana knew he would, but her timing had been perfect. She hadn't heard a word.

When she got back to Amy's room the nurse was there checking the IVs. "I thought you'd gone home," she said.

"How is she doing?"

"As well as can—"

"Be expected," Diana finished for her.

"I'm sorry, I know how meaningless that must sound, but it's the truth." She touched Diana's arm and looked directly into her eyes. "Your sister has been through a rough time. We've done what we can to help; now it's up to her."

She'd received more compassion and understanding from a stranger than she had her own
father. "I'm going to stay with her tonight. Is there
somewhere on this floor I can get a cup of coffee?"

"I'll get one for you out of the break room. You
don't want to drink the stuff that comes out of those
machines."

Finally she and Amy were alone. Diana pulled
the chair next to the bed, reached through the bars,
and took Amy's hand. "Remember that summer
Mom sent us to the camp where they were supposed
to teach us how to be ladies, and we short-sheeted
that old witch who wouldn't let us room together? I
met a woman today who reminded me of her. She
was—"

Diana talked nonstop for the next hour. It wasn't
as hard as she'd anticipated, especially when she
found herself being led from one memory to the
next, visiting places in her mind she hadn't been in
years. She smiled a lot at the memories, fighting the
voice that whispered they might be all she and Amy
had.

She had no idea that she'd fallen asleep until a
feeling that someone else had come into the room
woke her up. She sat up and looked at the doorway,
squinting at the light. "Who's there?"

"Travis."

She blinked. Her eyes adjusted. It really was
Travis. "What are you doing here?"

"I came to see my sister."

Sixteen

"How did you find us?" Diana asked.

He came into the room and dropped a duffel bag behind the door. "I started calling hospitals until I found one that had an Amy Winchester."

She stood and placed herself between him and Amy, a deeply protective streak surfacing. "What's the real reason you're here?"

"I told you," he said patiently. "I wanted to see my sister."

She looked into his eyes, seeking a hidden motive. Fatigue and confusion were obvious, but she could detect nothing else. "Did you tell your mother you were coming?"

"She knows I left, but not where I was going." He raked his hand through his hair, bringing a semblance of order that disappeared when he dipped his head and wiped the same hand across his face. "After you left I started thinking about what you'd said. One thing led to another, and here I am."

It was obvious he hadn't come there to impress her. She'd heard more compelling speeches when friends had been pulled over for speeding. "I probably should warn you that she doesn't look . . ." She moved away from the bed. "I don't know why I'm bothering. You'll see soon enough for yourself."

Travis stood at the foot of the bed and stared at this stranger who was his sister. Diana was right, Amy didn't look anything like the pictures he'd seen at the restaurant. Still, despite the hospital trappings and her swollen features, he could see that Amy was a Martell. The discovery brought an unexpected, profound sense of loss.

He moved closer. He'd seen his share of battered people, men and women who'd fallen climbing mountains, skiers who'd lost control and slammed into trees, a lifetime of accidents on the farm, but none of the others had affected him the way seeing Amy did. It didn't matter that he hadn't even known she existed two days ago. She was family.

"Why is that wire coming out of the bandage?"

"It monitors the pressure inside her head."

"How is she doing?"

"As well as—" Diana's voice broke. "She's alive. That's all I really know."

"Why are you here by yourself?"

She was instantly defensive. "What did you expect, a party?"

Her response confused him. He'd been asking about her parents and when they might be coming back. He needed to know how they would feel about having him around.

"I'm not the enemy, Diana. I came here to help." It wasn't the exact truth, but close enough. He didn't understand himself why he'd felt compelled to be there, only that he couldn't stay away.

"What possible help could you be?"

It would be so easy just to turn around and leave. He'd seen Amy, had satisfied his need to know whether he would feel a connection. Why was he staying? "I can keep you company."

"What makes you think I need company?"

A monitor behind Diana sounded an alarm. Seconds later a nurse entered the room. She checked Amy and then the wires leading to the machine. "One of the leads came loose," she said with a quick, reassuring smile. She glanced from Travis to Diana. "Your father never mentioned you had a brother."

Diana was caught off guard. It was impossible to miss the interest in the look the nurse gave Travis. He wasn't the kind of man who appealed to her—he was too rough around the edges, too unpredictable. She'd never understood why women were attracted to men like him, but she knew she was in the minority.

"Travis is Amy's brother." The adoption had never been a secret. In the past few years her parents had done everything possible to distance themselves from Amy. They would be pleased to know that Diana was finally cooperating.

The nurse seemed confused, then obviously sorted it out. "Does that mean you're not from around here?" she asked Travis.

"Wyoming," he supplied.

"Is this the first time you've been to Minneapolis?"

"Yes."

She reset the alarm on the monitor. "It's too bad it had to be under these circumstances. Maybe you'll get to come back again when your sister can show you the city."

"I'm looking forward to it."

Diana watched Travis. He seemed completely oblivious of the signals the nurse was sending him. When she was gone, Diana asked, "How did you get in here?"

"An old trick—I acted as if I belonged."

She was angry that Dorothy wanted nothing to do with Amy and hurt that Travis had put his father's feelings above Amy's needs, but she couldn't spare the energy it took to sustain either emotion. "I don't care why you came," she said. "I'm glad you did."

"I'm not sure how long I can stay."

"Have you thought about what you'll tell Amy if she wakes up?"

"You mean 'when,' don't you?" he asked gently.

She had to be more careful. What if Stephanie was right and Amy could hear them? "I only meant if she wakes up before you have to leave."

"I don't know." He looked down at Amy and then up at Diana again. "I guess we should talk about it."

"There's something you should know about Amy. She can't be controlled. Once you tell her who you are, she's going to make up her own mind about whether to tell your father or not."

Travis gave her a slow, wry smile. "If you're reminding me that she's stubborn, I'm not surprised. It's one of those family traits I was telling you about before."

She wanted to know more about his family, things she could eventually pass on to Amy that would help her understand who she was. "Tell me about Judy and Faith."

"They're inseparable, more like twins than sisters. There's such a big gap between them and me and Sharon—" He stopped and thought about what he'd said. "There shouldn't have been that gap. If Amy had grown up where she belonged, none of us would be the same."

"And I wouldn't have been who I am if she hadn't come into my life." It was a sobering revelation. "I can't imagine my childhood without her."

Travis looked at Amy as if expecting her to join in

and tell her part of the story. "Why did you come looking for us, Diana? What went wrong here?"

"Amy needed something good in her life." She didn't know him well enough to trust him with more details than she'd already given him. "I was hoping it would be her real mother."

"Don't you mean birth mother?"

He was testing her. "My mother was never a real mother to Amy. A maid took care of her from the day she came home from the hospital." The next came hard. "What little love and familial feelings Eileen Winchester had in her, she gave to me."

"That's a hell of a burden to put on a kid."

"Amy never knew what it was—"

"I wasn't talking about Amy, I was talking about you."

She didn't know what to say. "I had it easy growing up. Everything I wanted I got."

"How can it be easy to see someone you love constantly mistreated?"

"I don't want to talk about this here." She didn't want to talk about it at all, but that would have required explaining something to him she didn't fully understand herself.

"You look exhausted. Why don't you go home and get some rest? I can stay with Amy until you get back."

Had the offer come from Stephanie, or anyone else in her circle of friends, she would have been grateful. Coming from Travis, it made her suspicious. "Why would you want to do that?"

"She's my sister, too."

"I'm sorry, but I find it a little hard to believe you've developed this instant, overpowering family tie to a woman you didn't know existed twenty-four hours ago."

"What do you think I'm going to do, wait until you leave and pull one of these plugs?"

The accusation was ludicrous, but it made her stop and think. Just what was she afraid of? "I wouldn't sleep anyway. I might as well stay."

"Then I might as well see if I can find another chair, because I'm not leaving, either."

A peculiar peace settled over her, as if another warrior had joined the battle, evening the sides. She wanted to give him something in return. "You couldn't tell in the picture, but Amy has your father's smile."

He seemed to know what she was trying to do. "He would like that."

Stephanie dropped by with doughnuts and coffee the next morning. She stood in the doorway and looked around the room. Travis was standing next to the bed; Diana was curled up on two chairs that had been pushed together, sleeping. "Who are you?" she asked Travis.

He put his finger to his lips and motioned for her to keep her voice down. "She hasn't been asleep very long," he said, motioning to Diana.

"Are you a doctor?"

He didn't know how much to tell her. "I'm a friend." He would have extended his hand, but hers were full. "Travis Martell."

Her eyes widened. "Amy's brother?"

Diana might not have told Amy why she'd gone to Jackson, but she obviously hadn't kept her trip a complete secret. "I got in early this morning."

Stephanie set the bag and coffee on the night-stand, then checked on Amy before she said, "Diana must have been surprised to see you."

"You could say that." He leaned against the wall,

his hands pressed to the small of his spine for support. The only sleep he'd had in two days had been on the plane, and he was beginning to wear down. "You must be Stephanie. Diana told me if you hadn't been with Amy, she might not have made it. Thank you."

"What's going on here?" She moved closer to Travis, keeping her voice at a whisper. "Diana said you people didn't want anything to do with Amy. What made you change your mind?"

He was getting a little tired of defending himself. Under other circumstances he would have countered the attack with one of his own. Instead he said, "It's a little too complicated to go into here."

"You don't have to do that, Stephanie," Diana said. "I grilled Travis when he got here last night." She stretched and let out a groan. "He passed."

"Would you see if you can talk her into going home and getting some real rest?" Travis said to Stephanie.

She gave him a quick assessment before turning to Diana. "You know, he's right," she said reluctantly. "You look like hell."

"I'll go home when you come back this afternoon," she said. "I don't want Amy to be alone."

Travis leaned the back of his head against the cool wall. "I told you I would stay."

"He is Amy's brother." Stephanie gave Travis a threatening look. "I'm sure he would call you if anything changes."

Travis fought an intense dislike for Stephanie Gorham. If it weren't for the number of times he'd seen his sisters form a defensive front to protect each other, he would give in to his feelings. He looked over to Diana. "Give me your phone number and your address, and get out of here."

"Why do you need her address?" Stephanie asked.

"So I can rob her when I know she's at the hospital."

"Come on, you two," Diana said. "Even if Amy can't hear you, she's bound to feel the tension."

Stephanie glanced back at Amy. "You're right. I really ought to practice what I preach." She picked up the coffee and handed it to Diana. "Since you're convinced Travis is okay, why don't you let me drop you off at home? Even if you don't want to sleep, you could take a shower and put on some clean clothes."

She waited until she'd tasted the coffee before she said, "All right—I give up."

"You can have the doughnuts," Stephanie told Travis.

At least he could be reasonably sure they weren't poisoned. "Thanks."

Diana went to the bed and leaned over the rail to give Amy a kiss. "I'll be back in a couple of hours. Don't do anything I wouldn't." She started to leave, then added, "By the way, the guy I'm leaving you with is your big brother. He has a lot to tell you, so be sure you pay attention."

Diana picked up her suitcase and looked at Travis. "You'll call me—no matter what it is? I want to know if she loses an eyelash."

"I promise."

Stephanie began grilling Diana as soon as they were in the elevator. They were almost home before Diana had finished telling her about the night she'd just spent with Travis.

"So you like him?" Stephanie asked.

"Yeah—I tried really hard not to, but I kept running out of reasons."

"Does coming here mean he's changed his mind about telling his father?"

Diana was so tired, she was numb. For the

moment the fatigue insulated her from her fear and gave her a temporary reprieve from grief. "He can't."

Stephanie pulled into the parking garage and stopped beside the elevator. "Why is it that everybody in this mess deserves protecting except Amy? Why does she have to pay the price for something her mother did?"

"You're beginning to sound like me."

"Have you come up with an answer?"

"Not an answer, but Travis did give me something to think about. What would it do to Amy if the family fell apart because she showed up?"

"Isn't that a bit melodramatic? Whatever made Dorothy Martell give Amy away happened twenty-six years ago. It's ancient history."

"I don't think the kind of lie she told has a statute of limitation."

Stephanie glanced at the clock. "I gotta get out of here." Before she drove away, she opened the window and called to Diana, "Page me if anything happens. If I don't hear from you, I'll see you at the hospital this afternoon."

Diana waved at the disappearing car, picked up her suitcase, and went over to the elevator. The first thing she saw when she opened the door to her condo was Amy's purse sitting on an antique hall table. The table hadn't been there when Diana left for Jackson.

Amy had been determined to fill every empty space, wiping out Stuart's memory by replacing all evidence he'd ever been there. She was adamant that there be an equal mixture of old with the new, otherwise Diana could get the feeling she was living in a department store.

Diana had tried but couldn't convince Amy she didn't care about such things, that she could be content with a beanbag chair and a table to hold her cup of tea while she read by the fireplace. But Amy was a nester. She liked having her "things" around her. She said they gave her a feeling of home.

Amy would like Travis. And she would like her father, too. The sisters might be a harder sell. When threatened by an outsider, they would be apt to stand by their mother, even if they had doubts about what she had done.

It would have been so much easier if the Martells had been crooks or lowlifes. Diana could have come back to Minneapolis knowing Amy was better off where she was. Now there would always be a lingering regret over the promise of what might have been.

And she couldn't even blame Travis or focus her frustration on him anymore. He was as innocent as Amy, pulled into a situation where there were no right answers. Under any other circumstances, she would admire that he was determined to protect his father.

Diana liked Travis. He was the kind of man she'd known only in books. Her heart broke that Amy would never be a part of her brother's life, that she would miss out on his tenderness and caring, on the basic goodness that had brought him to her bedside simply because it was the right thing to do.

Seventeen

Diana rolled to her side. She knew she'd overslept before she even looked at the clock. The short nap she'd planned to take before heading back to the hospital had lasted six hours. It was three in the afternoon.

Why hadn't Travis called to check on her? The thought that he might have given up and left was discarded as soon as it appeared. She'd known him less than a day, but already there were things about him so evident that they were a given, like snow in winter. More likely Stephanie had relieved him. Diana felt a quick stab of disappointment. She would have liked to tell him good-bye.

She made a quick trip to the deli for sandwiches. By the time she was back on the road, she was in the middle of rush-hour traffic.

This time when she stopped by the nurses' station to ask about Amy, the answer had changed from "As well as can be expected" to "The same."

She had her hand on the door to Amy's room when she heard Travis's voice coming from inside. *He was still there*. She stopped to listen.

"I think you and Sharon would really hit it off.

She's a lot like Diana. Not in looks, but in the way they . . ."

Diana's heart skipped a beat. Amy must be awake. But that didn't make sense. The nurse would have said something. She opened the door slowly and looked inside.

Travis sat with his back to her, his booted feet propped up on the nightstand, his arm snaked through the metal bar on the bed, his hand holding Amy's.

"They're both really pushy, too. Sharon used to boss Faith and Judy around as if she were a wrangler and they were part of a herd. I always thought she would be the one to take over the ranch. She was better at it than any of the rest of us. But then she married Davis and they started working in the store and that was that.

"Davis is a great guy, not anyone I would have picked for Sharon, but then I never liked any of her girlfriends that she tried to set me up with, either. Who knows what's going to get the old hormones dancing? Every time I start thinking this one's the one, I panic." He shifted in the chair, recrossing his ankles. "I want kids, lots of them. That means staying married at least long enough to see them grown and out of the house."

Diana had the uncomfortable feeling that her initial curiosity had become eavesdropping. She came into the room as if she'd just arrived. "You know, the nurse will shoot you if she comes in here and sees you with your feet up there."

Travis untangled himself and got up. "She already did." He moved the chair away from the bed, stretched, and grinned. "I promised she wouldn't catch me again if she promised to knock before she came in."

"I'm sorry about being late. I fell asleep."

"I figured as much."

She came over to the bed to check on Amy. "Where's Stephanie?"

"She called to say she got tied up at the newspaper, but that she'd be here as soon as she could get away."

"You should have let me know."

"Why?"

"So you could get some rest yourself."

He shrugged. "I'm all right."

"You know, I really hate that macho stuff. You've got to be every bit as tired as I was. Why not just admit it?"

He stared at her and shook his head in disbelief. "Okay, I'm tired. Satisfied?"

Was this what he'd meant about being pushy? "Amy's going to think we don't like each other," she said, trying for lightness.

"Do you really think she can hear us?"

The question surprised her. What was it that she'd walked in on if he didn't believe the same thing? "Don't you?"

"I don't know. I'd just hate to find out later that some part of her could be reached and no one tried."

"Have you thought about what you're going to do when she wakes up?" Diana asked.

"I've thought about it a lot. That doesn't mean I've reached any conclusions."

"Don't you think this is something we should talk about? I am involved, after all. You can't just tell Amy who you are without her wanting to know how you found out she was here."

"I understand why you're trying to protect Amy, but what makes you think you have all the answers, and that they're the right ones?"

"I know a hell of a lot more—" Diana glanced at Amy, then motioned for Travis to come with her to the end of the bed. "We can't keep doing this here."

He reached up to rub the back of his neck. "We do seem to get under each other's hide a lot."

"Why don't you get out of here for a while?"

Travis rocked from one side to the other, stretching his back. "Is there a hotel nearby?"

Diana couldn't think of any within walking distance. On impulse, she dropped the sandwich bag on the end of the bed and dug her keys out of her purse. "You can use my place."

Travis looked down at her outstretched hand. "I don't think that's a very good idea."

"Why not?"

"I don't know. I just don't."

"You'll be there, I'll be here. What's the big deal?" She put the keys in his hand. "Besides, this way I'll know where to find you if I need you." She dug through her purse again for her pen. After looking around for a piece of paper and not finding one, she tore the top off the sandwich bag and drew him a map. "You can use the bedroom downstairs and eat whatever you can find."

"I was hoping one of those was for me," he said, pointing to the bag.

"It wasn't, but I'm willing to share." She reached inside and took out the smoked turkey. "I didn't think you would still be here." She opened the wrapper, handed him half, and took half for herself.

"I had no idea how hungry I was until I smelled what was inside that bag." He consumed a third of the sandwich in one bite.

Diana took the pickles out of their wrapping and handed them to him. "They're the best I've ever tasted," she said.

"You don't want one?"

"No, you go ahead." He probably hadn't eaten since Stephanie brought the doughnuts. She felt guilty that she'd kept half the sandwich for herself. "Here, why don't you eat this, too. I can get something downstairs."

He smiled. "I hate eating alone."

"I can't promise you'll find anything but crackers and peanut butter at home. You'd better—"

"I can take care of myself." He put his hand on her shoulder. "I've been doing it for a long time now."

She eyed him. "Your sisters really spoiled you when you were growing up, didn't they?"

He laughed. "What makes you say that?"

"I don't know . . . you seem so comfortable around women, and you don't act the least bit surprised when they do something for you. There's no way one of these nurses would let me get away with putting my feet on that table. You not only get away with it, you talked one of them into being your accomplice."

He took a bite of pickle and shrugged. "What do you expect me to say to something like that? When they weren't driving me crazy, I liked having sisters."

Someone opened the door. It was Stephanie. She seemed nonplussed to find Travis still there. "How's Amy doing?"

"The same," Diana said.

Travis added, "I had a chance to talk to one of her doctors this afternoon. He told me that we shouldn't try to read anything into Amy not waking up yet. They would prefer she had, but just because she hasn't, doesn't mean she won't."

Stephanie looked at the pickle in Travis's hand. "So when should we start worrying?"

"I didn't ask. I don't like countdowns." He bent and pulled his duffel bag out from under the chair. "I'll do the midnight shift," he said to Diana.

"Why don't you go with him," Stephanie told her. "You've been here almost as long as Travis. You could use a break, too."

"I've only been here a half hour," Diana said guiltily. "Travis stayed with Amy today while I slept."

Diana would have sworn she saw a flicker of respect in Stephanie's eyes when she said to him, "Then I imagine you're anxious to get to your hotel."

He sent Diana a look containing the silent message that where he was staying was her story to tell. "Yes, I am."

"You might as well take my car," Diana said. "It's the tan Volvo a couple of spaces down from the elevator on second-level parking."

Travis nodded to Stephanie. To Diana he said, "I'll see you later, then."

"Are you out of your mind, just giving him your car like that?" Stephanie asked when Travis was gone.

"Not something you'd expect me to do, huh," Diana said thoughtfully.

"Not in a million years."

She gave Stephanie a half smile. "I think I'll wait until later to tell you what else I did."

Diana, Travis, and Stephanie settled into a flexible routine over the next three days, the determining factor being Stephanie's work schedule. Diana had postponed calling her office to tell them she was back in town. If there was a crisis brewing at work, she didn't want to know about it. More important, she didn't want to talk to anyone about Amy until she had something positive to tell them.

On Wednesday the doctors decided to try weaning Amy off the respirator. To everyone's surprise they succeeded on the first attempt. Travis went out and bought bottles of sparkling cider and paper cups. The entire unit helped them celebrate.

Thursday morning Diana and Stephanie were in a euphoric mood as they rode in together, Diana to relieve Travis, Stephanie to go to work. They were almost to the hospital when Stephanie let it slip that she was canceling a date with her mysterious new man that Friday to stay with Amy.

"I can't wait for you and Amy to meet him," Stephanie said.

Diana could have hugged her for the easy way she'd included Amy. "So how many dates are you up to now?"

"I honestly don't know. I stopped counting a couple of months ago."

In all the time they had known each other, Diana had never heard Stephanie as stimulated or seen her as animated when she talked about a man. "It sounds serious."

"There's just one problem: he's married. Well, kind of married," she added quickly. "They've been separated for over a year. She's holding up the divorce for some reason."

"I didn't know someone could do that anymore."

"Stan said that until he met me, he really didn't care how long she hung on."

Diana had a bad feeling about Stan and his divorce, but she didn't say anything. Stephanie was one of the smartest women Diana knew and had a cynical streak as big as the Mall of America. It was hard to believe she could be taken in, no matter how blinded by love. "Like I said, it sounds serious." She could not resist adding, "Just be careful."

"I will." She honked at the car in front of her after it failed to move on the green light. "You know me, I question everything."

"Don't break your date. Travis and I can stay with Amy."

"I don't mind—really. And Stan understands."

There was no way Stephanie would back out of a promise. The only thing to do was compromise. "Why don't you come in after your date? Travis and I can sleep in, and then one of us will relieve you, and you can sleep all day Saturday if you want." Not until she'd made the suggestion did it strike her that "after the date" could be eight o'clock the next morning.

"Do you realize how strange that sounds—you and Travis sleeping in?"

"Yeah, it sounds a little strange to me, too. But on that same note, I didn't mean to put a time limit on your date."

Stephanie laughed. "Is that a subtle way to ask how far the relationship has gone?"

"Well, it wasn't, but if you want to tell me, I'm not going to stop you." Their conversation was so grounded, so normal, it seemed almost surreal. She felt as if she were living in two worlds, the ever present fear and almost overwhelming intensity of dealing with Amy's coma and the ordinary everyday moments that made up her life away from the hospital.

"I've never gone to bed with anyone on the first date"—she glanced over to Diana—"until Stan."

"Wow." Diana let out a low whistle. "Don't worry about when you get to the hospital Friday, Travis and I will work it out."

"I'll be there by midnight. That way if you and Travis want to stop for a bite to eat on the way home, you'll still be able to find something open."

Stephanie arrived Friday night exactly at the

stroke of midnight. On the way home Diana and Travis talked about going out, but both decided they were too tired to bother.

The next morning Travis stepped out of the shower and heard the doorbell ring. He assumed Diana would get it and was puzzled when he heard it ring again a short time later.

He opened the bathroom door, stuck his head out, and called, "Diana?" She didn't answer. When the doorbell rang for the third time, he slipped into his jeans, buttoning them as he raced down the hallway. He tried to hide his half-naked state by standing behind the door as he opened it, one hand on the knob, the other finger-combing his still wet hair.

The woman who'd rung the bell took a step backward when she saw Travis. She looked at the number on the door. "I must have gotten off at the wrong floor," she said.

"Who were you looking for?" Travis asked.

She shifted her purse from one hand to the other. "I thought this was the Kennedy-Winchester residence."

"I don't know about the Kennedy part, but this is where Diana Winchester lives." He shoved his damp hand into his pocket. The top button on his jeans popped open. Deciding that as long as he stayed behind the door he was all right, he didn't bother rebuttoning it. "Did you want to see her?"

"Is she here?"

"She was about ten minutes ago. If you'll wait just a minute, I'll see if I can find her for you."

"Who are you?" the woman demanded. "And what are you doing here?"

The questions and the woman's tone stopped Travis cold. He looked at her again, more carefully this time. She was about the right age, wore clothes several steps above merely expensive, and carried a handbag previously owned by one of the world's exotic lizards. So this was the formidable Eileen Winchester. He wasn't impressed.

"I'm a friend of Diana's." Travis couldn't help adding, "And who are you?"

She purposely swept him with her gaze, then gave him a look that spoke volumes. She was not impressed with him any more than he was her. "I'm Diana's mother."

"Well, this is certainly a surprise. When did you get back in town?"

She frowned. "What are you talking about? I haven't been anywhere."

Travis was treading on ground he had no business walking. He had no right to interfere in the relationship between Diana, Amy, and their mother. He was battling the five days and nights he'd spent at the hospital trying to understand what kind of parents could abandon not only the adopted child they had raised as their own, but the one they still claimed to love. It wasn't just Amy who had awakened a protective instinct in Travis; as he watched Diana's daily struggles to put on a good front, she had become a part of it, too. There were times she'd hung on by her fingertips, needing someone to turn to, desperate for understanding and support from her family.

"You mean you've been here the whole time Amy has been in the hospital and you haven't gone to see her once?" He was careful to sound more incredulous than angry.

"How would you know whether—" She caught herself. "So, you're the one who's been making such a nuisance out of himself down there. You're not doing Amy one bit of good, you know. The nurses are considering having the administration ask you to stay away."

"Oh, which nurses would that be? Let's see, there's Denise . . . Kathy . . . Katelyn . . . Connor . . . Rick . . . but I'm sure it's not one of them. And then there's Paul and John and Shawn on the day shift, but they've been the most vocal in saying how important it is that someone be there with Amy as much as possible to let her know she's loved and missed." He rubbed his chin, feigning deep thought. "You know, for the life of me, I can't imagine any one of them as the manipulative type. If they were unhappy about something, they'd just come right out and say it." He gave her a penetrating stare. "Are you sure you had the right hospital?"

The look she sent back was filled with pure hatred. Eileen Winchester was not someone who lost graciously. If there had ever been a chance for them to make peace with each other, it was gone.

Before she could say anything in reply, something drew her attention. She looked past Travis. "Where have you been?" she snapped at Diana. "Why didn't you come to the door yourself? I was beginning to think—" She glanced at Travis. "Never mind what I thought."

"Mother—how nice to see you," Diana said coolly. She was wearing her bathrobe and pulled it tighter around her as she approached. "Out slumming?"

"Since you've chosen not to return any of my calls this week, you forced me to come over here to see you. There are some things we need to discuss."

Diana put her hand on Travis's arm in a possessive, intimate gesture. The unexpected contact sent a wildly intoxicating jolt through his body. It took a few seconds to figure out what was going on—Diana wasn't worried her mother would get the wrong impression; she wanted her to. He was more than willing to play along; he liked the idea. Giving Diana a tender, loving glance, he put his arm around her and drew her tight against his bare chest. She tilted her chin up to look at him. As if it were the most natural thing in the world, as if it had happened a hundred times before, he leaned down and kissed her.

Again, completely unexpected, there was the jolt of excitement, this time embarrassingly and uncomfortably centered in his groin. He liked having her in his arms, and he liked kissing her. A hell of a lot more than he would have expected.

"Are you through with your vulgar display, Diana?" Eileen asked.

Diana touched her tongue to her lips. Her bravado seemed to have been shaken. Still, she stared into Travis's eyes and managed a credible, "I don't know, are we?"

He couldn't read what was happening to her now, only that she looked as confused as he felt. "Would you like me to leave you alone with your mother?"

"Maybe it would be better," she said.

"Call me if you need me." They weren't empty words; he meant every one. He would relish the opportunity to slay dragons for Diana, especially this dragon.

"I'll be okay," she said.

When he was gone, Eileen went on the attack. "You gave up Stuart for that?"

"I didn't give up Stuart, Mother. He walked out on me."

"You could have gotten him back if you'd tried. You still could. He was desperate to get through to you. Leaving was the only way he knew how."

So her mother had talked to Stuart. What she wouldn't give to have been a fly on the wall during that conversation. "Is that what you came to tell me?"

"You'll ruin any chance you have to make a decent marriage if you don't get rid of that man. It's obvious he isn't one of us."

"One of us? What is that supposed to mean?"

"Do you really want me to spell it out?" She was clearly losing the battle to keep her temper, giving Diana the advantage. "He's common."

To call someone "common" was one of her mother's greatest insults, saved for people she truly disliked. "You don't even know him."

"I don't have to."

"Would it make any difference if I told you who he was?"

Eileen hesitated, sensing a trap. "I suppose you're going to tell me he comes from one of the Boston—"

"He's Amy's brother."

For the first time in her life, Diana had left her mother speechless.

After several seconds Eileen finally managed to sputter, "What could you have been thinking? How dare you bring a man like that here?"

"I didn't bring him, he came on his own."

"And I suppose the rest of the family will be parking their trailers outside the hospital in the weeks to come."

"You can be such a bitch," Diana said, more out of weariness than anger.

"Think about what you're doing," Eileen said. "All you have to do is look at Amy to know what her brother is like."

"I should be so lucky." She put her hand on the door. "Are you through? I have to get ready to go to the hospital."

Eileen straightened to her full five feet three inches. "Your father will be talking to you."

"He knows where I am."

Eileen turned to leave. She looked back at Diana. "How can you do this to me?"

At least she'd left off the "after all I've done for you" part. Diana had fallen for the line too many times to get suckered by it again. More important, she was running dangerously low on emotional energy. There simply was none left to spend on her mother. "I guess because deep down I'm just a heartless bitch, Mother. Which means I'm a lot more like you than either of us thought."

Eileen left without looking back.

Diana closed the door, turned, and found Travis waiting for her.

Eighteen

"You want to talk about what just happened here?" Travis asked.

Diana shook her head. "I have to get ready."

"Not so fast." Travis caught her sleeve. Slowly, deliberately, he brought her into his arms. For several long seconds he stared into her eyes, and then he kissed her. There was a moment of surprise before her lips yielded in response. The kiss deepened. She moved closer, fitting herself to the hard planes of his body. A sigh of loss escaped her throat when he brought his head up to look at her. Without saying anything, she touched the side of his face as if imprinting his feel into her consciousness. He kissed her again.

The moment was as magic as it was frightening. Diana had never been swept away by anything. She'd always prided herself on her control. What they were doing was insane, a result of emotions as battered during the past week as a tennis ball in a high school gym class.

Diana put her hands against Travis's chest to push them apart. "I'm sorry. I started something I shouldn't have. You had every right to think I was coming on to you, but I wasn't. Seeing my mother makes me do insane things sometimes."

"Are you through?" Travis asked patiently.

"Yes, I guess so." She'd ruined their fledgling friendship. The loss was like the string breaking on a shiny new helium balloon. All she could do was watch as the trust and respect they'd struggled so hard to build floated away.

"The reason I kissed you just now had nothing to do with what happened when your mother was here." He thought about what he'd said. "No, that's not right. It had something to do with it, but not what you think. I kissed you because I wanted to know if what I felt the first time was real."

If she had the sense God gave a mushroom, she wouldn't pursue the conversation. "And?"

"It was."

"You realize how crazy this is?"

"I wish to hell I didn't." He clasped his hands behind his neck in a frustrated, almost angry, gesture. "I don't understand how this could have happened."

"That's easy." At least it's what she kept telling herself. "We've been under a lot of stress. People do strange things when they're thrown together, especially as dramatically as we have been. This isn't real. It can't be. We've only known each other a week." She thought about what she'd said. "Actually, it's only been five days, six if you count Jackson, but we only saw each other for about an hour there." She was babbling. "Damn it, Travis. I can't afford to lose you as a friend."

"You won't," he said. "Nothing like this is going to happen again. I won't let it."

Instead of being reassured, she felt perversely disappointed. She wanted him to kiss her again, even knowing how destructive it might be. "Maybe if we'd met at another time."

"It would still be under the same circumstances. Amy will always be there. She's a part of both our lives now."

"I'm going to get dressed."

He put his hand out to stop her. "First tell me about this Kennedy guy."

The request puzzled her. "Why do you want to know about him?"

"Humor me."

"There isn't much to tell. He moved out about a month ago—when Amy got in trouble. I haven't seen him since."

"What would you do if he wanted to come back?"

"He won't."

"But if he did?" Travis insisted.

"I never loved him," she admitted reluctantly. "I think he was easy for me to be with because I didn't have to worry about being hurt if he left." She was still struggling to understand her and Stuart's relationship and why she'd stayed with him as long as she had. "I'm discovering I can't trust people who tell me they love me—except Amy. With everyone else, love is conditional."

"I'll remember that."

"Is that what you wanted to know?"

"Pretty much." Unexpectedly, the corner of his mouth pulled up into a grin. "Since loving you is out, would it be all right if I just said I liked you—a lot?"

He made her smile. "You can't say I've made it easy for you."

He stood perfectly still for a long time as his expression turned serious. "I'm sorry, Diana, it's not going to work. We can try to pretend what happened earlier didn't mean anything, but we started something today that isn't going to go away. No matter how much we want it to."

"We have to try. At least until Amy—" The telephone rang. Diana threw up her hands. "I have to get that. It could be the hospital." She went into the kitchen.

"I'm glad I caught you before you left," Stephanie said. "There's someone here who wants to talk to you."

Diana's first thought was that her father had stopped by Amy's room. "Who is it?" she asked, but Stephanie had already relinquished the phone.

"So . . . how was . . . Jackson?"

"Amy? My God, is that you?" Travis came up behind her. She turned to see if he'd heard. He was smiling.

"I think it's . . . me. But I'm . . . not sure. There's this . . . thing on my head."

"Don't talk anymore. I'm on my way." She grabbed Travis's hand and held on tight.

Stephanie took the phone again. "I haven't looked outside, but I'll bet the sun is shining."

"When did she wake up?"

"About a half hour ago. I would have called sooner, but this place has been a zoo with doctors and nurses coming in and out. And I wanted Amy to tell you herself."

"Is she okay?" Travis mouthed.

Diana smiled expansively and nodded. To Stephanie she said, "Give her a big hug for me."

"I think you should hustle on down here and give it to her yourself."

"You're right—I'm on my way." She hung up the phone. "Hurry up and finish dressing," she said to Travis. Instead of letting go of his hand, she pulled him along with her.

"I can't go with you," he said.

It was the last thing she'd expected to hear. "Why not? This is what we've all been waiting for."

"I still don't know how much I should tell Amy, or if I should tell her anything. If I show up at the hospital now, she's bound to want to know who I am. How would we explain my being there today of all days?"

Diana didn't want to leave him behind. It wasn't fair. "We'll think of something."

"There's nothing we could come up with that she would believe, Diana. This is too important a moment to include someone she's never met. If she gets the idea you're lying to her about me, she'll start doubting everything you tell her, including how well she's doing."

He was right. How could he know so much about Amy without ever having met her? "What will you do while I'm gone?"

"I should go back to Jackson, at least for a couple of days." He let go of her hand and folded his arms across his chest, as if beginning the process of closing himself off from her. "I have a lot of work to catch up on."

"You're not coming back, are you?" There was a calm certainty in her voice that belied the turmoil inside.

"I don't know," he said with brutal honesty. "I need some time to think. We both do."

Damn it, she didn't want him to be right. And she didn't want to lose him. Not now. "How long?"

"Whatever we do, it has to be the right thing for Amy. None of the rest of us count anymore."

"Not even your father?" she asked softly.

He didn't answer.

*   *   *

Travis began calling the airlines as soon as Diana left for the hospital. The earliest available flight to Jackson didn't leave until nine that evening. Rather than take the chance of running into Diana again, he hung around the condo until early afternoon and then went to the terminal. The first good-bye had left him drained. He didn't want to go through it a second time.

He bought several magazines to pass the time but couldn't concentrate on any of the articles long enough to get past the first paragraph. Finally he gave up and did what he should have done in the beginning.

His timing was almost perfect. He arrived at the hospital parking lot just as Diana came out of the building. She didn't see him right away, giving him the opportunity to watch her unobserved as she approached. He tried to imagine that they were strangers. If they'd never met, would he still think her eyes radiated the same sexy intelligence or that the way she moved was more graceful and erotic than any woman he'd ever known? Would her smile change his day from a five to a ten? Did his feelings for her color the truth or make it more clear?

She spotted him. Her unbridled reaction was a gift, a warming ray of sunshine he would carry with him for days. "I thought you'd be gone by now."

It was everything he could do to keep his hands stuffed in his pockets. Only knowing it wasn't the time or place to move to the next step in their relationship kept them there. "Me too."

She gave him a sheepish smile. "On the way to the hospital this morning I thought of a dozen things I wanted to tell you. Wouldn't you know, I can't remember even one of them now." She looked at him with unmistakable intimacy. "I'm so glad you're here."

"My plane doesn't leave until nine. I figured since we both had to eat, we might as well do it together."

God, when had he become such a coward? "The truth is, I came because I wanted to see you."

"I'm not having a very easy time with this, either." She ran her hand along her neck, lifting her hair off her collar, then tucking a strand behind her ear.

With an unexpected surge of desire, he wished it were his hand touching her neck. Even more, he wished he had the right to make the casual, intimate contact.

"You haven't asked about Amy," Diana said.

"I don't have to. I can see the answer on your face."

"She's going to be all right." She glanced at her watch. "If your plane leaves at nine, that doesn't give us much time for dinner."

"I'm not really hungry."

"Me neither."

The silence that followed should have been awkward but, like everything else between them, seemed natural. "It seems wrong not to do something to celebrate. You've been through hell this past week."

"No more than you."

"What about coffee and dessert?"

She thought a minute. "I've got a better idea."

Twenty minutes later, after a stop by the grocery store to pick up a loaf of nine-grain bread and a variety of leafy green vegetables, Diana drove to a small park with a large pond. With the exception of a couple reclining on a blanket, oblivious of everything and everyone around them as they absorbed the last of the day's sun, and a man walking his dog, they would have the park to themselves.

"I come here to have lunch sometimes," Diana said. "Mostly when I need to get away from work to think."

They got out of the car and went over to a bench beside the pond. When they sat down, it was as if a silent, beckoning call sounded to dozens of ducks and geese, who until then had been contentedly wading and swimming and plucking grass.

"From the looks of it, you've been doing a lot of thinking lately," Travis said as the flocks descended on them.

"It isn't me, it's the grocery bag." She reached inside and took out the bread. A cacophony of quacks and honks approved the action.

Travis laughed as one particularly bold goose waddled forward to help Diana with the wrapper, lifting her skirt several inches as he nudged his beak against her leg. "Precocious little guy."

She pulled out the heel of the loaf and gave it to him, rewarding his efforts. With a muted honk he ran for the pond. The others pressed forward expectantly. Diana turned the bread over to Travis and took out the vegetables. "Be sure to watch to make sure the shy ones get something, too."

With the flurry of activity surrounding them, it was impossible for Diana and Travis to think about anything but what they were doing. He luxuriated in the simplicity of the moment, taking pleasure in sharing the time with Diana.

Smiles and laughter came easily to them both, prompted by toes stepped on by webbed feet, fingers nibbled by too eager bites, and raucous antics to gain attention.

When the meal was over, order and calm were quickly restored. The ducks and geese went back to swimming and wading and munching on grass, and Diana and Travis slipped into easy conversation.

"How far is your office from here?" Travis asked.

She came forward and bent low to look past the branches on the ash tree beside them. "See that building with the narrow windows on top?"

Travis followed her direction. "The one behind the clock tower?"

"That's it."

"Impressive." He leaned back again. "Do you like working for Sander's Foods?"

"Sometimes—actually, most of the time. Things have been a little rough lately, but they'll settle down once we get past the launch." She propped her hands behind her head and closed her eyes, letting the sun warm her face. "I kind of fell into my job when a friend in personnel told me they were hiring and didn't care what my major had been in college. It was supposed to be temporary, something to keep me busy while I waited for an opening in one of the arts programs in the Cities."

Travis took the opportunity to look at her unobserved. Her skin appeared translucent in the early evening light, her profile enticingly flawless. "An arts program?"

She rolled her head to the side and smiled at him. "When I was in college I was filled with all these grandiose ideas about making the arts accessible to disadvantaged children."

"But somewhere along the line you changed your mind?"

"No—I got busy with other things, life mostly. Besides, Sander's Food is a great company to work for. They have a terrific pension plan."

"Come again?" He couldn't believe he'd heard her correctly.

"My, God . . . I sound just like Stuart."

"How long were you two together?"

"We dated a couple of years and lived together a little less than that."

"Whose idea was it not to get married?"

"Mine."

"How did Stuart feel about it?"

She was slow to answer this time. "I don't think he cared as long as we were officially engaged—and my parents approved the living arrangement."

Travis picked up a bitterness he hadn't detected before and wondered if Diana had begun to question the reasons she'd stayed with Stuart as long as she had. "Did Amy like him?"

"About as much as a wad of gum stuck to the bottom of her shoe."

Travis laughed. "I have a feeling that's a direct quote."

"Actually, she kept her feelings hidden pretty well when Stuart and I were together. I think she was afraid to force the issue and make me choose between them."

"And if you had?" He'd moved into territory that was none of his business.

She took a long time to answer. When she did, she turned to look him directly in the eyes. "Amy will always come first in my life."

Travis couldn't shake the feeling that what she'd said was as much warning as statement. To cover the sudden chill that had come between them, he looked at his watch. "I hate to leave, but if I don't, I'm going to miss my plane."

They gathered up their trash and dropped it in the container on the way to the car. Despite Travis's protests that he could as easily take a cab, Diana insisted on driving him to the airport.

As he stood on the sidewalk and watched her drive away, he was struck with the certain knowledge that they had become tied to each other in ways that had nothing to do with Amy. The idea both pleased and scared the hell out of him.

Nineteen

With a scheduled two-hour layover, Travis didn't get home until well after midnight. As he drove the nearly deserted highway, he thought about calling ahead to turn on the heater but decided a cold house fit his mood. He didn't want his life to seem easy, to be reminded how secure he was in his family position and in the community. But for the grace of God, and positioning in the birth order, he could have been Amy. She'd done nothing, contributed not a word or look or action, to what had happened to her.

Why had he been spared her fate? He couldn't accept that it was luck, good or bad. There was a reason. He had to know what it was if he was ever to be at peace with himself again.

By the time he crawled into bed it was five in the morning. He should have slept until noon; instead he was up and on the road by eight.

When he arrived at the ranch, he discovered his father had gone into town that morning and that his mother, as usual, had stayed behind. She met him at the door, a steaming mug of coffee in her hand. "You look like you need this more than I do." She smiled and handed him the coffee. "When did you get back?"

"This morning."

"Come in and tell me about your trip. Did you buy the mare?"

He'd almost forgotten that he'd told everyone he was leaving on a horse-buying expedition. "We need to talk."

"You sound so serious." She followed him into the house. "Is something wrong?"

"What did Diana Winchester say to you when she came here?"

Dorothy froze. "I told her to leave you alone." Then, as if realizing she could be assuming he knew more than he did, she asked, "Why do you want to know? Did she say something to you?"

"We've talked." Rather than come out with what he knew, he wanted to give her the chance to tell him herself.

The sounds of Felicia cleaning in the kitchen drew Dorothy's attention. She took Travis's arm and steered him into her office. Once she was seated behind her desk, she asked, "What did you talk about?"

Travis brought the cup to his mouth and stared at her above the rim. "I know, Mother."

"What do you know?" she asked carefully.

"That my sister isn't dead."

"Goddamn it—I warned her to leave my family alone."

"Considering she grew up with one of your daughters, don't you think that would be pretty hard for her to do?"

"That girl has nothing to do with us."

"Her name is Amy," Travis said.

"I don't give a damn what her name is. She's not a part of this family and never has been." Dorothy leaned forward and shot a penetrating look at Travis. *"And she never will be."*

Travis was too tired to get upset at the implied threat. "Why did you give her away?"

"That's none of your business."

He tilted the chair onto its back legs, something he knew would annoy her. "Would you rather I asked Dad?"

For the first time, she faltered. "It won't do you any good. As far as he's concerned, she's dead."

"And that's obviously the way you want it to stay. I'm willing to bet you would do just about anything to keep him from finding out what you did."

She grew wary. "What's that supposed to mean?"

He let the silence grow between them, waiting for her to figure it out for herself. "Why did you give Amy away?" he pointedly asked again.

"You couldn't possibly understand."

"Try me."

"You're taking the side of someone you don't even know against your own mother?" When he didn't answer, she gave him another shot. "I'll never forgive you for this, Travis."

"I guess that's something I'm going to have to live with."

"Have you thought this through? I'm the connecting link in this family. I'm the one who holds everything together. Without me the rest of you would just drift. Do you want that to happen?"

She was waiting for his reaction before deciding which direction to go next, but the words and attempts to manipulate were too familiar to have the desired effect on him. Travis had learned to hide his feelings around her, good or bad. It was a matter of self-preservation.

"Why are all the rest of you entitled to your mistakes," she said, sounding martyred now, "but I have to be held accountable for mine?"

She was good, better than anyone he'd ever known. "It isn't going to work this time, Mom. I need answers. If I can't get them from you, I'll get them any way I can."

"You couldn't possibly understand what I was going through back then."

"I promise I'll try." He leaned across the desk to take her hand, hoping the physical contact would reassure her. She purposely sat back, stuck her hands in her pockets, and glared at him.

"Don't try to make up to me. I told you, if you force me to do this, I will never forgive you."

He settled deeper into his chair. "Then why don't you just tell me and get it over with?"

"I was almost six months pregnant when I received word your father was dead. He didn't have to go to Vietnam, you know. He was married and had two children. The worst part was that he waited until the war was almost over before he decided he had to volunteer. He said it was his duty, that his father and his grandfather had fought for their country and, by God, he wasn't going to stay home any longer just because he could."

Growing up, Travis had tried to talk to his father about the war. Gus would never give any but the simplest answers—until one day when Travis was fifteen and the ranch was in the middle of a brutally hard winter. They were alone on horseback, looking for strays, when, without prompting, Gus started talking about the daughter who had died when he was half a world away. Travis had long ago forgotten the words, but the heartache and guilt in his father's voice he would remember forever.

"The rest of the country was out marching and burning flags protesting the war, and your father was at the recruiting office. I begged him not to go, but he wouldn't listen. He knew how hard it would be for me to stay here without him. I hated living so close to his parents; they were forever in our business. Harold would come right in without knocking—made no difference whether it was morning or night. Every time I'd go outside to work in the yard, Gladys would be at the window watching me.

"When they died, everyone said how remarkable it was that I made it through their funerals dry-eyed. Not one person—not even your father—guessed the truth. I was rejoicing in my freedom."

Her anger was fresh and sharp, as if it had been yesterday instead of all those years ago. And her secret wasn't as well kept as she imagined. Nothing she could say about his grandmother and grandfather would surprise him. Dorothy Martell held her bag of prejudices and resentments close, acting as if it were filled with diamonds instead of coal. A slight by someone more popular in high school carried as much weight as the banker who'd denied her the loan to start the sporting goods store. Travis had no doubt she would carry through with her threat to him.

"Why did you leave Jackson when you thought Dad was dead?" Travis asked.

Dorothy picked up a pen from the desk, held it between two fingers, and tapped it against the blotter. "Your grandmother never stopped crying the three weeks I stayed. She almost drove me crazy."

"What did she say when you told her you were leaving?"

"She begged me not to go. But it wasn't me she wanted to keep around, it was you kids. She said you were all she had left of Gus and she couldn't stand losing you, too. I told her I needed to be with my own family, and that I'd be back after the baby was born."

She tried to hide the smile that followed. "I might not have gone to college the way she did, but I was smart enough not to give something for nothing."

"Did you mean it, about coming back?"

She tossed the pen on the desk. "Your father left me without anything." Travis had unwittingly thrown fresh kindling on her smoldering anger. "He had a basic life insurance policy that just about covered what it would take to bury him, and the measly checks the government sent, but that was it. He told me we couldn't afford to buy anything more. He was right, we couldn't, not with what his father paid him. We lived like beggars. Everything the ranch made the two of them put right back in. Your grandfather had Gus convinced we shouldn't let the scrimping we had to do get to us, we were investing in our family's future. Which was all right, as long as Gus was alive. With him dead, I was tough out of luck. There was no way your grandfather was ever going to turn this place over to me. The only power I had was you kids. If I made it too easy to be with you, they would never appreciate the sacrifice I had to make to stay here."

"Let me get this straight. The real reason you left was to get Grandma and Grandpa to give you Dad's interest in the ranch?"

"You see? I knew it would be like this. You aren't even trying to understand what I went through."

"I'm sorry." They weren't just words, he meant them. He was sorry that he couldn't take her side, that he couldn't defend her, that he couldn't balance the loving, caring things she had done for the four children she had kept with the one she had abandoned.

"I wasn't just looking out for myself, you know. You kids needed protecting, too. It was your inheritance they were dangling in front of me to get me to come back."

"Wouldn't you have been in an even stronger position with three grandchildren?"

"I considered that. And if I'd had a boy, I probably would have kept him despite everything else."

"Everything else?" Travis repeated.

"I couldn't put all of my eggs in the Martell basket. I had to have a contingency plan in case they decided they could live without us after all. I figured finding a man who wanted to take on two children who didn't belong to him was going to be hard enough, three would make it damn near impossible."

There it was. The biological flip of the coin that had determined Amy's fate, made with emotionless logic. "I'm amazed you could be so clear thinking so soon after being told Dad was dead."

"I didn't have time to grieve. I was six months pregnant by then."

"Did Grandma Hart know about Amy?" He didn't understand why it mattered, only that it did.

"Of course she did. I never could have managed without her. She was the one who found the lawyer who arranged the adoption."

Travis wiped both hands across his face, suddenly, overwhelmingly tired. "I can understand why it would be hard for you to tell Dad about this now, but don't you think having Amy in his life would help him get over his disappointment?"

"Is that what you think this is all about? That I'm worried how your father will react?"

"It isn't?"

She made a dismissive wave with her hand. "Gus would forgive me anything."

Again she'd taken him by surprise. "Then where's the problem?"

Dorothy got up and walked over to the wall with all the plaques and honors she'd gathered for her

years of work with various state and local civic orga-
nizations and charities. Staring at her awards, her
back to him, she said, "I've worked too hard to get
where I am. I'm not about to let some pathetic
woman who couldn't make it on her own come in
and take it all away from me."

"What are you talking about? How is Amy going
to take anything away from you?"

She whipped around to look at him. "Don't play
dumb, Travis. You know as well as I do, once it gets
out that I lied to Gus about his daughter, I'll be as
welcome as a drought. Everyone around here thinks
your father's some goddamn saint. He could steal
money out of the poor box at church and people
would start a collection to give him more."

Travis was seeing a side to his mother he'd never
seen before, one he wished had never been revealed.
He didn't know what to say. He'd come to appeal to
the woman he'd believed her to be, not this stranger.
"I'm sure once everyone saw how sorry you were
they would—"

"It isn't going to happen, so there isn't any reason
to talk about it anymore." She went back to her desk
and sat down in her chair, rolling it forward as if she
were preparing to go to work. "Now unless you have
something else you wanted to say, I've got a dozen
things I need to get done this morning."

Travis stood and leaned over the desk, looking
down at her. "Just out of curiosity, how do you plan
to stop me from talking to Dad?"

She gave him the well-practiced, intimidating
look she'd used on her children their entire lives. It
was usually followed by, "Because I told you so."
To disobey carried the promise of some terrible,
mysterious consequences. "I forbid you to tell
him."

He blinked in surprise. "You actually think that's going to work?"

"Have you thought about what this will do to Gus?"

"That's the angle you should have worked, Mom." He put his baseball cap back on, adjusted the brim, and then flicked it with the tip of his finger to raise it a quarter inch. "You might have won me over if you could have convinced me you gave a damn about anyone but yourself."

"Why are you blaming me for what happened?"

"Who should I be blaming?"

"Your father. He knew he might be killed in that stupid war, but did he do anything to provide for his family in case he died? No, he was too busy playing hero to think about us. How was I supposed to raise three kids with what the government paid widows?" She paused to see if she had gained any ground, then added, "Everything I did was for you and Sharon."

"Is there anyone else you want to add?"

"You'll be sorry, Travis," Dorothy vowed. "And so will she if you bring her here."

An image of Amy in her hospital bed flashed into Travis's mind. "If you try to take any of this out on her, I'll consider it my personal mission to make sure every person in this state knows what you did."

"How can you do this to me?" She shot up and came around the desk. "Where is your loyalty? How can you cold-bloodedly set out to destroy your own mother?"

"How could you cold-bloodedly give away your own daughter?"

"It wasn't as if I dumped her in some alley. I made sure she was going to a good home. The man who adopted her was a doctor. They had lots of money. And they wanted her, I didn't. Damn it, I did what I thought was best. Why am I being punished now?"

He didn't want to see her side. And he didn't want to hurt his father. But what about Amy? Where did her rights come in?

"Maybe when Amy finds out, she won't want anything to do with us."

"You mean she still doesn't know?" Dorothy jumped on the news like a mosquito on a bare arm.

He considered telling her what Amy had gone through that past week but decided it wouldn't make any difference. "I wanted to clear everything here first."

"Don't tell her, Travis," she pleaded. "You'll only confuse her. She's built a life for herself where she is. Tell her and you'll destroy that life."

He didn't have to. If Amy continued on the course she'd already set, eventually she would succeed in destroying herself. In his mother's own perverse way, she had just convinced him that he didn't have any real choice.

"Do you want to tell Dad," he said as gently as he could manage, "or do you want me to?"

She backed away. "You're really going to do it? No matter what I say?"

"I'm sorry—"

"You're choosing her over me? A stranger over your own mother?"

"It isn't a matter of choice."

"If you do this, you're no son of mine. I don't want to see you here again—ever."

"Then you'd better stay inside and keep the curtains closed," he said. "I have no intention of abandoning Dad. As long as he's here, I will be, too."

Twenty

Travis was on his way into town to find his father when he decided he was tired of playing God. The role was one he'd never intended, the robes were too big, the decisions too hard.

Once he told his father about Amy, there would be no turning back. August Martell, more than any other man Travis had ever known, was an integral part of his children's lives. He could no more turn his back on one of them than he could leave a wounded animal to die on its own.

Travis sought a familiar refuge for the few remaining hours that his father could still believe his world was good, and right, and in order. He drove into the mountains behind his house, parked at the end of the narrow dirt road, and walked until he came to an opening in the forest. The meadow had a stream that ran year-round, fed from snow that never completely melted on the distant peak.

There was a rock here, cracked and chipped by centuries of water relentlessly filling every fissure, freezing, and expanding. Pieces had disappeared from the enormous boulder, leaving a near perfect chair, the arms cushioned by lichen, the seat by pine needles. Both provided insulation against the cold.

Whenever something was bothering him, Travis would come to this place to be alone and to think. Often he was here at sunrise. Sometimes it was as the day folded into itself, yielding to night. Always he came away with a sense of proportion, his troubles in perspective.

Today the sky was the warm blue of summer, the pines sporting fragrant new growth. It took only minutes for the squirrels and chipmunks that had disappeared at his approach to come out of hiding and go on with their business.

Given a choice, he would have been born when the Shoshone were the only residents of the valley, before the farmers and ranchers came to fence off the land and destroy the natural migration routes and feeding grounds of the deer and elk. His great-grandfather had passed down stories of the battles between settlers and elk, of a winter when a man had claimed to walk a mile on the dead and dying animals, some lying four deep. Now the elk were a tourist attraction, fed alfalfa during severe winters on a seeded and irrigated refuge.

When Travis had brought groups of people into the backcountry, he'd tried to give them a sense of what he believed Jackson Hole had been back then. He wanted them to feel the freedom and exhilarate in the danger of being someplace wild and untamed. When they went home he wanted them to remember how the stars looked without ambient light, to be able to close their eyes and hear the sounds of a living forest, to savor the adrenaline rush that came with seeing a wild animal living free.

His sister Sharon claimed pine tar ran through his veins, that he would be content living in a one-room cabin on a mountainside, his beard down to his knees, and a bear for best friend. She was only half-right. He needed people more than she knew. He was even beginning to think he was finally ready to settle down, whatever the hell that meant.

The need for someone to share his life must have been growing inside him for some time. It was the only way he could explain the strange attraction he felt for Diana. They barely knew each other and couldn't be more of a mismatch. Yet he hadn't been able to stop thinking about her since leaving Minneapolis.

Even with everything else that was going on, she was there with him, an ever present distraction. And it wasn't just because she was inextricably tied to Amy. Kissing Diana was what he remembered, and the way she wore her hair, and how he'd felt the first time she smiled at him.

There was an explanation for why he was attracted to Diana, something that would put his feelings into perspective and flatten the emotional roller-coaster ride. He just had to figure out what it was.

But that would take time, and right now his first priority was his father and Sharon. Travis had been willing to let his mother tell Gus about Amy, but not Sharon. He didn't want her ambushed with the news or prejudiced in the telling. If Amy decided to come there to meet them, Sharon would be a critical ally. She was the only sister who had been alive when Amy was born, old enough to know the promised baby had not come home with her mother, old enough to feel the loss.

The sun had moved behind Travis now. The trees cast long shadows across his rock. He was cold and had run out of reasons to stay.

He'd promised his mother time to talk to his father first and hoped to hell she'd taken him up on it. Travis didn't mind filling in the details, but there was no way he wanted to break the news. His father deserved an explanation, and his mother was the one who should give it to him.

Travis hiked back to his truck. On impulse, he stopped by the house to see if Diana had called about Amy. Disappointed there was no message, he walked out on the porch and was preparing to leave again when Gus pulled into the driveway. One look and Travis knew why he was there.

"I'm glad I caught you," Gus said.

Travis went over to meet him. "You want to come inside? I'll put on some coffee."

"Yeah . . . I guess I do." He took off his battered Stetson and tossed it on the front seat. Neither said anything as they went into the house.

Gus sat at the kitchen table while Travis made the coffee. Heated water dropped into a filter holding twice the recommended grounds; the pot had been turned to its darkest setting. Thick, dark liquid streamed into the carafe, filling the compact room with its heavy aroma. Travis removed a couple of mugs from the cupboard, added sugar to his father's and nothing to his own.

Gus took a long swallow before he put the mug on the table and laid his hand over the top. "You may not be able to cook worth a damn, but you make a hell of a cup of coffee."

"I had a great teacher." Travis pulled out a chair and sat opposite his father, his legs stuck out to the side, crossed at the ankles, his arm resting on the table. They might have been there to discuss the crops, or the weather, or buying a new piece of equipment. Only a subtle, unacknowledged tension set the afternoon apart from any other.

"I miss those camping trips we used to take when we'd tell your mom we were looking for strays," Gus said. "There's nothing feels as good as crawling out of a sleeping bag in the morning and standing in a patch of sun till it bakes the kinks out of your back."

"There's no reason we can't go again." At that moment Travis would have done anything to ease the sadness he saw in his father's eyes.

"I'd like that."

A silence grew between them, begging to be broken. Finally Travis said, "Mom told you?" It wasn't as much a question as a statement.

"Some of it." He took another drink of coffee. This time he held the mug suspended between his hands rather than returning it to the table. He stared into the dark liquid a long time, as if searching for what he would say next. "I came here to get the rest of it."

Because Travis had no idea what would be important to his father and what wouldn't, he started at the beginning. The days he'd spent with Diana learning about Amy through her eyes turned into a history not even he had been aware he knew. He told about Amy's childhood and how she had fought for attention and love that were denied her by the man and woman who had adopted her.

Gus asked questions, and when he could, Travis answered them. But there was a lot he couldn't tell his father, things that Diana either didn't know herself or had chosen not to share with him. He couldn't tell Gus what color Amy's eyes were, only that Diana had said her smile was like his. He had no idea whether Amy was shy or outspoken, whether she liked to read or what kind of music she listened to— more important, he had no idea who had given her the beating that had almost cost her her life, or why.

"What are you thinking?" Travis asked his father when the questions stopped.

"I never understood why I couldn't let that little girl go," Gus said softly. He looked at Travis as he tapped his fist against his chest. "She's been right here with me all these years. I always figured it had to be the guilt that made me hang on the way I did. I was so sure her dying was my fault, that if I'd tried harder to get out of that jungle sooner, your mother wouldn't have lost her."

Travis recoiled at the pain he heard in his father's voice. How could he know so little about this man he'd been with all his life? "You hardly ever talked about her."

Gus shook his head. "I couldn't."

"What do you want to do now?"

"It doesn't matter what I want." He stood and took his cup to the sink. "Whatever happens next is up to Amy." He stared out into the yard, his back to Travis. "Amy . . . It's a pretty name, don't you think? I knew a gal named Amy once. She was . . ." He took a paper towel, wiped his eyes, and blew his nose. When he spoke again it was as if he'd gone somewhere else, unaware that Travis was even in the room with him. "I knew she was going to be a girl. Right from the start I told Dorothy I wanted to call her Diana—after that Greek goddess. There was the prettiest moon I'd ever seen the night she was conceived. I just knew she was going to grow up to be someone special. When I found out she'd died, I think a part of me did, too."

Gus shook himself free of the memories and turned to face Travis. "I've never told anyone about the name thing." He crumpled the paper towel into a ball and tossed it into the garbage. "What do you suppose the odds are that she would wind up with a sister named Diana? Kind of makes you think there was some master plan playing itself out, doesn't it?"

Travis tried to imagine what Gus was going through but lacked the most basic understanding of what it would feel like to create a child and then have the child taken away.

For almost twenty-six years his father had struggled to find a way to live with a daughter's death. Now he had to find a way to deal with his wife's lies.

"What do you think, Travis? Is she going to want to come back to us?"

"I don't know," he answered truthfully. "She's got some problems she needs to work out."

Gus leaned against the sink and stared hard at Travis. "What kind of problems?"

Travis hesitated. There was no use pretending Amy had come away from her upbringing untroubled. "Diana said she'd talked to a counselor about Amy. He said it seemed to him that she was hell-bent on self-destruction."

"You mean she's trying to kill herself?"

"Not directly. You remember Jack Fender's son— the one who was always in trouble?"

"Yeah . . ."

"Amy does the same kinds of things."

"I still say that kid would have been all right if his dad had put his hand on his shoulder once in a while instead of always on his backside."

"Like I said, Amy rowed the same boat, right down to having the same kind of parents."

"You're going to have to make it a little plainer than that, Travis. I'm still not seeing the connection."

"Amy does things that get her in trouble, things that aren't good for her. Sometimes what she does is dangerous."

"Get to the point."

There was no way to soften the blow. "She's been in rehab for drugs and alcohol." Amy's arrest for prostitution was her story to tell. The important part was that Gus understand Amy's downward spiral and why she needed them now.

Drugs and alcohol were a fact of life in a town

like Jackson, where the wealthy and famous came to pay and play. "But she's all right now?"

Travis didn't know how to answer him. "Diana seems to think so, at least about the drugs and drinking." He couldn't let it go at that; his father had been lied to enough. "There's something else going on, Dad. I could tell you about it, but I'd rather let Amy."

"What did Diana say when you asked her why she came looking for us?"

"That Amy needed her real family."

"Did she say why now, after all this time?" Gus put the pieces together as he always did, slowly, methodically, and unerringly.

"Something happened that scared her. She decided she'd rather lose Amy to us than lose her forever."

Gus wiped his hand across his face. "Your mom doesn't want anything to do with her."

"I know," Travis said.

"Have you told Sharon?"

"Not yet."

"Well, we'd better get on it before your mother does. We're going to need her help when Amy comes home."

Travis had never loved or admired his father more than he did at that moment. "What about Mom?"

Gus pushed himself away from the counter. "What about her?"

"She's going to fight you on this."

"It doesn't matter." He started across the room, his limp giving him a rocking gait. "What she wants doesn't count anymore."

Travis had a sinking feeling the world he'd known hadn't just suffered a wound, it had been irrevocably laid to waste. What would it do to Amy when she found out she was the cause?

Twenty-one

Diana stepped out of her heels as she flipped on the hall
light and hung up her purse. It was ten-fifteen and
she hadn't eaten anything since lunch. Her feet hurt,
her head hurt, her back hurt, and yet she was still
smiling. Amy had seemed almost herself that night.
She was coming back a lot faster than any of her doctors had believed possible. They were even talking
about moving her out of intensive care and into a
regular room in a day or two.

While she and Stephanie were still spending
every spare minute at the hospital, it wasn't an
around-the-clock marathon anymore. Diana had
actually gone back to work that morning to attend a
meeting to review revised proposals from advertising.
She was surprised to discover she was actually able to
concentrate on what everyone was saying.

After the meeting she took Bill Summersby aside to
tell him about Amy. He asked all the right questions,
showed genuine concern, and told her he would do
what he could to cover for her, but that after all the
meetings she'd missed the first time Amy was in the
hospital, they desperately needed her to be at the office.

She headed for the kitchen, shrugging out of her suit jacket and unbuttoning the neck of her blouse as she went. She shed the jacket and her panty hose on the landing to be taken upstairs later when she changed clothes. A familiar, small stab of disappointment hit when she saw there weren't any messages on the answering machine.

Travis had been gone for four days and she hadn't heard a word from him. He hadn't said he would call, but she'd convinced herself he would—if not to keep in touch with her, at least to find out how Amy was doing.

Maybe he was waiting for her to call. He'd left both his work and home numbers under a magnet on the refrigerator with a note saying when he expected to be where. If she wanted to talk to him, why didn't she just pick up the phone and call?

Damn, how had their relationship gotten so complicated?

If she still hadn't heard from him by tomorrow, she would break down and call. What possible difference could it make who initiated the contact? She had a legitimate reason for wanting to talk to him. Until he made up his mind whether to tell his father or not, she couldn't say anything to Amy. Not that she would tell Amy about the Martells now. Even if the news was good, it was going to have to wait until she was out of the hospital.

Diana started opening cupboards, looking for something easy. There were lots of canned things—tomatoes, beans, olives—ingredients, not meals. She wasn't in the mood to order pizza, and the only thing in the refrigerator that she was sure wasn't on its second leg was lemon yogurt—Amy's favorite, but the one flavor Diana couldn't abide.

Somehow she was going to have to find the time

to go grocery shopping. Until then . . . until then, what?

She grabbed a bag of popcorn and threw it in the microwave. She'd had worse dinners. At least popcorn had fiber—and fat and salt, her inner voice reminded her.

The doorbell rang at the same time the microwave beeped. She glanced at the clock. Stephanie's date must have ended a lot earlier than she'd planned. Diana grabbed the popcorn and dropped it on the counter before she went to answer the door.

"What are you doing back here?" she asked as she opened the door.

But it wasn't Stephanie. Diana caught her breath in surprise. She'd tried to imagine how she would feel if Travis came back, never doubting she would be happy to see him but never suspecting a physical reaction that would push her heart into her throat and put her IQ on hold. "I'm sorry," she said. "I thought you were—"

"I should have called first." His gaze shifted to her untucked blouse and then her bare feet. He gave her a quick, apologetic smile. "From the looks of it, maybe it was a good thing my plane was late or I might have interrupted something."

She didn't understand. "What are you talking about?"

Travis shifted the strap of his duffel bag higher on his shoulder. "Obviously you had company."

"No, I didn't. I just got home from the hospital." She looked down at herself. "Oh, you mean because I look this way?"

"It doesn't matter," Travis said. "I just wanted to come by and let you know I was in town."

She tried not to, but she smiled. "You thought I had a man here with me?"

He shrugged. "It's possible you and Stuart might have decided to try to work things out."

"Would you care?" She was leading with her chin, something she never did.

"It really isn't my business to care what you do or who you see."

"Would you care?" she insisted.

He stared at her a long time before he said, "Yeah, I would."

"Now that we have that out of the way, why don't you come in?"

Travis stepped past her and dropped his duffel bag on the floor. They stared at each other a long time before he took her in his arms. Her soft cry of release was all the encouragement he needed. He kissed her as if they were longtime lovers, intimately and without restraint. Any thought he'd had to hold back or try to deny his feelings disappeared when she returned his kiss. The heat emanating from her was the most erotic thing he had ever experienced.

He didn't give a damn anymore if what was happening between them made sense or whether they were reacting to some emotional storm that held them hostage. She was strong, and she was beautiful, and she made him feel good just thinking about her.

He put his hands on the sides of her face and stroked her cheeks with his thumbs. With a half smile, he echoed her earlier statement: "Now that we have that out of the way, how is Amy?"

She put her hands over his. "I need a second to catch my breath." All her life she'd lived by a set of rules that told her what to feel and think and expect. She'd felt safe in their confines, even knowing her position was purchased with freedom. Travis wasn't a part of that world. He operated on instinct, acting as if freedom were his due. "Are you always so . . ." She struggled to find the words. "So . . . sure of yourself?"

"Was I wrong?"

She closed the door. "That's not the point."

"Then what is?"

"I've never known anyone like you." How could she explain what was going through her head? "What would you have done if Stuart had come back?" It wasn't what she'd intended to ask, but she wanted to hear his answer.

Travis smiled. "I would have wondered what in the hell you were doing with him when you felt the way you do about me."

"How do you know how I feel?"

"I can see it in your eyes." He stepped closer. His voice dropped to a low whisper when he said, "Just the way you can see it in mine."

A powerful yearning sent waves of heat racing through her body. He might as well have put his hand on her breast or between her legs. How could Travis do with words what Stuart hadn't been able to do in bed?

"This is happening too fast," she said, putting her hand on his chest and backing herself into the corner.

"If it had been up to me, it wouldn't have happened at all." He picked up his bag again. "I don't need this any more than you do."

"Where are you going?"

"To a hotel."

"Why?"

He gave her an exasperated look. "Are you serious?"

"Yes . . . no." She started to tuck in her blouse, then realized how foolish she looked. "I don't know what I want."

"Well, I do," he said gently. "But it's not going to happen until you're sure, too."

"Don't go." She added quickly, "At least not yet. I haven't told you about Amy."

He put the bag back down. "And I haven't told you about my father and Sharon."

"They know? I thought you weren't going to say anything. What made you change your mind?"

"First, how is Amy doing?"

"Fantastic. She's even beginning to look like herself again. That enormous bandage is finally gone, and she isn't that terrible gray color anymore. Her doctors are even talking about moving her out of intensive care in a couple of days." God, she was glad he'd come back. She'd missed him the way she did sunshine, not realizing how much until the rain had passed and the clouds were gone. For all the joy Amy's recovery had given, something had been missing. Now she knew what it was.

"I want to see her." He leaned his shoulder into the wall. "I need you to help me come up with something she'll believe that we won't have to explain later."

There were dark circles under his eyes. The trip home must have been hell on him. "Come with me to the kitchen and we'll talk about it. I just made some popcorn and I'm willing to share."

"Next time," he said. "If I don't find a hotel, I'm going to wind up sleeping here whether I want to or not."

She took his hand and led him down the hall to the spare room. "The shape you're in, I'm sure we can manage the night together. You can find a hotel tomorrow."

He tossed his bag on the bed. "Still, I don't think I'm going to kiss you good night."

There it was again, that damn heat. "Good idea."

*   *   *

Travis was still asleep when Diana went to work the next morning. She left him a note on the kitchen table along with a thermos of coffee.

> *Travis,*
>   *With any luck you'll sleep in until noon and we can meet for lunch. If you happen to get up earlier, you're welcome to anything you can find in the kitchen. I'm embarrassed to admit the offer is more challenge than generosity. Stay away from the refrigerator. Everything in there is either green or growing, and I don't want you winding up in the hospital, too. I know you're anxious to see Amy, but now that she's awake, mornings aren't a good visiting time. They have rounds and give baths and a hundred other things. Besides, we still need to come up with a way to explain you—which we can do over lunch. I rode in with Stephanie, so the car is yours. The keys are on the hall table. Call me after you read this, and I'll give you directions to the restaurant.*
> *Diana*

Travis glanced at the clock before he poured himself a cup of coffee. It was nine-thirty, and he was starved. He took a swallow and grimaced at the anemic liquid.

The phone rang. He considered letting the machine pick up, then realized it could be Diana.

It was his father.

Gus stammered for several seconds and then said, "I was expecting a machine."

"Are you all right?" He'd given his father Diana's number as a way to get in touch with him in an emergency.

"I was hoping to catch you before you talked to Amy. Have you told her anything yet?" Gus asked.

"I haven't even seen her yet. My plane got in late last night. I've only been up about five minutes."

There was a long pause. "You just got out of bed and you're answering the phone at Diana's?"

Travis closed his eyes and gritted his teeth. He'd been so careful not to let on to anyone at home how close he and Diana had become, and now he'd given it away by answering the damned telephone. "Don't go making something out of nothing," he said, trying for a light tone. "I was really tired when I got here last night and Diana let me stay in her extra bedroom."

"She sounds like a nice person."

August Martell was the most trusting man Travis had ever known. He hated lying to him, even by omission. "Why did you want to talk to me before I saw Amy?"

"I was thinking maybe it would be better if you put off telling her about us for a couple of days."

Gut instinct told him his mother was up to something. Travis turned to look out the window. There were thick black clouds moving in from the west. They mirrored the sudden shift in his mood. "What's wrong?"

"Sharon called and told me your mother chased Faith and Judy down in France a couple of days ago. They're on their way home, coming in sometime this afternoon." Gus stopped, took a deep breath, and let it out again before he went on. "There's no telling what she's said to them. Until I find out, I figured it might be best if Amy wasn't involved. I know you think she's going to want to wait a while before she calls, but I didn't want to take the chance."

"She's not going to call, Dad. At least not right away."

"Did something happen? Is she worse?"

"She's fine. But she's still in intensive care. I don't plan to say anything to her until she's a hundred percent again, or near to it."

"When do you think that will be?"

"I'll have a better idea after I see her this afternoon."

"You'll call me?" Gus asked.

Travis did some quick figuring, calculating the time difference and when he felt he would have a chance to call. "Where will you be tonight after supper?"

"At home."

"If I miss you for some reason, do you want me to leave a message with Mom? I wouldn't have to go into detail, just let you know I'd seen Amy and that she looked okay."

"She won't be there."

It wasn't the words so much as the way Gus had said them that alerted Travis. "Why not?"

"She's moved out."

Suddenly, overwhelmingly tired again, Travis pulled out a chair and sat down. "When did this happen?"

"A couple of days ago."

"You didn't say anything." He put his elbow on the table and braced his head with his hand.

"I figured you had enough on your mind. Besides, this is between your mom and me. I don't want you kids feeling you're caught in the middle or that you have to take sides."

Things were beginning to fall into place. He understood now why his mother had called Faith and Judy and why she wanted them to come home. The coffee turned to acid in his stomach. "Is Mom staying with Sharon?"

"Sharon told her she didn't think it would be a good idea for her to move in there. She's staying at Roger's place for now."

Roger was Sharon's brother-in-law, a computer nerd who'd hit it big producing nonviolent video games for teenagers. He had a house in Teton Village that had been featured in magazines both for its Frank Lloyd Wright type of architecture and for its innovative use of technology. Dorothy hated the place and had never been shy about saying so. Travis had often wondered if the knife she used for cutting wasn't honed with envy.

"I'm sorry, Dad. I never thought it would come to this."

"There's nothing for you to feel sorry about," Gus said harshly. "You did what you thought was right, and I'm damned proud of you."

"What if Amy decides she doesn't want to be part of our family after all?" Travis was beginning to wonder if there was going to be any family left for Amy to be a part of. "All of this would have been for nothing."

"Just knowing she didn't die is enough. All those years I blamed myself . . . "

His father's voice became so soft, Travis had to strain to hear the rest.

"I'm free of it now," Gus finished.

"Do you want me to come home to talk to Judy and Faith?"

"No, let your mother do that."

"They need to hear both sides." There were times his father's belief in fair play bordered on naiveté.

"They will, in time."

Travis knew it was useless to push any harder. "I'll call you tonight."

"God, I wish I were there with you. I've got so much I want to tell her."

"Yeah, I wish you were here, too." Travis told him good-bye, hung up, and said a silent prayer that someday Amy would want to listen.

Twenty-two

The first wave of patrons at the restaurant were women who came in together carrying shopping bags. They talked nonstop, scanned their menus when prodded by a waiter, and drank white wine. Second came men and women dressed in gray and navy and black business suits. They greeted each other with enthusiastic handshakes and expansive smiles, studied their menus in silence, and drank designer water.

Travis looked over his menu, decided on his choice—a Reuben sandwich—and then tried to guess what Diana would order. He settled on the Chinese chicken salad with the dressing on the side.

As he'd been doing since he was seated, he glanced up when he saw the door open. This time his effort was rewarded. Diana came in wearing the seemingly obligatory suit, only hers was tan with narrow blue stripes, cut to hide the curves underneath. For Travis it only fed his imagination.

Diana waved off the hostess when she spotted him. Her smile was that of a lover's, intimate and excited, as if for her he was the only man in the room. Somehow during the wary dance of getting to know each other their hearts had bypassed their minds. Something cataclysmic would have to happen to wrest it away.

Travis had dreamed this moment, not as a child, but as a man—one who'd begun to believe it would never happen.

He stood and held her chair, a politeness he knew but rarely used with a contemporary. She rewarded him with another smile.

"Have you been waiting long?" she asked.

"No," he lied.

"People kept stopping me on the way out of the office. All hell is breaking loose with the new ad agency." She picked up her menu.

"So what can you do about it?"

She lowered the menu and studied Travis. "You don't have to do that."

"Do what?" he asked.

"Pretend you're interested."

"I never do. My sister insists it's one of my many flaws."

"Which sister?"

Travis could see the question had cost her. Diana had admitted over popcorn the night before that she was only now beginning to realize what it might be like to have to share Amy. "Sharon—she thinks it's her job to mold me into a socially acceptable human being."

The waiter came to take their orders. Diana chose the pasta special until she heard what Travis was having and decided to have a Reuben, too.

Travis shook his head. "I had you figured for a salad," he admitted.

"Why?"

"Because you're so skinny."

"I'm not skinny," she said defensively. "It's just the way this suit is made. It hides my—"

"I'm sorry, I meant to say thin. See what happens when I don't have a sister around to correct me?" Travis asked.

"It's not your fault. I promised myself I wouldn't do that anymore."

"What in the hell are you talking about?"

She picked up her water and took a drink, putting off answering him. "Stuart used to call me skinny whenever he thought I was putting on weight. It was his way of telling me I needed to go on a diet."

"I don't play those kinds of games, Diana. How much you weigh or don't weigh doesn't mean a damn to me. What I care about is more basic. I want to know what you look like naked . . . and what your eyes are like when they're hooded and hungry." His gaze dropped to her breasts and then to her waist. "I know making love to you can't be as good as I've imagined, but that doesn't keep me from thinking about it all the time. Like right now. I'd even skip lunch to find out what's underneath that horrible suit."

"What makes you think it can't be as good?" she challenged. "And what's wrong with this suit? And what do you mean, *even* skip lunch? I'll have you know I'm worth at least a week of meals."

He laughed. "Now there's the real Diana Winchester. Where was she when you were living with that jerk Stuart?"

"I don't know. I've asked myself that question a hundred times since he left."

The waiter returned with a basket of bread and an ornate bottle filled with olive oil. With a practiced flourish, he poured the oil onto their bread plates, making a circle with an X in the middle. When he finished he put the bottle on the table, made a slight bow, and left.

"I never have the heart to tell them I prefer butter," Diana said, watching the oil merge into a small pond.

His mind was miles away from what to put on bread. He shouldn't have said what he had about wanting to make love to her, especially after last night. It was tempting to pretend whatever was happening between them was an island off to itself, neither affected nor influenced by the storm surrounding Amy, but he was too much of a realist to buy into it for long. He'd experienced lust and understood its elements. This wasn't it. He wanted Diana, but he wouldn't be content with her body alone.

"I've lost you," Diana said.

"No, you haven't."

"You know, you shouldn't tease me like that. What would you do if I took you seriously?"

"Try me," he said.

"We shouldn't be doing this."

They were the words he needed to hear. "You're right. It's the wrong place . . . and the wrong time."

Travis didn't want bread, and he sure as hell didn't want it dripping with olive oil, but he needed something to do. He reached inside the basket and broke off a corner of the fragrant sourdough. He offered the first piece to Diana. She shook her head. He dipped a corner and took a bite. "I was just thinking how different my life was two weeks ago."

"I don't let myself do that," she said. "I'd go crazy if I did."

"One day at a time, huh?"

"I'm afraid to look too far ahead. There are too many things I can't control that could change my life forever."

"Like?"

"Your father and sister. You still haven't told me

how they reacted when you told them. Was Gus as hurt as you thought he'd be?"

He gave her a shortened version, ending with, "Right now he's most concerned about Judy and Faith being forced to take sides. He doesn't want Amy to come home and find herself in the middle of a battle."

"That sounds so strange—come home. Amy has never been in Wyoming."

"Do you think it would it be better if they came here?"

Somehow the idea had never occurred to her. She'd always imagined Amy going to them. Not until she thought about it did she understand why. Minneapolis was a prison for Amy. She didn't need visitors, she needed to escape.

"No," Diana said. "She'll want to go there."

When the waiter brought their sandwiches they began to eat without talking, as if glad of the opportunity to focus on something else.

Finally Diana broke the silence. "I won't be able to go to the hospital with you this afternoon. There's a meeting at work that I can't get out of, and . . ." She hesitated telling him about the phone call from her father and his insistence that she meet with him and her mother that afternoon. "And another thing I can't get out of. I was going to have the nurse tell Amy why I wasn't there, but Stephanie said she was dropping by the hospital around two and that she would take care of it." She picked at her coleslaw, her appetite gone. Giving up the pretense, she put her napkin on the table and sat back in her chair. "I'm going to need the car this afternoon, but I'll come by the condo and pick you up as soon as I can get away."

"Is there a reason you don't want me to go to the hospital by myself?"

There was an edge to the question that Diana

didn't understand. "Don't you think it would look a little strange if you just showed up? What will you say?"

"I'll tell Amy I'm a friend of yours."

"Someone who gets their kicks out of visiting strangers in hospitals?" She hadn't meant it to sound as sarcastic as it came out.

"Give me a little credit, would you?"

"I just think it would be easier if you waited."

"Easier for whom?"

"Amy, of course," she said defensively. "She's the only one I'm concerned about."

"You're acting as if she's your personal property."

"I care what happens to her. I'm not about to let some—" She caught herself, but not soon enough.

"Some what, Diana? Outsider?" He, too, laid his napkin on the table, the meal ended. "You keep forgetting, I'm her brother. If you wanted to keep Amy all to yourself, you never should have come to Wyoming. The Martells take care of their own."

A rage swept through Diana. "If that were true, we wouldn't be here, would we?"

He flinched. "No, we wouldn't."

The anger left Diana as quickly as it had come. "I'm sorry."

"I don't know what came over me."

"Me either." She looked at him in wonder. "I've fought *for* Amy all my life, but this is the first time I've ever fought *over* her. It feels so strange."

"Was that what it was like for you two when you were growing up?"

"I know it sounds perverse, but my parents are the reason Amy and I are so close. I don't think we could have overcome the five years between us any other way. I'm all she has." And she's all I have, Diana realized with startling clarity.

"Not anymore," Travis said gently.

Why was it so hard for her to let go when this was what she'd hoped for Amy? "Do you want me to call Stephanie and tell her she doesn't have to stop by the hospital?"

"Just tell her I'll be there, too."

Diana took a deep breath. "I guess I'll see you later, then."

"What time?"

She had no idea what her father wanted, let alone how long it would take. "I honestly don't know, but you probably shouldn't look for me before five." She glanced at her watch. Her meeting started in fifteen minutes.

He reached in his pocket and pulled out her keys. "Go on," he said. "I can find my way to the hospital."

She didn't want to leave. "Are you sure? It won't matter if I'm a few minutes late."

"I'll see you tonight, Diana."

She pushed her chair back and stood. "How can you afford to be away from work so long?"

His answer was too quick and too easy. "I'm the boss."

It didn't happen often, but every once in a while Diana saw behind Travis's facade. Always, she liked what she saw. She couldn't shake the feeling that somewhere there was a flaw, something to balance the good.

Travis spent his first half hour at the hospital trying to find Amy. The nurses in intensive care told him that she'd been moved to another wing but were too busy to stop what they were doing to look up precisely where. Travis tried several floors before he finally gave up and went downstairs to the visitor information desk.

On his way to the elevator again, he passed a cart filled with flowers waiting to be delivered to patients. The idea of doing something to mark the occasion of Amy leaving intensive care appealed to him. He doubled back to the gift shop. Because he had no idea what she liked, he chose the bouquet that appealed to him. It was filled with an assortment of colors and shapes, as if someone had walked through a garden and picked whatever happened to be in bloom.

By the time he got to Amy's room, he'd begun to wonder if the flowers had been such a good idea after all. Were they more than a simple "friend" of Diana's would think to bring? Even considering the attendant problems that would come with telling Amy who he was, Travis was anxious to get it over with. He didn't like keeping the truth from her.

He was almost relieved when he got to Amy's room and discovered her asleep. There were two beds in the room: Amy's, which was near the window, and one that was unoccupied, by the door. Travis put the flowers on a shelf opposite the bed, then quietly went to get a closer look at his sister.

She wasn't connected to anything anymore, not even an IV. There was a square gauze bandage on the side of her head where they'd shaved her hair and painted the skin orange. Otherwise she looked no more sick or in need of hospitalization than he did.

Out of a peculiar need to prove to himself she was alive, he touched the back of his finger to her cheek. He couldn't decide whether the physical resemblance was as strong as he thought or simply something he wanted to see. In sleep, with her high cheekbones and firm jaw, Amy was obviously Judy's sister, but the thick, arching brows and slightly upturned nose made her damn near the duplicate of Sharon. He tried to imagine what it would feel like to have a brother somewhere who looked like him. Would he resent the seeming intrusion on something so individual or feel a connection?

He'd attempted to prepare Sharon, but how could you prepare someone for something like this? On the surface there was an undeniable family tie. It seemed impossible that the similarities would stop there. But how could they go deeper? Sharon and Amy had been raised in different worlds. They shared genetic codes, not experiences.

Maybe when his mother actually met Amy, when she looked at her and saw how much of her other daughters were in this one, it would make a difference.

And maybe pigs would fly and that damned tractor the mechanic had flown out to fix would stop giving them trouble. Travis shoved his hands in the pockets of his jeans and stared out the window.

Amy wasn't sure what woke her, but even before she opened her eyes, she knew she wasn't alone. She listened a long time and then heard something—a chair being moved, someone sitting down. It wasn't Diana. She knew this as surely as she knew her sister was hiding something from her.

Finally curiosity overcame fatigue and she worked her eyes open, moving the lids a fraction at a time. It was amazing how much effort and concentration it could take to do something so simple.

The first thing she saw was an enormous bouquet. The flowers could only be from Diana. No one else knew how she hated the stiff arrangement that usually came from florists. Besides, Amy had elicited promises from both Diana and Stephanie that they would tell no one she was in the hospital. She'd even had Diana put a message on her machine saying she was out of town so no one would start looking for her.

Her gaze shifted to the window and then to the

chair. A man sat forward and gave her a slow smile. She was sure she didn't know him, yet there was a peculiar feeling of familiarity.

"How are you feeling?" His voice was soft, almost liquid. And it was warm, like a verbal caress.

Was he one of her doctors? She frowned. "Fine."

"Do you need anything? I saw a nurse walk by a couple of minutes ago."

"Do I know you?" She must not have asked very loudly because he got up to move closer.

"My name is Travis Martell. I'm a friend of your sister's."

"Is Diana here?"

"She had a meeting this afternoon, but she wanted me to tell you that she'd get here as soon as possible."

There was something about his voice, a memory she couldn't quite snag. "Why do I feel as if I know you?"

The question clearly made him uncomfortable. "I came to see you several times when you were still in intensive care. Maybe you recognize my voice."

"Maybe." It seemed a little farfetched, but there had to be some reason for the crazy connection she felt. A thought struck. "You said you came to see me in intensive care?"

"Yes," Travis answered warily.

"They only let family visit there."

Now he really did look uncomfortable, like a cat that had just realized there was no way down from the roof. He shrugged. "They must have changed the policy—Stephanie was there as much as I was."

"She told them she was my sister." She waited. He didn't say anything more. "What did you tell them?" she prompted.

"Why don't we talk about this later? You look tired, and I have—"

"What did you tell them?" Amy insisted. She was suddenly scared but couldn't fathom why.

He tried to smile. The effect was more ominous than reassuring. "I said I was your brother."

It was then she remembered the phone call she'd received less than five minutes before she'd blacked out, the one that had sent her racing down to Stephanie's apartment.

Amy looked at him, long and hard. At last she asked, "Are you?"

Twenty-three

Helen opened the kitchen door for Diana when she was still coming up the walkway. She put her finger to her mouth, motioning for her not to say anything. When Diana was closer, Helen whispered, "There's something going on. Be careful."

Diana didn't know whether she was just too tired or had been through too much in the past month to let the warning scare her. "Whatever it is, I hope it's worthwhile. I had to duck out of an important meeting to get here."

Helen took Diana's arm, as if by touch she could convey what words had failed to do. "I've never seen your father like this. He was yelling and using language I've never heard him use before, not even that time you wrecked his Mercedes."

Normally her father expressed anger with silence and a cold, intimidating stare. "Where is he?"

"In the living room with your mother."

Diana went inside. Her hushed voice became a whisper. Eileen would fire Helen if she caught her talking to Diana about "family" business. "Do you have any idea what's going on?"

Helen shook her head. "I'm sorry. I tried to find out so I could warn you, but nothing they said made sense. Your father kept going on and on about some check, and your mother just kept saying she'd only been trying to help."

Diana smiled. The reaction left Helen wide-eyed in surprise. "Don't worry." Diana gave the older woman a quick hug. "I can take care of myself on this one."

The living room was Diana's least favorite room in the house. The decorator had furnished it in a rigidly formal style, copied from something Eileen had seen in a book about the rich and famous. There was twice the furniture needed for comfort and far too many "things" sitting around. While the work was in progress Diana made the mistake of telling her mother that the photographs she used as a guide weren't actual depictions of the rooms, but arrangements put together by the photographer to fill empty spaces. Eileen had never forgiven Diana for the comment or for being right. The room that had been her showcase became an embarrassment, something that in her stubbornness she could never admit or change.

Eileen sat in the obscenely expensive copy of a Chippendale chair, her back to Diana. Carl stood at the fireplace, his arm resting on the mantel between two Staffordshire dogs.

Carl looked up and spotted Diana at the door. "You're late."

Knowing it would annoy him, she looked at her watch. "Actually, I'm early. By two minutes."

"Close the door," he said.

She did, standing with her back pressed against the raised panels rather than moving into the room. "You wanted to see me?"

He glared at her. "What did you do with the money?"

She wasn't going to make it easy for him. "What money is that?"

"You cashed the check your mother gave Amy." When she started to say something, he held up his hand. "Don't try to deny it. I've talked to the people at the bank and they told me exactly how you manipulated them. I've investigated and I know the money isn't in Amy's account and that it's not in yours. What did you do with it?"

"What difference does it make?"

He whipped around to face her, moving so abruptly that his arm hit one of the ceramic dogs and knocked it over. Eileen jumped up and let out a scream. She stretched out her arms in a futile attempt to catch the dog before it hit the hearth. Failing, she turned on Diana. "See what you did?"

"Would you forget the goddamned dog?" Carl shouted.

In all the years she'd been growing up, Diana couldn't remember her father ever raising his voice to her mother. She waited to see the reaction. Instead of a retaliatory outburst, Eileen sat back down and started crying. Today was a day of firsts.

Carl turned on Diana again. "I'll tell you what difference it makes. That's my money, and I want it back."

"Amy's name was on the check. As far as I'm concerned, that makes it her money."

"She said she didn't want it," Eileen said, her gaze fixed on the shattered dog.

"Then why did you leave it with her?" Until that instant, Diana had managed to keep her distance, viewing the battle as an observer rather than a participant. Now, remembering the morning she had found Amy unconscious in her apartment, she was deep into the fray.

"I told you that I didn't care if it took every dime we had, I would see to it that your father never had to go through the shame and horror he did when Amy was arrested."

The speech was for her father's benefit, but as far as Diana could tell, it had little effect. "If you're through"—she looked from her father to her mother and back again—"I'd like to get out of here before rush-hour traffic starts."

Carl took several steps toward Diana, as if he meant physically to stop her. "You're not going anywhere until you tell me what you did with that money."

"It's somewhere you can't get to," Diana said. "Threaten me all you like, there's no way I'm going to give—"

Carl raised his hand as if to hit her. Instantly consumed by rage, Diana knocked his arm aside. "Don't you ever even *think* about hitting me again."

"Where you're concerned, I'll do whatever I damn well please. You're my daughter."

"And that makes you think you own me?"

"Don't you use that tone of voice with—"

"Do it again, and I swear to God I'll have you arrested."

Eileen joined the fray. "How dare you talk to your father that way! Apologize to him right now."

"He should be the one apologizing to me!" Diana shouted.

Carl took several steps backward. "Get out of here. And don't come back. I never want to see you again."

Eileen let out a gasp. "You don't mean that, Carl. Diana is—"

"The hell I don't. Let her keep the money if it's so important to her, but it's the last she'll ever see from me."

"Diana, say something to him," Eileen begged.

The shock was too new, the wound too deep, for her to respond. How could her father cut her out of his life, just like that? She had to get out of there. Reaching behind her, she blindly sought the doorknob.

"Don't walk out of here thinking I'll change my mind," Carl warned her. "Unless you come back with my money, I don't want you to come back at all." He waited. When she didn't say anything, he went on. "Do you understand?"

Diana looked at Eileen. "Mother?"

"You never should have taken that money," Eileen said.

Somehow the statement made what had just happened easier to accept. If her mother had given her even a small show of support, Diana would have tried to make peace with her father. Now she saw that it was useless. She and her parents would never understand each other, and now they'd lost even the will to try. Her anger gave way to a profound sadness as she made her way through the house and out to her car. The tears came when she drove away and realized it was likely for the last time.

By the time Diana arrived at the hospital, she'd stopped crying. She spent a few minutes in the parking lot repairing her makeup. It wasn't that she cared whether Amy or Travis saw that she'd been crying; she didn't want them to know why. Not yet. Not while the wound was still bleeding.

After the fight with her father and a day at work where she'd begun to develop a real fear that if she didn't find a way to spend more time at her job, she wouldn't have it much longer, she needed Amy and Travis to balance the bad with some good.

With any luck, Amy had been awake long enough for Travis to talk to her and for them to get to know each other a little. How ironic that on the very day Amy met someone from her new family, Diana had lost her old one.

A nurse stopped Diana as she entered the intensive care unit and told her Amy had been moved. In her excitement at the news, she almost missed seeing Travis sitting in the waiting room on Amy's new floor. He was hunched forward, his elbows on his knees, staring at something she couldn't see.

Even in profile, he was so handsome that he took her breath away. The way he moved, the way he talked, the way he smiled—they had become the ingredients of her dreams. She had no business feeling this way about him. Travis Martell had come into her life at the wrong time, bearing the wrong name.

"What are you doing out here?" she asked.

"We need to talk."

"In a minute. I want to see Amy first."

He stood, took her arm, and pulled her into the room. "Bad idea."

"What's wrong?" She tried to read his expression. He was upset; her heart skipped a beat. "Did something happen to Amy?"

"We can't wait any longer, Diana. We've got to tell her who I am tonight."

Relieved, she laid her hand on his chest, using touch to reassure, taking as much as giving. "It's too soon. We agreed we should wait until she's out of the hospital."

"Amy has her own agenda. She's not going to wait for ours."

"What are you talking about?"

He put his hand on hers. "She's already got this thing half figured out for herself. She took one look at me and started asking questions. I wasn't about to lie to her, so the only thing I could do was leave."

"She couldn't have just guessed who you were. You must have said something that tipped her off." Diana slowly lowered herself to the sofa. "Something happened to you—what was it?"

She looked up at him. He couldn't know her well enough to read her moods. "I'm fine, just a little tired."

"I don't believe you."

His concern touched a responsive chord. She had to be the most pathetic person in the world to be so easily toppled by a caring look. Tears burned the back of her throat. "Can we talk about this later?"

He didn't answer right away. "I didn't want to tell Amy until I talked to you, but you don't have to be there."

"She's going to have a hundred questions."

"I'll answer what I can, the rest she can save for you." He sat down next to Diana and took her hand. "It's going to work out."

She was beginning to need him, and it scared her because she didn't want him to see her this way. Instead of responding to his touch, she freed her hand and folded her arms across her chest. "I want to be there when you tell her."

"Then we should do it now. It would be a mistake to wait any longer."

Diana nodded but didn't move. "She's going to be furious when she finds out."

"Why?"

"Because I promised I would stop interfering in her life."

"She'll get over it."

Diana turned on him. "I'm getting a little tired of you acting as if you and Amy are longtime friends when you don't know the first thing about her."

He stood and stared down at her. "I'll listen if you want to talk. I'll stay if you want company. But I won't let you use me to work out your frustrations." He left time for what he'd said to penetrate before adding, "Now are you coming, or am I going in there alone?"

"I'm coming."

Amy was on her side, her back to the door, when she heard Diana's voice. She'd hoped for more time to figure things out before seeing her sister again, time to work through her anger or, failing that, to reduce it to a manageable form. Now her rage was like some mutant bacteria, invading every thought, devouring every attempt to modify her reaction with reasoning. She kept telling herself Diana had acted out of love, but it didn't help. No matter how altruistic the motivation, Diana had made a decision that wasn't hers to make. She had taken the one thing from Amy that had belonged solely to her. And there was no going back, no way to right the wrong.

"Amy?" Diana said softly.

For an instant Amy considered closing her eyes and pretending to be asleep, but that made about as much sense as trying to dodge raindrops. The confrontation was inevitable. Why put it off? She rolled to her back and carefully adjusted her head on the pillow until she could see Diana without twisting her neck. Travis was there, too. She tried, but she couldn't keep from looking at him.

Her *brother* . . . How strange it seemed to see him actually standing there. In all the years she had put herself to sleep creating her "real" family, her favorite fantasy was the big brother who loved and took care of her.

"How are you feeling?" Diana asked.

"Manipulated."

The hopeful look disappeared. Diana glanced at Travis and then back to Amy. "How did you figure it out?"

"Does it matter?"

"No, I guess not. I just thought we would have more time."

Amy hadn't expected Diana to capitulate so readily. "Sorry to spoil your plans."

"Diana thought we should have a chance to get to know each other," Travis said.

"Oh, I see. . . ." Amy struggled to keep the hurt out of her voice. "That way if you didn't like what you saw, you could just pack up and go home. I wouldn't know I'd failed your test, and my feelings wouldn't be hurt. How considerate."

Travis shoved his hands in his back pockets, rocked back on his heels, and gave her a slow, sad smile. "If I hadn't seen your mouth moving, I would have sworn it was Judy talking. I used to think no one could have a chip on her shoulder as big as hers, but you just proved me wrong."

"Who's Judy?" Amy asked.

"My sister—your sister. The one born right after you. You look a lot like her. I guess it only makes sense that you'd act like her, too."

Without conscious thought, Amy touched her cheek. She had a sister who looked like her. . . . All the years she'd wondered what it would be like to see a piece of herself reflected in someone else's image, she'd always imagined it would be her mother. Since she was old enough to understand what it meant to be adopted, she had looked into the faces of strangers, hoping that one day someone would look back in recognition.

"I have a sister?" Amy said. Not until she saw the reaction in Diana's eyes did she understand how hurtful the words sounded. It was too late to take them back and too soon to convince Diana they were a reaction, not a feeling.

"You have three." Then, as if realizing how insensitive he, too, sounded, Travis added, "Actually four, including Diana. Back home, you have one older, two younger."

An enormous weight settled on Amy's chest. It hurt to breathe. When she'd grown too old to sustain the fantasy that she'd been stolen as a baby, she had made up a dozen reasons her mother had given her away. Always she had done so against her will. Amy had never considered the possibility her mother might have other children she'd kept. Humiliated at being the one child singled out, Amy couldn't ask the next, obvious question. Why?

Amy turned to Diana. "I want to talk to you—alone." Travis hesitated and then said, "I'll be in the waiting room."

When he was gone, Diana moved closer to the bed. "How did you know?"

"A woman called while you were gone. Before I had a chance to tell her who I was, she told me she had come across some more information about my sister's family and did I want her to send it directly to me or to continue to work through Stephanie."

"Why did you wait until now to say something?"

"I'd forgotten about it until Travis showed up this afternoon. The call came just before I went down to Stephanie's and blacked out."

"I'm sorry you had to find out that way."

"*You're sorry about the way I found out? That's it?*" Amy wrapped her hand around the metal bar beside the bed and struggled to sit up. "My whole life I've only had one thing that was mine alone—my real family. It was my right to look for them, Diana, not yours. You took that away from me."

Diana held her arms open helplessly. "I only wanted to help."

"Help who? Not me, certainly."

"Of course it was you," Diana countered. "Why else would—"

"Maybe you were looking for someone to take me off your hands?"

"That's not fair."

The glue that held Amy's emotions in check was disappearing as fast as summer hail on asphalt. "Fair has nothing to do with whether it's true or not."

"You're my sister. I love you."

"You used to love your pony, too, but your life was a hell of a lot easier when Mom made you get rid of it." Amy didn't have the strength to stay upright any longer. She fell back against the pillow. "I'm not blaming you, Diana. You have every right to feel the way you do."

"Stop that. You don't know what you're talking about."

Amy put her arm across her face, closing herself off. "I'm tired. I want to go to sleep now."

"I didn't tell you what I was doing because I wanted to find out what kind of person your mother was first."

"She didn't want to see me, did she?"

"It's a complicated situation," Diana said.

Amy moved her arm to her forehead and looked at Diana. "Did she want to see me—yes or no?"

"No," Diana admitted.

All Amy's life she'd nurtured a fantasy so special, it was saved for the moments without light or promise or hope. Somewhere was a woman who loved and dreamed about the little girl she'd given away, a woman who said a prayer every night that someday her daughter would find her, a woman who would cry when they met and beg Amy to become a part of her life. Now the fantasy was gone. There was no place left to go in her loneliness.

"Go away," Amy said. "I want you to leave me alone."

Diana moved closer. "Not until you've heard me out."

Amy turned to face the wall. "Nothing you can say will make any difference."

Twenty-four

"*Amy just needs some time,*" Travis said as the elevator doors in Diana's apartment building opened. "She's been through a hell of a lot this past month."

He was repeating himself, but he didn't know what else to say. Since they'd left the hospital Diana had made every attempt to convince him she could handle Amy's anger, but he still didn't believe her. She had a look about her that reminded him of a dog that had been abandoned in the woods and expected to fend for itself—lost and confused, its eyes reflecting the innate knowledge that death would be as slow and painful as it was inevitable.

As they stepped inside, Diana flipped on the light. "You're probably hungry. We should have stopped by the store."

"We passed a Chinese restaurant on the way here. How does takeout sound?"

"I think I'll pass." She hung up her purse and unbuttoned her jacket. "My stomach's a little upset."

"You have to eat something."

A flash of anger squared her shoulders. "No, I

don't. It's my stomach and my life. I can do as I damn well please with either of them."

"You want to beat me up for caring, go ahead," Travis said easily. "But I'm not sure what good it will do. When you get up tomorrow morning Amy's still going to be mad at you for meddling, and I'm still going to be here waiting for her to get well so I can take her back to Wyoming with me. You can't undo what's been done, Diana. You're just going to have to hang on and ride it out."

"This has been a really shitty day," she said. "I don't care about anything right now but getting past it and starting over again tomorrow. If you want Chinese, go ahead and order it. I'm going to take a bath and go to bed." She started down the hall. When she realized Travis wasn't following, she turned and looked at him. "What's wrong?"

"I don't think it's a good idea for me to stay here tonight," he said, his voice low and husky.

"Why not?"

"Because you're not ready for what would happen if I did." It was foolish to try to deny what he was feeling or how much he wanted her.

She started to protest, then stopped. "Where will you go?"

"I don't know, probably one of the hotels near the hospital." He opened the door and stepped into the hallway.

"I liked having you here," she admitted softly. "I'm not the solitary creature I want everyone to think I am."

If he stayed, their relationship would change, the complications becoming burdens, the pleasure tempered by the need for secrecy. As much as he wanted her, there was nothing he would not do for her at that moment, including walking away.

Travis put his hand on the door to pull it closed behind him. "I'll see you at the hospital tomorrow."

She waved, her smile melancholy. "Let me know where you are."

"As soon as I get to my room I'll call." He closed the door before he could change his mind about leaving.

Travis was about to get into a taxi when he realized he'd left his bag upstairs. He let the cab go and headed back to the elevator. Diana didn't answer his knock or the bell. Deciding she must be in the shower, he was about to let himself in when the door opened.

"I'm sorry it took me so long," Diana said. "I was in the bedroom."

She'd changed into a dark green robe that she held closed with her hand. Her cheeks were flushed, and there were dark smears of mascara under her eyes. She'd been crying, hard. A dozen emotions hit at once, riding on a wave of protectiveness. "Why were you crying?"

"I don't know. It just started." Her eyes filled with fresh tears. "I can't seem to make it stop." She tried to smile but failed. "Kind of scary, huh?"

He cupped her face with his hands, wiping the moisture from her cheeks with his thumbs. Diana had gone through the dark hours at the hospital with Amy in a stoic calm. To see her break down now tore at his heart. How could he have been so wrapped up in his own world not to have seen this coming? He brushed a kiss on her temple, saying softly, "I'm sorry. I shouldn't have left you. Not tonight."

She turned her head to press her cheek against his hand. "Why did you come back?"

"I forgot my bag."

The words grounded her. She tightened the hand that clutched her robe. "I'll get it for you."

Travis stopped her when she moved to leave. He looked deeply into her eyes. "Don't bother. I'm not going anywhere." With a natural, fluid ease, he brought her into his arms.

For long seconds she held herself rigid. Finally, her private battle lost, she let go. Deep, shuddering sobs followed the release. Once started, the tears were impossible to stop. She fit herself tightly against him, wrapping her arms around his waist, holding him the way she would fraying straps on a parachute.

At first Travis believed the storm was nothing more than a release of pent-up emotions, a safety valve for the unrelenting pressure Diana had been under the past month. But it was soon obvious that something more was going on. When the sobs lessened, replaced by deep, exhausted breaths, Travis leaned back to look at her. "It seems there are some things we need to talk about."

She reached into her pocket, took out a tissue, and wiped her eyes and nose. "I'm sorry. I've never done that before."

"What's going on, Diana?"

"I don't know. I guess everything just caught up with me at once."

"Tell me if you don't want to talk about it, but don't lie or try to shine me off like some stranger who just wandered in off the street."

"I told you—I had a bad day. It's not worth talking about."

"This is more than a bad day," he persisted.

Her gaze dropped to the second button on his shirt. "I'm falling behind at work. . . . If I don't do something to catch up, it could mean my job." She slowly circled the button with the tip of her finger. "And I had a fight with my parents this afternoon," she added softly. "I can't talk about it—not yet. It's too soon."

"You must wish you'd never started this thing with Amy."

"No, you're wrong. Even with her mad at me, I'm convinced finding her family—finding you—is the one thing I've done right."

A tear lingered at the corner of her eye. Travis touched his lips to the spot, tasting the salt, taking in her sorrow. She put her arms around his neck. Without words she brought her mouth to his, parting her lips at the last second.

He responded with a swift, explosive hunger, his tongue seeking the sweet recesses of her mouth, his throat rumbling with a deep, primitive release.

Travis had kissed many women in passion, in moments before, during, and after lovemaking. Never had he felt the way he did now. It was as if he had somehow taken Diana into himself, as if she'd become as clear a part of him as his heart and mind. The contact was pure and intimate and deeply sexual. He could feel her essence in his hands and in the air he breathed. He was warm where he'd been cold, on fire wherever her body touched his.

"I want you, Diana." He combed his hands through her hair and kissed her again. "I don't give a damn if it's too soon."

"Yes. . . ." She rocked forward on her toes, stretching to meet his kiss.

Seconds later he let out a frustrated groan. "I don't have protection."

"I do," she murmured against his lips.

The words sent sharp, sweetly painful electricity to Travis's groin. He was filled with a wondrous ache to find release inside of her. His hands slid across the back of her robe and along her sides, relaying the message that she wasn't wearing anything under the thin satin.

He opened the robe, exposing a narrow path of creamy skin. She made no effort to hide herself or shy away when he laid his hand against her breast. The tender flesh yielded invitingly to his touch. His thumb passed over the hard, ripe point of her nipple. She arched her back in response to the caress.

Diana caught her breath when he traced a thin, fiery path from her neck to her breast with his tongue. She was ready for him; more than that, she was impatient. Her hands worked his shirt from his jeans and slid underneath to caress the firm muscled flesh across his back.

He was unlike the men she'd known all her life, his strength quiet and sure, gained from work, not from the machines in a gym. He moved with grace and confidence, touching her, making love to her without awkwardness or hesitancy. When his hand moved between her thighs and his finger dipped into her moist cavity, it felt as if the intimacy had been predestined, as if she had been waiting for that moment forever.

She worked the buttons on his jeans, feeling his heated shaft straining to be free. He moaned when she wrapped her hand around him.

Travis stared at her with an intensity that left her trembling. Without saying anything more, he picked her up and took her to the guest room, gently laying her in the bed he would never sleep in again. What they had begun, what they would do, was a commitment, an unspoken promise. There would be no turning back.

Diana watched as Travis stood beside her and stripped off his clothes, his body reflected in the light coming from the hall. He was built like a swimmer, with broad shoulders and narrow hips, his legs long and powerful. The men she had known before Travis fought their battles in an urban wilderness, their armor of choice suits and ties or lab coats and stethoscopes. She understood them, their hopes and dreams, the motivations that drove them. He was a mystery. For all the compassion and tenderness he had shown with Amy, there was an undercurrent of danger about Travis Martell; turbulent water flowed beneath the surface calm.

When he finished undressing, he eased himself down beside her. They fit together effortlessly, as if molded by a master sculptor. She was ready and urged him to come to her, but he held back. With exquisite care he explored her body, finding the secret places that with a touch destroyed her inhibitions. His tenderness and caring gave her an erotic freedom she had never before experienced. There was no intimacy she could or would deny him.

Finally, the anticipation turned into a mind-numbing need, and he entered her. She welcomed him with an urgency that destroyed all possibility of subtlety.

Travis drove into her with abandon, feeling the need for release build within him until every other thought vanished. When the climax came, the room spun around him in an iridescent haze.

Their descent was slow, without need for words. A sense of home settled through Travis that had nothing to do with where he was, but everything to do with who was beside him. He pulled her closer into his side and touched his lips to her hair. "Tell me what happened to you today."

Diana didn't want her job or the fight with her parents or Amy's accusations to tarnish their night. There would be plenty of time later to tell Travis how her world had crumbled that day. Now all she wanted him to know was how glad she was that he had come into her life.

She propped herself up on her elbow. Before she could analyze what she was going to say and let the rational side of her brain convince her it was too soon, or that the timing was all wrong, or that she might drive him away, she said, "I think I may be falling in love with you."

He looked so stunned, she would have given everything she owned to buy back the words. But it was too late; the damage was done. "I'm sorry, I never should have said that. It just came out."

He brushed the hair back from her face, tucking it behind her ears, focusing on the inconsequential to give himself time. He didn't understand how he'd come to feel the way he did about Diana, how one day he'd realized he needed her as much as wanted her. She had filled an emptiness inside of him with a joy that was like a door opening to the rest of his life. He knew innately that he could live without her, but he knew just as surely that his life would be a shadow of its promise if she weren't there to share it with him.

Finally, when he was sure he could trust his voice, he said, "I think it's just possible I may be falling in love with you, too."

Her lips trembled as they pulled into a smile. "When did this happen?"

"I'm beginning to believe it always was," he said softly. He brought her back into his arms and kissed her with an aching tenderness. "We just had to find each other."

"I'm so glad you waited for me."

He looked longingly into her eyes. "I didn't have any choice."

Twenty-five

———

The next morning the phone rang as Diana got out of the shower. She picked it up in the bedroom at the same time Travis answered downstairs. It was Stephanie.

"Travis got there kind of early this morning," Stephanie said after he'd greeted her and hung up.

"He's staying here again." She would reveal that much; the rest she and Travis had decided should remain their secret until Amy was out of the hospital and had had time to deal with all the other dramatic changes in her life. "It's easier than a hotel."

Surprisingly, Stephanie didn't pursue the subject. "How's Amy? I didn't get a chance to stop by last night."

"She's out of intensive care . . . and she knows Travis is her brother."

"How did that happen? I thought you weren't going to tell her until she came home."

"She figured it out for herself, with the help of a phone call from Margaret McCormick."

"I don't understand."

The towel slipped. Diana tucked it up higher under her arms. "It's a long story, I'll fill you in later."

"Can you meet me for lunch?"

"It's not that important, Stephanie, just complicated. The story will keep."

"This is something else," she said mysteriously. "I hate to ask, especially with everything else you've got on your plate, but I really need your advice."

She'd planned to meet Travis for lunch, but Stephanie so rarely asked anything that Diana couldn't deny her. "How about that Italian place near the newspaper?" She looked up and saw Travis standing in the doorway, smiling. Her immediate reaction was to check that the towel hadn't slipped again, but before she did, she remembered how painstaking and thorough he had been in coming to know her body the night before and how foolish she would look trying to hide it from him now. A flush at the memory warmed her. "Twelve-thirty okay?"

"I'll make the reservation," Stephanie said.

"See you then." Diana hung up the phone. "I'm sorry," she said to Travis. "I couldn't tell her no."

He came across the room, sat down on the bed next to her, and handed her a cup of coffee. It was as if they had shared the morning ritual a hundred times before. "Trouble?"

"I don't know." She took a drink. The powerful black liquid hit the back of her throat like a shot of alcohol. She swallowed, then coughed.

"Too strong?" He took the cup and put it on the nightstand.

"No, not at all."

"Liar."

"Well, maybe a little."

"It takes a while, but you'll get used to it." He glanced at his watch. "What time do you have to leave?"

"What did you have in mind?"

"The same thing that's been on my mind since the first time I saw you."

"Now who's lying?" Without touching her, he had ignited a deep and intimate response. Almost without conscious thought, she swayed toward him, her breasts hot and swollen and aching with the need to feel his hands on them. "I'll bet you don't even remember the first time you saw me."

"At the restaurant." He leaned forward and licked a drop of water from her shoulder. "You had your hair down around your shoulders and your nose stuck up in the air. Who could have guessed, huh?"

She touched a small scar on his chin and then another on his temple. There was so much she didn't know about him. So much to learn. "I don't believe in love at first sight."

"Neither do I." He gave the towel a gentle tug. It landed in her lap.

"Then what is this that's happening between us?" She put her hand on his arm.

"Proof that we were both wrong?" He moved her hair out of the way and kissed the hollow behind her ear.

"Maybe it's just lust." She slipped her hands under his shirt. "Did you ever think about that?"

"No."

"How can you be so sure?" She was ready to explode with wanting him, almost beyond caring what name to give whatever it was that drove her.

He caught her chin and made her look at him. "What are you afraid of, Diana?"

"Losing you," she said with more honesty than she'd intended.

"There's no way I'll ever let that happen."

"Promise?"

He answered with a deep, plundering kiss. For the moment, it was enough.

*   *   *

Stephanie was waiting for Diana when she got to the restaurant. "Did you see Amy this morning?" she asked as they were being shown to their table.

"I decided not to go until this evening. She was pretty upset with me yesterday." Diana sat down and laid her napkin on her lap. "Travis is spending the day with her." She gave Stephanie a quick rundown of the confrontation between her and Amy the day before, ending with Travis's attempted role as peace-maker.

"That guy can't be real. No one that nice is."

It was as hard for Diana to keep a secret from Stephanie as it was to go a month without chocolate. Still, Diana had to give it a try. "He's either real or a damn good actor."

"Do you think he'll be able to talk Amy into going back with him for a visit?"

"I don't know. She's going to be even more upset when she learns what's happened to the Martells since they found out about her. There's no way we're going to be able to convince Amy the breakup wasn't her fault."

"Who would have thought this thing could get so damned complicated?"

Diana smiled wryly. *And getting more complicated every day.* "Is everything okay with you?"

"Yes—no, that's not true. Everything is not okay."

"Which is why you wanted to talk to me, I take it?"

"I'm really sorry to be dumping this on you, especially considering everything that you've got going on right now."

"Would you please not do that? I don't know what I would have done if you hadn't been there for me this past month. At least let me try to be as good a friend to you."

Before Stephanie could say anything more, the waiter came for their orders. When he was gone she sat back, took a deep breath, and plunged in. "There isn't any easy way to say this."

The breezy facade slipped, allowing Diana a glimpse of the deep worry that had brought Stephanie there. "Then stop trying to find one and just spit it out."

"I'm pregnant."

Diana's mouth dropped open in surprise. She was at a loss for words. Of all the things she might have guessed, this would have been the last. "I don't know what to say," she admitted.

"I felt the same way when I found out. Picture this—I even asked the doctor the classic stupid question: 'How did it happen?'"

"Have you told Stan?"

Her reaction said it all. "Yeah, he's having a hard time understanding why I think it's a problem."

"He wants you to have an abortion." It was a statement, not a question.

"He says I'm being hypocritical to believe in pro choice for everyone but myself. He did everything but come right out and say I was trying to use the baby to trap him and that I'd planned the whole thing."

"Then he doesn't know you very well." The words brought her up short. *No better than Travis knows me.* He had no idea what she thought or how she leaned politically, let alone something as basic as her opinion of bringing an unwanted baby into the world.

"He's not the only one. I thought I knew him, but it's obvious I don't have a clue. Oh, I know what he likes in bed, and which restaurants are his favorites, and how he thinks the Vikings will do next season, but I don't have any idea how he votes, or who his favorite writers are, or how he feels about the environment. God, how could I have been so stupid to let myself believe I was in love with a man I didn't even know?"

Diana avoided answering. It was something she didn't want to think about. "I take it marriage is out?"

"He never had any intention of divorcing his wife." She let out a self-deprecating laugh. "All this time he's been using her as a safety net. My God, can you believe I swallowed that old line? How could I have been so blind?"

"Would you stop beating yourself up? You made a mistake. We all do—including me. Remember Stuart?"

"Thanks, but it's not company that my misery needs, it's advice."

"I assume you're talking about the baby?"

Stephanie straightened the napkin on her lap, then the silver on the table, then her water glass. "I can't look at any of this dispassionately."

"I'm not sure you should listen to anything I have to say," Diana told her. "Look at the mess I made when I tried to help Amy."

"Not everything done out of love turns out the way you want, but I'll take love over reason anytime." She moved to make room for the waiter to deliver her pasta. "Besides, something tells me everything is going to work out even better than we thought for Amy."

"I hope you're right." Diana speared one of the shrimp scattered across the top of her salad. It was tough and tasteless. She sat back and studied Stephanie.

"What?" Stephanie asked when she looked up and saw Diana staring.

"I'm trying to imagine you a mother."

"Pretty hard, huh?"

"Your life would be completely different."

"That's not what bothers me," she said.

Her answer surprised Diana. "Then what does?"

"What if I was a terrible parent? You can really screw up a kid if you don't know what you're doing. Look at Amy."

"Are you worried about being able to love this baby?" Diana asked.

Stephanie blinked in surprise. "That thought never even entered my mind."

"Then stop worrying about it. My mother could have made a hundred mistakes with Amy. They wouldn't have mattered if she had just balanced them with a little love."

Stephanie wasn't convinced. "I've got some savings, but there's no way I could afford to quit work and stay home to raise a child. She'd be with strangers more than she was with me. What kind of life is that?"

"I don't know." On the rare occasions Diana had thought about her and Stuart having a child, the same questions had plagued her. "Why don't you ask some of the people you work with who have kids? It's not as if it's a unique problem."

"Are you saying you think I should keep the baby?"

"No," she said carefully. "What I'm saying is that I think you should do what you always do when you have a problem. Figure out exactly what's bothering you, and get Mike Jones to help you research the answers. We could talk about this until the day they wheel you into the delivery room, but you're not going to be satisfied until your mind confirms what your heart is already telling you."

"And that is?" Stephanie asked.

"Since you haven't even mentioned adoption, and you won't have an abortion, it seems a little obvious, don't you think?"

"I did consider adoption. I know a couple who just got a little boy after waiting five years. You wouldn't believe how excited they are. The way they show him off, you'd think they invented babies."

"But?" Diana asked, already knowing the answer.

"What if my baby went to people like your parents? I couldn't stand it if I thought she wasn't loved. What if they joined some cult with her, or taught her prejudice, or told her it was all right to wear fur?"

"There's always an open adoption." Diana understood now that it wasn't advice Stephanie needed, it was someone to act as a sounding board. "You could arrange to meet the couple first to make sure they came up to your standards."

"It wouldn't work. If I knew who they were, I'd never be able to stay away."

"Are you listening to what you're saying?" Diana asked.

"I never pictured myself a single parent."

"I doubt many people do. Given the choice, I'm sure most women would prefer bringing up their child in a traditional family setting."

"Me and Murphy Brown," Stephanie said without humor. "Single-handedly setting out to destroy the moral values of an entire generation."

Unknowingly, Stephanie had pushed one of Diana's buttons. "I never want to hear you say anything like that again. The people who spout that crap are looking for sound bites, not solutions. They're the same ones who are going to damn you if you have an abortion, criticize you if you give your baby away, and condemn you if you keep her. Did you ever hear one of them talk about the father of Murphy Brown's baby, or even suggest he should be held accountable in some way? These people belong back in the Middle Ages. I think we should—"

"Whoa," Stephanie said. "I get the picture." She reached across the table and took Diana's hand. "I'm really glad you're on my side."

"Was I coming across too strong?"

Stephanie grinned. "Maybe for the military, but not for me."

The waiter came by to check their progress. When he saw how little they'd eaten, he frowned and glanced back at the long line of customers waiting to be seated.

"His tip just dropped five percent," Stephanie said.

Diana laughed. "Now there's the Stephanie Gorham I know and love."

The hospital parking lot was full by the time Diana arrived that afternoon. She circled the block, waiting for an opening, thinking about her lunch with Stephanie. She'd decided not to tell Amy about the baby, at least not right away. If the decision was more proof that she couldn't resist interfering in Amy's life, so be it. Her heart did a funny little skipping beat as she walked down the hallway. She was scared, a feeling she'd had for Amy in the past, but never about her.

Diana didn't know what to say to make things better between them. Travis insisted Amy just needed time, but Diana had a gut feeling that it was going to take something more. Amy had trusted her completely, a gift she'd given to no one else. Until they could find a way to get past the broken trust, nothing else mattered.

The door was open, the room filled with late afternoon sunlight. Travis sat in a chair by the window, writing something on a spiral tablet. Amy was asleep. Diana stared at the two people who constituted the very soul of her world. At odd moments she could see a physical connection in a smile or glance or the way they held their heads when deep in thought. The recognition always came with a start and brought with it the bittersweet realization of how different all of their lives would have been had Gus not been reported dead.

Travis sensed her standing there. When he looked up there was no surprise, only intimate welcome. He got up to meet her, glancing at the bed before giving her a quick kiss.

"How was your lunch with Stephanie?" he asked softly.

"Interesting." She looked into his eyes. How could she have missed the gold flecks in the blue or how long his eyelashes were? Her chest ached with joy at being with him again. And then a cloud moved across her thoughts. Surely this was the way Stephanie had felt about Stan? "I'll tell you about it later."

Travis glanced at the still sleeping Amy. He took Diana's hand and led her into the hallway before he smiled and said, "We had a good day. Amy never stopped asking questions."

"What did you tell her?"

"The truth. I don't want her blindsided with anything when she comes home."

The "home" gave her pause. "Amy agreed to go back with you?"

"She said she needs some time to get used to the idea first."

"I agree."

"I don't understand what good it will do to wait."

The statement made her irrationally angry. "After all she's been through, the last thing she needs is to land in the middle of your family fight."

"It isn't just my family, Diana, it's Amy's, too. She's a part of us now. That means she has to take the bad along with the good."

"You make it sound as if she's going to move to Wyoming."

"We've got a lot of years to catch up on. That's not something you can do by phone."

Diana took a step backward, as though distancing herself from him could negate what he was saying. "Amy will never leave Minnesota." She shook her head to reinforce the words. "She'd go crazy living in Wyoming. She wouldn't last a month."

"Who are you trying to convince, Diana, me or you?"

"What's that supposed to mean?" she snapped.

"Do you want to tell me what's going on here?" Realizing they were both talking too loudly, Travis put his arm around her and steered her down the hall toward the waiting room. "Why did you look for us if you didn't want Amy to be a part of our family again?"

"I didn't expect you to take over her life." Instead of sitting on the couch where he could sit next to her, Diana took one of the single chairs.

Travis lowered himself to his haunches in front of her. "You started something you can't control," he said gently. "Amy is in charge now. What happens next is up to her—which is exactly the way it should be."

The fear that dogged her for the past week finally had a name. "I don't want to lose her."

"You won't."

He sounded so sure of himself. "How do you know?"

"She loves you." He stood and held out his hand. "I've had her all to myself today. Now it's your turn."

"Where will you go?"

He pointed her toward Amy's room. "Grocery shopping. I like popcorn, but not every night."

Twenty-six

—

Spicy, mouthwatering odors greeted Diana when she opened her front door. Not until that moment did she realize how hungry she was. As if on cue, her stomach rumbled.

Travis stepped out of the kitchen and waved to her with a wooden spoon. "You're early. Dinner won't be ready for another half hour."

"Amy was tired. I decided to let her sleep." She stepped out of her heels and dropped them and her jacket on the stairs as she passed.

He wasn't fooled by her seeming cheerfulness. "I take it the visit didn't go well?"

The hurt was so great, had anyone else asked the question, she would have lied. "We were like strangers. Every time I tried to talk to her about you, or your dad, or what happened when I went to Jackson, she told me she didn't want to hear about it."

"She probably resents you knowing more about her family than she does." He took her in his arms, resting his chin on the top of her head. "But something tells me what's really bothering her goes a lot deeper. Somehow she's gotten it in her head that she's so different from the rest of us that she won't fit in."

"Did she tell you that?"

"Not directly. It was just a feeling I got from the kinds of questions she asked." He let her go with a quick kiss and poured them each a glass of wine. "I considered telling her I already knew about the problems she's had in the past, and that they didn't matter, but then decided it might be better to let her have a secret or two." He handed Diana her wine.

It was a merlot. She preferred white wines, but there was no way he could know something like that. The likes and dislikes of a person came with time and familiarity. She took a sip and was pleasantly surprised, took another and decided she actually liked it. A small, private smile followed. Had Travis known her preferences, she might never have discovered they weren't as rigid as she'd thought—at least not about wines. "Don't tell me you're a wine connoisseur, too."

His eyebrows rose in question. "Too?"

"It was just a comment. I know so little about you that—"

"Ask me anything." He pulled out a chair and motioned for her to sit down.

"Who's your favorite singer?" She had no idea why she cared or why she'd asked that question.

"It's not the singer so much as the song." He opened the oven to baste the pork roast.

"Television program."

"You got me there. The set I had gave out on me a couple of years ago. I keep saying I'm going to buy another one, especially when I hear people talking about something great they've just seen, but I never seem to get around to it. Maybe when I run out of things to read. But with the stack of books sitting on my nightstand, I don't see that happening any time soon."

He was the first person she'd ever met who didn't own a television set. "You don't keep up with any football or baseball teams?"

"If there's a game I want to see, I go to one of the sports bars in town. Otherwise I listen to it on the radio."

"Okay, if you were stranded on an island, what one thing would you take with you?"

He gave her a wicked grin. "That's too easy. . . ."

She'd read about people's toes tingling, but not until that moment had she experienced the sensation herself. "I'm serious."

"So am I." He tossed the pot holder on the counter, leaned down, and gave her a kiss that left no doubt just how serious.

She put her arms around his neck and let him pull her to an upright position. "How long before dinner?" she murmured after the second kiss.

"I thought you wanted to get to know me better."

"Oh, I do. . . ."

He pulled back to look at her. "I will make love to you anywhere and whenever you want. It's damn near all I've thought about this past week. But we have time, Diana," he said tenderly. "I'm not going anywhere."

"I can't shake the feeling I'm going to lose you."

"You're mixing me up with Amy."

Diana leaned into him, resting her head on his shoulder. "She's been mad at me before, but never anything like this."

"Put yourself in her place. How would you feel?"

"I'd be furious," she acknowledged.

"But you'd get over it."

"I'm not as stubborn as Amy." She could feel the

soft vibration of laughter in his chest. Taken aback at his reaction, she looked up. "Ask any of my friends. They'll tell you I'm the most easygoing person they know. I stayed with a man I didn't even *like* because I didn't have the backbone to create the scene it would take to throw him out."

"You're describing someone I haven't met," he told her. "If the real Diana Winchester is this acquiescing rag doll you'd have me believe, who was the woman I met in Wyoming?"

"Even sheep stand up for themselves when they're threatened."

"Then who is the woman I made love to last night?"

"I told you, yesterday was a really bad day for me. You caught me at my worst."

He released her and took a step backward. "Why are you doing this?"

"What am I doing?"

"Trying to drive me away."

"What gives you that idea?"

"Relegating the best thing that ever happened to me to the result of a really bad day for you. What in the hell do you expect me to think?"

"Everything has happened so fast between us. How can it be real?"

"How much time are we talking about before our relationship is real to you? Six months? A year? If that's what you need, I can wait. I told you before, I'm not going anywhere." He pulled out a chair and sat down. "But humor me, would you? What's going to happen in six months? How is it going to make a difference?"

"At least you'll know something about me by then—the real me." She sat in the chair opposite him. "And I'll know more about you."

He leaned over, grabbed a notebook off the counter, and handed it to her. "I started this for you while Amy was sleeping. I have a ways to go, but it's a beginning."

She looked inside and saw there were several pages filled with loose-flowing handwriting. "What is it?"

"A crash course on the likes and dislikes of Travis August Martell. I had a feeling we were headed for something like this."

Maybe he knew her better than she wanted to admit. "Your middle name is Augustus?"

He laughed. "Don't worry, there isn't some long-standing family tradition that the name has to be passed on to the first son."

The implied meaning wasn't lost on her. Instead of feeling rushed or cornered, she felt a liquid warmth that he had casually assumed his child would also be hers. "What about the firstborn daughter?"

"Marigold."

"Marigold?"

"Yeah—after my great-great-grandmother."

She smiled. "Liar."

"Come here." The statement was as much demand as invitation.

She got up, rounded the table, and sat on his lap. He put his hands on the sides of her face and kissed her, long and thoroughly. "We have time, Travis," she said, echoing his earlier statement.

He kissed her again. "Yes, I know . . . at least an hour if we turn the oven down."

"Let me do it for you."

"Anything to make you happy."

"Anything?" She moved to straddle him, hiking her skirt up to her hips and then stretching to reach the temperature gauge.

"Name it." He worked the buttons on her blouse free.

She smiled. "Can't—don't know the words."

"Then I guess you'll just have to show me." His finger traced a path along the lacy outline of her bra.

She caught her breath when his hand moved lower. "Now that I can do."

Three days passed before Amy would do anything but turn her back on Diana when she came to visit. Finally, after Diana told her that she wasn't going to leave until they'd talked, Amy broke down. First came the anger, then the hurt. After more than three hours of listening as Amy poured out her soul, the healing began.

Even though it was well past midnight, Travis was up and waiting for Diana when she came home that night.

He met her at the door, kissed her, and said, "I take it Amy finally decided to talk to you."

She nodded. "For a while there I wished she hadn't."

"Have you eaten?"

"I'm not hungry. A glass of wine would be nice, though."

They went into the kitchen, where Travis poured the wine and directed Diana to put cheese and crackers on a plate. "I haven't seen Stephanie in a couple of days," he said. "Is she all right?"

"She broke up with the guy she'd been dating." The incomplete answer had been automatic. Diana considered Stephanie's pregnancy a confidence, even if not requested. But a sudden, compelling curiosity prompted her to tell Travis. "She's pregnant."

Travis let out a low whistle. "That's a tough one."

"What do you think she should do?"

"I don't make those kinds of judgments for other people, Diana. There's no way I'll ever experience what Stephanie's going through. I'm not about to give advice on what she should do."

"I'm not asking you for advice. I want to know what you think."

"I think she's got a damn hard road ahead of her no matter what she does."

"She won't even consider giving the baby up for adoption."

"Because of what happened to Amy?"

Diana chuckled. "And because they might be the kind of people who wear fur."

"A principled woman." He moved three kitchen chairs out on the balcony, two for sitting, one to use as a table. The roar of the motorized river of cars below had settled to a level of a rock-strewn stream; still the sounds were as alien and intrusive to Travis as the call of an owl or coyote would be to Diana were they sitting on his deck at home.

"The stars are incredible," she said, settling into her chair.

He looked at a sky so washed out with ambient light that he barely recognized it as the same one they had at home. "Have you ever seen the Milky Way?"

"When I was a kid, but not in years."

"There's a special place I go in the mountains behind my house that I want to take you someday. At times the moon looms so big and bright, you'd swear you could reach out and touch it." There were a hundred things that would be made new again seeing them through her eyes.

Diana leaned forward, bracing her elbows on her knees. "Amy's upset that I've seen Jackson before her."

"She needs someone to work out her frustrations on—you're an easy target."

"I knew she'd be miffed when she found out I'd gone behind her back to find her family, but I had no idea it would go this far." She took a sip of wine. "Does she say anything to you about it when you're there?"

"She never even mentions your name," Travis said gently.

"I'm not surprised. She's as hurt as she is angry. Thank God she doesn't know about us." Diana looked at him. "You haven't said anything, have you?"

He shook his head. "I figured she's got enough to deal with right now. When she comes home from the hospital we can—"

"No, not even then. Not until she's had a chance to get to know you better. She has to feel as if you're really hers before she can share you with me. I know it sounds crazy, but all our lives it's as if I've been at the head of the buffet line and she's been given the leftovers. This time Amy has to come first."

"We're never going to be able to pull it off, Diana. Five minutes after she sees us together she's going to know how I feel about you."

"We have to find a way to keep that from happening. She's going to be a long time forgetting, or forgiving me as it is."

"She's just scared."

"No, it's more than that." She sought a way to explain something that was more feeling than substance. "Amy's different somehow. I can't quite figure it out yet, but it's as if she's in the middle of this peculiar metamorphosis. She's either growing up, or growing old, or maturing, or . . . I don't know what's happening to her, only that she's changing." Diana struggled to find the right word. "She's become contemplative. No, I think 'introspective' is a better way to put it. Neither one is anything like the old Amy."

Travis propped his feet up on the railing. "She's had a lot to think about lately."

"All the way home I tried to convince myself I was making a big deal out of nothing." She picked up a piece of cheese and put it back again. "If you knew me better, you'd know I don't usually do that. I'm more inclined to try to make something really important into an everyday occurrence." She looked over to him and smiled sheepishly. "I've done a lot of things lately that I don't usually do."

Travis took her hand and gave it a gentle squeeze. "Give Amy a couple of days. After what the two of you have been through, you're both entitled."

Diana didn't say anything right away. She tilted her head back to look at the stars, hoping one would fall and that she could make a wish. "We've always been so close," she said, a catch in her voice. "Now it's as if there's a wall between us. I keep trying, but I don't know how to make it go away."

This time, Travis didn't have an answer.

"I can't lose her." Diana's voice dropped to a soft whisper, almost as if she had slipped into prayer. "She's my best friend, Travis. I don't know what I'd do without her."

The rest of the visits with Amy that week grew progressively better. By Thursday she seemed to have put her anger behind her. On Friday Diana had even elicited a smile when she brought the Steiff teddy bear she'd found at an antique store on her lunch hour. Still, there was an awkwardness between them, one they didn't talk about.

She and Travis still visited in shifts, deciding it

would be easier for Amy to deal with them one at a time. Stephanie popped in whenever her schedule allowed.

By Monday the doctor had started mentioning that Amy would be released soon, though he refused to give a specific day, saying it all depended on her continuing improvement.

Keeping her and Travis's relationship a secret from Amy proved harder than Diana had thought. At least a dozen times during each visit she had to stop herself in the middle of a sentence when she realized that finishing would reveal something that would lead to questions. Amy seemed not to notice—or if she did, she didn't say anything.

Wednesday, Diana was in the middle of a meeting at work when her assistant interrupted to tell her she had an urgent phone call.

She raced to her office, her heart in her throat at the possibilities that came to mind. "Yes?" she said, grabbing the receiver before she'd rounded the desk to sit down.

"I'm sorry to pull you out of your meeting," Travis said. "But this couldn't wait. The doctor told Amy that as long as there was someone there to help her, she could go home this morning. She told him she would be living with you for the next few weeks, and that I would be there to take care of her during the day."

"That's been the plan all along. I don't understand why—"

"I can't leave here without Amy. And once we get there, I can't come up with a way to get my things out of your bedroom without her seeing me."

"Oh, my God. How much time do I have?" She not only had to come up with an excuse to get out of her meeting, she had to find a ride, since Travis had her car.

"I'll drag this out as long as I can, but don't count on much more than an hour. It's taken me almost that long to get away to call you."

"An hour isn't enough."

"It has to be—Amy's already threatened to leave without me if I don't start moving a little faster."

Twenty-seven

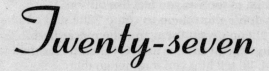

Travis settled Amy into the car and got in the driver's side.
"How does it feel to be out in the fresh air again?"

Amy rolled down the window. "Unbelievable."

"Want to drive around a little, see some of the sights?" As if there were anything she hadn't seen a hundred times before.

"Not today."

"Tired?"

"A little," Amy admitted. "It comes over me all of a sudden. One minute I feel as if I could go all day, then I'm so sleepy I can hardly keep my eyes open."

"Did the doctor give you any kind of time frame when you could expect to be back full strength?"

"He said if I didn't try to rush things, I should be feeling my old self again in a couple of weeks." She turned to look at Travis. "Why do you ask?"

"Dad wants to know. Actually, it's practically all he talks about anymore. He's anxious to see you, but it's hard for him to leave the ranch without a couple of days to make the arrangements."

"He's planning to come here?"

Travis purposely took a wrong turn. "Sharon told

him she didn't think it would be fair to ask you to come all the way to Wyoming. She's going to fly up with him as soon as you feel like visitors."

"I don't want them to come," she said emphatically. "I don't want them anywhere near here."

His heart went out to her. "Then next time I talk to Dad, I'll tell him you'd rather go there."

"Will he be upset?"

"Only that he'll have to wait a little longer to see you, but he'll understand."

"What about Sharon?"

Travis smiled. "Dad will probably have to sit on her to keep her in Wyoming. She's never been known for her patience."

Amy adjusted the seat belt where it crossed her shoulder. In what Travis had come to recognize as a nervous gesture, she reached up to touch her hair, making sure the shaved spot was covered. "Have you talked to Faith or Judy since they got back?"

Travis wasn't fooled. What Amy really wanted to know was whether he'd talked to their mother. "Sharon told me they were staying at the ranch, and that Faith was trying to figure out Mom's bookkeeping system."

"I took a couple of semesters of accounting in college. Maybe I could—" She ran her hands down the crease in her pants and looked out the side window. "Listen to me, would you—already butting in where I'm not needed."

He thought of a dozen trite, meaningless platitudes that he could use to try to reassure her but knew nothing he could say would do any good. "I'm not going to pretend that when you come home you're going to slide into your place in the family and we'll all go on as if you'd always been there."

"Maybe it would be better if I didn't go at all."

"Better for who? You? Me? Dad?"

"Everyone."

"We can't go back to the way we were, Amy. Whether you come home or not, none of us will ever be the same. You aren't responsible for what's happened to the family, and you can't undo what's been done. Whatever you decide, it has to be because it's what you want. No one else matters."

"What happens if I'm so different from the rest of you that I can't ever fit in?"

"And what happens if a meteor strikes the airport just as your plane is landing?" he asked. "If you have to worry about something, that's as good as anything you've come up with so far."

A small, sheepish grin played at the corners of her mouth. "You're really good at this."

"I don't know what you're talking about."

"This big brother thing."

He laughed. "If I am, it's because I've had lots of practice."

"Are the others like you?"

"I'm going to leave that for you to decide."

They drove several blocks in silence before Amy took note of their surroundings and frowned. "Where are you going?"

"To Diana's," he said as if stating the obvious.

"This isn't the way."

He had no idea where he was but hoped he'd gone far enough out of the way to give Diana time to get home. "I wondered why I didn't recognize any of the buildings we passed."

"Turn left at the next corner."

Amy guided him through a residential area with homes on the shabby side of stately, past a large shopping area with red, white, and blue bunting hanging off the light standards, and into an industrial area, where they picked up the highway and headed south.

"Dad would like you to stay at the ranch when you come home," Travis said after he'd merged into the traffic. "I told him that should be up to you."

She didn't say anything for several seconds. "I guess if I'm going to do this, I might as well go all the way. My being there is either going to work or it isn't."

"Nothing is that simple, Amy. Just like here, there are going to be good and bad days. I don't want you grabbing the first plane back to Minneapolis if things start getting rough."

"You don't have to worry about that. I've decided no matter what happens in Wyoming, I'm not coming back here."

She might as well have told him she was moving to South America and joining a cult. "Does Diana know this?" he asked carefully.

"I just made up my mind this morning."

"That's a pretty big decision. Maybe you should give it some more thought."

"There's nothing here for me anymore."

"What about Diana?"

"Other than Diana."

"What about your friends?"

"They're part of my past." She traced the lifeline on her left palm with the index finger of her right hand. "We used to have things in common, but not anymore."

"If you decide you don't like it in Jackson, where will you go?"

She curled her hand around her finger, as if symbolically bringing her old life to an end. "I don't know . . . I never thought about living anywhere else before." She looked at him and smiled. "I guess I'd better start thinking about it, huh?"

It wasn't threat, or defeat, or compromise Travis

heard in Amy's voice. It was a declaration of independence. "Promise me you'll give us a chance."

She tried to keep the smile, but her lips held a telltale quiver. Tears formed and pooled behind her eyelashes. "No one wants this to work more than I do, Travis," she said. "I won't give up without a fight."

Diana left Stephanie's apartment, glanced at the digital numbers above the elevator, and saw that the car was on the lobby floor. Rather than wait, she took the stairs, arriving out of breath and only seconds before the elevator doors opened and Travis and Amy got out.

"You're home," Diana said, forcing a smile. She hated that she was lying to Amy again. "I've been pacing the floor waiting for you."

"We would have been here sooner, but Travis took a wrong turn." She came across the hall and gave Diana a quick hug. "Shouldn't you be at work?"

"I wanted to be here when you got home." She held the door open and stepped aside for Amy to enter.

Travis gave her a questioning look. "I took everything down to Stephanie's," she whispered as he passed. "You can pick it up later when we know which hotel you'll be staying at."

He had a bag containing Amy's personal things in one hand and a vase of flowers in the other. "Where do you want me to put these?"

"In here," Amy said, indicating the spare room.

"How do you feel?" Diana asked.

"A little tired, but it's great to get out of that place. I think I would have walked home if Travis hadn't been there to give me a ride."

"Are you hungry?" The invisible barrier still stood between them. "There's soup and things for sandwiches."

"They wouldn't let me leave until I had lunch," Amy said. "But Travis hasn't eaten anything."

"I'll get something later," he said.

Diana glanced at her watch and then at Travis. "I couldn't get the rest of the afternoon off. Would you mind staying with Amy until I get home tonight?"

"I don't need a keeper," Amy said testily. "And you didn't have to take off work to be here."

"Sorry, Ms. Winchester," Travis said, "but as I recall, having someone here with you was one of the conditions of your release." To Diana he said, "I planned on staying."

"It's good to have you home." She gave Amy another hug, ignoring the stiff response. "I'll be back as soon as I can get away."

"It's good to be home," Amy told her automatically.

"I love you." Diana forced the words past a knot in her throat.

"You'd better get going." Amy released her and took a step backward. "You've already missed too much work because of me."

Diana brushed her hand across Amy's cheek. "Take care of yourself."

"I'll make sure she does," Travis said.

When Diana was gone, Amy turned to Travis. "She must like you."

He put his arm around her shoulders and led her into the kitchen. "Now why would you say that?"

"She let you use her car. As far as I know, she's never done that with anyone else. She didn't even ask you for the keys when she left. Which means she let you have her spare."

Travis couldn't tell if she was testing him or simply making an observation. "How about a cup of tea before your nap?"

"What nap?"

"The one you're going to take as soon as you finish your tea."

"Are you this bossy with everyone, or should I consider myself special?"

He pulled out a chair and indicated she should sit in it. "If you asked Sharon, she'd probably tell you it was everyone."

"Do you think she'll like me?"

He'd been honest with Amy about her sisters, letting her know that Faith and Judy were going to be slow coming around, but that she could look to Sharon to be an ally. "Just last night she asked me the same thing about you."

"What did you tell her?"

"That I was sure you would hate each other on sight."

Amy recoiled in surprise. "Why would you say—"

"I'm *kidding*." He should have known she would take him seriously. Everything was serious to Amy now. "I told her if she liked what she saw in the mirror every morning, the two of you were going to get along fine."

Amy got up, filled the kettle with water, and took two cups out of the cupboard. "You really scared me, Travis. If you hadn't told me you weren't serious, I don't know what I would have done."

"I'm sorry. I shouldn't have—"

She turned and gave him a mischievous wink. "I'm *kidding*."

Travis laughed. "I have absolutely no doubt you and Sharon are going to get along just fine."

Diana stopped by the bakery on her way home to pick up the carrot cake she'd ordered that afternoon to celebrate Amy's homecoming. When she arrived at the condo she found Amy asleep and Travis on the balcony, a mug in one hand, the phone in the other.

He looked up when he saw her at the sliding glass door and signaled he would be with her in a minute. While she waited, she put the cake in the refrigerator, stepped out of her shoes, and took off her jacket.

Travis came in as she was pouring herself a glass of iced tea. "Is she awake?" he asked softly.

Diana shook her head.

He put the phone back in its cradle, glanced down the hall, and gave her a quick kiss. "How was your day?"

"The usual." It had been hell. Nothing had gone right—from the meeting she'd missed to an urgent shipment from the Nebraska office that had been lost in transit. But she didn't want to talk about her problems at work. "How did it go with Amy?"

"She was a little surprised to see how well I knew my way around your kitchen, and wanted to know how I'd charmed you into letting me borrow your car, but other than that, we got along fine."

"I take it she was satisfied with your explanations?"

"She's so worried about meeting the family, I don't think she can take in much else."

"Was that your dad on the phone?"

He shook his head. "One of my guides. Things are starting to get a little backed up at TMO with me gone."

"A little?" She offered him a taste of her tea.

He took a drink and handed it back. "All right, a lot. As soon as Amy's able to stay by herself, I'm going to have to get out of here."

"I'm sorry, Travis. I know I'm imposing on you, but everything is in such a mess at work right now, I'm afraid if I take any more time off, they're going to be looking for someone to replace me."

"I thought I heard voices," Amy said from the doorway. She yawned. "When did you get home?"

"About five minutes ago," Diana said. "How are you feeling?"

Amy yawned again before answering. "Like there's an empty hole where my stomach should be. Can we send for pizza?"

"Sounds good to me," Travis said.

It was on the tip of Diana's tongue to insist Amy eat something more nutritious, but she stopped as she heard the words echoing in her mind. God, at times she could be such a drag. "Sounds good to me, too."

Twenty-eight

━━━

By Thursday Amy was feeling well enough to go grocery shopping with Travis. She pushed the cart while he tossed in cans and boxes. When they arrived home, Amy insisted she would fix them lunch. After they'd cleaned the kitchen, and she still had enough energy to beat him twice in a row at gin rummy, Travis folded his cards, dropped them on the table, and said, "You need a keeper about as much as a bee needs a map."

Amy gathered the cards and shuffled them once before putting them back in the box. "That's what I've been trying to tell you and Diana, but you're both so hardheaded you refuse to listen."

"How are the headaches?"

"I haven't had one since Monday." She liked that he worried about her. "I'm beginning to think I must have been allergic to the hospital."

"Well, if I'm not needed, there's no reason for me to stick around. I might as well go home and get back to work."

She'd known this day was coming, but it didn't make it any easier. "I'm going to miss you."

"How long?"

She frowned. "How long what?"

"How long before you come home—to Jackson?"

"I'm not sure. There are some things I have to do here first."

"You have to have some idea. A week? A month?"

"What you really want to know is if you're going to have to come back and get me."

"Something like that."

She tore the top sheet off the tablet they'd been using to keep score, wadded it into a ball, and tossed it into the trash. "Don't worry, I'm not going to change my mind."

"I've been thinking about your decision not to come back to Minneapolis."

"What about it?"

"You're putting an awful lot of pressure on yourself. All this time you've been worried about whether the rest of the family will like you. What if it turns out you don't like them? Maybe it would work out better if you kept the first visit short, a week or two, then you could come back to Minneapolis for a while and visit the family again in a couple of months."

"Leaving Minneapolis isn't something that just came to me, Travis. I've given this a lot of thought." Since waking up from the coma, she'd thought of little else.

"Have you talked to Diana about it yet?"

She'd come up with a dozen reasons not to—the time wasn't right, Diana was too busy, there were other people around. They were excuses, ways to postpone hurting the one person who deserved it the least. "Not yet," she admitted. "But I will—soon."

"Something tells me she's not going to like the idea."

Amy knew Diana wouldn't like it. But she knew

something else, too. Once Diana got past the initial surprise, she wouldn't fight anymore. Diana loved her enough to let her go. "So, when do you think you'll be going back?" she asked, purposely changing the subject.

"Tomorrow night."

"So soon?"

"We lost one of the guides who's been with us almost since the beginning. If we don't find someone to take his place before next week, we're going to have to cancel his trip. You can imagine how well that would go over."

"One of your guides died?"

Travis laughed. "Nothing that dramatic. He broke his leg skydiving."

"That's dramatic enough for me. I'm surprised you let your employees do that kind of thing while they're working."

"They're an independent lot, Amy. They pretty much do whatever and whenever they want." He stood and took their empty glasses to the sink. "Now why don't you take a nap while I call the airlines."

She was tired and had been headed that way anyway, but she couldn't resist saying, "First you tell me how well I'm doing, then you tell me to take a nap."

"I want you bright-eyed when Diana comes home."

"First—I'm going to put an ad in the paper for my car. How much do you think I should ask?"

Travis had used Amy's car a couple of times when Diana had needed hers at work. "I think a better question would be how much you should offer to get someone to take it off your hands."

"It runs. It has to be worth something."

"Just because something *can* run doesn't mean it should," he said.

"So you think I should junk it?"

"The sooner the better. Why do you think I borrowed Diana's car to go shopping today?"

"All right, I will—as soon as I don't need it anymore."

"I thought you said you'd seen enough of hospitals."

"It can't be that bad. You drove it."

"Twice," he said. "After that I decided I'd be safer walking down the middle of the highway."

"All right, all right—I give up. I'll call a junkyard first thing tomorrow."

He gave her a gentle shove toward the guest room. "And I'll leave here a happy man."

That night after work, Diana caught a ride home with Stephanie. "How are you feeling?" she asked.

"Not bad. A little sick to my stomach sometimes, but nothing like what my cousin went through when she was carrying her first."

"Have you told your mom and dad?"

She turned to check traffic before merging into the next lane. "I started to, but decided to wait until after I'd been to the doctor. I have an appointment next week."

"How do you think they'll take it?"

"Not well. My father likes to think I'm still a virgin. For the first time since I moved here, I'm glad they live three states away."

"They'll come around once the baby arrives. How could anyone not love a baby?" The statement had been automatic. She looked at Stephanie. "I can't believe I said that—me of all people."

"I'm not worried how they'll respond to the baby," Stephanie said. "I just hate to have them disappointed in me."

"Have you heard from Stan?"

"He left a couple of messages on my machine last week, but I'm not ready to talk to him yet." She slowed as the traffic began to build. "Enough about me. How's it going with your folks? Did you tell them about Travis?"

Diana hadn't said anything to Stephanie about the fight she'd had with her mother and father, figuring she had enough problems of her own. Now, rather than lie or sidestep the question, she gave Stephanie a brief rundown.

"Wow," Stephanie said after the telling. "This just gets better and better. How long do you think they'll stay mad at you?"

"Unless I do something to pacify them—which means giving them back the money—it could be forever."

"And are you going to give it back?"

"Not in this lifetime."

"Have you thought what you're going to do with it?"

"I had planned to give it to Amy," Diana said. "But I don't think there's any way I could talk her into taking it now. I don't even want to try anymore."

"Then why keep it?"

"Stubbornness, pure and simple."

Stephanie laughed. "I suppose that's as good a reason as any. The money's not going anywhere. Someday you'll come up with the perfect way to spend it." She pulled into the underground garage. "Amy's car is gone."

Diana looked at the visitors area where the Pinto had been parked that morning. "Wouldn't it be great if someone stole it?"

Travis was in the kitchen on the phone when Diana came in. She glanced through the crack in Amy's door as she passed and saw that she was asleep. It seemed as if a pattern had formed.

"Yes, that's right," she heard Travis say. "One way, whatever you have open tomorrow night." He waited. "Eight forty-five is fine."

A quick stab of disappointment forced Diana to catch her breath. Travis was making arrangements to leave. He hadn't even told her he was going. She came into the kitchen.

"Travis Martell," he said, and spelled his last name. After reading out a credit card number, he hung up.

"You're leaving?" Diana asked.

He took her in his arms. "I'm sorry. All hell is breaking loose at—"

She put her finger to his lips. "You don't have to explain. I know you'd stay if you could."

"Amy's doing fine. By Monday she'll be up to staying on her own without any problem."

"I'm going to miss you." She laid her head against his chest. She desperately didn't want him to go.

Travis stopped to listen when he thought he heard a sound coming from the hallway. Relieved when it wasn't followed by another, and that they still had a few moments alone, he pressed his face against Diana's hair, breathing in its clean smell.

The words he needed to say hung heavy between them. The love he felt for Diana wasn't meant to be a long-distance kind of thing. He wanted to go to bed with her at night, wake up with her in the morning, and know that she would be there always, through the good and the bad, the children and the grandchildren. He understood that he had no right to ask her to give up her home and the career she'd built for herself, but there was no way he could survive in Minneapolis. They had to find a way for their worlds to merge before their lives could.

Until he had an answer, he couldn't ask the question.

"I want you to come to Jackson with Amy. There are places in the mountains I want to take you where you won't see another human being for days. Places where the water runs so clear and cold you'll swear you can hear it crack when it hits the rocks. There's so much I want to show you, Diana."

She leaned her head back, looked up, and kissed him. She was filled with a deep ache to have him make love to her. Since Amy had come home, and Travis had moved to the hotel, they hadn't had more than a few minutes alone. They needed time and a place where they could close out the reality that kept them from putting their love into words and from expressing hopes too fragile to withstand practicalities.

A low groan escaped the back of Travis's throat as he deepened the kiss, opening his mouth to taste her, to make her a part of himself. "Come back to the hotel with me tonight," he murmured against her lips.

She'd never wanted anything more in her life. "Let me call Stephanie. I'll see if she can stay with Amy."

Diana had the number half dialed when Amy came into the kitchen. She stood at the doorway and stretched. "I must have slept longer than I thought," she said. "I didn't even hear you come home."

Diana hung up, deciding the call could wait a couple of minutes. "I tried to be quiet."

"Did Travis tell you he was leaving tomorrow?"

"We were just talking about it."

"I thought maybe we could do something special to celebrate his last night in town—if that's all right with you."

Diana cast a quick look in Travis's direction. "Of

course it is." How could she say no? "What did you have in mind?"

"We bought some steaks at the store today. Travis could barbecue. You could make scalloped potatoes, and I'll fix a salad." Her voice picked up enthusiasm as she went along. "I think we should invite Stephanie, too. She and Travis will probably never see each other again. This way she'll have a chance to tell him good-bye."

"What do you think, Travis?" Diana asked, fighting to keep the disappointment from her voice. "Are you up for a going-away party?"

He shoved his hands in his pockets. "Sure—why not?"

The next day Diana was late picking Travis up to go to the airport. She'd left work early so they'd have time to stop for a bite to eat. More important, she'd wanted a chance to say good-bye in private. Then, halfway home, for the first time in her life, she'd had a flat tire. The auto club promised to send a truck "right away." Right away turned into an hour.

Even though he had promised to call the next day, Amy had trouble letting Travis go. She walked them to the door, and then the elevator, and then finally rode down with them to the garage.

"I feel like a heel leaving her," Travis said when they were finally on their way.

"I've never seen her like this," Diana said. "She usually tries to hide her feelings. I'm surprised she didn't insist on coming with us."

"I think she knew it was beyond her energy level."

"That wouldn't have stopped the old Amy."

"Do you suppose she knew we wanted to be alone?"

Diana shook her head. "I've left a couple of openings to see if she'd picked up on something. She hasn't."

Diana took the surface streets to avoid the worst of the Friday rush-hour traffic, but finally had to give up and take the highway. Despite her attempts to save a few minutes for them to say good-bye, by the time they arrived at the airport it was too late to do anything but drop Travis off at the terminal. She got out of the car to stand with him while he checked his bag.

"The best-laid plans . . . ," she said, forcing a brightness she didn't feel. She wanted him to remember her smiling.

He dropped his bag on the sidewalk and took her in his arms. "Promise me I won't have to come back here to get you, that you'll come when Amy does."

"I'll do what I can."

A man in a blue uniform came up to them. "Excuse me, sir, are you checking this bag?"

"Yes." Travis released Diana and dug in his pocket for his ticket.

The man scanned the flight information. "If it's important your bag gets to Jackson the same time you do, you might want to consider carrying it on."

Travis looked at his watch. "I had no idea we were this late."

Diana was struck with a sudden, deep need to tell him that her life would be as empty without him as her sky was without the Milky Way. Neither would ever be the same to her again. She put her hand on his arm and started to tell him when he leaned over and kissed her.

"I've got to go." He was already moving away from her when he said, "I'll call you tomorrow."

She stood frozen as he went inside, her gaze

locked on his retreating back. Then, as if drawn by her longing, he stopped, turned, and came running back. He shouted, "I love you," as the glass doors opened to let a frantic man slip through.

She shouted back, "I love you, too." But the doors had closed again. There was no way he could have heard her.

Twenty-nine

———

Diana and Amy were in the middle of an indulgent pancake breakfast the next morning when Travis called. Amy hopped up from the table and had the receiver in her hand before Diana could get her chair pushed back.

"How was the flight?" Amy asked.

Diana sat back down and reached for her coffee. She picked up a section of the newspaper and tried to focus on an article about wolves in Yellowstone Park. Fleetingly, she wondered whether the rancher in Travis would be for or against reintroducing the natural predators and how that would conflict with the naturalist in him. She had so much to learn about this man she loved.

"I feel great," Amy said. "There's no way it's going to take another two weeks to get back to where I was. Even Diana said she thinks I'm way ahead of where the doctors told me I'd be."

Even Diana. She felt like an outsider. When had she been relegated to that category?

"I will," Amy said. And then, "You too . . ." Then, finally, "Call me when you get back." She hung up the phone and turned to Diana. "Travis said to say hi."

"He didn't want to talk to me?" Diana struggled to hide the disappointment.

Amy looked puzzled. "I'm sorry, I didn't even think to ask."

"That's okay. I'll catch him another time." She folded the paper she'd been reading and returned it to the stack. "I was just wondering if he made his plane all right. We got there late."

"He didn't mention it."

It was everything she could do to keep from grilling Amy. "Did I hear you say something about Travis going somewhere?"

Amy topped off their coffee before sitting down. "He and his dad—" She flushed and made a face. "I can't seem to get the hang of thinking of him as my dad, too. Anyway, they're going to someplace called Pinedale to see if Travis can talk an old fraternity brother of his into helping out at the ranch while Travis gets the guide thing straightened out."

She tried to take a bite of toast but couldn't get it past her lips. "How long will he be gone?"

"A couple of days. He said he'd call as soon as they get back."

Diana couldn't ask anything more without being obvious. "So, what do you want to do today?"

Amy considered the question. "Why don't we go for a ride? We could pack a picnic, and a blanket, and drive until we get hungry."

"And spend the rest of the day finding clouds that look like people," Diana finished for her. It had been one of Amy's favorite things to do when she was growing up.

"Let's borrow Stephanie's bird book. Do you still have your binoculars?"

"Stuart took . . . No, wait a minute. They were in my closet." Diana got up to look. She was halfway to the stairs when she remembered something she'd been meaning to ask Amy. "What did you do with your car?"

"I sold it."

"Who would buy—" She decided to leave the rest alone. She couldn't decide whether she was more surprised that Amy had given up her treasured piece of trash or that she'd actually found someone willing to take it.

"Travis found a junk dealer who paid me twenty-five dollars and towed it away free."

She should have known Travis was involved in this. "So now I guess we should add car shopping to our list of things to do."

"It can wait. I've got other things to do first."

Diana didn't understand. Amy's independence was tied to her transportation. "You can use the Volvo until you figure out what you want to do."

"I'm impressed. First Travis and now me."

"What's that supposed to mean?"

"You used to be so hard-nosed about people borrowing your car, and now—"

"I've learned there are more important things in life."

Amy smiled. "It's about time."

The weekend was the best Diana and Amy had spent together in longer than either of them could remember. They drove north for their picnic, laughed over dumb jokes, and ate potato salad with their fingers when they discovered they'd forgotten to pack utensils. That night, they cried over *Casablanca* and consumed a dinner with marginal nutritional value.

On Monday Amy got up early and drove Diana to work. She said she had some things to take care of at her apartment but didn't elaborate. When she picked Diana up later that evening, she was unusually quiet and asked Diana to drive.

"How was your day?" Diana asked. Before she slid behind the wheel, she took off her jacket and heels. Once inside, she turned the air conditioner on high. The heat and humidity both hovered at ninety, making her feel like one big piece of human flypaper.

"Interesting," Amy said.

Diana decided not to push. "What sounds good for dinner?"

"Whatever you want. I'm not very hungry."

"What about gazpacho? It's too hot to cook anything."

"That sounds fine."

They rode the rest of the way in an easy silence. Diana glanced at Amy occasionally to see if she'd gone to sleep but always found her staring out the window.

As soon as they arrived home, Amy headed for the bathroom, and Diana went into the kitchen to get something to drink. She was on her way upstairs when something in the living room caught her eye. Transfixed, she stood and stared and tried to make sense out of what she was seeing. No matter how she came at it, she couldn't come up with a reason Amy's clock would be sitting on her bookshelf. Finally, she tapped on the bathroom door and asked, "What is your clock doing here?"

A minute later, Amy came out. "I want you to take care of it for me."

"Why me? What's wrong with keeping it at your place?"

Amy looked down at her feet, avoiding Diana's questioning look. The lightheartedness of the weekend had become a shadow usurped by the night. "We have to talk, Diana."

A seed of fear burst in Diana's chest. A clear, compelling voice told her she didn't want to hear what Amy would say. "Give me a minute to get out of these clothes." She started upstairs. "You know, it just hit me that we haven't been to Roberto's for pasta in months. How about we skip the soup and—"

"I think it would be better if we stayed in tonight."

The fear became a lump, cold and hard and heavy. "It was just a thought."

When Diana came downstairs again, Amy was in the kitchen making iced tea. "Good idea," she said too cheerfully.

Amy turned and braced her hands against the counter. "I moved out of my apartment today."

"Why?" Before Amy could answer, Diana asked, "Where?"

"I guess moved out isn't quite accurate. Actually, I called that group that builds low-income housing for the homeless and had them come and take whatever they could use. Which turned out to be nearly everything. What they didn't take, I had that thrift store near the mall come and pick up."

"You gave all your furniture away?" Diana tried to make sense out of what she was hearing, but Amy might as well have told her she had sprouted wings and could fly. "Why would you do that?"

Amy folded her arms across her chest, the motion seeming more to hold herself together than to close Diana out. "I didn't want to put it in storage, and I liked the idea of a fresh start—all the way around."

"What aren't you telling me?"

"When I leave, I'm not coming back."

Diana could barely breathe past the pain that filled her. She'd assumed Amy would want to visit Wyoming. It had never occurred to her that she would stay there. "You don't mean that."

"I've thought about it a lot, Diana. I know what I'm doing."

"But this is your home."

Instead of answering, Amy let Diana's words hang in the air between them.

"What if you don't like your new family? What will you do then?"

"Start again—somewhere else."

Diana's legs wouldn't hold her anymore. She pulled out a chair and sat down. "I wish you had talked to me about this first."

"Don't you think it's about time I started making my own decisions?" Amy asked gently.

"That's crazy. You've always made your own—"

"No, I haven't, Diana." With a sigh, Amy sat down, too. She reached across the table and took Diana's hand. "I've leaned on you my entire life. If I'm ever going to be a whole person, I have to learn to stand on my own."

"Why does it have to be in some other state? Why can't you do it right here?"

"This isn't a whim. I'm fighting for my life."

And I'm fighting for mine, Diana wanted to shout. They might not be genetically linked, but Amy was her family—according to her father, her only family. "I don't know what to say to you."

"There's more," Amy said softly.

Diana withdrew her hand and put it in her lap. "You might as well tell me now and get it over with."

"I have to do this alone."

"Do what alone?" Before Amy could answer, Diana knew. It was okay, she could live with Amy's need for independence. "You don't want me to go to Wyoming with you?"

"Please, Diana . . . you have to listen to me. Really listen. With all your heart." Her voice caught. She blinked to rid her eyes of sudden, blinding tears. "All my life you've been my strength. Whenever I felt I couldn't go on, you were always there to pick me up. I couldn't have made it this far without you."

"But?" Diana knew she didn't want to hear what would come next, but like the horrified passerby of an accident, she couldn't turn away.

"I don't know what it's like to stand on my own," Amy said.

"Put it in words I can understand."

"I have to go to Wyoming alone, and I have to be there alone. Until I'm sure I don't need you, I can't see you, or even talk to you."

It was as if a shaft of ice had been laid along Diana's spine, draining all the heat from her. Amy was as much a part of her as her arm, or leg, or heart. She couldn't be whole without any of them. "Are you doing this because you're still mad at me?"

"Diana . . . don't—" The rest was caught in a sob. "I love you. I would trade my life for yours."

"Then I don't understand why you're doing this."

"I've been given a chance to start over, to become someone I might even learn to like someday . . . someone you could admire. Do you have any idea how much that means to me?"

"I love you, too, Amy. How can you expect me just to let you walk out of my life without a fight?"

"You love me, but you don't admire me. You have to let me have this chance to change your mind. We won't be apart forever. I couldn't do that, not even if I had to stay the way I am now for the rest of my life."

"I still don't understand how cutting me out of your life is going to help you."

"If I get knocked down, you won't be there to pick me up. I'll have to do it all by myself. If I can't run to you with my problems, I'll have to solve them myself. If I make a mistake, I'm the one who's going to have to fix it. And if I fall on my face, I'm going to have to bandage my own bloody nose. Most of all, if I start drinking again, I'm either going to have to stop on my own, or let it destroy me."

It was hard for Diana to feel anything beyond her own heart breaking, but she couldn't ignore the desperate look in Amy's eyes or the conviction in her voice. "How long?"

"I don't know. I'm so scared I can't think much past meeting my mother for the first time." Amy fixed her gaze on something outside the window. "Did Travis tell you she hasn't changed her mind about wanting me?"

"She's not worth beating yourself up over."

It was the wrong response. "That's for me to decide, Diana."

Diana was on the outside; it was as if Amy had already mentally moved into the circle of her new family. If this was a glimpse, a hint, of what Amy had felt her whole life, it was a more profound loneliness than Diana had ever imagined. "I'm sorry," was all she could think to say.

"I know what I'm asking is hard. As soon as I know I can make it on my own, I'll call you."

"Things will never be the same between us."

Amy gave her a small smile. "I'm hoping they'll be even better."

"I'm going to miss you," Diana said, yielding ground.

"Not nearly as much as I'm going to miss you." Amy looked out the window again. "You have to promise that you won't try to see me, or call me—that no matter how long it takes, you'll wait for me to call you."

Feeling as if the words were being torn from her, Diana said, "I promise."

"Wait—that's not all."

"What more could you want from me, Amy?"

"Promise me you won't call or write or see Travis, either."

The mental blow left her as stunned as if it had been physical.

Before Diana could say anything, Amy went on, "I know you've become friends. And I know that if you stay friends, it will be impossible for you to keep from checking up on me. The break between us has to be complete."

Still Diana said nothing.

Amy turned to look at her. "Promise?"

The innocence in Amy's expression told Diana everything she needed to know. She had no idea what she was asking. Diana could scarcely breathe through the pain. Loneliness settled over her. Love and happiness became the prizes in a spinning wheel of fortune where she'd been given the questionable right to choose the winner—Travis, Amy, or herself. Only she didn't know the rules. Should the prizes go to the most needy, the most deserving? If so, the decision had been made for her a long time ago.

Diana looked into her sister's eyes. "I promise," she said softly.

Thirty

Diana lived in a bittersweet haze the next two days while Amy glowed at the prospect of her second chance at life. As the day she would leave drew closer, Amy continued to grow stronger and more determined. While Diana exulted in the change, she mourned the reason. If she'd required proof that Amy was right about having to face her future alone, she had it every moment they were together. Instead of the hoped-for change of heart, Diana saw a constant reinforcement of the impassioned reasoning Amy had already given her. Slowly, inexorably, Diana was made to face something she desperately did not want to believe—Amy had to learn to stand alone before she could lean on someone without losing a part of herself in the process.

In a remarkable show of determination, Amy talked her doctor into releasing her on Wednesday. As soon as she left his office, she made arrangements to fly out of Minneapolis the next morning.

Diana drove her to the airport, refusing to give in to the childish, selfish voice that demanded she remind Amy who had been her sister first, who had stood by her the longest, and whose heart had broken at the thought of losing her. Even for someone as known for her patience as Diana was, the time Amy had requested to build the foundation for her new life seemed objectionably long. What if the weeks slipped into months? Would it make the time go faster if she marked the days on the calendar the way prisoners did?

As they moved through the terminal, further conversation was impossible. They had nothing to say to each other that they hadn't said a dozen times already. Only fear contained Amy's joy. Only hope kept Diana from sinking into the depths of depression.

The attendant called for boarding. Diana managed to stay dry-eyed when she kissed Amy goodbye. She even found a smile when she wished her Godspeed.

Later, after the plane was loaded, Diana couldn't force herself to move, not until the attendant closed the ramp door. It was as if she were afraid to give whatever fates controlled her destiny the chance to shrug and say to themselves that Diana Winchester didn't care enough about her sister to stick around to see if she would change her mind at the last minute.

But the door closed without Amy running back up the ramp.

In a fog, Diana went to the window to watch the plane taxi to the runway. She remained there, her nose pressed to the glass, her gaze fixed on the gleaming silver wings, on the powerful engines, on the long row of windows filled with people looking back, staring at the plane until it was airborne . . . until it became a tiny speck . . . until it disappeared forever when she blinked.

Amy was gone, sworn never to return, her life begun anew.

Diana took the long way home, seeking comfort in the familiar. Nothing seemed the same. She felt no ties to the people in the parks, no welcome in the neighborhoods. She'd lived in the Cities all her life, yet she felt like a stranger. Where before she'd been tied by roots generations old, now there was only a sense of isolation. All that held her here now was knowing she had nowhere else to go.

Thirty-one

As soon as Diana arrived home from the airport, she broke her promise to Amy. She'd known from the beginning there would be this one exception. Afterward she would do everything she'd been asked, would abide by all of the rules, but she would not turn away from Travis without first telling him good-bye, not even for Amy.

They hadn't talked since his return to Jackson, both by circumstance and by desire. Her one opportunity, when Amy was in the shower, she'd let the machine pick up. She hadn't known what to say then, how to explain that she'd chosen Amy over him. That wasn't accurate, there had been no selection process, no scale to weigh the value of one choice over the other, but the results, the sense of loss, the heartache, were the same as if she'd engaged in a battle where only one could come out the winner.

Diana took the portable phone out on the balcony and dialed Travis's home number. He answered on the second ring.

"It's me," she said.

"God, it's good to hear your voice again. Where are you?"

There was too much space around her. She needed to be held, if only by a room. She went back inside. "At home."

"What are you doing there? Isn't your plane supposed to be landing in a couple of hours?"

She moved into the bedroom Amy had been using and sat on the corner of the bed. "Amy's coming alone."

A long time passed before he asked, "Whose idea was that?"

"Hers."

"I knew she'd decided not to go back to Minneapolis, but she never said anything about—"

"There's something I have to tell you, Travis," she said. "It won't be easy to hear, and even harder to understand, but I need you to listen with your heart as well as your mind."

Travis walked over to the window and looked at the Douglas fir seedling he'd planted that morning. It was Diana's tree, something to celebrate her first day there with him, something they could watch grow together. "I'm not going to like this, am I?"

"No more than I do."

The telling took only minutes. He listened without comment, taking in what she was saying, refusing to accept there wasn't a way around the chasm that Amy had inadvertently opened between them. But then slowly, sentence by sentence, a wall of logic and emotion began to grow. True or not, Amy could never have left Diana behind if she hadn't believed with every fiber of her being that she had to.

"I didn't know what else to do," Diana said. "I had to let her go."

"How long have you known?" He didn't know why it mattered, only that it did.

"A couple of days."

"Why did you wait until now to call me?"

"I needed time—and I promised Amy I wouldn't."

"She made you promise you wouldn't talk to me?" He couldn't stop looking at the tree.

"I know what you're thinking, but she doesn't know about us."

"Then why—"

"The break has to be clean."

"How is she going to know if we talk to each other?"

"Maybe she wouldn't, but I would. I promised I'd do this for her, Travis. She's never asked me for anything. Not once." Her voice cracked. "Not even when that son of a bitch beat her up."

"Did you see this coming?"

"No. Even if I had, it wouldn't have made any difference."

He couldn't let it go. There had to be a way for them to be together. "You don't have to break your promise. I'll come to you." As soon as he'd said the words he felt how wrong they were. "I'm sorry. I know how much pressure I'm putting on you, but I can't accept this the way you obviously have."

"I've had more time. We just have to keep reminding ourselves it's only a couple of weeks."

He didn't buy it, not for a minute. "It took your parents years to do what they did to Amy. Even if my mother wasn't here ready to do battle with her the minute she stepped off the plane, it would take a hell of a lot longer than a couple of weeks for Amy to find what she needs."

"It doesn't matter. And it doesn't change the promise I made."

"You don't believe it's only a matter of weeks any more than I do."

"Then months," she acknowledged.

He still didn't buy it. "Why are you acting as if we'll never see each other again?"

"Probably because you've only been gone for a couple of days and it feels like an eternity," she said softly. "I guess that's what happens when you love someone."

He leaned his shoulder into the wall, shaken by words that filled him with a bittersweet joy. "What am I going to do without you?"

"The same thing you did before you met me."

He couldn't fight her anymore. "Wait for me."

"Always . . . forever."

"I love you, Diana."

She didn't say anything for a long time. "I understand what love is because of you." Her breath caught in a quick, muffled sob. "Take care of Amy for me."

And then she was gone.

Amy leaned forward in her seat, her gaze fixed on the mountains and the valley floor as the plane began its descent into Jackson Hole. As she had been doing for nearly an hour, she nervously folded and unfolded the top of an uneaten package of peanuts. Her stomach recoiled at the thought of actually eating them, of putting food of any kind in her mouth. Even the club soda she'd had earlier had taken effort to get down. It was as if her fear had gathered into an enormous knot in her stomach.

Finally, the plane was on the ground and had taxied to a stop. She unbuckled her seat belt and stepped into the aisle. As she began to move toward the door, she realized a transition had taken place.

Now, instead of walking away from her past, she was walking toward her future.

Travis was waiting for her. He came forward, enfolding her in a bear hug that took care of any lingering doubt she had about being welcome. "Dad decided to wait for us at the house. He thought it might be easier if you weren't overwhelmed by everyone at once."

"You came alone, then?" Amy asked.

"Sharon's waiting for us in the car." He wanted to ask about Diana but decided it would be better to let Amy take the lead. He took her carry-on bag and guided her toward the luggage pickup.

"I managed to get everything I own into two suitcases," she said.

She hadn't told him about giving everything away until after it was an accomplished fact. He would have preferred that she'd taken things more slowly, that she hadn't jumped off the cliff until she had a safety net in place, but it seemed that wasn't Amy's style, at least not the style of this new, determined Amy. "No second thoughts?"

"A couple, but not what you'd suppose. I knew it would be hard to leave Diana, I just didn't know how hard."

"I thought she was coming with you," he said, reluctantly playing along.

"She's taken care of me my entire life. I decided it was time I took over the job myself."

"If that's true, she didn't seem to mind."

"Maybe not, but that didn't make it right. I'm hoping that without me around to take up all of her time she'll meet some really terrific guy, get married, and have half a dozen kids."

Travis started to say something when he saw Sharon headed their way.

"I couldn't wait one minute longer," she said,

extending her hand to Amy. "Hi, I'm Sharon—your big sister."

Amy took her hand. "I'm Amy."

"Of course you are. I would have recognized you anywhere." Sharon cupped Amy's face between her hands and looked into her eyes. "Wouldn't you know you'd be the pretty one."

Amy had her mouth open to protest, "But I'm not—"

"You're wasting your time," Travis told her. "Sharon never loses an argument. She's the most stubborn—"

"Don't listen to anything he tells you about me," Sharon said. "He's upset the Martell sisters have gained an even bigger advantage." She slipped her arm through Amy's. "When it was three to one, he managed to get a word in once in a while. Now that there are four of us, he won't stand a chance."

Travis had always admired Sharon, but never more than at that moment. With an understanding heart, and an economy of words, she'd brought Amy into the family.

"We'll wait for you out in the car," Sharon said to Travis. To Amy, she said, "I brought some pictures of the family. Nothing great, just us kids when we were growing up, but they're kind of fun to look at. Especially the ones of Travis. Wait till you see what he looked like when he was ten. His was skinny as a fence post and all ears." She looked at Travis and smiled. "Of course he's the best-lookin' guy in Jackson, now. Except for Davis, of course."

"Before Davis would marry her, he made her sign a piece of paper swearing she'd tell everyone how handsome he is," Travis said.

Sharon laughed and put her arm through Amy's. "Don't believe a word he says."

"My suitcases are green," Amy called out as she was led away. "With a piece of orange tape around the handle."

"Dad's almost worn out the carpet pacing back and forth waiting for you to get here," Sharon said. "He can't wait to see you. Faith is at the house, too. She brought a present, and then decided that was a dumb idea, so she took the present back, and got flowers instead. Be sure and act surprised. She'd shoot me if she knew. . . ." Her voice faded as she led Amy out of the terminal.

Travis smiled at their retreating backs. A kindling of hope sparked into fire in his chest. Maybe everything would work out after all. With a family to love her, it wouldn't take long for Amy to discover the inner strength that had made her the survivor she was. After that, she would be eager to have Diana back in her life again.

And he and Diana would be together again.

"Travis—what are you doing here?"

He looked up to see Joyce Lockford, a friend of his mother's, headed his way. "Meeting my sister."

"If I'd known, I would have had you pick up Jack, too. His car is in the shop, and he had to fly out yesterday for a meeting in Casper."

"Is he still trying to make up his mind about buying that bull?"

She nodded and looked to the ceiling in long-suffering frustration. "How's your mother? I haven't seen her around lately."

The question grounded Travis as hard and effectively as lightning hitting a hot-air balloon. How could he have believed, even for a minute, that with his mother waiting to do battle, Amy's road home could be smooth?

Thirty-two

———

Diana sorted through her mail as she headed for the elevator. She smiled when she spotted the "love note" Stephanie's daughter, Rachel, had stuffed through the slot. Her refrigerator was covered with similar missives, the collection dating from the day her one-and-a-half-year-old godchild had received her first box of crayons. While Diana was convinced she saw real talent in the creations, Stephanie insisted they were nothing more than the frustrated ramblings of a child whose real goal was to create her masterpiece on the living room wall.

Less interesting, and certainly less fun, was an assortment of advertising flyers, magazines, and bills. In the mix were a couple of letters that held promise. The first was an announcement of the upcoming dinner and auction to benefit the battered-women's shelters of Minneapolis and St. Paul. The evening's special honoree—Diana Winchester.

She smiled, a little taken aback but pleased. The organization had an old and somewhat archaic tradition of not revealing the name of that year's honoree before the invitations were sent out, automatically

assuming everyone would be as pleased with the
choice as the committee. She'd had no idea she was
even in the running. There were a dozen volunteers
who'd put in more time and effort that past year—
but, of course, none who'd also donated two hundred
and fifty thousand dollars in the name of a sister she
hadn't heard from in almost two years.

In reality, her mother and father should be the
ones being honored. Diana had never intended to tell
them what she'd done with their money, partly
because she never had the opportunity, but mainly
because she didn't want to revisit the end of their
relationship. But they'd found out. Diana was never
sure whether it had been through the newspaper or
one of her mother's friends. The source wasn't
important; what mattered was the phone call that followed. Her mother took the role of messenger, her
father the scribe. Diana's decision to humiliate them
in such a public fashion could mean only one thing:
she had chosen to make the break from them permanent and irreversible.

She stuck the letter into her purse on her way to
the elevator, stopping to dump the flyers in the trash.
After hitting the up button, she went back to the mail.

The typewritten, cream-colored envelope she
found under a credit card application looked like an
invitation or announcement.

The innocent look of the envelope lulled Diana
into doing something she hadn't done it almost two
years. She slipped her finger under the back flap,
reached inside, and pulled out the handwritten note
without checking the return address first.

A breath-stealing jolt hit when she opened the
letter and saw the handwriting. For a long time Diana
did nothing but stare at the paper. Finally, Amy's
tightly written letters became words.

Diana,

How can it be so hard to actually pick up pen and paper to write to you when I've mentally sent you a letter every day I've been here? In my heart I've shared every joy and heartache, every fear and accomplishment, and as crazy as it sounds, I've felt you were here with me, giving me the push I needed to get up some mornings and the encouragement I needed to stay.

When I left, I said you wouldn't hear from me until I got my act together. Well, don't break out the bubbly just yet. I'm doing okay, but there are still days I want to walk out the door and never look back. The one thing I finally know for sure is that I don't want to go one more day without you in my life. Especially not now.

I've met someone, Diana. His name is Peter Drennan. He says he loves me, and the remarkable thing is, I believe him. He wants to get married, but I told him he would have to meet you first.

Can you—will you—come to Jackson? Next weekend would be perfect. It's Sharon's thirtieth birthday and we're having a big party for her here at the ranch. Everyone is really anxious to meet you. I talk about you all the time.

Please come, Diana. I love you and miss you more than I can say.

Amy

How like Amy. Just when the void of not seeing or hearing from her had ceased being a constant ache, she was ready to reestablish ties. A dozen emotions fought for dominance. She was angry Amy had taken so long, relieved the waiting was over, and terrified of the changes that had occurred in both of their lives. What if there were too many? What if they had so little in common they were like classmates at a high school reunion who ran out of things to say after "How are you?" and "What have you been doing?"

And what of Travis? Why hadn't Amy mentioned him? They'd been friends, after all. Or so Amy had believed.

What would sustain her if she discovered he hadn't waited, that he'd found someone else?

God, when had she become such a coward?

The door that led to the garage opened just as the elevator arrived. "Diana—hold up a second."

Diana turned to see Stephanie juggling Rachel on one hip, a bag of groceries on the other. She stuffed the letter and the rest of the mail in her oversize purse, then crossed the lobby and took the baby while Stephanie got her own mail.

Rachel Gorham was the one bright spot on what had been a bleak two years for Diana. Even now, it was impossible not to return the eager, toothy smile the wiggling little girl bestowed on her. When a chubby hand came up to investigate her earring, she ducked before the inquisitive fingers could snag the gold loops.

The pink elastic band that circled Rachel's head slipped, leaving tufts of black hair sticking out every which way. Diana clucked softly as she captured the still grasping hand and nuzzled Rachel's cheek. "Didn't anyone tell you that you're too young to have a bad hair day? I guess we're just going to have to talk to that mother of yours and tell her what we think of these headbands."

"Now what are you telling my daughter?" Stephanie asked, dropping her mail into the grocery bag.

"We decided the headbands have got to go."

When the elevator came Stephanie waved Diana inside. "And what would you suggest I do instead, tape a note to her forehead telling everyone she's a girl? We discussed this gender thing just the other morning, didn't we, Rachel? I promised her she wouldn't have to wear pink anymore as soon as she promised she'd grow some hair."

Diana buried her nose in Rachel's neck and waited for the inevitable squeal of delight. "I can't believe anyone could be dumb enough to think these gorgeous, flirty eyes could actually belong to a boy."

They arrived at Stephanie's floor. Instead of getting out, she gave Diana a suspicious look. "Something's wrong. What is it?"

Stephanie's perceptiveness could be downright scary at times. Diana would have sworn she'd done nothing to give herself away. "I'll tell you about it later."

"It's not something at work, is it?" She didn't wait for Diana to answer. "My God—you heard from Travis."

Diana shook her head. "Amy."

The door started to close. Stephanie put out her hand to stop it. "She called you at work?"

"She sent a—" Diana shifted Rachel to her other arm and reached in her purse for the letter. "Here, you can read it yourself."

Stephanie reached for the paper at the same time the door jerked against her hand. She moved to break the light beam. "Why don't you come inside? We can—"

"Not now. I need some time alone. I have a lot of things to think about."

"I'll give you an hour. Rachel will be ready for bed by then, and we can talk without being interrupted."

"Maybe tomorrow."

"You have to eat. I'll fix—"

"Do you remember when you told me I should let you know when you were being pushy?"

Stephanie's eyes widened in surprise. "Me? Act pushy? I can't imagine I would ever do anything like that."

Diana decided to take the stairs the final flights to her condo. She got out of the elevator and walked Stephanie to her door, handing Rachel over when it was opened. "I'll let you know if I change my mind and decide to come down after all."

"I don't feel right leaving you like this."

Having a friend like Stephanie could be both blessing and curse. No one knew her better. Amy had once, but the two years since they'd seen each other seemed a lifetime ago. "I'll be fine."

Rachel squirmed out of Stephanie's arms and ran into the apartment with a rocking, bow-legged gate. "I didn't get a chance to read the letter. Did Amy say anything about Travis?"

Diana shook her head. "Nothing. She wants me to go to Jackson next weekend—for a lot of reasons."

"Are you going to go?"

"I haven't decided." As soon as she said the words, she knew she had.

The surprise must have shown on her face, because Stephanie immediately said, "I think you just did."

"You're right."

"And?"

"How could I not go?" She felt as if the door she'd been trying to beat down for two years, the one she'd believed held all the answers, had suddenly swung open. "All this time I thought I was being so understanding about the reasons Amy had cut herself off from me, but I just realized that under all my altruistic posturing, I never believed a word she said." The revelation left her shaken. She was unable to go on.

"Which only means you're human after all," Stephanie said.

"Amy's letter caught me off guard. I felt this amazing hurt and anger that I didn't even know existed until then. I have to go, to make peace with her." Diana frowned. "I think it's the only way I'll ever make peace with myself."

"What about Travis?"

"What about him?" Diana asked.

"I don't want you going there not knowing anything about him, wearing your heart on your sleeve."

"I'd have to be an idiot to think he'd waited, not after the phone calls I never returned, and the letters I sent back unopened." She'd been like a recovering alcoholic back then, knowing that one slip, either an answered call or an opened letter, and she'd never be able to keep her promise to Amy. When the weeks turned into months and she finally realized the separation was not the temporary one they'd all believed it would be, it was too late. Travis had stopped calling. The reasons she assigned his silence kept her from initiating the call herself. If he had gone on without her, she didn't want to know. Better to keep the dreams that got her through the night.

"Remember who you're talking to here," Stephanie said. "I know how much you love this guy. You haven't even looked at another man in two years."

"Maybe seeing him with someone else is what I need to get going on my own life again." As if that were really possible. Thanks to the notebook he'd left behind, she knew him better now than she had two years ago. Instead of her love diminishing with time and distance, it had grown stronger.

A crashing sound came from the direction of the

kitchen, followed by a frustrated wail. "Don't go away," Stephanie said. "I'll be right back."

"You take care of Rachel. It's time I took care of myself." Diana headed for the stairs, the words echoing in her mind. Wasn't that exactly what Amy had wanted, to take care of herself?

Thirty-three

Instead of immediately heading back to the ranch after picking up Diana at the airport, Amy drove north to an overlook on the side of the road. A creek, once bordered by trees and owned by beavers, wandered its own unhurried path to join the Snake River. A sense of timelessness permeated the mountains and valley floor, putting day-to-day worries into the perspective of aeons. Amy came to this place whenever she wanted to be alone to think.

The ride there had been unnaturally quiet, as if she and Diana no longer knew how to communicate on any but the most impersonal levels. They could talk about the economy or the upcoming elections, but not about the new nail polish Amy had tried that morning or whether Diana had ever carried through with her threat to donate the two-carat diamond engagement ring Stuart had given her to the Humane Society.

"Why did we come here?" Diana asked.

"To give you a chance to say what's on your mind without other people around." She opened her door. "Let's walk down to the creek. You're probably tired of sitting."

They got out of the car and began to walk down the path in silence. After about a hundred yards Diana finally burst out, "I'm mad at you, Amy."

"I know, and I don't blame you."

"Oh, no, you don't. You're not getting off that easy." She shoved her hands in her jacket pockets, then immediately took them out again, a conductor directing her frustration. "You gave the impression in your letter that even though you were about to become engaged, you were still unsure of yourself, that you were still struggling to fit in. I get here and what do I find? This glowing picture of health and happiness."

Diana stood back and looked Amy over. "I've never seen you look better than you do now."

"Thank you—I think."

"It wasn't meant as a compliment." She walked ahead, turned, and went back on the attack. "Why did you wait so long to get in touch with me? Were you so busy with your new life you couldn't find the time to squeeze in one lousy phone call?"

The anger didn't bother Amy. The pain behind the defensive posturing broke her heart. "I'm sorry. I never meant to hurt you."

"Why didn't you call?"

"Until about a month ago, there wasn't a day I didn't want to run away from here. If I'd called and you had even hinted that you wanted me to come back, I would have been on the first plane."

"What happened?" Concern overrode anger. She came back down the trail toward Amy. "What did they do to you?"

Amy stared at Diana a long time before she said, "Ah, my sweet, wonderful sister, always ready to mount your steed and rush into battle to defend me even when you'd rather be wringing my neck. Do you see now why I couldn't call you? What I needed was someone to listen, not help."

With almost brutal clarity Diana finally understood what Amy had been trying to tell her all this time. "You needed a friend, not a sister."

"It wasn't your fault. I let you take care of me all of my life, and then changed the rules when I decided it was time I grew up and started taking care of myself."

"I'm proud of you," Diana said. The next didn't come easy. "And I'm jealous."

Amy looked stunned. "Why would you be jealous?"

"I liked taking care of you." The admission surprised her as much as it did Amy. "I wanted you to need me."

"I'll always need you."

"But not the same way."

"Does that bother you?" Amy asked carefully.

"No. It's just going to take some getting used to." Diana thought about it a little longer. "I think I'm going to like being your friend."

"Damn it, Diana. I swore I wasn't going to cry." She wiped twin lines of moisture from her cheeks. "And now look at me."

Diana reached for her purse to give Amy a tissue before she remembered she'd left it in the car. "Sorry, I guess you'll just have to use your sleeve."

Amy smiled. "I love you."

"I love you, too." Diana put her arm around Amy and they started back to the car, their heads tilted and touching, their shoes scuffing the packed trail. "Now tell me what's been going on here."

"Are you sure you want to know?"

"I can take it." She gave Amy's shoulders a squeeze. "I need practice if I'm going to learn how to listen and keep my mouth shut."

On the drive back to the ranch, Amy gave the highlights of the attack Dorothy had mounted against her. True to her nature, instead of stealing away silently, or looking for a way to heal the wounds, Dorothy had done everything possible to discredit the daughter she had abandoned. It was almost as if she thought that by doing so, she would be able to justify her own behavior all those years ago. According to Sharon, Dorothy even managed to convince herself that with Amy gone, the path would be clear to restore her life and her family to the way they had been.

Dorothy had hired a detective to investigate Amy's background, going all the way back to sixth grade. Instead of releasing her ammunition all at once, she'd doled it out to friends and Amy's impressionable younger sisters in dramatic pieces, each timed effectively to shatter the small trust Amy had managed to build in the meantime. The gossip around town ran from curious to indignant. Family friends were divided as much by age as by loyalty.

Dorothy became the champion of those who believed in the sanctity of the home and saw Amy as a destructive force. They listened to Dorothy's list of Amy's shortcomings, from her drug and alcohol addictions to her arrest for prostitution, and labeled her a money-grubbing, self-serving intruder. They considered Gus pathetically blinded over his joy at discovering he had another daughter.

Not until Gus announced cheerfully to any and all who would listen that one of his children finally had the good sense to want to take over the ranch did Dorothy give up the battle and move back to Ohio to be with her mother. Judy left with her but returned within a month. She took an apartment in town and went to work part-time in the store with Sharon.

Divorce papers arrived two months after Dorothy left Jackson. Gus turned them over to his attorney to see if a settlement could be worked out that wouldn't involve selling a portion of the ranch. No one held out much hope.

During the telling, Diana asked questions but made little comment. Amy could see the effort had cost her, but that she took pleasure in succeeding.

They came to the turnoff for the ranch. Amy eased the car onto the gravel road. "Just about there."

"It looks the same," Diana said.

Amy glanced at Diana and smiled. "I forget you've been here before." She slowed for a jackrabbit. "Ever think I'd be happy living out in the wilds like this?"

Diana laughed. "Not in a million years."

"I can't wait for you to meet Carter."

"Carter?"

"My nephew." Amy had never been around a baby before Carter and was fascinated by everything about him. "Sharon's baby."

"I'd forgotten she was pregnant." Diana started to tell Amy about Rachel but decided to save it for later.

"You want the latest on Travis?" Amy asked.

"No," Diana said, too quickly. Then, in an attempt to cover her mistake, "I'm sure he'll be at the party this evening. We can catch up then."

Amy settled back in her seat, surprised and a little bemused to discover she'd been right about Travis and Diana. The mystery was how long it had taken to figure it out. "He called yesterday and said he would be late."

"Does he know I'm here?"

Amy didn't miss the effort it cost Diana to ask. "I didn't tell anyone you were coming. I wanted it to be a surprise."

Diana turned to look out the window. She was trapped in a prison of her own making, bound by the lies she and Travis had told to keep their relationship secret and the two years they had been apart.

That evening Diana worked her way across the room, smiling at a woman she'd been introduced to earlier whose name was either Mandy or Sandy and nodding at a teenage boy wearing a silver-and-gold belt buckle as big as a dinner plate. This was the first party of its size Diana had attended where everyone obviously knew and liked each other. The odd thing was that she didn't feel like an outsider in their midst. It was almost as if being Amy's sister made her a Martell, too, no matter how convoluted the connection.

Diana had been welcomed into the family with enthusiasm from all except Judy, who'd been polite but reserved. After initial surprise at her unexpected appearance, Gus enthusiastically took her bags to the guest bedroom and insisted it was hers for as long as they could talk her into staying. With anyone else she would have passed off the invitation as a somewhat trite social nicety; with Gus she believed every word.

Minutes after meeting Sharon, she felt as if they'd known each other all their lives. In the beginning, Faith had been more reserved, polite, but not as easily won over. She didn't open up until after lunch, when they were alone and she began asking Diana questions about her job with Sander's Food. Ironically, Diana was everything Faith wanted to be—or so she thought. She was eager to experience life in a big city, to work in the atmosphere of an international corporation, and to discover for herself the world she'd heard about secondhand from the wealthy tourists who visited Jackson.

Diana stepped out of the crush of people in the living room into the relative quiet of the hallway. She pulled up her sweater sleeve to look at her watch. Travis was two hours late.

She moved to the window beside the door and looked outside. Maybe he wasn't coming. The thought created an odd mixture of relief and disappointment. She should have just asked Amy about Travis and saved herself the anxiety of wondering what she would do if he walked in with another woman. She'd never be able to hide her feelings. He'd know what she was thinking the minute he looked at her.

At least she didn't have to make a public spectacle of herself. There was no reason anyone else had to know how long she'd held on to her impossible dream.

She opened the front door, glanced around to see if anyone was watching, then slipped outside.

"I should have made her listen to me," Amy said as she stood in the far corner of the living room and watched Diana leave. "It's not fair that she has to go through this waiting."

Peter put his hands on Amy's shoulders and turned her to look at him. "If Diana had wanted to know about Travis, she would have asked."

"I know. It's just—"

"It's just that you want her to be as happy as I am," he said tenderly before he brought her into his arms. "By the way, I really like her. We had a chance to talk before the party started and she's everything you said she was."

She laid her cheek against his shoulder. "It would be so perfect if Diana and Travis really were in love with each other." Amy hadn't recognized the tiny, telltale signs that Diana and Travis had given off unconsciously, until she and Peter had fallen in love.

The looks that lingered a fraction too long, the smiles that expressed the joy that came simply with being in the same room with someone, the caring touches, and the longing that left an emptiness only the other person could fill.

She'd been devastated to discover what she'd done by keeping them apart. In a rush to make amends, she'd told Peter she was going to call Diana the next day and clear the path for her and Travis to get back together again. As usual, Peter had raised the hand of reason, saying it was up to Diana and Travis to work things out between them. Amy's role, if she were to have one at all, could be no more than catalyst. Sharon unknowingly cooperated by agreeing to celebrate a birthday she would have just as soon forgotten.

Peter rested his chin on top of her head. "I'm afraid you're setting yourself up for a fall, Amy."

She knew he was right, but it didn't matter. Two years ago she would never have imagined herself where she was now, in the midst of a caring family, about to become engaged to a man who'd fallen in love with her with his eyes as open as his heart, a man who didn't give a damn who she'd been, only what she was.

Even knowing it wasn't hers to give, Amy wanted Diana and Travis to have what she had. She put her arms around Peter's neck, rocked up on her toes, and gave him a kiss. "I'll be right back."

"Where are you going?"

"Out on the porch."

"Your being there won't make it happen," he said.

"I know."

He took her hand. "I might as well go with you."

She looked up at him as she wound her fingers

through his. Good or bad, he would always be there for her. "I love you."

He kissed her again. "How did I get so lucky?"

"Luck had nothing to do with it, cowboy." She grinned mischievously. "It was seeing you walking down the road in those sexy, tight jeans."

He laughed. "Last week you said it was the after-shave."

Amy leaned against the porch railing as she looked for Diana. "Do you see her?" she asked Peter.

"Over there." He came up behind her and put his arms around her waist. Diana had wandered across the yard to the barn, where Peter's golden lab, Bercut, had enticed her into throwing a stick for him.

"Here he comes," Amy said. She looked up as Travis's pickup made the turn and headed toward the house. A lump formed in her throat. She leaned into Peter, using him for support. "I should have told him she would be here. What if he decided to bring someone?"

"It's too late now."

Her panic grew as the truck neared the house. How could she have missed the possibility Travis might bring a date? Her gaze fixed on the cab, but the setting sun reflecting off the window prevented her from seeing inside. She closed her eyes, then opened them again as soon as she heard the truck pull to a stop. Travis got out, spotted them on the porch, and waved.

Across the yard Diana's hand froze in midthrow. The dog turned expectantly, waiting for the stick to fly by. The instant he caught sight of Travis, he took off in a tail-wagging rush, the stick forgotten.

The mental pictures of Travis that had sustained her the past two years were images she'd assumed had become enhanced with time. She couldn't have been more wrong. Travis in the flesh was more powerful, and far more handsome, than she had remembered. How could she have forgotten the seemingly effortless way he moved? Had she been too busy two years ago, too involved with Amy, to realize how simply looking at him made her feel, or had she purposely forgotten in an effort to protect herself?

Diana nervously wiped her hands on the sides of her slacks as she waited for Travis to notice her. At least he'd come alone. She knew now that she wouldn't have been able to bear it had he brought another woman. She'd waited all this time because she'd had no other option. She loved him and always would.

Travis scratched the lab's ears. "Some watchdog. You're supposed to—" The rest died in his throat. He stood perfectly still, as if trying to convince himself that what he was seeing wasn't an apparition.

"Diana?"

Unable to trust her voice, she nodded. After several seconds, Travis started toward her. The dog seemed to sense what was happening and, instead of following, stayed where he was.

No words were spoken. None were necessary. Everything Diana needed to know she could see in Travis's eyes. He'd waited for her. With a fierce longing and palpable hunger, he reached for her and took her in his arms.

"Are you really here?" he asked in a choked whisper.

"Yes . . . finally."

He leaned back to look at her, holding her face between his hands, staring into her eyes. "I need something to convince me this isn't a dream."

"I love you."

"You always tell me you love me in my dreams."

"I want you."

"That, too."

"If you don't shut up and kiss me, I'll—"

He didn't wait for her to finish. The kiss he gave her expressed an aching need that went beyond the physical. It was as if he wanted it to erase the pain of the past, to always have this moment.

"I was so scared to come here," she told him.

"Why?"

"I didn't know what I'd do if you'd found someone else."

He touched his lips to her temple, her forehead, the tip of her nose. "That's not possible. There is no one else for me. There never will be." Effortlessly, in a joyous release, he picked her up and swung her in a circle. "I intend to spend the rest of my life proving to you that we were meant for each other."

"Is that a proposal, Mr. Martell?"

"No, this is." He put her down and lowered himself to one knee. "Will you marry me?"

With a laugh, Diana joined him. She threw her arms around his neck. "Yes. A thousand times, yes."

"Why are you crying?" Peter asked Amy.

"I never understood how much Diana loved me . . . until this moment." She turned to look at him. "I must be pretty special to deserve that kind of love."

The feeling was a wondrous gift—one that would last a lifetime.

Read These Novels by Award-Winning Author
Diane Chamberlin

BRASS RING

Claire Harte-Mathias's world is shaken when she is unable to prevent a tragedy from occurring. Confused and frightened, she is caught in a devastating struggle between terrible secrets and life-altering revelations. In her fight to uncover and accept the truth, she discovers that the past, present, and future are intertwined in a way she is powerless to change . . . or forget.

LOVERS AND STRANGERS

Torn apart by the death of their little girl, an estranged couple is forced to confront the painful truth that, one way or another will seal their fate forever.

FIRE AND RAIN

A compelling drama that delves into the deepest reaches of the human heart to reveal its darkest secrets.

PRIVATE RELATIONS

Kit and Cole have a friendship so valuable that neither is willing to risk it by acting on the intense attraction between them. But like a strong wave, their passions inevitably crash and force them to choose between love and all else.

KEEPER OF THE LIGHT

Three people are caught up in a whirl of love, passion, and deception that could destroy their lives and only one person can help them.